An Evil Ki

. . . In his heart is a blind desire,
In his eyes foreknowledge of death . . .

When the cause of a fire is investigated in vacated Victoria Crescent, not only are the charred remains of a vagrant discovered, but also the headless, mummified body of a young woman called, *Vicky,* by the officers involved. Could there have been a connection between these deaths? Could Jacob Bisset, the last owner of the house, be involved with either crime?

To Detective Superintendent Mike Hallows and his team, it seems unlikely since Bisset has been severely disabled for many years.

While Detective Chief Inspector Roy Kennet sets about searching for *Vicky*'s identity and the means of her death, Detective Chief Inspector Liz 'Ferret' Ireton begins enquiries into Bisset's background. Piece by piece the jigsaw of his life comes together, revealing a loathsome picture.

As Kennet and Ferret pursue parallel investigations, a blackmailer grasps at opportunity. With another death, Hallows joins his team on the front line in the search for a fearless, ruthless killer.

Also by Robyn Sheffield

DEADLY PURSUITS
A KILLING TERM
THE PARTING

AN EVIL KINDLING

Robyn Sheffield

BLACKTHORN

CRIME

First published in 1998
by Blackthorn Crime
an imprint of Penlin Publications
Sorrel House Lee Ilfracombe Devon EX34 8LL

British Library Cataloguing in Publication Date.
A catalogue record for this book is available from the British Library.

ISBN 0 9533660 0 6

Typeset in 10/14pt Palatino by Exe Valley Dataset, Exeter.

Printed in Great Britain by Devonshire Press, Torquay.

This book is dedicated to the memory of
STEPHEN DAVID PENN
1962–1998
A loving and honourable man
who died suddenly in his sleep without reason.

The characters, organizations, locations and situations
described in this book are entirely imaginary
and bear no relation to any real persons,
places or actual happenings.

AN EVIL KINDLING

CHARACTERS

POLICE OFFICERS	ABBOTS HILL, HELENBOROUGH
Detective Superintendent Mike Hallows	Detective Sergeant Rob Curtis
Detective Chief Inspector Liz 'Ferret' Ireton	
Detective Chief Inspector Roy Kennet	Detective Sergeant 'Scotty' Scott

THE FRIENDS

Josh Elwood	Senior Partner of Earle, Elwood & Davis, Estate Agents
Keith Hawes	Physiotherapist, owner of the Fitness Centre
Anne Hawes	Physiotherapist, Keith's wife and partner
Dr Oliver Wyland	Head of Earth Sciences, Helenhall University

OTHERS

Huey Alcott	Ex Security Guard, University Hospital
Cllr. Lester Barraclough	Neighbour of Keith Hawes at Roxleigh
Ray Bedworth	Fire Investigation Unit Officer
Jacob Bisset	6 Victoria Crescent and Green Vale Nursing Home
Quentin Dyer	West Hillington
Kate Elwood	Josh Elwood's wife
Patrick Elwood	Josh Elwood's son
Martin Falder	Reg Falder's son
Reg Falder	Builder
Isla Hallows	Wife of Mike Hallows, sister of Iain Sinclair
Gina Hawes	Social Worker, Helenhall University
Neville Howard	Anne Hawes's father
Frank and William Lilly	Window cleaners
Detective Inspector Merrison	Retired Police Officer, Abbots Hill
Dr Duncan Milo	Helenhall University
Stan Parkin	Dealer in Second Hand Furniture
Charles Saville	Grandfield Development Company
Bernard Scofield	Forensic Entomologist
Prof. Iain Sinclair	Consultant Pathologist
Devin Slade	ViewPoint, Hillington
Libby Stratten	ViewPoint, Hillington
Linda Thorne	Assistant and Secretary to Josh Elwood
Detective Inspector Turley	Hillington Police Station
Richard Webber	Sally Webber's brother
Sally Webber	Student, Helenhall University

PROLOGUE

Night, and the fire prospered in the house, feeding hungrily on old timbers. Then, with a mighty roar it escaped, exploding through the roof in a sheet of livid flame as gas ignited.

The entire terrace of stagnating cottages shuddered in the blast. Neighbours, snatching for what was most irrationally precious, raced in panic for the street. They gathered on the far pavement in a strange array of undress, their eyes fixed on the yellow darting tongues that reached through roof ribs and licked greedily at the flaking brick of a communal chimney.

Glass was shattering with the violence of pistol fire and they huddled closer as if their hour was called. Held in thrall with the dancing fury mirrored in their horrified eyes, they scarcely heard the distant siren of the summoned fire engines.

Later, when the search for bodies became possible, two severely charred remains were discovered in the dripping, steaming ruin. Attending Forensic and Fire Investigation Officers had no hesitation in declaring that the fire had been deliberately set. Traces of an accelerant, paraffin the hydrocarbon, had been found.

Establishing identities had been assigned to Detective Inspector Jim Merrison. Initially, Merrison believed the bodies were of two university students, Sally Webber and Carol Reynolds, since the young women had been renting the cheap accommodation. However, jewellery worn by one of the victims had not belonged to either woman. Post-mortems took place. Dental records and blood groups were checked. One body was definitely that of student Carol Reynolds, while the other, in possession of the jewellery, was confirmed as being of Gina Hawes, a social worker attached to Helenhall University. Merrison learned from Gina's distraught husband that she had been helping Sally Webber through some emotional crisis.

There had been immediate concern for Sally and a rush to

find her. It was established that late on the evening of the fire at Briers Way, she had been seen walking along the tow path of the Nean. Fellow students, drinking in the gardens of the Riverside Inn on the opposite bank, had recognized her. With no further sightings, Merrison had called in the Under Water Search Unit. The divers had checked along an extensive area of the fast flowing river, but Sally Webber's body had not been found.

Carol's and Gina's deaths excited full media coverage when Merrison, on interview, spoke openly of murder not accident. However, as time moved on, with lack of police progress in the investigation other news took precedence. It slipped into history and most of Helenborough's urban population forgot.

Merrison, close to retirement, had to live with failure; with continuing chagrin at his inability to close the file on the Briers Way deaths. No years would distance his memory or dull that of Iain Sinclair who had been junior to the pathologist involved at the time. While Merrison was bitter, Sinclair remained intrigued.

It had not been Sinclair's task to show that the women had been dead before the fire was started. The fire had been so rampant that means of death had not been established.

Even ten years after the murders, when Merrison had become accustomed to receiving his pension, Sinclair still dallied with details of the crime. As he leaned over the stone parapet of Canongate Bridge, the opaque waters of the Nean had the effect, as always, of conjuring up recollections. If he had been chief consultant of pathology then, would he have acted differently from his predecessor? It was an unanswerable question. He always sighed at this point: he liked confirmation and certainties, that was his business. Had knife blows been delivered in a frenzy? And had both women, not one, died from cuts to the throat? Certainly the attack on Gina had been the most violent, for her blackened remains had shown that her head had been completely severed from her body.

PART ONE

Chapter 1

Detective Chief Inspector Liz Ireton sat on the sill of the tall, narrow window, curled her fingers around her mug of black coffee and grimaced at the chaos around her. It was true. Moving was hell. She felt she had been packing for weeks. Now it had come to it, when she was actually about to collect the keys of her new flat, she had a weird sense of grief that came from appreciation that she would be losing the security of the familiar. This cramped, rented place had been home since she had split with Mac.

Never get involved with another copper, not one who has a silver tongue, not one with good looks – and especially not one from your own nick. More fool her for not taking on board good advice. More fool her for not listening to her boss, Mike Hallows, when he dropped hints that questions were being raised, that Mac could be a rotten apple. More fool her for not getting out sooner, before their violent finale. She looked at the back of her right hand as she held the mug. The jagged scar that diagonally bisected it was no longer a raised livid line. It had mellowed to a wriggle of flattened white rope.

Her eyes returned reflectively to the living room. Its faded wallpaper and unstylish furniture had witnessed a chain of very solitary exultations and griefs. Now it was on with the new. Had she shown a creative flair with carpets and curtains?

Bound to a mortgage. Here must be confirmation of how she felt about her work, colleagues, and Helenborough. A summation of how it was at Abbots Hill Police HQ as one of a team under Hallows – so why was she in this odd mood, massaging uncertainties?

She felt a weak November sun on her back, stretched slowly under its warmth then finished her coffee. In the tiny kitchen she washed up the mug. Time to head into town. Quite suddenly, doubt and fatigue dropped away. There was a sense of release. Her blood coursed in a rush of gleeful excitement. 'Yes!' she shouted jubilantly and punched the air.

Liz Ireton darted across North Way, entered the pedestrian-friendly High Street with its bus-access-only, and turned into Goldsmiths Walk. Earle,

Elwood and Davis, Estate Agents, had a prime corner site; one foot in the historical quarter of the city, the other in the new Guildhall Shopping precinct. They were an old established firm, customarily simply called Earle's.

She had met Josh Elwood in the previous May when he had been incidentally involved in a case under investigation. So frequently had she seen him in her search for the ideal flat that they had arrived at first name terms. He called her Liz as did her boss. The majority at Abbots Hill, however, called her Ferret, a name dispensed by a canteen wit shortly after she had arrived.

'I trust he's in.' She poked her beaming face around Elwood's private secretary's door.

Linda Thorne laughed. 'He wouldn't have missed giving you the keys for the world. Go on through.'

Ferret took four more strides along the narrow corridor towards the rear of the premises and turned sharp left.

'Heard you coming, Liz.' Elwood was bouncing the keys on a strong, fair-skinned palm. He stood up, dropped them into her open hand, then bent to collect something from close to his feet. 'Thought you deserved this.' He was passing her a bottle of champagne. 'Thanks for sticking with us. This firm does try to do its best for its customers.' He winked: 'The old fashioned values. You know.'

'Well, if this is a regular thing I'll accept. Don't know who I'm going to share it with, though. I haven't had time to be sociable beyond Abbots Hill.'

'Get settled in, and then Earle's will attempt a remedy.'

The flat had been part of a conversion of a two-floored quay-side warehouse. It was more than decades since the River Nean and its short canal had fulfilled an active maritime role, and even then the river had not played a crucial commercial part in the city's growth. Now her building rubbed shoulders with a maritime museum. There were displays under cover, and assorted antique boats tied up against the quay for visitors to scramble over. The advantage of Quay House was that it was superbly quiet, even when the museum had its influx of visitors, while being only a quarter of a mile from the city centre and Abbots Hill.

She let herself in through the outer security door with its entryphone, and ran up the short flight of stairs to her tiny landing and front door fitted with two security locks, chain and spyhole. There was always the chance that some offender would entertain thoughts of revenge when fortified with booze or drugs. Being on the first floor made break-ins more difficult and the brightly lit outer entrance would discourage night time skulkers who had thoughts of rushing you as you found your key.

She unlocked the balcony door, slid it back and stepped, proprietorially, on to her narrow balcony. Below, in reflection of the sky, the soft grey waters of the Nean flowed steadfastly towards the estuary and the sea less than eleven miles away. Would she be able to smell the brine when the wind blustered inland from the south?

She hauled herself back from dreamy loitering. She carried the champagne into the kitchen and used the telephone extension there. 'Warings? . . . Elizabeth Ireton, 2 Quay House – just to confirm that the carpets can go down this afternoon.'

Outside again, she checked her key in the garage lock and then returned to where she had parked her car. It was back to the old flat to collect cleaning gear and most of her kitchen stuff.

From the direction of the museum came a loud, protesting yell and then two other voices, rising in greater volume. The jarring noise funnelled between the museum building and the moored craft towards Ferret, as she wandered in the direction of the locked high, spiked, wrought-iron entry gates. Winter opening time was not for another hour. Leaning her elbow against a metal scroll, she watched through the tracery as the three approached. The two flanking men were marching the middle one forward, assisting him by the arms while he dragged his heels.

The vagrant had enjoyed a dry place to doss for the night. There were so many homeless on the streets; a high proportion of them youngsters. Some had walked out of acceptable homes, while others had bunked off when pressures there had been too abysmal to endure. There was talk of building a hostel, but funding was tight . . . when was it not? And right now, with her new keys in her pocket, she felt the guilt of the more fortunate.

But this bag of filthy clothes being frog-marched towards her was not young. She recognized him: Huey Alcott.

'How did he get in?' she asked as the gate was opened. Alcott was given a sufficiently firm shove to propel him beyond it, before it was locked again.

'We had the service entrance open yesterday,' one answered as they walked away. 'He must have nipped through then.'

'I'm cold!' Alcott whined and hugged his once good overcoat around him.

'You're so full of anti-freeze, I wonder that you notice,' she said and then added with more compassion, 'At your age, you should be showing more respect for your old bones – you know the Sally will give you a bed *and* a bath. God you stink!'

'I like to be on my own,' he answered with some hauteur and began to shuffle off.

'So where are you going now?'

'The gardens by the hospital.'

'You used to work there?'

'Security. You know that,' he added belligerently.

She did. She knew that past colleagues often brought out sandwiches and cups of tea for him. He was no problem in the grounds unless he got very drunk, then he had to be evicted. He looked tired, wizened and frozen, this morning. In her shoulder bag she had a Mars Bar. 'Here. Eat this and get going.'

'Money'd be better. I want a nip of something.'

'Chew that. Consider your misfortune and then hop it.'

He watched her walk away, observed with bloodshot eyes the boyish slimness, the lively tread, the heavy gold-brown hair worn shorter than shoulder length. Images of his daughter escaped from the locked drawer of memory. It was so long since his world had crumbled.

He felt the sweats starting . . . he *needed* that drink. Bloody Mars Bar! He scowled at the bar, resting on the ingrained grime of his open hand and then saw the coins. Two pounds? He tested each on his teeth. They were real.

Detective Sergeant 'Scotty' Scott was driving, and unhurriedly. Their day had extended well into late evening, but since their case was now nicely buttoned up, they felt relaxed.

'Fancy a beer?' he suggested, taking a short cut around the broad green of Cathedral Close.

Ferret opened her eyes to see where they were. 'Probably go to sleep over it – it'd be a waste.' The Royal Hotel was coming up on their left, with cars overflowing from its park and along the road side for some considerable distance. 'What's on?' she asked.

'A Patronus dinner.'

'Oh, an all-guys do.'

'They pay hand-over-fist for their grub. Raise a packet for charity. You need loot, clout or to be personable to be a member.'

'Personable?' She yawned through a smile. 'Now I know why you're not with them. Hey!' She tapped his arm. 'Slow up. Three are coming out.'

'You want to be nosy?' He slowed to a halt twenty feet back from where the flight of steps from the hotel entrance met the pavement and where a woman waited at the open door of a car.

Ferret lowered her window. A cluster of timber-framed buildings on either side of the Georgian hotel acted as a sounding board for the men's voices. On the still, cool air, their quiet tones carried with startling clarity.

Arms linked, they strode forward on to the wide flight of steps, smiling benignly at each other. They had had a good time; drunk a little too much and laughed a good deal.

'I know two of them,' Ferret whispered. There was Josh Elwood and Oliver Wyland, a lecturer at the university. She had met him at the same time as first meeting Josh. 'Who's the shortest one?'

'Keith Hawes. He owns and runs the Fitness Centre with his wife, Anne. That's her by the car.'

The three had paused as one man on the top tread.

'They're pissed.' Scott sniggered. 'One'll end arse down.'

They were more sure footed than he supposed.

To the three, the descending steps must have seemed like an invitation to tap and dance. Elwood's ungainly attempt to impersonate a hoofer brought a giggle from Anne.

'Stand back and let the younger set have a go!' Hawes ordered and began a respectable stamp, hop and skip. Wyland joined him, making a reasonable partner in the double act.

Ferret elbowed the grinning sergeant. 'They're not bad.'

The two who danced had begun to whistle and clap a rhythm.

Anne rushed forward. 'Hush.' Suppressing her laughter, she collected Elwood and urged him into the back seat of the Rover.

With well synchronized steps, Wyland and Hawes were now tapping down two treads and springing up one.

'Keith! Bed time.' Anne lifted her skirt a mite.

'Oh, very nice.' Scott's grin had widened.

'Boo-ba-de-doo. What a lucky me.' Hawes's croon ended in a chuckle. 'Exit, car, old man!' he called to Wyland

The Rover eased away from the kerb.

'Pity there was no encore.' Ferret smothered a further yawn. 'We should have clapped.

The early days of November had been either cold or showery, with the added seasonal offering of intermittent fog. With today overcast, dusk had settled early on Helenborough.

Ferret's angle-poise lamp pooled brightness over a thick file on her desk. She had been working through it for so long that her neck had stiffened and she rubbed at the muscles absently.

The outside phone rang. She groped, colliding with a cup of cold coffee.

'DCI Ireton.' Her response was crisp, automatic.

'Liz? You sound terrifyingly efficient.'

She recognized the speaker and smiled faintly. 'Good. Keeps people like you, Josh Elwood, in your place.' She shared his chuckle.

'Thought it was about time I prised you away from Quay House. Do you play badminton?'

'Inexpertly, yes.'

'Would you like to make up a four? Patrick and I often have a game at the Leisure Centre. My son's ambition is to run me ragged. Kate will come too if you can join us.'

Ferret hadn't seen Josh's wife since the Helenhall investigation in the spring. She had felt diminutive beside her, not that Kate was particularly tall or that Ferret was markedly small, it was just that Kate had a covetable willowy poise. Had it been this and Kate's dark good looks that had first attracted Josh? It was unlikely. As a widower with two much loved children, Josh would have been drawn more probably to qualities suited to their needs: Kate's equable nature well threaded with quiet fun.

'When were you thinking of going?' She stretched for her diary.

'This evening any good?'

'Oh . . . I've got a stack of paper to clear.'

'Hard luck. If it weren't for Linda's efficiency I'd be saying the same. We'll try for next week.'

'. . . Look forward to it. Tell Patrick, from me, to do his worst.'

Elwood's laughter lingered in her mind. It elbowed aside some of the day's irritations.

Josh Elwood was reminded, as he picked up a low return near the net, that badminton could be one of the fastest and most exhausting pursuits in the athletic world. This evening his forty-three years were telling. He was lumbering against the agile speed of his seventeen year old son.

Patrick was almost the mirror of his father. Both Elwoods were nearly six foot tall. Both had keen pale-blue eyes, thick blond lashes and brows, and fair wavy hair. Both had open strong square faces. When Patrick filled out replication would be complete. Josh Elwood gave the impression he could carry any burden.

Well aware of his father's fatigue, Patrick grasped the advantage. Every shot was placed to force Elwood into the maximum run. He dealt with a high shuttle, slamming it down the centre line.

Elwood got to it, dropping a low return over the net.

Patrick took a long quick stride, struck and sent it high and deep.

Elwood, running back, turned to take it on his back hand. At the moment of impact something excruciating happened in his leg. His agonized yell rebounded from every wall.

Long before expected, Kate heard her husband's key in the latch.

'Josh?' She hurried into the hall and gasped: 'What have you done?'

Elwood swapped Patrick's shoulder for the support of hers. 'Must have pulled a muscle.'

With him hopping, they reached the sitting room and a settee. She swung both his legs up, pushing cushions under the injured one.

'I'll fetch you two paracetamols.'

'And a whisky – for shock. We strung on the L-plates: Patrick drove home.'

'Dad!'

Elwood could grin at such indignation. His leg already felt less uncomfortable and the crack was designed to ease Patrick from a nagging sense of guilt.

Sports injuries were an everyday fact of life, and it was this theme that Kate and her husband later pursued.

'I'll ring Keith tomorrow.' He added with humour, 'See if the Fitness Centre matches its reputation.'

'Does Keith offer discounts to old friends?' she joked, and perched on the arm of a chair where he now sat, his leg raised on a footstool. 'No way. We've both moved on from being broke.'

'Then you have been magnanimous in the past? My, my.'

'I'm not all hard edges, as you well know.' He twitched a lock of her straight waist-length hair affectionately. 'I bore all the costs for his and Gina's first home. He was working at the hospital and pretty strapped for cash. That must be twelve years ago – a couple of years before Gina died at Briers Way.'

'Murdered: dreadful! What was Gina like?'

Elwood scratched his jaw reflectively and felt the rasp of an emerging growth of evening beard. 'In height and colouring, similar to Keith: around five-eight, with shortish medium brown hair. She was full of strong opinions. Good at her job, I believe, dealing with the personal problems of Helenhall's students. Her closeness to their age must have made it easier to communicate.'

'Did you like her?'

'Not my type. Lacked cuddle qualities . . . ' And reaching sideways he brought her down to him.

Josh Elwood was forced to hobble into the firm's office at a quarter-to-nine. He paused at Linda's open door. 'Bring today's mail through.'

Gathering his opened morning's post, she followed him and watched him push his door back with the irritable jab of one not accustomed to being unfit.

Elwood, who disliked bulky pockets, tossed his personal keys on to his desk and sank gratefully into his chair.

Linda Thorne looked pointedly towards his injured leg.

'Badminton,' he informed her, keeping to simplicity. She nodded, appearing satisfied.

She had been his personal assistant since the time he had been widowed, but seldom had their conversations transcended the office. She could have been a robot, she thought; he only responded to her efficiency.

She flicked her head in a moment of discontent, sending soft waving hair swirling. Reaching beyond her shoulders and a lustrous red, it was like a beacon which overcame the disadvantage of her small stature. She knew her head could turn heads. It was her natural colour; not mildly ginger, but vivid, glowing close to crimson. She was proud of it and her alert green eyes proclaimed a present-day assurance.

As Elwood began to scan the letters, Linda's gaze roamed. She knew this room so well. Over the years, she had spent hours in here, waiting on important clients, checking Josh had the necessary papers ready on his desk, dealing with more sensitive documents kept in the four-drawer cabinet placed midway along the wall to her right. The only mystery lay in the contents of a metal cupboard on the door wall that was always locked.

What did he keep in it? Her curiosity had heightened over the years. Patronus papers? Probably, since he was an executive officer for the Order. Was it true, as rumoured, that membership fees were based on income? Was every man's financial worth held in ledgers here?

Her eyes returned to Josh's bent head. Each soft wave was like a contour on a familiar map, yet she had never been able to touch, to stroke. Her feelings were no different now from the first day at Earle's. She had the familiar tightening in her chest as if she would choke from love. And he had no idea, not then, when he was free . . . and certainly not since Kate had entered his life. If only I had been bold in those early days and made him aware, she thought, sadly breast-beating. But it was all too late now. The only thing that had changed was her resolve. No more treading water, she must make her own destiny. She would kick or join the devil, she no longer cared which.

Elwood had arrived at the last letter.

'You've no appointments until twelve,' she reminded him. 'Mr Saville for the Grandfield Development Company will be calling then. You'll have time for some physiotherapy treatment. Shall I contact Mr Hawes at the Fitness Centre?'

'It's OK, I'll phone him.' Having kept some letters back from the main bulk, he looked up: 'I'll give you a call when I've made some notes on these.'

She collected the rest but didn't move.

'Yes?'

'Driving must be uncomfortable. Shall I play chauffeur?'

Carelessly he brushed the suggestion aside. 'I can manage. You'll be more valuable here.'

She nodded and turned away.

He missed her sigh, a sound of soft finality.

Keith Hawes was sleek in a vibrant, healthy way. Slim framed and hard shouldered, he could have been an elegant clothes peg for any high class glossy. It was in their heights that the more solidly formed Elwood felt the only advantage. Against him, Hawes looked as if he was standing on a lower step.

'Josh! So I've got you as a patient at last!' Hawes led the way to a sitting-cum-consulting room furnished with tasteful restraint situated at the rear of the Fitness Centre. Elegantly proportioned, its tall window looked over an acre of immaculate grounds.

Sliding up on to a high couch, Elwood eased both trouser legs above the knee.

Hawes had a light but assured touch. 'A strain – a minor tear of muscle fibres. As you can see it's quite swollen, with some slight bruising. Aspirin or paracetamol will take care of the ouch! factor. We won't bandage it, the injury's not severe enough to warrant support. The best treatment is rest and a cold compress to reduce the swelling. We'll do that now, it'll make my bill appear more justified.' Hawes's mouth curled in a smile: there was always something of the mirthful schoolboy about him.

'Have to forget the resting. We're busy.'

'Well, do your best. Come into the treatment room. We can jaw there over a coffee.'

The touch of cold against hot bruised muscles made Elwood gasp. 'You enjoyed that,' he accused.

'Of course.' Hawes chuckled, gave the compress a final glance and then reached for the cafetière. 'What are the chances Patronus can raise enough money for an over-night hostel? There are so many youngsters sleeping rough in Helenborough.'

Elwood said with quick passion: 'We must give it a good shot.'

He accepted his coffee, sniffed with half closed eyes. Strong roasted and the best; but from Keith it wouldn't have been anything else.

Hawes said: 'I've heard Barraclough's looking for outside funding. He's been a good councillor. Finger in every pie, of course.'

'True.' Elwood grinned agreement. 'Oh, thought you'd like to know – it's no longer a secret – Victoria Crescent in entirety has been bought by the Grandfield Development Company.'

Hawes showed momentary surprise. 'Where Gina and I lived? Really? What are they going to do with it? It was on a slow decline when we bought number 4; its price and the park opposite were the only attractions. The crescent has to be pretty shabby by now.'

'Very. Empty and boarded up except for number 6.'

'Jacob Bisset's place?'

'Yes. He's just moved out. Relented, at last, and transferred to a nursing home: Green Vale. In his state of health he should have been the first to go. Obstinate, disagreeable...'

'So he hasn't mellowed. Didn't like help: said he'd live in that house forever despite his degenerative illness. So what do Grandfield intend to do with the row?'

'Restore the good-looking fronts, gut and rebuild the interiors, then sell them as up-market city desirables. The view of the park will provide the icing to a dignified cake.

It was growing colder. The clouds had dispersed leaving a high, open night sky. The vast ceiling of stars above Huey Alcott were bright as tinsel frost. Less drunk than earlier in the day, he shuffled along Victoria

Crescent looking for the house. Somewhere quiet to suit a loner, he had been told as he huddled in an unlit bus shelter on hospital ground. The only house not yet sealed up, he had heard from the person bending close to his ear. There would be a drink there in the front room.

The wan glow from the few street lamps touched boarded window after boarded window, and then his bloodshot eyes saw light reflected from glass. With his slight energy evaporating, Alcott tottered along the garden path of number 6 and leant against the solid front door. It swung inwards, bringing him lurching into the wide entrance hall. He stumbled forward. In the front room weak shadows from glazing bars stretched across boards scattered randomly with ancient discarded newspaper and abandoned shabby carpet.

Close to the fireplace he could see a new bottle of vodka. Reaching for it, he clasped it to him like a lover.

Alcott's legs had had enough of walking. He sagged down on to his haunches, then stretched out along the floor, resting his back against the projecting wooden column that supported the mantel.

Fumbling off the cap, he drank half the vodka in greedy, dribbly slurps. His eyes closed. He was tired . . . tired . . .

Alcott slipped into unconsciousness, the bottle still clasped in the possessive vice of his dirt-encrusted hand.

He was unaware of an approaching, soft foot-fall or the flashlight scanning his face. He failed to hear sheets of age-yellowed newspaper being crumpled into kindling, or to feel a square of carpet being folded over him with one end fed into the fire basket now laid with the paper.

A match was lit. The paper and carpet took flame with little hesitation. In minutes they were burning well, the carpet producing a dense acrid grey-brown smoke as the flames ran along its slack, soiled weave. With breath held, the visitor pulled faded velvet curtains across the windows allowing the blaze to grow in private and did not breathe again until the sitting room door was softly closed.

The front door was shut with an echoing snap of its Yale lock. Beneath his shroud of fire, Alcott slept on undisturbed.

The digital alarm clock placed on the table close to Mike Hallows's side of the bed, always gave a little clonk before it let rip. Most mornings it was the clonk that woke him, but not this morning. The detective superintendent was suffering from a deficit of sleep.

Hallows silenced the noise with an accurately stabbed finger, then he squinted at the clock's face: six-fifty. Where was Justice, he mumbled, to allow morning to arrive so soon? He stretched further and found switches for the small lamp and the radio. It was his custom to catch the local morning news before stumbling, leaden footed, to the bathroom. He pulled his hand back into the warmth, lay still and straight in bed and listened to the jingle that preceded the weather report.

In response to the sound of the reporter's bell-tones, Isla rolled over and wrapped herself around her husband.

' . . . Temperatures of just above freezing were expected to rise slowly . . . '

He smiled in the half light. Much the same could be said of Isla, but then there was more of him, considerably more, to maintain a robust warmth. He raised his head a mite and glanced down the length of the bed. Enveloped by their marital quilt, his covered form resembled a long-barrow under cropped turf. At the extreme end of the bed, over the cylinder of his solid punch-bag torso which mercifully had no mid-life belly sag yet, he could just see his size eleven feet jutting, shaping a lesser mound.

As Isla snuggled her head closer, her slender nose striking cold against his stubbly jaw, his attention sharpened to the news.

' . . . a vagrant rescued from a blaze . . . empty house in Victoria Crescent . . . University Hospital . . . unnamed man found to be dead on arrival . . . Next summary will be at eight a.m.'

Minutes later, while cleaning his teeth, an activity that could not be perfunctory since he was married to a dentist, he ran over the report of the fire again. An officer from the FIU would be looking over the building. It was routine with a fatal injury, or when the attending fire officer was uncertain over cause.

Hallows spun the tap, filled a glass and swilled his mouth. He spat directly down the drain. Most likely the investigating officer would be Ray Bedworth. He patted his mouth with his towel, rinsed the basin, then stared at his sullen morning expression in the mirror. Interesting character Bedworth – he coerced his dark, wiry hair peppered with white to lie flat – nothing ever appeared to rattle him. His wasn't an enviable job; horrendously dirty and frequently dangerous.

Detective Sergeant Rob Curtis had barely set foot in Hallows's room at Abbots Hill when he faced a barked question:

'Got the name yet for the vagrant who died in last night's fire?'

Against the great bear bulk that was Hallows, Curtis was more hound. He was sinewy, full of quick movements. A trim dresser, he liked well-cut shirts and suits and a shine on his leather shoes. He was a thirty year old policeman with an address book full of women's names, but he was married to his job and that romance showed no sign of tarnishing. Like the thick skinned salesman he could appear, Curtis had an answer for everything.

Hallows's bark was standard; he was always peptic in the morning. He wore the mood as an overcoat which could be discarded if the day improved.

'Huey Alcott,' Curtis said with his usual irksome chirpiness. 'Well known wino of this parish, and still clutching his bottle when found. DOA when they wheeled him into University Hospital. Lucky for Grandfield Developers one of our patrol cars spotted the blaze so quickly. The fire service contained it . . . just two rooms burned out. Ray Bedworth's taking a look.'

'Thought so.' Hallows pulled forward a stack of files, wrinkling his nose at what had to be faced. 'That it?'

'Nothing that'll get you away from that lot, guv. It was a night much like any other. Oh, a druggy thought he could walk on water. Found he hadn't the knack. Drowned.' Only a swift sniff conveyed that Curtis cared.

The elliptical shape of the municipal park had dictated that the road at its narrow southern boundary should be a crescent. Victoria had been queen for no more than ten years when the houses were built there, facing on to this generous acreage that gave the illusion of country dwelling. The seven properties were identical outside with short front gardens fenced from the roadway by blunt spear-topped railings. They were constructed of blue-red brick, with windows nearly flush with the walls beneath handsome stone architraves. Their front doorcases were slightly 'Adamish' in style, topped with pretty fanlights and off-set. One window to the left gave light to hall and staircase, two to the right, provided the drawing room with a view of the park.

The principal rooms were of a generous size, tall ceilinged and decorated with a happy riot of high plasterwork friezes where flowers, shells and ribbons capered luxuriantly.

What Ray Bedworth saw when he pulled into the curb outside number 6 conveyed nothing of the pride of those first years. Fashion and desirability had changed, leaving the houses to spiral into decline.

Bedworth opened his car door, completed buttoning the jacket of his protective uniform and exchanged shoes for boots. He locked the vehicle out of habit and put on his obligatory helmet.

Not a road to be used as a short cut by traffic, it lay silent and deserted except for five mildly inquisitive people who had gathered, following the news. A uniformed constable stationed at the open gateway was huffing warmth into his gloves and watching them.

Bedworth gave him an acknowledging nod, ducked beneath the yellow tape strung slackly across the entrance and then considered the smoke damage on the exterior face of the building. From the sitting room's window-heads, ugly, densely black daubs reached to the windows above. Similar grim bands of soot had coated the brick above the first floor bedroom's windows and caked the metal gutter. Beyond this the lichenous tiles had been scorched clean in a ragged arch.

Bedworth pushed back the front door which bore scars of forced opening by the fire crew, and stood in the wide outer hall that gave on to the stairs. He sniffed experimentally. This first impression registered nothing sinister, only the taint of burnt wood, paper and fabric.

All internal doors had been found closed by the crew and they had reported that flame and smoke had been efficiently contained. At first glance Bedworth didn't have cause to argue with this. There was only moderate smoke contamination in the hall and stairwell. Watchful for any weakness in the floor, he walked through to the rear of the property. The same could be said for these downstairs rooms too. The walls were discoloured and there was a strong stench of smoke, but that was all. And even the water damage had been restricted. He wasn't sploshing through puddles as he walked back to the inner hall and the entrance to the front sitting room.

From the doorway of the blackened gutted room, the signs looked straighforward enough. Fire travelled upward from the source which made pinpointing its origin relatively easy. Very close to the tiled fireplace was a circle of extreme damage. Floor boards had been consumed and the upper exposed surfaces of the joists wore a charcoal crust.

He tapped his boot, sounding out the strength of the floor just inside the door. Hearing a dull and hearteningly solid response he took a positive step into the room. Water still dripped from the exposed charred floor joists of the room above.

A drop splashed on to his face. Absently he brushed it away leaving a streak of dirt across permanently untroubled features. He was intent on tracing the course of the flames. They had ignited the wooden fire surround and then eaten into high rising shelves-cum-cupboards on either side of the chimney breast. Only metal remained: defunct angle brackets jutted. Having gathered fury the flames had made short work of the ceiling. Above him the bared joists had been reduced to matchwood. He squinted through, screening his eyes from splattering water. The maximum damage in the bedroom involved the fireplace wall. No skirting, no mantel, no cupboards, nothing of wood was left. The deeply moulded plaster work of lusty flowers and curvaceous leaves above the door was intact, but much of the cornice showed cavernous fissures.

At the cracked windows large brass curtain rings trailed a few shreds of fabric. On the floor too, there were fragments of scorched carpet . . . a man had died here. Bedworth's passive face creased in a sympathetic grimace. It was soft furnishings that killed: so much suffocating smoke.

So how did the fire start? Not this time through an electrical fault, all the services had been disconnected. And no vandals had been here making bonfires. There was no concentration of burnt debris on the floor. That left arson or an accident.

He looked critically at the boards he would have to cross to where the fire had started. There was some consolation in knowing there was earth not a cellar beneath. He stepped forward, moving along the joists gingerly to where they stuck out from beneath the consumed boards like umbrella spokes.

When near enough to the ignition point he plucked slack into his trousers and squatted.

Using a thin bladed knife and forceps, he collected samples for analysis from charred wood and soil. Traces of an accelerant could have seeped and remained unburned. Like a wine buff sniffing for a rich bouquet, Bedworth's nose dipped into each evidence envelope. Science might disagree, but experience told him neither petrol nor turpentine were present.

The cold of the building was beginning to chill, and he banged his gloved hands together before running up the dog-leg stairs to look at the front bedroom from a different angle. It was the focal room off the spacious half landing.

The door had been thrown back to allow a jet of water to quench the fire. Bedworth looked in. There was nothing new to be learned from the blackened shell.

Satisfied that the fire had only one origin, Bedworth took the remaining stairs to complete his inspection. Dust lay thick in the smaller bedrooms. Clouds puffed up from floor boards and from yellowing brittle sheets of newspaper left like rejected underlay. 'Stupid,' he muttered a fireman's disapproval.

Bedworth, in all respects thorough, ended by checking alcove cupboards built by some handyman on either side of jutting chimney breasts. He opened each set as he toured the upper floor. Mould, encouraged by damp and long neglect, blackened their interior walls.

To a more sensitive man, the property would have roused some melancholy: a home of fading memories, decades of laughter, joy, tears. Bedworth only felt the cold and slapped his arms against his sides.

In the last and smallest room he glanced out at a tidy but cheerless rear winter garden, then pulled back the left hand alcove's cupboard door. A single clothes hanger stirred, swinging gently on its rail. Dust swirled in answer to a draught. There was no mould here and he supposed that the warm flue from the kitchen below must have kept the damp at bay.

Presuming this applied to the final cupboard he reached for the door nob. Unlike its partner, the door stuck. He tugged. It resisted and then swung outward in a rush.

Bedworth stared, astonished. Phlegmatic in the face of all disasters, he remained totally composed as he bent forward for a closer look. The mummified, headless body was sitting, legs drawn up, its back resting against the plastered brickwork of the chimney. Beneath a grey cobweb veil it was clothed in pants and bra which demurely covered shrunken leathery skin. Intrigued, he cautiously touched her arm. Her flesh was as hard as stone.

The opening door, daylight: Bedworth was unexpectantly engulfed by a wave of fluttering downy wings. He sprang back with a roar of horror. Moths! He hated bloody moths.

He thundered downstairs, beating at the air and himself, at moths that didn't cling or follow. At the front door he found sufficient control to halt.

When his heart had stopped pummelling his ribs he stepped outside.

The waiting constable, wanting to have tedium relieved with a few casual words, came forward. He was disappointed.

'Expect the cavalry,' Bedworth warned and left.

Hallows slipped into first gear and pulled out of Abbots Hill alone. He could manage well enough without Curtis on this trip. There were no witnesses to speak to, no notes to be taken, no rapid decisions to be actioned. Urgency was not the imperative here; solving this elderly crime was going to be a matter of steadfast plod.

Helenborough was tight with traffic as usual. He knew the city well. He turned north-west, taking minor roads which were as familiar as the lines on his hands. The low fitful November sunshine stretched in feckless brilliance across open squares and roof tops. The quiet back-streets, columned with street lamps and telegraph poles, were a lattice of etiolated shadows. Pedestrians hurried forward, hugging their coats about them, but once he was inside the car the sun carried a semblance of warmth.

The handful of curious had been tactfully herded to the end of Victoria Crescent. Only word of the fire had brought them out, not whispers of a mummified body. The media were not having this information until it suited Hallows.

He looked for a space to park. Cars belonging to SOCOs were racked in an almost complete line along the curb-side.

Reaching for a soft felt hat which he seldom wore, Hallows slammed his door and faced the uniform row. Homes come to crumbling desolation were depressing. There was a sense of architectural parody about the place. It was as if the forsaken street, facing the winter bleakness of the park, mimicked a ghost town in a western. Sudden eddies of wind sent plucked, bleached tufts of weed leap-frogging across the gardens.

The same light wind nipped his ears. Hallows hitched up his collar, slapped on his hat and made briskly for the front door of number 6. A SOCO stepped out to meet him.

'Duty Home Office doctor has come and gone, sir. We've checked over the hall, stairs, landing and the bedroom, taken initial stills and video of the body but nobody's touched her yet. Knew you and the entomologist would want to take a look first.'

'When is Scofield expected?'

'Any time, now.'

'Right. Seen Bedworth? He said he'd meet me here.'

'Not so far.'

'OK.' Hallows cocked his head towards the hall. 'So show me.'

Ray Bedworth returned to the house as Hallows emerged. 'Mike . . . ' Bedworth, his warm breath spilling out in a vaporous cloud, thumbed towards the upstairs. 'This one's more British Museum stuff.'

'Can't argue with that.' Hallows's voice was remote, unhappy. 'Was the fire down to carelessness?'

'Looks that way.'

'That's something. With a decapitated body, albeit old, in a house that then takes fire, well, I have to consider a connection. So how?'

'Newspapers, threadbare carpet . . . Maybe the vagrant was lighting a fag. Maybe he tried to light a fire. Guess Sinclair, as senior regional pathologist, will be involved with the mummified body if not with him.'

Hallows scowled into space. How long did it take for a body to become mummified? Undoubtedly his brother-in-law would do the post-mortem; he would find the challenge irresistible.

Bedworth was saying: 'I'll drop by Abbots Hill. I presume you'll want a statement.'

Hallows nodded. 'Ask for DS Curtis.'

He kicked his heels for only a few minutes before a time-worn and far larger car than Bedworth's pulled up. Hallows watched as an orbicular figure climbed out. Goatee-bearded Bernard Scofield puffed up the slight incline of the path and extended a hand. It was uncomfortably warm and soft to the touch.

'Great day!' the Forensic Entomologist boomed.

'Only for some,' Hallows muttered, considering the woman's pitiless end.

It seemed incongruous, Hallows thought, observing Scofield at work with forceps, specimen jars and high powered lenses, that one so large should be dealing with elements so small. 'Well?' he said at last, having heard much Aahing and Oohing, and knew he was about to receive a general lecture on bugs besides, hopefully, learning something of more practical use.

Scofield stepped back from the source of his enthusiasm and began addressing Hallows as if he had no more knowledge than a ten year old. Hallows let him run on. It would cost more time, trying to stop him.

'Insects can provide important information even when a corpse has completely dried out.' Scofield gave a fulfilled man's beam. 'The larvae of the clothes moth – naughty little devils amongst your best suits – also feed on corpses in this condition; on dried hair and skin, as does a particular beetle which extends its diet to sinew and bone.' He bent close to the corpse again. 'Moths encase themselves in protective tubes. Excellent examples here; care to see?'

'No, thanks.'

Scofield gave him a disappointed glance and continued as animatedly: 'I'll confirm of course later, but I'm fairly certain there are thirteen kinds of clothes moth present but even give or take one or two, the body has undoubtedly been here for some considerable time.'

Hallows pounced: 'How long?'

'Ten years. Your pathologist will have his own opinion, naturally, but I'm generally right.' There was no conceit in the remark.

'Ten?' the detective repeated. Scofield nodded. 'I suppose you wouldn't like to offer an opinion as to the month she died, would you?' Hallows had asked the question somewhat facetiously and now paid with open-mouthed surprise.

'No problem. There's a particular fly – very interesting – quite rare. It only lays its eggs on fresh corpses, and only in May. There's evidence of its pupal stage here. Do have a look,' Scofield urged, offering a lens.

Hallows moved back, 'I'll take your word for it.' and left smartly.

The teams were gathering in the Incident Room. Two information boards, one designated to each case, were set up at either end of a long wall. Each carried known particulars and a photograph. Huey Alcott's sulking image had come from Records. SOCO had provided the photograph of the mummified body; a profile of anonymous, dry, contorted flesh. For ease of reference the body had to have a name and the Coroner's Officer had called her *Vicky*. The title resurrected her as a person.

When Hallows entered the packed room, clerical staff and officers were leaning against the furniture or perched on desk corners, talking in a low buzz. There was a fidgety expectancy in the air.

'Two deaths in one house,' he said as the company fell quiet. 'Bedworth of FIU thinks the fire was accidental. I hope so. Murder in an empty house in an abandoned road, opposite a park whose gates are locked at night . . . where are the eyes that might have seen something?'

He began outlining points as he saw them. 'Presuming *Vicky* was murdered, rather than that her body was mutilated after she had died from natural causes, we have to consider the following: Ten years or so on, is her murderer still alive, does he live in this area still or has he moved away? If still in this area, has he heard the news of the fire and does he believe she was destroyed in the flames? Or, did he set the fire himself with the intention of disposing of *Vicky*'s body and, either accidentally or on purpose, did he kill Huey Alcott while arranging the blaze? If Alcott was intended to die, was this a crime linked with the mummified body or do we have coincidence here, a fluke of fate, that brought Alcott to meet his death at number 6? And, if Alcott was destined to die, how was he encouraged to visit this house, sited as it is, some distance from his normal patch?

'Let's take Alcott first. Liz...' He looked to the centre of the room and met Ferret's keen eye. '. . . you and Scott check Alcott's background. Enemies. Who might have wanted him dead . . . ?'

She mouthed: 'Right.' already planning ahead.

'Now for *Vicky*.' Hallows focused on number 6. 'Obviously the last owner of the house, Jacob Bisset, should be in the frame, but I'll come to him in a minute. In respect of our unidentified deceased, DCI Roy

Kennet-' he searched for him and saw a hand raised at the back of the room -'Roy, you'll lead that area of the investigation.'

Kennet had been chewing the end of a pencil and staring at the floor. Inactivity didn't suit him. He was shorter than Hallows but still moderately tall with a hard-boned irregular face that was pleasant for all that. His hair, which lay heavy and with a wave that would fall across his brow, was more muted chestnut than red. His eyes suggested an indolent nature since he viewed the world for the most part from beneath half-closed lids, however, those who received his full unshuttered gaze confronted his best feature; they were the deepest, brightest brown, which could fix one with an unambiguous intensity.

Hearing what was allotted, he tossed back his head and straightened up. 'You'll be liaising with Professor Sinclair, guv?' It was confirmed. 'So when we know height, age and colouring, we can check through Missing Persons. Is it fact she died in the May?'

'Scofield had no doubt. He's also dated death as ten years ago but we'll be more circumspect until we hear from Sinclair. We'll look back fourteen. Discovering *Vicky*'s head has to be crucial to identification, but after so long-' Hallows shrugged at improbability -'well, we'll need some luck. We'll start with the house and its garden: take them apart. We have to be looking for a sharp implement too, Roy. More details on that when Sinclair's examined the neck wound.'

'Guv, I'd like to go for a long shot. I understand all seven houses in Victoria Crescent are to be gutted. I'd like to turn them over.'

There was a shocked silence before Kennet's suggestion drew a substantial muted chorus of groans. Some wag began to sing: '*Wider than a mile!*'

An angry flush tinted Kennet's jaw. 'Leave it out,' he growled through the subsequent laughter.

It was a hell of long shot, but since murder, statistically, was most often a local affair, Hallows went with the idea. 'Square it with Earle's and the new owners.'

This settled, Kennet said: 'House-to-house is going to be tricky. We could be chasing Victoria Crescent's past residents all over the UK. I'll hold back on that until we can be near positive about the year. Of course we could come at it from the Bisset angle . . . '

Hallows halted him: 'Bisset isn't likely to be our prime suspect. Apparently he's been crippled for years from osteoporosis – the exact number we'll have to look into – unusual in men. He can't climb stairs. Liz, I think you'd better see him: the softly-softly touch. If he's clearly not involved we don't want to upset the man. Link with Roy over other previous occupiers of number 6.'

'Right, guv.' She glanced back at Kennet.

He nodded; there had never been any rivalry between them, nor sex. He enjoyed the company of women, had had a number of satisfactory, short-term affairs and now, in his mid-thirties, considered that degree of commitment was as far as he would ever venture. As to Ferret, while she was assuredly attractively female, on the job he tended to regard her as one of the blokes.

'What about the press?' the appointed press officer asked. 'Better to make an announcement about *Vicky* than have a leak.'

'Let's keep it to ourselves for a while.'

The press officer looking sullenly uneasy.

'Alcott's death will provide a blind until we're ready,' Hallows added. 'I'll have a word with the coroner for a delay in her inquest. Any other questions? No? Right, all to it then!'

Noise and activity broke out.

Hallows cast about for his sergeant. 'Rob?' Curtis snaked forward through the shifting crush. 'Keep at Forensics over the woman's few clothes. Vintage, style, quality; manufacturer even. Something as soon as possible. They're our only jumping off point.'

With Curtis one stride behind in his substantial wake, Hallows marched in the direction of Iain Sinclair's office with a hope that Sinclair would be found there. Hallows had no desire to confront his brother-in-law with a cadaver near by, yielding up its secrets.

Sinclair had been host to the unknown woman for only a few hours when Hallows arrived at University Hospital. 'I hope you're not expecting to learn how she died yet.' Scowling, Sinclair glanced up from where he wrote. 'There's a queue for my time. People die with regularity, you know.' Sinclair's Edinburgh accent grew proportionately more noticeable with fatigue or shortness of temper. He was scrawling his signature at the bottom of a lengthy, detailed report. A collection of half empty tea cups, littering a nearby table, suggested he had been in the department more hours than was its due, but there was nothing stale about his appearance.

Sinclair looked immaculate in his whites, as immaculate as he would in his charcoal three-piece suit when he left the hospital for home at the end of the day. Apart from his hooked nose, he had clean-shaven refined features which were capped with sleek, silvering hair. Curtis was taken with the way his pale, much scrubbed hands moved. They were quick and startlingly decisive. He had no doubt Sinclair could dispose of a troublesome fly at first swat.

'I'm not rushing you.' Hallows had responded so tranquilly Curtis, for a moment, wondered if he was with the wrong man. 'She's waited ten years,' he continued, 'a few more hours won't make much difference.'

'Ten years, you say. So you're a member of the scientific service now, are you?' The Scot was thrusting a copy of the report into a large brown envelope.

Curtis searched Hallows's face for signs of rising ire and saw none.

'Bernard Scofield gave an opinion.'

'Scofield?'

Hallows nodded blandly.

'Well, we'll see.' There was no animus in the statement.

Then it dawned on Curtis that these two men were engaged in an odd form of ritual joust born from mutual respect and kinship.

'But you've had a look at her already? Admit it.' The slightest of smiles curled at Hallows's mouth. 'That's why you're pushed now.'

A grin began to creep across Sinclair's face. 'Of course I have. External features. X-rays. PM itself is going to be tricky – however . . . '

'So what have you got so far?'

Pulling a fresh buff file towards him, Sinclair flicked back the cardboard cover to reveal initial notes.

He informed: 'The body is desiccated, shrivelled, brownish-black in colour. The anatomical features are well preserved despite larval activity: skin still clings to much of the shrunken frame and there's a good sample of hair in the pubic area. The head was severed close to the time of death in a very precise manner – you're looking for a fine bladed knife. No damage to the third cervical vertebra. She was white and a brunette. She would have been around five-foot eight inches tall and I'd hazard she was in her early twenties. No scars that I've discovered so far . . . ' He looked up daring anyone to ask for more. They had had their allowance.

'But how does it happen; mummification, that is?' Curtis asked. 'I mean, Helenborough is hardly your Egypt. No hot sun, no hot sand, no drying winds.'

'Quite. So it must be down to where she was left immediately after death. I gather the cupboard was upstairs next to a much used chimney. Therefore the body remained in a constantly warm environment with a generous amount of drying air circulating around it. The tissues would have dried out gradually without the smell of putrefaction . . . but yes, Sergeant Curtis, I grant you, it is pretty unusual.'

'Is Bernard Scofield right about the ten years?' Hallows asked.

'It's too early for me to say, however-' Sinclair raised his shoulders in a resigned shrug -'Scofield knows his bugs.'

Hallows changed subject: 'Are you doing the PM on Huey Alcott?'

'Past tense.' Sinclair picked up the large envelope. 'Your report's in there. Nothing to suggest foul play. Partial burn damage. Signs of the heavy drinker: bloated appearance, vitamin deficiency, poor circulation. He might well have wanted to light a fire, November is a damp, chill month. Since he had severe liver damage, he had only a very limited span ahead. The vodka bottle's been sent for a contents and fingerprint check as routine.' Sinclair paused reflectively. 'Looked seventy; was closer to fifty. Hardly recognizable since . . . '

Hallows cut in: 'You knew him?'

'Passingly – years back. He was on the hospital payroll. Started drinking and was asked to leave. Don't remember any details.' He scratched his chest absently. 'Found any trace of the matches?'

'Matches?' Hallows frowned.

'Well, Alcott was hardly likely to carry a lighter,' he scoffed and flapped the envelope, 'You'll read there was no intense incendiary damage to the body, so they couldn't have been in his pocket. Yet Alcott, at his level of poverty, would have regarded them as a precious possession surely? Almost as important as the vodka bottle he was clutching so determinedly while engaging with death. Even if mentally confused, he would have kept them close by.'

Vicky's desiccated remains waited on a ceramic slab for Prof. Iain Sinclair.

'This is the body I saw when called to number 6, Victoria Crescent at . . . ' The first officer at the scene gave formal identification. He moved back. There were enough people mustering around *Vicky*.

Sinclair was flanked by an assisting pathologist, two mortuary technicians, a medical photographer and his assistant, an entomological specimens officer, a forensics laboratory officer and a scenes-of-crime officer.

'The trouble is-' Sinclair indicated for the photographer to take introductory shots before the first incision was made -'Mike Hallows would like me to be very definite about the year of death, and unless something unusual turns up, it's going to be impossible. The X-rays revealed no fractures and the body shows no signs of operational scars, so there's no evidence to take him delving into hospital records.'

The photographer stepped back and the scalpel was raised. 'Now, let's see what we can find. Once mummification is complete,' he was explaining to the company in general, 'no further organic changes can take place.'

The team worked in recurring succession: incisions were made, internal structures exposed, photographic records taken and contents of various organs with tissue samples collected; this last achieved with particular difficulty due to the husk-like state of the body. The unique experience drove out all thoughts of other conversation. All that could be heard was a discussion over what was being painstakingly revealed and the voice of Sinclair dictating his findings into the overhead microphone.

Nearly four hours later, much longer than would be normal for a recent death, the post-mortem was over.

'Wonder what the Super will make of that? Though it's hardly a motive.' The photographer's remark was directed at whoever might be listening as he removed the final film from his camera.

'Time was when it was,' the assisting pathologist pronounced, but refrained from explaining to what attitude exactly he alluded.

Sinclair, not contributing to the debate, tossed his protective clothing into a laundry receiver and walked purposefully to his office.

The phone on Hallows's desk produced only a brief noise before he lifted the receiver. 'Iain – you've done it? So?'

'I can't confirm or dispute what Bernard Scofield has said about time. If he says May, then May it's likely to be. If he says ten years ago then he's on his own. I can neither support nor deny that date. Since there is no other apparent cause, death probably occurred through some trauma to the head. The removal of the head came after death.'

'Trauma? Natural or homicidal?'

'Find the head and I'll tell you. But I know which I'd back. Removal of the head with such precision does not indicate panic or feverish fear.'

There was a pause when Sinclair listened to Hallows's even breathing. The pathologist held back on his best shot, waiting for the question that would bring its release.

'Then you found nothing helpful?'

'I didn't say that.' Sinclair heard Hallows snort. 'She was pregnant with a foetus of ten weeks. Perhaps when you find the father you'll have your murderer.'

'Ten weeks, you say. Not long into the pregnancy: could be the man who fathered the child didn't know.'

DCI Kennet entered the bright display area of Earle's with its glossy photographs and looked around for a member of staff not engaged with a client. Linda Thorne, catching sight of him from the open door of her office, came down the short, separating length of corridor when Kennet asked to see one of the bosses.

'Mr Elwood's free, but he's going out very . . .'

Kennet cut in: 'I won't keep him long.'

Elwood, rising too sharply to greet his visitor let out a very audible wince. He was instantly apologetic. 'Pulled a muscle playing badminton with my son. I've an appointment at his school imminently – A-level discussion – so I can't spare you much time.' And, as if to enforce the point, he checked his watch.

Kennet, who could be obsessional over the profitable use of time, pushed on: 'Am I right in thinking Grandfield Development Company have bought Victoria Crescent?"

'Quite correct.'

'In absolute confidence: we need to examine the properties. This will involve lifting floor boards and turning over the gardens. Who should I contact?'

'Floor boards? Gardens? Good grief!' Josh Elwood's eyes, with their fair lashes so long they could have been effeminate on a man less assertively male, narrowed from surprise. 'Whatever for?'

'I can't disclose the reason. Now, Grandfield's man is . . .?'

'Charles Saville.' Elwood scribbled the name and telephone number on a piece of paper but hesitated in placing the information into Kennet's waiting hand. 'He won't want any publicity.'

'Nor do we, sir.'

Parting with the paper, Elwood shot his cuff: 'Lord, the time!'

'I'm off.' But even as Kennet turned away Elwood was clearing his desk in a flurry.

Kennet glanced through Linda Thorne's open door in passing. She was touch-typing and gave him a darting smile. But it was not the recollection of her smile, pleasant as it was, that Kennet carried with him into the street. It was the image of a glorious halo of red hair that filled his mind's eye. It diminished the red tones of his own to complete insignificance.

And thoughts of hair colour took him to *Vicky*. If she had been as distinctive a colour as Elwood's assistant it would immediately narrow the field when they began their hunt through Missing Persons.

Linda heard Josh Elwood's door bang. She sprang up, meeting him in the corridor. 'Letters?' she asked.

'I've signed a batch.' He tugged on his overcoat in a whirlwind of haste. 'Get them in the post as soon as possible.'

'Of course.'

He took a quick step away and staggered. 'Shit! This damned leg!'

'Josh! Can I give advice? Go home when you've been to the school. Rest. You've got no late appointments.'

He moved again warily. 'It makes sense . . . so I'll see you tomorrow.'

Half an hour later, alone in his room, she began folding his letters and sliding them into their envelopes. This done, she walked to the four drawer cabinet to file associated documents. She was pulling open the second drawer when a glint of metal close to eye level distracted her.

On the cabinet top, partly hidden by the abundant, ribbon-leaves of a chlorophytum, lay a ring of keys. Josh had been atypically careless. She glanced at them periodically as she slotted away the remaining papers, then carried them to her own desk where she placed them squarely in its centre. His car keys were on a separate ring, otherwise he would have been back long ago. These keys were for the office, its safe, his private cupboard, and his house.

What to do?

There was no equivocation.

On the point of ringing his home, Elwood rang her: 'My keys. I dashed out in such a rush . . .' His tone hinted at self reproach rather than concern. 'Can you drop them off at the house after work?'

'Yes, no trouble. But don't expect me too soon, I have some late night shopping to do.' Such a lie.

She slid her finger through the ring and gently twirled the keys.

New dictum: no more missed opportunities. She felt elated, like a traveller bound for a new and exciting land.

When the staff had left for home she would open that cupboard.

Smoke curled lazily upward from forty cigarettes lit eagerly after a morning of deprivation in other regions of the building. The ceiling of Abbots Hill's canteen, repainted white only recently, was already hinting nicotine-yellow.

Ferret and DS Scott carried their loaded lunch trays towards a free table close to a window which she surreptitiously opened a crack. At any moment she expected a yelled complaint above the clatter of crockery and intermittent laughter. None came which saved an argument.

Heads butting in order to hear, the two discussed their morning.

'The hospital couldn't ignore a letter saying there was drink in Huey Alcott's locker, even if it was unsigned,' Ferret said. Point proven when they found a whole bottle of whisky and a quarter-full one, yet his duty partner in Security remains convinced Alcott only drank at home.'

'Well he should know, they worked nights together long enough. That's why they could agree to do the outside turns alone, checking stores, dressings refuse and the like.'

'Pity the letter went missing.' She grimaced as she swallowed a mouthful of chicken pie. 'Grief this is salty!'

'Widowed, daughter abroad, few friends outside work, Alcott had to have been bloody lonely.'

'He didn't deny the whisky was his.' Defeated by the pie she wolfed down beans, carrots and peas. 'Maybe he was too miserable to care anymore.'

'What an existence since then; drunk most of the time and surviving on food hand outs from hospital mates.'

Ferret filled glasses of water. 'He was always seen with a bottle. Someone had to be supplying. Where did it come from?'

Scott took a noisy quenching sip. 'You couldn't leave booze in a shed or a derelict house, some other dosser would get wise and find it.'

'So how would Friend Giving play it, forgetting for a moment a reason for offering handouts?'

'Our guy – it has to be a bloke! – would want to be assured, first, that the supplies were available on demand, second, they couldn't be lifted by other parties, and third, they could be paid for without his making a personal appearance.'

'Sounds like a fix with a corner shop, to me. A certain side door where he could collect. An arrangement that started before Alcott's addiction took a complete hold.'

Scott looked at her eyes, the darkest of grey, often playful but now glittering with certainty. He wasn't about to disagree: 'Then we're considering premises away from the city centre, but not too far from Alcott's pitches. He ranged between us, in Peel Square, the hospital grounds and the quay.' He pushed his plate aside, then heeled his way back from the table with sturdy legs. Legs that had, before he had joined the police, carried him efficiently over army assault courses while he roared at other marines to do better. 'Want a coffee?'

'Mm, thanks.' She watched him join the slow moving queue. He was quite short for a copper but square, solid, with a thick bull neck and powerful shoulders. His face, beneath dark close-cut hair, was hard and unquestionably ugly until he smiled. No one in full possession of their senses would mess with Scott. And he was one of the kindest men she knew.

He planted a brimming black in front of her, sipped his white and resumed talking: 'While you're seeing Bisset, I'll organize shop calls with Alcott's photo.' He blew soft ripples across his coffee. 'Wonder if the hospital personnel file will produce anything?'

'I set more hope on the Management Committee's minutes taken shortly before Alcott was fired. If he had been discussed in committee, it should have been noted.'

Scott reached for the sugar bowl.

'You've given it up.'

'Yes, in coffee – but not direct.' And he pushed a cube into a grinning mouth. 'Now, reasons for Alcott being supplied with liquor. He must have got wind of somebody nicking from the hospital. Drugs, food, linen.'

'That's one scenario. But what if his death is linked with *Vicky*? Perhaps he saw something and didn't, at the time, realize its significance. Important then, to keep his mind blurred by encouraging an accelerating habit. A man pickled isn't going to think through details. But Friend Giving would always see Alcott as a risk. His death and the incineration of her body would be the only satisfactory conclusion.'

Situated on the somewhat meandering River Nean, Helenborough's occasional outcrop of hills came as a surprise with their abrupt and unexpected heights where they sprang from the old flood plain.

To the south-east of the city, the road Ferret followed had risen steeply, cutting a straight course through a mid-sixties housing estate. At the crest, the march of semis had dwindled into pasture. She had a sudden open view: the descending road, a Tarmac drive, dark against the lighter shade of lawns, and a large, cream-walled house.

Even when first built Green Vale could have had nothing to recommend it architecturally. Now, eighty years on, when extensions had been added willy-nilly, only its many windows showed something of an agreed form.

She left her car parked among a dozen others, hurried up a flight of three wide steps with a dividing wheelchair ramp and, cupping her eyes against incidental reflection, peered through the glazed front door. The entrance hall, with inviting chintz-covered chairs and bowls of fresh flowers, was empty.

Prodding a bell-push marked *Visitors*, Ferret picked a wisp of fluff from her corduroy trousers and waited.

A nurse in darkest blue arrived immediately and unlocked the door.

'Chief Inspector Ireton? We spoke on the telephone. I'm Sister Parke. I've told Mr Bisset of your intended visit and about the fire.'

'How did he take the news?'

'He ignored me. Not unusual. He's bitter at giving up his home.' She led the way into the east wing past numbered doors spaced along a wide corridor. 'There.' She pointed. 'Just knock and go in.'

The rectangular room, of a good size, was dominated by two immensely tall sash windows located on one long wall. The furniture was plain, smelt strongly of polish, and just sufficient to cater for basic needs: sleeping, eating, sitting to look at the grounds or sitting to watch TV. While adequately comfortable, such stark impersonality depressed Ferret. Had Jacob Bisset no photographs to stand on his bedside table, or paintings to enliven the walls? What did he read? She could spot no books other than one that was leather-bound and bulky, lying on his lap and partly concealed by his loosely held hands as he sat at the further window.

'Thank you for seeing me,' she said, took a dining chair and placed it close by.

He ignored her entirely as she settled herself, bag at her feet, notebook on knee. She followed his gaze, saw the close cut lawn and a distant tended circular bed where roses had been brought to uniform barbed sticks by winter pruning, and wondered how sustained would be the pleasure of this view over the grey months ahead.

While his oval face was parchment white and skeletal, there was still some indefinable quality present that hinted of a once good-looking man. He was fully dressed, wearing peat-brown trousers and a greener toned Harris-tweed jacket. This hung from his shoulders, emphasizing his shrunkenness. A slight doming of his upper spine had brought his head, well capped with dark straight hair, jutting forward over his chest.

His translucent skinned hands with their knobbly joints remained motionless on the book.

Quite suddenly he turned his head, confronting her with cold unblinking eyes. 'Who set light to my house?' he snarled.

Ferret caught her breath at the unexpected hostility but there was something else, beneath the words, that had her hackles rising.

Outwardly unruffled, she said: 'Yours? I thought you'd sold it.'

'So, what else am I to call it?'

She was struck by his voice: such a marked phonetic clarity.

'A vagrant got in.' She moved on briskly: 'You've been told I'm here to ask questions about the property. When did you buy it?'

'Fourteen years ago. Why the interest?'

'To assist with a series of enquiries we're making.' A panacea of a reply given, she realized, too readily, for he picked his words as a chef might select a knife.

'Time on your hands?' he said. 'Nothing better to do? Nobody in Helenborough to harass? Short of paper to file? Get on!'

His dark, deepset unwavering eyes were as hard as nail heads and she was reminded of a preying reptile. She shifted fractionally in her chair. 'Who did you buy it from?'

'A large family: can't remember the name. Earle's handled the sale, ask them.'

She would. 'And you occupied the entire house?'

'Yes, until I was defeated by the stairs. Ten or eleven years ago I had a builder put in a bathroom on the ground floor. I had the first floor cleared and forgot about it.'

'So you didn't let out the upstairs rooms?'

'I did not. I like my privacy.' The words danced solos in their clarity.

'What was the name of the builder?'

'Fenner, or something like that. Are you sure you're a police officer? You sound like a busy-body from social services.'

She bit her tongue. He was goading her. He didn't require reminding that the social services had been instrumental in helping him to preserve his independence for so long. She would be speaking to them about him in due course.

She continued levelly: 'Did the nurses and home helps have keys?'

'No. I kept the front door unlocked until I went to bed.'

'So that friends and neighbours could come and go?'

He gave a derisive snort: 'I don't have friends. Finished?'

No friends. She could believe it if he was always as crabby as this. But it was the pellucidity of his speech that increasingly intrigued her. She inquired about his neighbours before they had accepted Grandfield's offer and moved away. She was not surprised to learn that he had frozen them off. 'And you resisted those early offers to buy your house, negotiated by Earle's?'

'Why should I have moved? Why should I have been inconvenienced?'

'But then your health deteriorated further and you had no choice but to come here?'

He shrugged: 'It would seem so.' Glinting crystals of tone.

Ferret found she was listening to the sound of him, independent of meaning. Such musicality, such perfect diction. 'What did you do for a living before you became disabled?'

He turned from her abruptly, looking again out of the window. She saw that the roses were lost, hidden by an early creeping dusk.

She waited, obstinate for an answer.

He took a long time to reply: 'Before this living death? Too long ago to recall, and nothing to do with you.'

A living death . . . With a shiver, she was brought back to his condition. Dear God, what must it be like, her mind raced to ask, to be in constant fear of breaking bones, to be imprisoned inside a treacherous body? She said with compassion despite disliking him: 'It must have been distressing, having to give up most of your possessions.'

He glanced at her warily and seemed better satisfied when she reverted to pattern, asking: 'Who arranged for your house to be cleared?'

'Earle's. They're very good at arranging such things.' It was no advertisement. There was no intimation of praise.

Out again in the car park with the nursing home behind her, its windows ablaze with lights like a great ungainly ship aground on a ghostly sea, she took off her jacket and shook it with vigour. The action was as near as she could get to washing. In some inexplicable way, Bisset had succeeded in making her skin creep.

She couldn't yet be finished with him, not until she could show that *Vicky* had been placed in the cupboard after the time he had become unable to climb the stairs.

Earle's would be closing before she reached the centre of Helenborough. Talking to the agents about the sale and clearance of Bisset's house would have to wait until tomorrow.

Back at Abbots Hill, with a coffee close to hand, she began a search through a register of local builders. Bisset had said Fenner. She found no such name, but there was a Reg Falder who specialized in house alterations. Hoping she had the right man, she arranged to see Falder early the next morning.

It was nearly seven. Ferret leaned back in her chair, stretched her setting joints, then slowly raked her fingers through her hair. She ought to see Hallows before signing off. She drained her cup, then ambled in the direction of his office.

The sound of his absently drumming pencil trrrap-tapped along the stark corridor and she guessed he was reading his way through a never lessening mountain of case reports.

'Scotty's still combing through the hospital's staff file on Alcott,' she said.

Hallows looked up, beetle-browed: 'And Bisset?'

'Lovely man – chews wormwood between meals!'

He listened to what she had learned, then tossed his pencil aside with finality. 'Going home?' She nodded. 'I'll walk downstairs with you. I need five minutes change of air.'

As they emerged through the swing doors on to Peel Square, they met the ever present swamping sound of its traffic. Neither of them saw Dr Oliver Wyland.

On the point of drawing away from the kerb, Wyland glanced back towards the police station and recognized Ferret. It had been six months since they had last spoken when she had interviewed him at Helenhall. If Wyland had known that he, Elwood and Hawes had entertained her and Scott quite recently with their dancing on the steps of the Royal Hotel, he would have shaken with carefree laughter.

She left Hallows, turned downhill towards the quay and entered Bear Street at a cracking pace.

Wyland moved off, intending to visit the Mitre. Bear Street was on his route. He passed her, then stopped. 'Hi! Remember me?' he called through his opening window as she came alongside.

She turned abruptly, then recognition relaxed her face. 'Of course. Dr Wyland.'

'How's your crime-drenched life?'

'Interesting.' She smiled.

'Like a lift?'

'No, but thanks.'

'You're welcome.' He echoed her smile, then pulled away.

She watched his car turn left and disappear at the next junction. 'Oliver Wyland,' she murmured slowly. 'What is it with you?' And she stepped out again, trying to ignore her sudden racketting pulse.

A squat and solid rather than imposing building, the exterior of the Mitre Inn indicated little of its ancestry. Until the dissolution it had been a monastic property. Then it had slipped into decay until the nearby university grew in importance when its many visitors required a convenient inn.

In recent years the Mitre had become a popular stamping ground for Helenhall University's senior staff. Beneath its stout beams there was room to stand in groups or sit at the numerous small tables and gnaw over in-house rancours and gossip. While not particularly smart, it served Ruff's Russet, a choice real ale, and offered sound food from its bar and in its more intimate restaurant.

Neville Howard, Anne Hawes's father, sat at the bar idly revolving his glass as he considered the menu. He was a quiet, courteous man, known for his shrewdness and sensitivity. The years had treated his features kindly; while life's lines had deepened, his face had mellowed to a kind of beauty. The moderate arrogance of his middle-age had vanished, only to be hinted at by a firm and jutting jaw. His hair remained thick but was now totally white. He was a little proud of it, and of his figure. A slim man, he was still very upright.

It was boredom, not ageing, that was his enemy since retiring. While registrar to the university, he had never indulged in any consuming hobbies and none, other than a little walking, were enticing him now. In want of some conversation the widower had taken to eating his evening meals at the Mitre because of its popularity with former colleagues.

He spotted Wyland approaching: 'Oliver, having your usual?' Howard had known Wyland a long time: watched him progress to earn a distinguished and far reaching reputation. In his mid thirties and invariably dressed as casually as his students, he headed the Department of Earth Sciences.

Wyland tossed his black leather jacket on to a bar stool and sat on another, saving Howard a crick in the neck when talking up to his six-foot-four. No longer the spindle he was in his youth, Wyland was still markedly lean. Cupping his hands over his face, he blew out fatigue, then scooped his dark hair back from his brow in a gesture of release.

'A Ruff's would be a life-saver, Neville, but only a half. I'll be driving home to Roxleigh on a very empty stomach.'

'Missed lunch again. Why not eat here, with me?' Howard pushed the brimming amber Ruff's closer to Wyland.

'I can't. Too much to do. I lost time with a visit to Abbots Hill. Two of my students were a mite foolish during Rag Week.'

'What! Nothing that will harm the university?'

'No, no. You can relax.' Wyland took an appreciative swallow.

Howard watched Wyland gazing into the glass with a suggestion of a smile that had nothing to do with patterns created by the thinning foam. He was content to wait: Wyland was, in most instances, open by nature.

'I'd just left Abbots Hill when I had an encounter of an agreeable kind.'

'Ah . . .' Howard encouraged.

'DCI Ireton. She investigated the campus attacks last May. Bold grey eyes, face like an elf: an attractive elf. Yes ... definitely attractive.'

There was a tantalizing pause.

'And?'

Wyland tinged his neat finger nails against his glass. 'Don't know if she's attached. Wondered whether to invite her out.'

'Well, if you do, for goodness sake don't start comparing her with Kate.' Howard's tone became impatient: 'Better, perhaps, if you two had divorced acrimoniously. Brought children into the world and argued over them like the rest of the nation. You might then be more willing to forget her.'

'Don't act the cynic,' Wyland scolded good-naturedly. 'As to passing on my genes . . . you have to like babies to procreate and I'm not sure that I do.' He changed the subject: 'I'm promised a house-warming party invitation from Anne and Keith. Will you be there?'

Howard's nose crinkled: 'Too old for parties. Too noisy. Too crowded. Too many faces I don't know. Mostly Anne's wealthy patients, no doubt.'

'Do I detect a chime of disapproval? You should be relieved the Fitness Centre is a success. Keith poured a lot of money into it.'

'I am, of course, but they work such long hours. I see so little of Anne. Anno domini, Oliver, anno domini.'

'Well, have a word. She probably regards you as being ageless, not in the autumn of your years.' Wyland drained the last of his beer. 'Thanks for that. My call next time.'

Regretfully Neville Howard watched him leave and wondered what kind of husband Oliver Wyland might have made for Anne, but that brief affair had been so long ago, well before he had met and married Kate. Eleven years, was it? It was before the fearful murder of Gina Hawes. And now Anne was married to idolizing Keith.

Oliver, Keith and Josh Elwood: death and sadness had touched all three friends. Elwood's wife had also died, leaving him with two young children. Then incomprehensible Fate had made Kate want to divorce Oliver, whose affection had never faltered, and marry Josh. But no one could deny Lucy and Patrick Elwood had gained a loving mother.

It was a rare occasion. Keith and Anne Hawes had allowed themselves an evening free and were leaving the Fitness Centre together.

'Am I forgiven?' Hawes asked without seriousness.

'No.' But she laughed, a sound that was soft and melodic. 'You are the limit. Fancy putting a bundle of invitations into your coat pocket and then forgetting to post half of them.'

'Not half,' he protested, 'Only four that needed stamps.'

'Just as well I found them before I got to the cleaners. You men! all with stinky clothes. Oliver's fault, wanting to bake potatoes in Lucy's Guy Fawkes fire. If Josh has heard about our party he'll think he's been cut.'

'Not Josh. He'll have guessed there's been no more than a technical hitch.' He heard a theatrical sniff. 'Delivering the invitation will set things straight.'

Elwood's large Edwardian semi-detached house, designed like its neighbours to rise imposingly from higher ground, but only a short distance from the road, had drive space for only one car. Second cars were parked in the road. Hawes was surprised to find a good sized kerbside gap conveniently near.

Choosing to wait in the car, Anne pulled off her gloves and began to select a cassette. Her smooth, firm-skinned hands were without jewellery except for her narrow gold wedding ring. It was inappropriate to wear rings at work, as inappropiate as it was to have long nails. Hers were kept rounded and very short.

A weak street lamp stretched Keith's shadow to giant size as he left the path and sprang up the steps to the Elwoods' front door. She watched him reach for the bell, then he turned and waved. She waved back, but doubted he could see her in the deeper darkness of the car.

She had slotted in some Mozart when the door opened. A cheerful, wide beam gave Keith cogent form before he disappeared inside. In the car it was growing cooler. She tugged at the collar of her grey soft-wool coat and pinched it in so that it hugged against her high cheek bones. She felt some warmth returning except to her small, straight nose. She could live with that, but not with chilling fingers.

She started to feel for her discarded gloves when, from behind, head-lights at full-beam cut across the car's interior. The light was no sooner there than gone as the vehicle parked. Anne watched for the driver as the car door slammed. A woman walked briskly past. She recognized petite Linda Thorne as she, too, sprang up the steps and then stretched for the bell.

Kate had teased Hawes as she led him into a rear sitting room. 'You're not checking up on your patient, surely?' Her husband reclined, his legs extending along a settee. 'Looks decadent, doesn't he? So why the pleasure of an unexpected visit?'

'Ah, please note that I am looking hang-dog.' Hawes's amiable face held not a dash of shame. 'We're having a party and I've forgotten to post this.' He dropped an envelope on to Elwood's lap.

Elwood withdrew the elegantly printed card, read it and passed it on to Kate. 'House warming. Do we deign to go?'

She made a brief pretence of displeasure. 'Well . . . We surely do. So you are pleased with the house?'

'It couldn't be better for . . .'

The door bell rang and Kate hurried to answer it.

The bright escaping light from the hall lent fire to Linda Thorne's hair. She gave a trifling toss of her head. The effect was glorious; of shimmering flames.

Kate felt a spasm of irritation: the woman knew.

She stood back. 'Go through, Linda.'

Linda had not been in this rear sitting room before. It was small, furnished modestly, comfortably. It suggested sheltered family intimacy, a sense reinforced by the slight lingering smell of a nourishing home-made leek soup. A pang of envy brought a very physical pain; she wanted all this.

'Your keys.' She passed them to Elwood but it was to Hawes she turned, his moneyed friend, and offered a sensual smile.

Hawes enjoyed the moment, then pointed to the keys. 'You don't mean to say you left those behind, Josh.' His charming laugh would not be contained. He turned to Linda: 'I made a social gaffe. So, Linda, do you like house warmings?' His brow arched. He sparkled amusement. 'Will you join us?'

Linda's mouth opened a fraction in brief astonishment. She would have wanted, but to be given . . . 'I'd be delighted.'

It was a pretty mouth, Hawes decided. However, he could admire it with detachment. No woman could hold a candle to Anne. 'Our pleasure. Now I must go. Anne's in the car. Can't keep my love waiting, she might deny me my rights.' And with an exaggerated wink he left them.

Chapter 2

Reg Falder's modest bungalow lay at the end of a cul-de-sac and some distance from similar properties. It stood back from the lane behind a hedge of holly and a garden wearing the overgrown look of autumn. The builder's yard, on adjoining land, was hidden by taller holly allowed to grow as a screen.

Falder was loading copper piping into the back of his pickup when Ferret drove into the yard. She wondered if it was inconvenient, living as he was on the margin of Helenborough. But then she supposed bulky materials were more likely to be delivered to the work site.

He stood resting his back against the side of the vehicle, watching her as she walked from her car. Falder was close to forty with a full and heavily lined face. It was as if sadness had visited and then refused to leave. He was not a tall man but square, sturdy. His navy jerkin strained and failed to meet across his chest. His arms were as thick as hawsers beneath the checked shirt.

She saw he was eyeing her with some surprise and guessed he had expected a policewoman of more substantial weight, equating brawn with strength, forgetting the value of speed. Ferret, dressed as usual in trousers, roll-neck sweater and crisp cut jacket, was built to run.

He said: 'Glad you're on time. Can't hang around, I'm short-handed this morning.'

'I know how it feels, chasing a shrinking day.' She smiled and he relaxed as a quiet man would who was happier on his own than dealing with people or authority. 'Did you do work for Jacob Bisset of 6 Victoria Crescent, about ten years ago?'

'Yes. Come into the office.' His office was a small flat-roofed brick building overlooking his back garden.

She had hardly stepped inside when she heard a child's voice calling and laughing. Through the dusty window she saw a tiny girl skipping across the lawn to a rabbit's hutch placed near the dividing fence. Her piping voice carried clearly as she chattered to the white doe while pushing a carrot through the mesh.

Ferret had ambiguous feelings towards small children. With no strong maternal instincts, most times she could remain detached, but occasionally she would warm to one. As the fingers of the child's free hand tried to reach and stroke the soft fur while the rabbit nibbled at the carrot, Ferret was aware of that rare tender response.

'My youngest.' Falder's weather-brown face softened. He lingered, watching her, and then remembered the time and became brisk.

Central, on an elderly desk, the details relating to Bisset rested on a spread sheet of drawings for a house extension. He ran a calloused finger along the date line of the job sheet. 'Got the go ahead after the Christmas-' his finger pointed -'ten years back. Started work end of January. Put the new bathroom in where the back scullery used to be. Not difficult. Didn't have to chase Bisset for the money.' He passed her the copy of the receipted bill. 'Received his cheque at the end of Feb. Not seen him since.'

'What did you do about the bathroom upstairs?'

'Nothing, except check there were no leaks and the piping was lagged. He wanted the heating turned off to most of the rooms up there, and I didn't want the bloke flooded out from a burst pipe. Had the floor boards up where necessary.'

'Did you have to go into the alcove cupboards?'

'Yes, that's where the planks ended.'

'Every cupboard in every bedroom?'

'Yes.'

'And they were empty? Nothing stored there?'

'Nothing.'

'Just now you said: most of the rooms?'

'Yes, well, the front bedroom still had a few bits of furniture in it.' He screwed up his eyes trying to recall. 'A good sized room, that one. Nice bit of moulding over the door: chrysanths, birds and the like. Clever bloke who did it; I'm not much good on the fancy stuff. The wife would have liked it, I remember thinking. Stunning flowers. Anyway, there were rugs in there, a heap of cushions, a carved chest – bloody heavy. Had to move the lot. There was an easy chair – might have been two – bit hazy. It was a long time back.'

'No bed?'

Falder shrugged. 'No. Perhaps he wanted to discourage people from staying.' He looked towards the garden again, where an elderly woman had appeared and was pegging out washing. 'Know the feeling,' he said ruefully.

She grinned and left to see Bisset's doctor.

Kennet met Curtis carrying three cups of coffee with infinite care into Hallows's third-floor office. He helped himself to one, took a sip, found it too hot and planted the cup on the narrow window sill. He had come to report progress.

He began: 'Charles Saville, representing the Grandfield Development Company, is being surprisingly cooperative for a business guy who counts delay and accumulating costs. We can lift floor boards, strip down what we like so long as we respect the stucco work. He's offered us skips and a couple of their workmen's cabins: they'll make a good blind. Our blokes will be able to eat and wash up on location.'

'So when are you going in?' Hallows sniffed his coffee before tasting it. It didn't smell much like coffee, but then constabulary instant never did.

'This afternoon. We'll start with number 6. Hope it doesn't rain.' Kennet glanced out of the window at a sky of unremitting grey. 'The garden could turn into a mire. Someone's been keeping front and back in good order. We're chasing up a name.'

Satisfied, Hallows turned to Curtis: 'What about *Vicky*'s clothes?'

Curtis, revolving a packet of biscuits, looking for the pull-tab, shook his head. 'I'll give Forensics another ring closer to midday.' He yanked. A shower of crisp crumbs scattered across Hallows's carpet. 'Ahh! Sorry, guv.'

'Not again.' Hallows grumbled and beckoned for the packet.

Curtis grinned, passed it, and then focused on *Vicky*. 'I presume she was deprived of her head to avoid identification through her teeth. Was she a tart? Running drugs? Since her murderer didn't remove her hands that has to mean . . .'

'. . . no fingerprints on record.' Kennet took a biscuit and then returned to the window. 'I've checked. They're not.'

Curtis moved on: 'Would Bisset have been physically capable of removing her head ten or so years ago, never mind getting rid of it?' He dashed a crumb from his tie. 'As to risking keeping an uncovered corpse under his roof, that would be boneheaded, for Pete's sake. And we haven't heard he's off his chump.'

'Don't have to be mad to be bad.' Kennet quoted the cliché absently. He looked down on bustling Peel Square. The little café opposite was getting busy with early shoppers needing a break.

Curtis shrugged agreement. 'Perhaps she was law-abiding. Either way you can't argue it's unusual for a murderer to get rid of the victim's head.'

'Get rid . . .' Kennet turned from the view, he was not part of that morning out there, the meetings, the pairings, the inconsequential chat. He wished for a moment that he could be, he might feel less gloomy, less disagreeably solitary. 'The head could still be at number 6, under the floor boards or buried in the garden. Of course, it could have been burnt in the grate.'

'Impossible, if Bisset's not involved.' Curtis, all pep and certainty, paused to drink his coffee.

Hallows seldom interrupted when these two were shuttling views. He waited for Curtis to resume.

'SOCO found no trace of blood in . . .'

'. . . the rooms left untouched by the fire. Quite.' Irritably Kennet then added the unnecessary: 'That's why I'm looking elsewhere.'

Curtis's eyes narrowed: why stroppy? There was no asking Kennet, he'd flare. Well, shit, attitude. 'Yes, but don't you see, that would mean the body was dumped out of convenience.'

Hallows put aside his cup with the finality of whistling time: 'Scrubber or paragon. Malignant friend, or stranger, until we know when, we're treading water. We have no time scale and won't have until Liz sorts out the Bisset angle. Sinclair won't deal in guess work other than chancing she was probably killed by a blow to the head. He's made it quite clear he can only help us with her fingerprints, blood group, DNA profile and the fact that she was a healthy, young, expectant mother who died shortly after eating a pizza and salad.'

Linda Thorne, having just shown Charles Saville of Grandfield's into Josh Elwood's room took some minutes for herself. She crossed to the outer office, noted the reference from a large property advertisement for a Grandfield conversion and collected an information pack.

Behind her closed door she spread the contents. Since delving into Josh Elwood's cupboard, photocopying some material, keeping other items, she had spent a considerable time thinking. Now she knew not only what she wanted, but how it was to be achieved.

A tense and impoverished childhood had bred in her the desire for security. A home, bought not rented as now, could bring that providing the financial arrangements were favourable and later income guaranteed. She wanted somewhere not just decent, but modestly impressive to live.

Shillington Court, with luxury two and three bedroom apartments and landscaped grounds extending to the Nean, answered her longing. An apartment, at a tailor made price, was going to be negotiated between herself and Josh Elwood. Of course he would have to make a deal with Saville, but Charles Saville was not in a position to be negative, not with the knowledge she held. Blackmailers were open to being blackmailed themselves.

Having ticked off Reg Falder and Bisset's doctor from her interview list, Ferret turned her car towards the centre of Helenborough. It was Earle's next. The traffic worsened. The city was as thick with vehicles as wasps collected on a basket of over-ripe plums, and the drivers were as tetchy. She left her car in the rear yard of Abbots Hill and walked to the agents.

She arrived only minutes after Charles Saville had left. Elwood was engrossed, writing at his desk when she tapped on his open door.

'Liz! Not wanting to move out of Quay House already?' Elwood joked and, unwisely, sprang up. 'Bloody hell.' Pain seared through his leg and he clutched at the arm of his chair.

She regarded him with a not unsympathetic, lop-sided grin: 'That'll teach you to doubt my love-affair with my home. So what happened? Are you the victim of a tantrum thrown by a dissatisfied client?'

It had eased and he laughed, beckoning her towards a seat: 'Earle's don't have dissatisfied clients. Badminton . . .' he said and explained what had occurred. 'So what brings you here, if it's not about Quay House?'

'6 Victoria Crescent. I'm after information on Jacob Bisset and previous owners.'

'Isn't DCI Kennet dealing with Victoria Crescent?'

'We have different areas of responsibility. Can you confirm the date you sold the house to Bisset?'

'Mmm, should be able to.' Elwood used the internal phone and two well handled files were brought in. 'We run a cross reference system: PURCHASER and also PROPERTY.' He flicked through the pages of Bisset's file. The date of occupancy agreed with that given by Bisset's doctor. The Vernays had owned the house prior to Bisset.

'How long had the Vernays lived at number 6?'

'Eight years.' He gave their address since they would have to be seen.

Having covered Hallows's time allowance for the occupancy of the house she turned to the present. 'Mr Bisset's GP told me it was thanks to you that Bisset agreed to sell up and move into the Green Vale Nursing Home.'

Elwood made a gesture of mild dissent: 'I'd rather believe it was down to our joint efforts. All I did was point out the turmoil that was going to erupt around him once Grandfield began working in the crescent.'

'Mr Bisset said you were responsible for arranging the house clearance.'

'We contacted Parkin & Son: they had dealt with him before.'

That meant Stan Parkin. Ferret knew him. Parkin wobbled along a fine line between nicked goods and honest dealing. Nothing hot had ever been found on his premises. 'When was the previous time?'

Elwood rustled papers. 'February, ten years ago, when Bisset was planning to live solely on the ground floor. . . . Like a coffee?'

'Thanks, if it's quick.'

Linda watched Ferret leave and chose now to challenge Josh.

'Abbots Hill haven't got two detectives investigating the fire in Victoria Crescent, surely?' She collected the two empty coffee cups on to a tray and balanced the files alongside.

'Liz Ireton seems to be more concerned with the history of the building.'

As so often, she looked down on his bent head.

'Interesting,' she said and took the tray into the corridor. She returned, closed the door with a sharp snap and had his attention. 'I'd like a private word.'

He gave an offhand shrug. 'All right.'

'DCI Ireton was asking about Jacob Bisset.'

'So?'

'Then she'd be interested to learn just how you and Charles Saville persuaded him to sell.'

Elwood didn't move. Not a muscle twitched. But a nerve had been touched. His pale eyes blackened. It was as if a shutter had dropped.

'I'm not sure what you mean.'

Linda continued with a quiet arrogance: 'His stubbornness in refusing to sell to Grandfield was threatening to become a nightmare, wasn't it? His staying could ruin the original concept for the crescent and besides, they didn't want to have to work on the properties piecemeal. That would escalate costs.'

Elwood's voice was perfectly controlled: 'Go on.'

'You called on him often, then came back here muttering that he was still sticking. We all knew his views.'

'Bisset enjoyed his independence. I could sympathize with his wish to stay.' His tone mirrored the sentiment.

'You were far more in sympathy with Grandfield's wishes,' she countered. 'Delay could blight all future contracts coming from their company; the efficiency of this firm would be in question. You had tried to coax Bisset to sell with increasingly generous offers.'

'Standard policy,' he pointed out.

'But you found something that was a greater persuader than money. You used fear to drive Bisset out.'

'You have an over fertile imagination, Linda,' Elwood said smoothly.

'No. I have evidence. I have a copy of a letter . . . you, sharing a worry with Charles Saville. And then there's the photograph.' Unmistakably he blushed. She sighed out of pity for his stupidity: 'You really shouldn't hoard, Josh. Relax, I don't propose to tell tales to DCI Ireton – not unless you frustrate my wishes. I want two things of you: a no-dismissal clause in my contract together with an improved salary, and an apartment at Shillington Court: my choice, my price.'

The blush had faded leaving an unhealthy pallor.

Silence. Elwood touched his dry tongue to his lips.

Waiting patiently for him to concede victory, Linda could just detect noises from the street. Life might have momentarily stopped for Josh Elwood but not for those others out there. They progressed, as she intended to.

Elwood did not move for some minutes after Linda had swanned out of his office. He felt the paralysis of shame and fear.

She had broken faith – used his keys!

Coming out of shock his first instinct was to ring Saville. He stretched an unsteady hand for the phone and then halted. Saville would not be available until late afternoon. He must carry this alone.

How reliable was Linda's promise not to talk to Liz Ireton? Since she was so positive over what she wanted, perhaps what she had discovered was safe. But this was not the only question hammering in his mind. What else in his cupboard might she turn to her own use? Besides personal items there were papers he held for Patronus and among these, the financial status of members.

The adrenalin ran. A pulse beat at his temple. He checked his diary: free for an hour after lunch. He could forget eating. He would get rid of Linda, send her to Shillington Court to indulge in a two hour dream. With the rest of the staff told he should not be disturbed, he would go through the cupboard. He must try to deduce what else she might have copied or taken.

Much later, when alone, he'd shred everything not essential to hold.

At Abbots Hill, as the morning passed, Hallows grew irrationally more impatient. The early days of an investigation always affected him like this. While others were out there, asking, listening, he was still here committed to shunting paper.

He thrust himself away from his desk and stomped to the window.

A token patch of blue gave way to a continuous ceiling of low cloud. There was nothing to be seen beyond the irregular plain of red and grey roof tops. If it was a brighter day and he had binoculars he might just be able to make out Wendle Woods on the rising western boundary of the city.

A car horn blared and he glanced down at a snarl-up of cars. Somebody was yelling barbarically as they got moving again.

Helenborough was a warren of roads and to a stranger they all seemed to end at the river. The locals had a saying: It took a long shadow to reach Wendle Woods. Was some mercantile navigational aid being suggested, he wondered, or was an overview the best means of arriving?

Sounded like his province . . . the overview.

Was the *Vicky* case going to be as baffling as Helenborough's road system? Would they be forever coming upon the river? With the trail so overgrown by time, did they have the remotest chance of arriving at Wendle Woods?

'Guv?'

Hallows glanced towards the door. He hadn't heard Curtis arrive.

'Got it!' The sergeant was triumphant. He flapped a bunch of faxed papers bearing the logo of the Department of Forensic Science. '*Vicky*'s clothes.'

'Helpful? The underwear was in poor condition.' Hallows sat with the pages squarely in front of him.

'Darned good, considering. They've included drawings detailing design, style and trimmings. Should help in pinning down the year they were made. As for manufacturer . . .' Curtis was tense with excitement. From behind Hallows's left shoulder he just held back and allowed him to find the appropriate page. 'You see she was a size twelve.' He leaned heavily against Hallows's shoulder as his blunt square-nailed finger prodded at the detail. 'Can you believe it? Under all that dirt the fabric was a cream figured silk. Both bra and briefs were made by Lareine.'

'Lareine,' Hallows echoed. He moved his shoulder, felt Curtis ease back, and glanced up at the narrow enthusiastic face.

'Yes. Classy number. Would have set the budget back a few quid.'

Hallows, reading the details for himself, merely grunted. Yet he knew only too well about the cost. As an occasional surprise for Isla, he had sunk inhibition and walked across the plush carpets of Nichol's lingerie department to purchase gossamer items in a size ten for his wife. They had been married for a little less than a decade and he was pleased to maintain a courtship. He was in no way buying forgiveness for his unsociable hours; he was fortunate in that these were always graciously and unconditionally forgiven. Iain Sinclair's sister, as poised as Iain was precise, was a most tolerant woman.

'Shall I get after their design and marketing people?' Keen to draw attention to every detail, Curtis pressed forward again, more strongly this time.

Hallows, ignoring the force across his shoulder for the moment, twitched pages to and fro, paused to read, and came to the drawings again.

'Well, guv?'

Into Curtis's ear, which Curtis appreciated suddenly was a breath too close to his boss, Hallows said tartly:

'Since you look as if you're maintaining a claim to this angle – why not?'

Back in her car, Ferret headed for the seedier commercial byways of the city. Litter filled the valley of the curb to her left. A paper bag took air and blew in front of her across the road.

She was looking for a narrow entrance. A down-at-heel caf and there it was, the lane to Stan Parkin's warehouse branched off between two high crumbling brick walls; a black hole like a gap in a row of teeth.

The battered furniture van was standing in the dank courtyard, its doors open wide.

She parked. He didn't appear.

'Stan!' Ferret's voice vibrated from the blank back walls of surrounding buildings.

Parkin, a sallow skinned man with prominent cheek bones and lank hair, reversed from the crammed interior of the van and halted at the top of the dropped tailboard. 'What is it?' he yelled over his shoulder and then saw her. 'Oh, its you! Well, I'm busy. No time for jawboning.'

'Who says I'm not?' She thumbed for him to come down. He did so peevishly. 'You moved stuff out of 6 Victoria Crescent, recently.'

He sniffed: 'Bisset's. What of it? Earle's asked me. It's all pretty duff. Won't get much for it.'

'So you haven't sold any of it yet?'

'Ain't 'ad time to price it up. It's still in the warehouse.' He flicked his narrow head in the direction of a long-time disused chapel that was now graced with that name. The building appeared as neglected as the sunless weed-invaded yard in which they stood. The slipping roof tiles were prevented from making a final departure by soft, cushioning ridges of moss. The sagging guttering was a bed to grass whose dead, fluttering seed stalks described a forgotten harvest.

'I'd like to see the recent inventory and also one of a clearance you made for Bisset ten years ago.'

'Ten years ago! Don't want much, do you?' And he headed off towards a room that jutted towards them and had once served as a vestry. Even Parkin could not bring himself to call this an office. It was a hideous confusion of abandoned small household objects. There was hardly room to walk from the outside door to a peeling leather-topped desk which partially blocked the entrance to the main building. Just as well Parkin was skinny, Ferret thought, her nose pinching at the disagreeable fusty air. A man of Hallows's solidity would never squeeze through the gap.

Parkin scratched his head thoughtfully, opened a drawer, changed his mind and rummaged at the bottom of a cupboard. 'Must be your lucky day,' he grumbled and pushed a yellowing ledger her way. He retrieved a scrap of paper from his jacket pocket. The second inventory of goods cleared recently from Bisset's house had not yet been entered in a book. Both lists were dated. 'I'm taking these to make copies,' she said, side-stepped towards the interior door and looked across the congested nave of the building. 'Where have you put Bisset's stuff?'

'Want to refurnish your place?' he gibed and pointed to an untidy stack close to the west door.

She picked a route through an obstacle course that marked, in tables, chairs and cupboards, a cross section of human need. There seemed no order to the way Bisset's effects had been unloaded. She checked the list against the small mountain that confronted her and pointed to what was visible of a brass bedstead. 'I'm not in the market, but you'll get a bob or two for that.'

'Perhaps,' he answered off handedly.

She spotted a revealing twitch at the outer corner of Parkin's left eye. She would have asked the next question anyway: 'Is it all here?'

'Course it is,' he said, spreading his arms expansively.

'You're coming over too strong, Stan.' While he looked wronged she took a list supplied by Earle's from her bag. 'I'll call: you point.'

He shifted sulkily, but did as bidden.

She left the bulkier items until last. She ticked off the brass bedstead, then: 'Chest: oak with carved side panels.'

Parkin moved around the stack, shifting a chair, a fireguard, a small bookcase.

She waited, letting him continue to rummage, allowing him to look more and more ridiculous in the pretence of searching.

He glanced up and met her mocking eyes.

'All right, Stan. The pantomime's over. Now show me where you've hidden it.'

He shrugged amiable defeat and led the way to where rolls of carpet were stacked at an incline against the north wall. The chest was just visible in the cavern they made.'

'Very snug,' she said drily. 'I want to see inside.'

'You would,' he muttered and tugged it out. 'It's empty.' Lifting the heavy lid, he proved the point.

'What was in there when you took it out of Bisset's house?'

'Do me a favour,' he snapped. 'It was bleedin' empty then. Everything was empty. The trouble with you is you mix wiv the wrong people. Now, can we get on? I've got a big job lined up. Won't get finished at this rate till you've knocked off and 'ad yer supper.'

'Play a different record, Stan. Which room was the chest in?'

'Upstairs front.' He leaned into it and propelled it beneath the carpets again.

'I presume you're squirrelling . . .'

'. . . 'cause I've got a buyer lined up. Yea.'

'Well I've got news for you. You don't sell any of Bisset's stuff till I give you the OK.'

'Hang about. I've got a living to earn.'

'You'll manage.'

Ten minutes later she rested Parkin's ledger on the wing of a chair and hunted for the decade-old entry under Bisset. She found his name against 11th January. If in nothing else, Stan Parkin was precise over his simple book keeping. 'Think hard, Stan. Did you empty all the upstairs rooms ten years ago?'

Having been on the premises so recently his memory had been adequately jolted. 'Yes, apart from a few bits he wanted left in the front bedroom.'

'The bedrooms had built in cupboards,' he was nodding, 'did you clear them all out?'

'Course I did. Nothing much was stored there, more's the pity. Good bits can come out of cupboards.'

She grimaced privately. A mummified body hardly qualified. 'Did you check the bedroom cupboards again this time?' she said unemphatically and watched his shifty eyes for any tale-telling changes. There were none. He was innocent of a horrifying knowledge.

'Didn't bother,' he was saying. 'I knew Bisset couldn't climb stairs and it was obvious straight off that the rooms hadn't been used, well, all except the front, that is.'

She masked interest: 'The room you'd left furnishings in before?'

'S'right. No dust there. Thick on the other bedroom floors it was.'

'So who'd been up there? Did Bisset say?'

'Him? Don't be funny! He wouldn't tell you his middle name if he was hanging by his thumbs.'

Parkin's view of Bisset's character, if more colourful, was in accord with others heard today.

She continued: 'So on this recent list, which items came out of that room? And don't kid me on! You're not the only one who's eyeballed the contents.' She didn't say when. It was ten years since Reg Falder had worked in the house.

He said: 'The chest.'

'Was it locked, by the way? Does it have a key?'

'Nah.'

'Go on.'

Impatiently Parkin pointed out an easy chair, cushions, and a pile of four or five small rugs.

She lifted the corner of the top one, glanced at the pattern of the second, then let it fall back again. Dust, in a small cloud, puffed away from the heap. She coughed and looked at him sidelong: 'And you're still saying that the front bedroom was remarkable for its lack of dirt?'

'I know houses.' He was offended. 'I know when rooms are used or not.'

It was nearly two o'clock when Ferret left Parkin. She had a great, yawning hole in her stomach and knowing that the canteen at Abbots Hill would have a depleted lunch menu, she walked to the Dog and Duck, Abbots Hill's local. It lay in a side street, its two bars opening straight off the pavement. It was plain and functional; wheel back chairs, settles, thick plank-topped tables, red tiled floors, leaping fires behind high copper fenders and burnished copper skuttles full of coal. And it smelt of Brasso and lavender wax if you got there early enough before the smokers lit up.

Ferret preferred the Saloon, there was more chance of getting a seat.

Scott, who had been of a similar mind, was leaning against the counter. 'What are you drinking?' His hand went to his hip pocket.

'It's my call.'

For once they didn't argue.

They were both ravenous. They carried their pork chops, peas and hills of chips plus beers, to a side table and ate in virtual silence.

With her empty plate pushed aside and her glass brought forward, Ferret said: 'Anything in Alcott's hospital personnel file?' She eyed Scott's remaining three chips and stole one.

'Oi!' He grinned. 'Zilch, but reading the Management Committee's minutes taken over the four months before he got the boot, there should have been. There are references to letters of complaint received from a member of staff. The complaints were taken on board. The committee's secretary issued the statutory warnings: two verbals followed by a written.'

'Why weren't Personnel instructed to act?' She swirled the last inch of beer and drank it.

'Personnel's senior had left and had yet to be replaced.'

Preoccupied, she rolled the tapered glass between her palms. 'And it's clear that these letters were to be filed by Personnel?'

'Crystal. The minutes don't name who complained and the committee are saying they can't remember now who blew the whistle.' He drained his glass and then snapped beckoning fingers: 'Aren't you telling me anything?'

'You can read my interview statements,' she teased, but left him with a parting nugget. 'Looks as if our entomologist could be right.'

*

All over Helenborough the street lights had begun to flicker on. The road to Green Vale was lined with stammering morse. Jacob Bisset sat motionless, looking out on to the darkening garden. Suddenly the room was bathed in an eerie livid light. The sky, which minutes earlier had been a solid leaden sheet, was dyed crimson from a setting sun: a sun out of his view. Such blazonry left Bisset entirely unmoved. He was more interested in the time, his awaited tea, and an expected visitor.

The tall man, arriving in Green Vale's car park, was affected, however. He turned westward. The sombre cloud-base had unexpectedly divided as if knife cut. He paid homage to the colours which burst across the sky: crimson, blush-reds, orange to a focus of dazzling gold too intense for the eye. Once he would have reached for his camera, now it was sufficient to absorb.

The gape in the clouds closed. The valley was abruptly dark, very dark.

The elderly man, with distinctive thick white hair and aquiline nose, became melancholy as he crossed to the front door of the nursing home and rang the bell. While the sun marked the world out in days; measured a time of endless futures, he saw no brilliant tomorrows for himself. To endure, he lived each day mechanically: the only way with his kind of emptiness.

'You're expected?' A nurse in a hurry let him in.

'Yes. By Mr Bisset.'

'I was told.' She showed him quickly to Jacob Bisset's door and went herself into a neighbouring room. It was the first visitor she could think Bisset had received and, as she secured the window locks and drew her patient's curtains with a brisk tug, she wondered if he was an old friend.

She was aware of muted growling tones: the rumble of an argument coming from next door.

Since Bisset seemed to thrive on quarrelling, she returned to the needs of her patient but, when the dispute grew louder, the two of them listened.

Jacob Bisset's perfect speech was becoming shrill like the harsh whine of a drill. Odd words became clear . . . something that should have been done had not been done. Suddenly his visitor roared. From fury or anguish? The nurse could not tell, but saw danger. A slap and Bisset's bones would crumble.

She ran to intervene.

On the point of bursting into his room, the door swung violently inward. Brought off balance, she was thrust against it by the sweep of a long arm as the elderly man rushed away.

Recovering, she hurried to Bisset's side. He was a fearsome colour, almost purple with a glaring fire in vulturine eyes.

She stared, intimidated: 'Are you all right?'

'Damn fool question!' His words came out in a froth of spittle. 'Confined here and dealing with unreliable dolts. Get out! Get out and leave me alone.'

In the last shred of daylight, DCI Roy Kennet, clad in protective overalls, sat down on a floor joist and rested his broad back against the wall of Jacob Bisset's front sitting room at Victoria Crescent. All the charred floor boards had been removed. The substructure of wooden cross members looked like the scraped ribs of a butchered carcass. He stared at the opposite wall. What had been the purpose of the metal tubing the blaze and then his team had revealed? It was not a relic of early plumbing or of a gas supply. Open ended, it started three feet from the floor, passed upward in the angle of the protruding chimney breast and the wall, where it would have been hidden within the tall bookshelves, then through the ceiling and into the fire-gutted room above.

He turned on his torch and let the beam follow the tube's route into the burnt out alcove cupboard of the bedroom. It ended two-thirds up the wall. It had to have been a conduit for conveying something, but what?

'Not stopping here all night, are you, Roy?' one of the search team asked from the doorway.

Kennet muttered, no, and hauled himself upright then lit his way, joist by joist, to the front door. He carried a dull, deep-rooted ache between his shoulder blades and recognized this was down more to disappointment than fatigue.

They had probed every crook and cranny of the ground floor and dug up over half the garden. No decaying skull had been discovered. No blood stains either, yet, if *Vicky* had been decapitated close to the time of death she must have bled considerably. Tomorrow morning, failing a find here, they would begin a painstaking search of the rest of the crescent.

At this gloaming hour of the day Kennet was visited by pessimism, but he felt a strange sadness as well. As he paused with his grimy-gloved hand on the door he recognized that he had become protective of *Vicky*. He wanted to see some honour paid to her body: he wanted to see justice done.

Elwood had pushed work Linda's way, giving her no time to refer to the apartments seen at Shillington Court. He couldn't talk. This afternoon he would have choked he was so full of spleen. He had to learn to be civil.

She came into his room, fastening her coat: 'Not leaving yet?'

Elwood glanced up. There was something different about her. A vitality. A gleam in those green eyes. She was walking tall, he thought bitterly, thanks to his gross carelessness.

'No,' he said, shuffling paper. 'I'm meeting Kate in an hour.' He bent the truth, then redirected conversation. 'Liz Ireton rang. She was asking about Bisset's effects. We had an oak chest on our list. She wanted to know if it had been locked and whether we had the keys. David made the inventory. Is he likely to be over his cold and back here tomorrow? Our copy is as unhelpful as the list we gave her.'

'We've no keys. David should be back. It's hardly pneumonia. Doubt it's a cold he has anyway. He does the minimum, we ought to get rid of him.'

We, was said with a proprietorial ring that incensed him.

'Eating out?' he asked, wishing her swiftly off the premises.

'Don't I always?' she said easily.

He remained motionless until he heard the outer door locked.

Elwood had rung Kate to say he would be home later than usual. When he appeared she asked, not what had detained him but rather, what was he carrying in the black plastic bin bag?

He was straight with her. 'Private papers I've shredded. Now I want to burn them. What the staff don't see, they don't question.'

She found matches and he prepared his small bonfire where Lucy's Guy Fawkes had recently perished. In the light spilling from the house, the contents of the bag made a ghostly white mound against the dark scorched earth. The thin strips caught quickly. Photographs and letters took flame, glowed red and became ash in minutes.

'Why so much caution all of a sudden?' she asked when he returned to the kitchen.

'The Order of Patronus is not quite the stuff of the Masons, but we do have our secrets. As a senior executive, it's up to me to protect them. Weeding out inessential stuff has been long overdue. Anyway it's done now and I feel better.' They were empty words. They were said for her.

He now knew exactly what Linda was holding in respect of himself and Saville. There was a letter returned by Saville when he had called to reinforce an argument. It damned. Then there were photographs. The irony was that one had been in an envelope addressed in his own hand to Detective Superintendent Hallows at Abbots Hill. Another, predating his marriage to Kate, had gone. He had taken the shot, and should have disposed of it when asked, but sentimentality, and humour at the time, got in the way. In addition, he strongly suspected that Patronus papers detailing each member's financial status had been examined.

Today he had said goodbye to all peace of mind.

Should he warn those others whom Linda might now target? He was inclined to wait and watch rather than usher in anxiety, perhaps needlessly.

As for himself and Saville, they were well caught. The apartment she chose and the price she would suggest would not be opposed. The financial arrangements would be kept in-house.

Like Elwood, his friend, Dr Oliver Wyland had delayed going home.

Since returning from a meeting with the university's purse holders, Wyland had quartered the carpet in his severely practical study at Helenhall: sofa to ceiling-high overloaded bookshelves, door to window and overflowing desk, his long legs making a doll's house of the space as he chewed over what had been said.

The Research Finance Committee, having read his meticulously detailed funding application for his project for next year, had called him and other applicants for interview. Wyland had known that competition between the Faculties would be strong and it had ended with himself and the physiologist, Dr Duncan Milo, in a play off. The fact that Wyland had already scored a success with a project for the police force, tagged Kite by the officers, had carried little weight despite its bringing in a useful financial return.

He and detestable Milo had each been given six months to explore commercial avenues and run a pre-project programme. Upon assessment of their results, plus, it was emphasised, their record within the university, a final choice would be made.

Wyland was determined to meet the challenge and win, but he was also a realist. He had to face what it would mean if muck-raking Milo did get the funding. It could bring a pall of gloom to his own department. His students boiled with the questing spirit, they were ambitious, they looked to their careers, the value of their names in the scientific and academic literature. It was their enthusiasm that gave the extra zest to his work. Damn it, now Kate had gone his life offered little else.

He opened his window and leaned out into the darkness. The tree-dotted lawns of the campus might have been a hillside of grazing sheep for all he could see and might have believed too, if it were not for the purr of traffic noise from the city's roads and the unholy orange halo it wore at night. Money, he reflected, or rather the lack of it – what it made a man do. Desperate needs encouraged desperate measures.

The air struck cold on his face with a hint of damp. He withdrew, pulling the window closed.

Home? He reached for his jacket thrown on to a chair. Did he really want to drive out to Roxleigh yet? What pleasure was there in an empty house and with little in the fridge to compensate for a day of sketchy eating.

No, he'd have a meal in town first.

It was past seven o'clock when Ferret and Scott had parted in the high-walled car park at the rear of Abbots Hill.

She had fancied a change from the utilitarian fair at the Dog. She drove along Bear Street, turned away from the quay and headed downstream for the Riverside Inn. She craved something toothsome, chicken with Gruy re and prawns, with hot, perfectly cooked vegetables.

The bars had been tarted up to look olde-worlde-cottagey but the hospitality was genuine. The place was pretty full, locals mostly, she judged, unlike the late spring and summer when students from Helenhall made the snug and the beer garden their own.

Ferret ordered. The dish arrived and having popped a hot sprout into her mouth, she carried her tray between a press of diners to the only free table that filled the minutest space by a window. Once squeezed into her seat she peered beyond her reflection into the deserted and dismal garden. Two lonely strings of coloured lights threaded parallel routes through incidental leafless trees to the opaque water's side. A slight wind must be blowing off the Nean. They swung gently in rainbow arcs.

Her mind drifted back ten years as she shook folds from her napkin. She remembered how students and regulars had packed into the garden after the fire at Briers Way. How the booze had passed their lips unconsidered while they watched in fascinated silence as the river had been searched for missing Sally Webber.

Her involvement with the case had been minimal. She had been drafted in to Helenborough for a few weeks on general duties, a WPC working for her sergeant's exam.

She tucked into her meal. Food, for her, was a real pleasure. Nothing, well, practically nothing, dampened her appetite.

She was about to spear her last bitesome prawn when some idiot rocked her table.

'Steady!' She grabbed at a tumbling pepper pot as the spare chair was taken.

'Sorry for the earthquake.' Oliver Wyland's smile was apologetic.

Her heart performed a wilful somersault.

'Long legs, small space,' he added. 'May I join you?'

'Join me?' she said tartly, 'I think you have already.'

Last May the man's playful, inviting smile had jolted her into a spin. Now, again, her pulse was racing furiously. It was ludicrous. She wasn't panting for some warmth: for love. And yet, if Providence had brought him here, there was little harm in a tease, a small revenge for being unsettled.

'Moreover-' she contemplated his shins wedged against the table legs - 'I doubt you could extricate yourself even if I did object.'

She fixed him with a steely QC's stare.

It was a pretence she felt certain he would recognise, but even so, she was relieved when she saw amusement crease his eyes. They grinned in unison and she eased the table further her way.

Ferret watched with interest the exactness with which he unloaded his tray and arranged plates, napkin and cutlery. He had chosen a mixed grill to be followed by apple pie, a course she generally waived. 'Are you always so precise?' she asked when the operation was complete.

Wyland made a slight *moue* as he considered the question. 'Guess I am. I do like order. It prevents one overlooking things.' He began to eat, his attention resting on her more than his food. 'But the same principle must apply to your job, too.'

'Oh, I'm meticulous over my work, but at home . . . Well, I have a stack of excuses for some sloppiness. Long hours, fatigue . . .'

'Justified, I should think.' He paused and looked at her intently but his question was delivered casually enough: ' Do you ever have a whole evening off?'

'Of course, Dr Wyland,' she said brightly. 'All work . . . You know.'

'Makes Jill dull.' He was running his knife blade around the chop, carefully separating tender meat from bone. 'Then by that token, you've been logging up plenty of free time.' The compliment had slipped off his tongue uncontrived.

She enjoyed it, but any answer, smart or otherwise, was foiled.

He was adding quickly: 'And for heaven's sake call me Oliver! I presume you have a first name, Chief Inspector, or does your birth certificate read DCI?'

She laughed outright. 'My boss calls me Liz when things are going well.'

'That's Hallows?' He saw her nod. 'We've met. Through *Kite,* I hasten to add.' He smiled again, that smile. 'Fortunately, departmentally, I don't have anybody to please but me. I'm responsible to Helenhall's hierarchy, naturally, and it pays to be of good behaviour.' He was playing with words, words that she might use. 'Or they could cut funds for research or wave me goodbye.'

'And research is important to you?' She watched him exchange his empty first course plate for the apple pie.

'As life. Always has been.' His angular attractive face clouded.

Her curiosity was immediately aroused: 'There's a problem?'

'An annual one. How funds are to be awarded. There was a meeting this afternoon. Instead of deciding today, a colleague and I-' mistrust of Milo brought a passing grimace -'are in a contest situation. It's bothersome.' He looked at her intently again, his dark, deep-set, expressive eyes not leaving her face, even as he shrugged anxiety aside: 'But since I have weeks to fret, I don't have to do it all tonight.'

She was so disconcerted by his continuing attention, she focused on the pie. Crisp flaky pastry, a crust of sugar, a wedge of deep apple. 'Is that good?'

'Judge for yourself.' Deliberately Wyland exchanged spoon for fork, cut a portion and lifted it to her mouth.

Ferret hesitated for an instant, then accepted the morsel. 'Mmm,' she confirmed, 'Very.' then distanced herself, leaning far back in her seat. This was a game which involved people played and, even given that her emotions were in libidinous disarray, she wasn't sure yet if she was ready for a new commitment.

She had been at home for only an hour when her phone rang. It was the duty sergeant at Abbots Hill. 'Ferret, Dr Wyland rang. He wanted your number. I said, *can't do it,* so I've got his. Ready?' He dictated it.

She sat with her legs dangling over the arm of her easy chair and considered the piece of paper. Decision time . . .

Recollections revolving around Mac had eased in recent months. It had been all highs or the pits with him. Sweet memories were few, almost suffocated by the bad, but it was these that gave her pain: the loss of the good times. Was Oliver Wyland OK? Was Oliver Wyland safe? She didn't want to face that kind of gutting hurt again. Yet, he might be fun, and she needed some fun; she'd been a solo act for too long.

She returned to the phone and dialled his number.

'Ah, Liz! A friend's holding a house warming tomorrow. Keep me company.'

Chapter 3

A white mist, thick as gathered muslin, clung to fields and gardens on the extreme boundaries of Helenborough. Since dawn it had masked the course of the river Nean, drifted in gentle billows across the dew drenched lawns of the Riverside Inn and engulfed river bridges which carried traffic into the heart of the city. Approaching Canongate Bridge, the oldest of these, where the water always raced beneath its three stone arches, Hallows needed to turn on the lights of his car.

The *Vicky* case, just now, was as ill defined as the vehicle in front and the pedestrians on the path to his left, and he looked forward to the imminent meeting with his immediate officers to discuss their next moves.

Liz Ireton arrived in his office and took a chair. Rob Curtis arrived and settled his narrow rump on the window sill.

Kennet was late.

Hallows pulled his chair closer to his desk, tapped his pencil irritably against a bare portion of wood and glared at the open door. When Kennet failed to materialize he said: 'Well, let's kick off with Alcott. Do we have an accidental death, or not, Liz?'

'It's looking like not, guv. Alcott had been getting hold of booze on a regular basis, too regular to be nicked. Could be that the payer was tired of shelling out. At the moment we're trying to pin down where his drink came from. There was nothing helpful on the vodka bottle.'

It was ever thus, Hallows thought, and heard speeding feet.

'About time,' Hallows grumbled as Kennet rushed in. 'Well, shut the door.'

'Sorry, guv. Been at Victoria Crescent.' Kennet pushed the door closed then leant, puffing and pink-faced, against it. He had sprinted from the car park. The exertion had transformed his scattering of freckles. Mere ghosts of childhood normally, they had become as obvious as amber paint spatters. In those few minutes before they vanished again, his serious face shed years: a brief visitation of the lighter-heartedness of youth.

'Bisset's place?' Hallows said, pushing on.

'Yes. Had an early morning meeting with a metals expert from Forensics. Something odd's turned up.' Kennet produced photographs of the tubing which linked the front sitting room to the first floor bedroom. 'Any thoughts?' he asked, handing them around.

They pored over them, tossed ideas, but had no conviction they were right.

'I'll talk to Reg Falder who plumbed in Bisset's second bathroom,' Ferret suggested. 'Does it predate Bisset, Roy? Would it go back fourteen years to the previous owners?'

Kennet shook his head and a wave of hair slid towards his eye. He brushed it back impatiently. 'No. The SO I've just left was describing changes in gauge. He maintains this couldn't be a day older than thirteen years. Apparently it's standard industrial conduit.'

'Industrial?' Hallows queried.

'It's easily obtained. Commonly found in factories and large office blocks. It's rodent proof.' Kennet pointed up to the suspended ceiling tiles. 'We've probably got it above those, carrying power leads and telephone lines.'

Hallows looked from the ceiling to Ferret: 'Be interesting to hear what your builder has to say.' He hurried them on again. '*Vicky*, Liz?'

'Everyone dealing with Bisset confirms he was unable to negotiate stairs ten years ago, and before then only with considerable difficulty. The worst affected part of his body is his lower spine. Stan Parkin and Reg Falder confirm the cupboards were empty at the time the new bathroom was installed, so *Vicky* couldn't have been in the cupboard longer than ten years. She might, however, have been placed there more recently.'

Hallows reached for the forensic entomologist's report: 'Got the answer to that one. According to Scofield: based on surveys of similar reported cases where mummification time was in no doubt and where insect activity had been scrupulously plotted, the body has to have been in the cupboard for *at least* nine years.'

'Bingo!' Curtis stood abruptly.

Hallows was not surprised by the sudden move. The clay was up for Curtis, and his sergeant would have his eager eye on it, no matter what.

Kennet was as brisk: 'Good! Now we can complete our Missing Persons search.'

Absently Ferret wriggled the toe of her shoe into the short pile of Hallows's carpet. Her face darkened as she viewed the prospect of the disagreeable. 'I'll have another talk with Bisset.'

Hallows's sensitive ears detected an odd dead note. 'Yes?' He encouraged her.

She made an attempt at lightening up: 'It could be interesting . . . seeing how Bisset takes the news that he's had a dead house-guest for ten years.'

What he heard left Hallows unconvinced, left him instead, wondering what was going on. He could feel her dislike of the man. Her aversion was so palpable his skin prickled. He followed with the obvious: 'I'll join you when you see Bisset.'

With that settled, he said to them all: 'So if Bisset was in ignorance, we're looking for someone who knew a good deal about his domestic circumstances.' He heaved himself upright and began to wander. 'We're looking at friends . . .'

'Bisset maintains he has no friends,' Ferret cut in. 'That said, Stan Parkin thought the front bedroom had been in use. I'll ask at the nursing home if anyone's visited Bisset since I last called.'

Kennet came in with problems concerning Bisset's past neighbours: 'Tracing people is proving difficult. The properties have changed hands quite a bit. Incidentally, it was the guy who lived in number 7 who looked after Bisset's garden.'

The pool of information grew. Ferret said: 'I've learned nothing from social services except that Bisset was difficult. On the medical side, Bisset's GP told me that, ten years ago, he arranged with the hospital for Bisset to received a course of physiotherapy treatment at home. Keith Hawes – he now owns the Fitness Centre – took it on . . .'

For a moment Curtis stopped listening. He had a flash of recollection. He kept his mouth shut though, until he could check out a file.

'. . . Bisset ended the treatment when Hawes's wife died.'

Hallows's heavy face was all cynicism. 'Out of consideration for Hawes? Doesn't sound like the Bisset I'm coming to know.'

'Quite,' Ferret said coldly. 'My guess is that he was protecting his privacy. Gina Hawes was murdered, guv. Her body was found after a house fire in Briers Way. The case is still open. When our officers were enquiring into the marital side, as routine, Bisset cut connections with Hawes. Bisset's reported to have been obsessional about his privacy.'

'Sounds as if he's done time.' Kennet's tone inferred certainty.

She nodded: 'My thoughts too. I'll look into it. While I can't see him implicated in *Vicky*'s death, he could have been involved with something else while at Victoria Crescent. I'd like to talk to his immediate neighbours. Do you mind?' She turned to Kennet. This was his ground and it would be insensitive to barge in. Auburn haired, hot tempered, the accepted formula and exact for Kennet, but he'd have good reason to flare.

'Help yourself.' He smiled. 'You've got the gardener there as well.'

Hallows became the focus again. He had assumed the taut stance of a man who knew where he was going and would enjoy being on the move. He said: 'It'll spread the work load if Rob and I talk to Keith Hawes, see what light he can throw on Bisset.' He sensed Curtis stir, twitching to be off. 'Later today, Rob,' he said pointedly. 'Anyone anything else to add, before we break up?'

'One thing,' Ferret paused, groping beneath her chair for her bag. 'When Stan Parkin cleared Bisset's house, he took out a large, carved oak chest. Stan said it was empty but . . .' She see-sawed her hand. '. . . you know Stan. I'm awaiting confirmation from Earle's.'

'Scott can chase them up. If he's not satisfied he can follow through with a second call on Parkin. I'd rather we saw Bissett sooner than later.' He looked at the men: 'That it?'

'Only a thought . . . about the undisturbed dust. It doesn't make sense.' It was Kennet. 'If people were using the front bedroom of number 6, why didn't they have a snoop in the other rooms? Ray Bedworth's not rare, it's instinctive to prowl and open cupboards.'

Curtis, whose mind could be more serpentine than his sinewy body, offered an instant facetious suggestion, 'Perhaps they were half-cut: beyond caring about their surroundings.'

'My car or yours, guv?' Ferret asked as she and Hallows walked into Abbots Hill's rear yard. The mist persisted, with no wind to waft it away. It hung over the high brick wall like finely teased out wool.

'Yours,' Hallows said, content to let her handle snorting vehicles behind, ditherers in front, and kamikaze motor cyclists weaving between the queue of bumpers. He squeezed himself into Ferret's Civic and offered no advice as to which route they should take: she knew the city as well as he did.

She gave him a side-long glance as she took to the back streets. Would he ask her about her aversion to Bisset? Mike Hallows was uncomfortably good at reading her and far more sensitive to the needs of others than his brusque manner would suggest.

She had a lot to thank him for. He had saved her from far bloodier injuries from Mac than a slashed hand. It was strange that while anticipating how Mac might crack while under weeks of investigation – whisky, fright and broken vanity were a deadly mix likely to blow control – he couldn't have known exactly when. Yet one evening some sixth sense had him race to her flat.

Mac had grabbed her. He was furious, wild and on a power trip, wielding a jagged bottle. He had dragged her into the garden, tearing at her clothes while promising "grievous" with the bottle.

Next thing, Mike Hallows had Mac spread-eagled, eating dirt.

She wouldn't bring charges and Mike hadn't pressed her. He took her to A & E to have her hand stitched while Scotty poured coffee into Mac.

Hours later Mac had sobbed remorse and relief.

She made a left turn and then took another glance at Hallows. She was pleased he remained quiet. No doubt he considered meeting Bisset would serve better than quizzing her.

She drove through the thinning tentacles of Helenborough's older peripheral estates, entered the most recent development on the hill overlooking Green Vale, and met thicker mist where the last straggle of houses ended.

The sudden view that emerged as they dropped down towards the nursing home was quite extraordinary. Muted greens, muted browns, muted greys. Tree trunks and hedge rows were being decanted from the fine white fog. Bare branches of beech and oak stretched and disappeared like fading apparitions.

Most of the worst of Green Vale's architectural features were lost in the creeping ebb and flow of the dense moist air.

Even as she parked, her spirits were sinking deeper under an unsupported prejudice.

The nurse who let them in told them of Bisset's visitor: 'We were to expect a tall, elderly, white haired man. No name was given. He arrived near tea time, as we were securing windows for the night.' She led them part way to Bisset's door. 'They had a ding-dong of a row. Something left undone, I think. The man took off like a scalded cat.'

To her knock, Ferret heard a clear, sharp: 'Come!'

Bisset was sitting in exactly the same place as before, looking through the second window on to dew-drenched lawns. And as before, he had the same book on his lap. He was closing it as she introduced Hallows. He said nothing, paid no attention to them as they collected chairs from the dining table and positioned them to his left, Hallows sitting diagonally behind Ferret.

As she let her bag slide to the floor, she took more note of the book. Bisset's white skeletal hands were flattening across it. It was bound in brown leather and similar in size to a Victorian family bible. It had an integral leather strap and lock which was now fastened. She wondered about it and guessed it to be an album full of family photos.

'Reminiscing?' She inquired pleasantly.

His fingers, with their smooth translucent skin, fanned over the tooled cover so that very little was left to be seen.

He looked beyond her, regarding Hallows with a small, suspicious pout.

Ferret wondered at herself. Even through his silence Bisset was fuelling all the wrong feelings in her; to her core she vibrated animosity. It was a wonder it didn't show.

She forced out a standard phrase . . . made it sound gentle: 'We won't trouble you long.'

Bisset's reptilian, unblinking eyes rested on her.

She opened her notebook: 'Now . . .'

'Seconds or minutes, it's all the same.' Bisset's voice rang with its unforgettable clarity. 'You're invading my space. Ask what you must and go.'

Ferret's foot, tucked underneath the hard seat of her chair, twitched its irritation, but her tone remained equable: 'After the fire, we found two things of interest in your house.' She produced photographs of the conduit: 'What can you tell me about this?'

'I thought we'd decided it wasn't *my* house any more.'

No sweet sound could temper the viciousness of the sneer.

Ferret had not been born to be mild, yet only Hallows knew she seethed. He had spotted the reflex jerk of her foot. There was no hint of tension as she tapped the photographs in an insistent demand that Bisset look at them.

He did so, considering each. 'I've no idea what it is, or who installed it,' he said. Unexpectedly, a humourless twist appeared at the corner of his mouth: 'And you can be certain I, personally, did not. Do-it-yourself is one of those hobbies I've had to forgo.' His eyes were on her face again, renewing a piercing attention: 'So, what else puzzles you that has you trespassing on my time?'

'In a bedroom cupboard . . .'

There might have been a fleeting contraction of Bisset's pupils, but whether this was from curiosity or some other emotion, neither officer could decide.

'The cupboards were emptied ten years ago,' Bisset said with pedantic clarity.

'Have you been upstairs since then?' Confirmation was what she wanted.

An irregular, ugly flush enlivened Bisset's pale face. 'A senior officer, are you?' The rush of fury affected his throat. It constricted. He spoke deliberately, in measured time, his voice harsh as jetting steam: 'Obviously, you didn't climb through ability. Presumably you have been sleeping with someone of influence to reach your rank . . . you stupid bitch!'

Influence! Stung by the insult into a moment of paralysed silence, Ferret sensed the heat of Hallow's rage.

She heard his voice. He sounded calm enough.

He was saying with exaggerated slowness: 'Mr Bisset, you have made it abundantly clear that you always prefer to be alone. We will respect that wish when you have answered Detective Chief Inspector Ireton's questions. If you do not answer satisfactorily, we will return again – and again – until you do. Is my meaning clear?'

Bisset's eyes had flashed briefly towards the big man. He now gazed lengthily, thoughtfully, at his hands, turning them this way and that before he began to stroke the hard cover of the album.

When, eventually, he looked again at Ferret, it was with unconcealed loathing. 'Very well, we'll continue to play your game. I will ask you, with complete indifference, what you found in a bedroom cupboard, and you can tell me. So . . . ?'

Could he see that same sentiment in her own eyes? 'We discovered the headless mummified body of a woman.'

The pallid mask that was Bisset's face began to change. Incredulity registered there. He made an odd gasping noise as he started to laugh; a strange roaring sound that held no suggestion of joy.

'What's so funny?' Hallows asked as the repellent sound subsided.

'Life, just life. And now I presume you want to know who she is. Well, I have not the remotest idea. Nor do I care.'

Ferret took pleasure in reminding him: 'Mr Bisset, lack of interest will not remove you from my enquiries. Who had access to the upstairs rooms?'

'Tinker, tailor, soldier . . .' He mocked. 'Anyone who could climb there.'

She persisted: 'Well, let's narrow it down. Forget nurses and home helps. I'd like the names of private citizens who visited, those people who could be called friends.'

His eyes had left her, at last. He looked into infinity. 'I will give you a definition of friendship,' he said with donnish care. 'A friend is one with whom one enjoys mutual affection and regard. I terminated all friendships a long time ago.'

'I see.' It was the sound of acceptance, but she was not quite finished. 'So who, Mr Bisset, did you quarrel with here, yesterday afternoon?'

'Did I quarrel with someone?' He almost smiled. 'I don't recall.'

Hallows leant on the roof of her car as she slotted the key in her door: 'You haven't heard me say this, but I'm surprised he's still alive, and I don't refer to his bone condition. It's hard to imagine Jacob Bisset ever being a warm-hearted human being but, after that little speech about friendship, perhaps he was.'

The car radio crackled into life. She yanked the door wide, knelt on her seat and spoke to Control. Hallows was left standing outside.

'Message from Scott from Stan Parkin's warehouse,' she said, letting him in. 'Stan's taken a vicious beating. It's touch and go. Poor little sharpie,' she muttered. 'As for the wooden chest, the guy at Earle's confessed he didn't check it when he made the inventory. It might have been locked. It might not have been empty. Only Stan would know.'

'And now Stan's been got at. A connection?'

'No idea right now.'

'Reg Falder for you next?'

'Yes, see what he knows about the ducting, then Bisset's neighbours from Victoria Crescent.' Suddenly she grinned wickedly. 'Perhaps they liked Bisset.'

'Tell me another.' He could smile with her, they had distanced themselves from the man for a while.

Linda Thorne did not speak to Josh Elwood on a personal level until some time after Detective Sergeant Scott had left Earle's. Elwood was furious with the slap-dash way the inventory at Victoria Crescent had been completed and had spent half an hour reading the Riot Act to David, the employee concerned.

She made Elwood a coffee, carried it into his office and closed his door.

'You've spoken to Charles Saville?' she asked.

A harshness had settled on Josh Elwood's normally genial features. It corrupted good looks, callously ageing him. 'He's agreed,' he said quietly, 'on condition you return every item you're holding.'

'I said yesterday that I would, but not until I've moved in.'

'Before then would show a greater degree of trust.'

'Oh, Josh.' She laughed in soft mockery. 'I'd be very foolish to do so. I'm not going to risk losing before I've won. Tell Charles I want to move in soon.' She breezed on: 'Now let's talk money. I've been considering my salary. I think we'll increase it by a third from today with a review in four months – quite a modest suggestion really.'

Fine lines at the corners of Elwood's eyes deepened with disgust: she had him bound and now the flogging had begun. He said evenly: 'Tim Davis won't wear it.'

'Josh, how you deal with your partner is a matter for you. Now, since I'm up to date with my work, I shall take an hour or two off. There's a party tonight to which we're both invited, and I want to buy a dress.'

'You're not still going?'

His look of incredulity brought her laughing again. 'Of course I am. It'll be lovely. Such an opportunity to meet new people.'

Curtis kept ducking his head out of his own office in an effort not to miss Hallows. For a big man, Hallows walked lightly. He might well pass by unnoticed and minutes were precious when Curtis was impatient to talk.

Hallows appeared and frowned interest at the fat file clutched in his sergeant's hand. As soon as he was seated, the file was down on his desk and Curtis turning pages with a damped enthusiastic finger.

'What is this?' He flicked Curtis's hand aside and turned back to check the front cover: 'SALLY WEBBER?'

'You remember Ferret mentioned Gina Hawes's death. Well, I got thinking. DCI Merrison led the inquiry. He retired as you transferred here.' Curtis, hands slotted in pockets, began to recite the story. 'Gina Hawes and Carol Reynolds died in a house Sally Webber and Carol had recently rented. Like Carol, Sally was a second year biology degree student at Helenhall.

'Word had it that Sally was depressed, possibly due to a breakup with a boy friend. She was secretive: no one knew who he was. Anyway, her work had taken a dip and her tutor insisted she talk to a counsellor. That responsibility fell to Gina Hawes. On the evening of the deaths, Gina had arranged to call on Sally at Briers Way. As you heard, there was a fire. Gas ignited. It exploded from the premises shortly after midnight. Bedworth believed the start of the blaze had been delayed. He thought the old candle trick had been used. You know: light the thing, skip, and when it's burnt low it ignites some inflammable material. Gina Hawes and Carol Reynolds were dead before the fire started.'

'Two bodies? What happened to Sally?'

'She'd disappeared. She was spotted by fellow students around eight-fifteen on the same evening, walking along the Nean's towpath. They were on the opposite bank at the Riverside Inn. Merrison had divers check the river: nothing. It was May. The river was flowing high and very fast. She could have been washed right down to the estuary and out to sea.'

'And Gina and Carol were positively identified?'

'Confirmed without doubt.' Curtis turned pages to the appropriate report. 'There were personal effects – rings and a brooch. And dental records matched the victims' remains.'

'So Merrison thought Sally Webber had killed both women.'

'Yes. Merrison had Hawes in the frame automatically, of course, but he had a foolproof alibi. With Hawes and a close friend of Carol's eliminated, Merrison was convinced Sally had been responsible for attacking both women with a knife.'

'Motive?'

Curtis shook his head. 'Nothing strong. Merrison wondered if Gina had said something that tipped her over the edge.'

'And then she set a delayed fire?' Hallows frowned: 'What reason?'

'A chance to get away, Merrison thought, and then she changed her mind choosing the river to end what she'd started.'

While Curtis became silent, Hallows recognized the familiar: a suggestion of triumph. Curtis had not quite finished.

Hallows could wait. He began turning pages for himself. He found a snapshot of Sally. He tilted it to catch the favourable light. She was a slim young woman, with an attractive oval face whose dense, curly, mid-brown hair was worn to nape length. Her expression was calm if slightly questioning, as if she was not sure the photographer was ready. She was wearing a dress that even he, with his limited knowledge, could identify as Laura Ashley, and over one shoulder was draped with an habitual carelessness a spectacularly large, fringed shawl.

The shawl interested him. He glanced down at the notes. Sally was no different from most young people of any decade who wished to make some kind of fashion statement. Whatever she wore, dress, skirt or trousers, it was always draped or trailed from her shoulders. It was as recognizable as a trade mark.

He lent away from the desk and eyed his sergeant: 'And this fire, with her disappearance, happened ten years ago.'

'Yes, guv.'

'So what are you holding back?'

Curtis, tense with excitement, flicked pages again. 'At the time Sally moved into Briers Way it was strongly rumoured she was pregnant.'

*

Before Ferret saw Reg Falder she wanted to learn more about Stan Parkin's condition.

At the final junction the lights were green; she made a sharp right and entered the higher of the two terraced car parks. The modern hospital, constructed in a series of cubes and moated by a considerable area of unrelieved grass, had a deceptive number of levels since the seventeen acre site was sharply sloping. Much of the earlier mist had cleared and all but the seventh and eighth floors of the central concrete tower block were visible. The operating theatres, if not consorting with heaven, were in a world of their own this morning.

Hooking her bag over her shoulder, she hurried towards the entrance to A & E. Some short way off a bus was picking up passengers. Huey Alcott's lonely death came immediately to mind. He had taken daily refuge in a similar but more distant shelter.

She followed directions and spotted Scott concluding a conversation with a doctor.

'Well, how is Stan?'

Scott's face wrinkled grimly. 'Alive, just, which beats me.' They were turning back towards the admitting hall. 'He looked as if someone had been playing cricket with his head. The lad who helps him was kicking his heels outside the warehouse when I arrived, fretting since Stan was always first there. Smelt odd so I put my shoulder to the door. Stan was lying by a pillar. Looked as if he'd been tied to it at one point. While we waited for the medics the lad had a scout around – knows the stock. Nothing was taken.' He caught her eye. 'No, not the chest either. I couldn't see signs of a break-in. Whoever did this must have caught Stan as he was locking up last night. There was a trail of blood . . .'

They paused and stepped nearer together as two patients in wheelchairs passed close to their heels.

'. . . from the door.'

She grimaced: 'So who's Stan been annoying?'

'I'll ask around. No point stopping here, it's going to be days before he's talking.'

Ferret swung into Reg Falder's yard and caught sight of him crossing through a low slatted gate into his front garden. She touched the horn.

He looked back, then waited on the paved path which remained greasily dark from the day's damp start.

He said cheerfully: 'You got a problem?'

'A little mystery.' And she showed him the photographs of the conduit linking Bisset's sitting room at the crescent with the bedroom above. 'Can you help?'

'Well-' he lifted his paint-speckled cap and scratched thoughtfully at a mat of springy hair -'no, no can't say I can. Didn't install it. Can't see a purpose for it. Sorry.'

'Never mind.' A child's giggle made her look towards the front door. Falder's little girl was running towards them. She grabbed her father around the legs and hugged him.

'Hey, you'll get all mucky,' he said. 'These are my working clothes.' But he made no attempt to separate her from him. Instead he tousled her short fine curls. 'Coming up to four – goes to play school now,' he told Ferret proudly. 'Loves it.'

'And the others?' she asked, offering her right hand to the small girl. The child looked at it, considered the scar with open curiosity and rubbed her finger along the white raised edge. Ferret glanced up and caught Falder's expression. His weather-beaten skin had contracted. It made a mimer's sorrowing mask of his face. She felt suddenly embarrassed as if she'd been caught crossing a private threshold uninvited.

His eyes were on the child. 'Off you go, Rosie. Go and see your mum.' He gave her a gentle push and she ran indoors full of bubbly chatter.

Ferret respected the silence that followed; it wasn't hers to fill.

Looking anywhere but at her, he said eventually: 'We had a twelve-year-old son who died in a road accident, and another who's . . . somewhere. He was coming up to sixteen, going to join me in the business – happy to – and then he took off. Went into town one evening and never came back. You people talked to his friends, but they said they hadn't seen him.'

'When was this?'

'Five years ago. He doesn't know about Rosie.'

'Doesn't'. So you have heard from him?'

'Four Christmas cards – *love, Martin.* – nothing else said. Posted in London.'

'At least you know he still cares, and if he cares he's going to want to come home sometime.'

'But why leave like that? There was no row. He took no stuff with him. I don't understand him doing such a thing.' He confronted her. His eyes were huge, pleading. 'I suppose you couldn't . . . ?'

'Make enquiries? He's an adult now and out of my area.' She saw Falder's shoulders settle in a dispirited sag. 'Look, I'm not promising anything,' she emphasized, 'but I'll ask a few questions, pull his file, see what info. we collected at the time. I have a pal in the Met, I'll speak to him. He'll probably hate me for this.'

Kennet had been so involved, working at a computer terminal in the Incident Room, that time had ceased to have significance. It was not until he had finished that he realized, ruefully, that he had been locked in one position for too long. However, there was satisfaction to accompany the pain, he thought, as he clasped his hands behind his neck and forced his spine out of its fixed bow. He had achieved what he had intended.

He picked up a short-list of names he had arrived at, whisked his jacket from the back of his chair and left to find Hallows.

While the computer was a godsend for producing data in a rapid and accessible form it did not have a chip that could replicate an experienced officer's intuition. The final analysis was down to gut knowledge.

'Got a strong possible from Missing Persons,' Kennet said, turning into the big man's office.

Hallows looked from Kennet's tired face that could so easily flush with annoyance, to a single sheet of paper he carried.

Kennet passed the list to Hallows. He had high-lighted one name in sharp yellow. 'I think *Vicky* could be Sally Webber.'

Hallows said nothing. Instead, his bushy eyebrows crooked an invitation for Kennet to read as he closed the file in front of him and revolved it.

Kennet saw: SALLY WEBBER. A flame of colour burst along his jaw. 'How?' he snapped.

'Rob Curtis has just pulled it from Records. As part of training he was involved with the riverside search. He remembered . . . meant he could leap-frog.'

Kennet wrestled with ignoble thoughts and just about won.

'Appropriate – for a riverside,' he said tartly. 'Inspiration v Perspiration. I wasn't here then.'

'Nor was I.'

Kennet's nod was grudging. 'Two converging viewpoints have to be useful.' It was a truth, totally acceptable, but for a while he would remain decidedly miffed. 'What I'd like to have, to tighten the knot, is the manufacturing date of the Lareine underwear. Have we heard yet?'

'I was about to call you.' Hallows reached for the *Vicky* file and thumbed back the cover. 'A Fax just received.' He quoted snippets from the top sheet: '. . . bra and briefs were part of a newly designed spring range . . . available from outlets in February ten years ago.'

Kennet realized he had been holding his breath. He exhaled noisily.

Mr and Mrs Lowe's sitting room was small and simply but comfortably furnished. Arranged around the cream-tiled fireplace with its small glowing pyramid of coal, was a settee in beige cut moquette and two matching wing chairs. Each seat-back was covered with a crisply starched linen antimacassar. A large television occupied one corner of the room and a glass-fronted cabinet full of china nick-nacks filled another. Close to the lace-covered window was a low mahogany-veneered table trimmed with scroll beading. An open copy of The County Echo lay on one end and beside it, in a chunky glass ash tray, rested Mr Lowe's briar. It had been between his teeth when Ferret knocked at the front door. A suggestion of smoke was seeping from the filled bowl as she was ushered into the room.

The elderly couple directed her to the least worn of their chairs.

'When did you move from Victoria Crescent?' she asked.

'Three months ago. We wanted somewhere smaller.' Bill Lowe glanced about him uneasily as if he'd lost something.

'Over there.' Ferret pointed to the pipe.

'Ah.' With his pipe at home between his teeth, he took a seat and stretched his slippered feet towards the grate. 'We lived in Victoria Crescent for nine years. Friendly people, apart from Mr Bisset.'

'You'd think, being disabled, he'd have been pleased for me to drop in, wouldn't you?' Mavis Lowe, a plump, sturdy little woman, rubbed her work-thickened hands together with impatience. 'I'd gladly have done a spot of shopping, a bit of dusting, that sort of thing, but we got the cold shoulder early on.'

'What about visitors? You would have seen them: your sitting room was very close to his path.'

'We don't like to be thought nosey,' the little woman said defensively, patting her wool skirt where the pleats overlapped.

'Of course not.' Ferret's smile encouraged. 'But it's awareness that makes Neighbourhood Watch schemes a success.'

There was a long frustrating pause. She had sympathy with their dilemma. A stiff social etiquette had been instilled from childhood, yet very humanly, they would so much rather talk.

'Well . . . ' Bill Lowe sucked on his pipe and gave way to desire: 'There were the regulars: doctor, health visitor, meals-on-wheels people. And a professional-looking man who used to call about once a week. We wondered if he was Mr Bisset's accountant or solicitor. Those were the only people we saw during the day.'

'Can you describe this professional-looking man?'

'Distinguished, as you'd expect. Dark suit, briefcase. Tall, with thick white hair. About my age: seventy.'

'You stressed, during the day. Were you aware of people calling on Mr Bisset after dark?'

'Sometimes,' Mrs Lowe said. 'If we hadn't pulled our curtains we saw people pass under the street lamp and come through his gate.'

'People? Groups do you mean? Young, middle-aged, elderly . . . ?'

'Not groups, no more than two together. One older. He was more of a regular. Round shoulders. Can't abide round shoulders when there's no good reason. As to the others . . . ' The various movements of Mrs Lowe's hands were as useful as litmus paper. She now circled her thumbs, indicating a marshalling of thoughts.

Ferret's toes curled as she waited with schooled patience.

At last the woman spoke: 'Bill and I used to visit the White Hart now and then. It made a change from the telly. One night, coming home, we heard a bit of a stir in Mr Bisset's doorway. A pair were shouting – awful raw noise – then one ran down the path and into the street. He collided with us.'

'The round-shouldered one?'

'No.'

'Did you get a good look at him?'

'Not really. Those street lights, well, they're very poor. But it was plain to see the lad was upset. His face was all shiny with tears.'

'Lad?' Over Ferret's skin passed a prickled warning. 'A boy, do you mean? How old, would you say?'

Bill Lowe scratched thoughtfully at his chin. 'About fifteen or sixteen. Thin little devil, I remember thinking. Ran off like a hare. When we looked back at Mr Bisset's house the door was closed.' He watched with a mixture of concern and curiosity as Ferret pulled a statement pad from her bag. 'Do you want to take all this down then?'

She hoped she was wrong. She prayed she was wrong. But the knot forming and tightening in her stomach told her she had stepped over the rim into a deep, dark and loathsome pit. 'Yes, Mr Lowe, I do.'

Ferret pulled away from the curb and headed for the second of Bisset's neighbours. He had lived at the end of the crescent at number 7.

By the time she arrived at Sam Westcott's home, the mist had cleared. A weak sun had emerged. It warmed her soul a mite, if not her body, as she pushed through his gate.

What she faced made her eyes widen. It was November, monotone November, yet here there was colour. Red leaves still clothed an acer, orange leaves dressed another. Two young trees, in purpling leaf, were laden with bunches of tiny, pure white fruit and a rose, with arching stems, was hung thickly with hips like bright red flagons. Clumps of kaffir lilies had weeks of flowering ahead and pink nerines looked positively smug in their hot spot beneath a window.

When you've heard something, when you feel you have just trodden in shit, when you long for something cleaner and brighter to touch your senses, then finding a garden like this does nothing but good.

Ferret rang Westcott's door in better heart.

Westcott had an office in a front room of his bungalow. A man close to her own age, he led the way lithely, swept a box of copy paper from a chair for her, and bounced down on to his own.

'Your garden's wonderful – when did you move here?'

'March. Treated myself to some quite mature trees: they've repaid with show.'

'March?' Roy Kennet had thought Bisset's garden had been cared for until recently. She asked: 'Did you continue to look after the garden at number 6 after you moved here?

'Yep, until I learned when Bisset was leaving. Seemed only fair, though thanks were in short supply.' Westcott's unhandsome face broke into a humorist's grin.

His broad desk was situated at right angles to the window, a place, she thought, ideally suited for watching his plants grow. But what did he do here to earn his crust?

The small square room was congested. There were the obligatory metal storage cupboards, fax machine, cordless telephone, three computers. Three? A laser printer and a colour photocopier.

'So what is your line?' She fished her pen from her bag as he carelessly sprawled. He appeared to have had no quarrel with life.

'Oh, I keep assorted irons in the fire. I offer a first aid service to people who are new to computing and get themselves in a mess. I upgrade systems for people wanting to advance but are terrified of uncovering the works. But most of the time I work freelance for a local printer's.'

She watched him curiously. He had become unexpectedly grave. He got up suddenly, turned his back on her and leant his folded arms along the window sill. As he stared out he had the appearance of a man engaged in a discussion with himself.

'Look-' he swung around -'I know you're asking about Bisset, but I also know what general enquiries could turn up. I've been in prison. Fifteen years ago. Sent down for hacking. I'd just left school and living with my mother at number 7. She's dead now. She didn't know what I was in to. It got out of hand. Been straight since.'

'Was hacking profitable?' The question was asked benignly.

Westcott began to relax: 'No. I was just a nuisance factor.'

'Thanks for telling me.' Her smile dismissed the matter. 'Now, Mr Bisset – how long were you looking after his garden?'

'Thirteen years.' He returned to his chair.

'Were you barred from digging in any part of the garden?'

'No. I could plant what I liked where I liked.'

'Living so close, you must have noticed his visitors. Who called apart from medical and welfare people?'

'I can't say I remember anyone. He must have been alone much of the time. Some evenings his radio was noticeably high; you couldn't have talked above it.'

'Did you ever see a tall, elderly man with white hair calling there?'

Westcott heeled his chair into a gentle turn. 'Oh, you mean the guy with the briefcase. Thought he was from social services.' The ready smile appeared again: 'Now he knew how to be polite. We exchanged views on the weather. Friend Bisset would have growled its irrelevance.'

'So you saw him at close quarters?' Seeing Westcott nod, she added: 'If I need to trace him, will you assist a police artist in making a drawing.'

'Sure.' His fax machine began zipping out a message and he rose to deal with it.

'Are you certain there were no other visitors? Did you see any one when you came home from an evening out with friends?'

'See . . . no. But he could have had someone staying there off and on. Sometimes there was a strip of bright light showing at the edge of the front bedroom curtains.'

Kennet had returned to Victoria Crescent to see the result of the final phase in the search of number 6. Where lawns and flower beds had been there were mounds, ridges and troughs of damp black sticky earth.

Kennet wondered why he was going through the procedure of scraping mud from his shoes along the edge of the door step. There wasn't a Welcome mat down, the house was a shell now, not a home.

The property had been dissected, scrutinized and had revealed nothing. He made a careful journey across the lattice of joists into the sitting room to look at the conduit again before it was removed. Forensics would examine it closely but he had no great hope of them finding anything helpful.

The sound of a car drawing up outside brought him to the cracked smoke-stained window. He watched Ferret close her door then look in his direction and wave. She grimaced at the garden then approached the house along the next door's path. He could just see her hop across the low dividing fence at the last moment.

'God, what a mess!' she called from the hall when her words echoed, faded and died to join other lost voices. Her small feet rested more securely on the joists than his and she arrived at his side quickly. 'How did it look before we opened it like a can of pilchards?' she asked.

'Apart from different wallpaper and paint, much like all the others. Want to have a look at one that's still whole?'

'Yes.' She pointed to the conduit and moved closer. 'Any ideas?'

'I thought it might have carried the TV aerial, but that comes down the outside and through the window frame.'

She was only partially listening. She was standing an arm's length from the lower end of the tubing, staring up into the bedroom above. Noting where the tubing ended, she concentrated on other details. The moulding over the bedroom door had attracted Reg Falder. She could see why. The carved flowers were so luxuriant a bee could have been misled and settled on a petal.

'How are you making out with Bisset?' Kennet was saying.

'I've got nothing that links him with the body, but . . . Well, I've a heap of odd ends.' She twisted around. 'Roy! Have that bedroom photographed from every angle, please, before Grandfield gets in here.'

'Sure. Does it feature?'

She sighed, hunching her shoulders: 'Wish I knew. Which of the other houses shall we look at?'

'Take your pick, I've keys for them all. Our guys have moved into 7 and 5.' He was already on his way to the hall.

'Then the next one down, number 4.' She followed but slowly and then stopped at the entrance to the room and looked back. 'Huey Alcott: rest in peace.'

The park opposite had the accepted forsaken appearance of winter. Grey leafless trees, empty flower beds, no children playing, no people walking their dogs behind its tall railings, and no sightseers in the road either, jostling to see men stripping houses.

In number 4, despite the boarded windows, Ferret could appreciate how Bisset's house would have looked: Front door, first entrance hall with broad staircase rising, elegant archway to second hall and entrance to Bisset's double windowed sitting room. She glanced in, then retraced her steps, running up the bare, hollow-ringing stairs to the wide first landing which led to the bathroom and to the master bedroom at the front. She entered the room, walking backwards slowly to the window wall while looking at the moulding over the door. The upstairs windows had been left uncovered and the detail of the plaster work was clear to see. The design, while beautiful, was quite different from Bisset's. 'Roy,' she called towards the landing. 'Have all the front bedroom mouldings photographed, please.'

'All of them? Why?' He yelled back, and hurried down the second flight of stairs from the smaller bedrooms to find out what was interesting her.

'I want to be sure they're all different,' she said. 'There are no alcove cupboards in here.'

'Nor elsewhere. Seen enough?'

'Mmm, apart from the scullery.' She shivered involuntarily. There was a seeping cold from months of the property standing empty. 'That's where Reg Falder plumbed in Bisset's second bathroom.'

The scullery in number 4 had been converted into a children's playroom with direct access into the back garden. There had been a swing. There was a tell-tale worn patch in the small lawn where tiny feet had scuffed at the grass. Beyond this lay a vegetable plot and a forlorn looking greenhouse, its white paintwork left to curl and flake. All three sides of the garden were either fenced or screened with tall privet.

Ferret nudged at Kennet to open the door. While he tried a selection of keys, she said: 'Have your guys talked to the last people to move away from here?'

'Yes. Nothing productive. The guv's seeing the owner who was here before them: Keith Hawes.' He had found the right one and heard the locking bar rasp back.

'Ahh! So Hawes lived in this house.'

'Right.'

They stepped through into the garden and, with nowhere else to go, they strolled towards the ancient greenhouse, a structure that had been absent from Bisset's garden.

'Do you grow vegetables, Roy?'

'Not me, but my dad does. Very keen. He grows tomatoes under glass.' He tried the door, found the wood sticking and was firm with it. Inside, the temperature was noticeably higher than in the house. They closed the door to appreciate the warmth. Empty flower pots littered the slatted staging. Old sun-bleached blinds hung in haphazard lengths from their anchor points along the sloping ridges.

'Dad whitewashes the glass.' Kennet looked away from the blinds to the dusty soil, digging a toe in and turning it over with a flick. 'Gutless stuff – doesn't look as if anyone has bothered with it for years.'

'Poor old greenhouse-' she grinned, feeling less chilled -'so unloved. Come on, I'm hungry. Let's take a chance on the grub at the White Hart.'

Hallows purposely closed his office door. He wanted some time with the Sally Webber file without interruption, without Rob Curtis popping in looking as if he had sold a flitch of bacon to a vegetarian.

He could see why DI Jim Merrison had opined that Sally had taken her own life by jumping into the river but, an hour later, Hallows now disagreed. He had reread the host of interview sheets and believed he had come close to understanding something of Sally's character. He considered she would have weathered the disillusionment of a lost love and arrived at a rational decision about the baby. And, as an indication of this, hadn't she already chosen to join Carol Reynolds in renting the house in Briers Way? She would enjoy a far more independent existence there than in the cloistered environment of the university.

Curtis and Kennet, independently, suspected *Vicky* to be Sally Webber. The date fitted and there was the link with Gina Hawes, though as to how or why . . . There were more ends here than with a cat-o'-nine-tails.

Well, at least Sally had one relative, a brother. When Richard Webber was traced, they could run a DNA test which would resolve the major question.

Inevitably, Hallows found himself thinking of Iain Sinclair. They should talk but, after so long, how firm would his recollections be?

Sinclair's office was far more comfortable than Hallows's functional own. The carpet was thicker and paler. There were full, heavy curtains at the window where he had blinds that had jammed so often he no longer dropped them. The walls were ringed with tranquil pictures of rural England: his carried maps of the city and county, and charts reminding him of the latest crime statistics. Even their desks, filing cabinets and chairs were pounds apart. In one corner Sinclair had a small hand basin and close by was a tiny refrigerator and a low, pine cupboard, both of which Sinclair had provided himself. A kettle rested on the cupboard top. Rather than making tea in the pathology staff's rest room, he could brew-up here.

Waiting for Sinclair to conclude a post-mortem, Hallows peered into the kettle. It had been filled and he switched it on. He took milk from the fridge and cups and tea pot from the cupboard.

When Sinclair joined him the full teapot was partially hidden, cosied by a clean hand towel.

'I hope that's a pot for two.' The Scot sat down with an exhausted thud. 'Is this a social call, I don't have a customer of yours here, do I?'

'I need to chat, yes.' Hallows remained standing by the fridge. 'I want you to think back ten years.'

Sinclair's eyes became watchful, interested: 'Is this to do with your mummified corpse?'

Hallows nodded.

'Have you decided who she might be yet?' Sinclair asked.

'Does the name, Sally Webber, ring a bell?'

'The young woman under suspicion in the Briers Way deaths,' Sinclair said instantly.

'Your recall appears to be matchless.' Hallows flashed a congratulatory smile and poured their tea.

'Recollection is one thing, accuracy is another.' Sinclair crossed to a cabinet where specialized or significant files of all ages were kept. He found what he looked for, made space on his desk and opened the folder.

He began fingering through pages that were fragile along their edges from much turning. 'I take it you haven't called out a copy of this yet?' he said and Hallows signalled no. 'My senior at the time did the post-mortem. You know me well enough, however, to appreciate I would be intensely interested.' Sinclair had arrived at the page he wanted and extracted the essentials. 'The bodies of two women were found in the house, some distance apart and in a severely burned state. They had been doused in paraffin.' He lifted his eyes for a moment: 'You'll have to read the FIU's report for details regarding the fire itself.' With Hallows confirming, he returned to the page. 'The women were dead before the fire started. The bodies were so badly burned that being precise over the exact cause of death was difficult. We can say they were not strangled or poisoned and there were no fractures. Since Gina Hawes's head had been severed, it's been generally presumed that both were attacked with a knife though, interestingly, there was no knife damage to any of the bones . . . '

'Not even to Gina Hawes's neck?' Hallows interrupted.

'None. Now, if we're right about the knife, the murderer was either lucky – or clever – my opinion. Sally Webber was a biology student which could be argued as relevant but, moving on, would she have been capable of a frenzied attack, as was believed?' Sinclair paused and his mouth pinched: 'As to that, I'm not in a position to say. However, the mummified body doesn't show the musculature needed for achieving spontaneous decapitation. Skeletal height and orthodontic evidence confirmed the identities of the two women, by the way.' He reach for his cup and drank the contents straight off.

'DNA evidence?'

'The deaths predated that procedure.'

'Of course. So we have the missing Sally Webber cast as villain.' Hallows, leaning forward with his elbows resting on his knees, considered his loosely clasped hands absently. 'And Gina was decapitated.'

Sinclair let him talk to himself. He strolled to the cupboard, uncovered the teapot and poured them more tea.

'And *Vicky* suffered the same fate.' The heavy policeman looked up. 'There are seven bones in the neck, aren't there? Was there any . . . '

Sinclair anticipated him: 'Similarity? In both cases the cut came between three and four. If the mummified body is shown to be that of Sally Webber, you'll be facing an interesting conundrum: deaths linked by the same modus operandi. So much villainy performed with a knife. But ten years on . . . Well, you'll need some luck to discover the truth.'

Scott walked into Ferret's room and with his foot, hooked a chair for himself closer to her desk. One of his shoe laces was working undone but for the moment he ignored it. 'There are no whispers that the low-life in Helenborough wanted to sort Stan Parkin out.'

'Then we hope he talks.'

'Probably won't remember,' he said and watched her pulling a face at his pessimism. 'We've had a touch of luck. A corner shop off Market Street was supplying Alcott with booze.' Before she could ask, he turned his thumb down. 'They didn't meet who paid. Cash was dropped through the letter box in response to a card left in the corner of the window saying how much was owed. A long standing arrangement. They say they can't remember how it started.'

She gave a derisive snort: 'They could have ripped off the one paying.'

'I got a strong feeling they daren't. Whether they tried it once and . . . ' He shrugged. 'Pity Alcott wasn't the confiding sort.'

'We'll still have to do the rounds of the down-and-outs. See if any dossed down in Victoria Crescent and in particular on the night of the fire.'

'It'll be as good as talking to space. Most don't know one day from another.' He rolled his foot casually and watched the lace slacken further. 'Anything come up relating to Bisset?'

'Odd bits. The tall man's visits to Victoria Crescent never coincided with the district nurse, home help or meals-on-wheels people. Josh Elwood was the only person they remembered calling on Bisset. It's Bisset's neighbours who say the tall man called regularly over the years.'

'Well, I can't see him being responsible for *Vicky*'s body being placed in a cupboard.' The idea struck Scott as farcical.

She agreed: 'Not the action of a friend, is it? And Bisset must be his friend or why maintain such a long association? We have to talk to him. I'm arranging for a drawing and description to be circulated. As to Bisset, there's no medical, DSS or employment record available for him before he moved into Victoria Crescent which has to mean . . .'

'. . . He's changed his name or he had it changed for him.' Scott shifted his feet in a little dance then bent to retie his lace. 'Looks as if we'd better ask him for his prints: very nicely, of course. Wonder if he'll wriggle? I'll see to it.'

The front door of the Fitness Centre, with its gleaming brass door knocker and handle, was unlocked. Curtis pushed it wide and followed Hallows into a large hall that was dominated by a huge circular mahogany table. At its centre rested a large blue glass bowl filled with a glorious living globe of tightly packed golden chrysanthemums. Close by was an elegantly printed notice to ring the bell to the right of the table.

Curtis leant his index finger on the brass button and a long-limbed receptionist, dressed in a crisp white shirt-blouse and knee-length navy skirt appeared. Curtis was a legs man. He looked at her well toned calves as she left to tell Keith Hawes of their visit, and wondered, with an expanding interest, if she pumped iron after hours, if she was single, if . . .

'Superintendent?' Keith Hawes looked mildly perplexed as Hallows stepped forward and introduced himself and his sergeant.

Considering the reception area to be unsuited to any kind of discussion, he led them briskly to his handsomely furnished consulting room at the rear of the ground floor. Its tall window, draped with an expensively heavy brocade, faced on to a stone terrace, faultless lawn and formal, rectangular, ornamental pond. The pond was too far away for Curtis or Hallows to see any fish, but both men could believe orfes, in shimmering, thriving splendour, would be there circling the two-tiered bronze fountain.

Hawes ushered them towards deep and heavily cushioned easy chairs.

While Hallows apologised for disrupting Hawes's afternoon, he was being encouraged to take one that was particularly low and accommodating. Committed, he sank into it and felt softly enfolded as if welcomed by a voluptuous woman. From being briefly disconcerted, he rallied. 'We're talking to everyone who lived in Victoria Crescent ten years ago,' he explained.

'Ten years ago-' Hawes's strong shoulders dipped wretchedly -'that was a hideous time for me.' He subsided back into his own chair. 'My first wife died under terrible circumstances.'

'Yes, sir, I know. I'm sorry we have to open old wounds.' Hallows was so deeply sunk, he had the sense of being held forever. He tugged himself forward so that, while his knees were level with his chin, at least his back was free. Curtis, he noticed, had perched side-saddle to take their notes. 'No doubt you will have heard about the recent fire at number 6. I must ask you now to treat the next piece of information in absolute confidence, since it has not yet been released. Our subsequent investigation has brought to light a mummified body of a woman in an upstairs cupboard.'

'Good God!' Hawes's jaw dropped.

'We haven't yet been able to identify her – her head had been removed. You're a medical man, you'll appreciate the difficulty.'

'No dental trace possible.'

'Quite. I'd like to talk to you about Jacob Bisset. His GP arranged physiotherapy treatment at his home.'

'Yes. The hospital management agreed only because I lived so near. You've probably learned he encouraged neither friendships nor callers. Gina practised the good Samaritan, but she never got past a first visit. And when she died . . . Well, he told me to sod off.'

'How disabled was Bisset at that time?'

'He could walk on the flat, but steps were impossible.'

Hallows nodded. 'A name's come forward: Sally Webber.'

'Sally? But she killed my wife!'

'It was suspected,' Hallows corrected. 'There was never any proof. How well did Mrs Gina Hawes know Sally?'

'We both met her several times, during the preceding December: casually, just a nod and a laugh. She was with a group of students and university staff who got together to provide a Christmas entertainment for the hospital. It was organized by Patronus. I wasn't a member of Patronus then. Gina roped me in to swell the numbers. As far as I know, Gina didn't see Sally again – no occasion to. Then her tutor got in touch. Gina thought it better to meet Sally off campus and that was why she suggested she call at the house in Briers Way.'

'That's helpful,' Hallows encouraged. 'Now, again, I apologise for reviving pain, but is there any possibility of you remembering events relating to you personally on that fateful evening?'

Hawes smoothed his hair in sudden weariness: 'It might have been yesterday. Merrison had me repeating the story so many times.' Echoes of those confrontations brought him turning abruptly to Hallows: 'Merrison had me down as Gina's killer. Husbands kill wives – QED. But I was where I said I was, so he had to look elsewhere.'

Hallows, saying nothing, waited patiently for his question to be answered. He heard Hawes sigh. It seemed to come from fathoms down.

Hawes said: 'Gina and I arrived home from work at the same time. We had a bite to eat. Now that detail, exactly what, does escape me. She said she had arranged to see Sally at Briers Way. It wasn't far. She said she'd walk. I had already planned to be out. I was meeting some guys at the Leisure Centre. She left the house about five minutes in front of me.

'The guys and I met as arranged. I worked out in the gym, showered, took a swim and then the three of us had a beer. We parted around ten-thirty. Gina wasn't home when I got in. It was a pleasant evening; I hung over the front gate waiting for her. Spoke to a few neighbours coming back from the White Hart. Around midnight I rang some friends to see if she had stopped by. They took the piss. Gina was very independent. You know Gina, go to bed! was their message. I was dog-tired and slept until seven-thirty. I . . .' he hesitated, his face reflecting torment, 'I can still feel that churning, clawing shock when I realized she hadn't come home. She was very casual about time, yes, but she would never stay out all night. I dragged on some clothes and drove to Briers Way. Can you have any notion of my feelings when I saw the burnt out house and police patrolling? Then I was asked to identify jewellery: Gina's wedding ring, a dress ring and a lapel pin which had been especially made for her.' Hawes's body tautened in a sudden violent shiver. 'God! How I wished it had been Sally!'

Hallows nodded understanding. 'A very natural reaction. But now I have to talk about Sally.' He watched Hawes. The explosive moment was gone, he was composed again. 'Did you see her after that Christmas?'

'I bumped into her at the hospital – January, possibly. She was having trouble with her tonsils. She was in for blood tests and hoping they'd whisk them out.'

'And did they?'

'No idea, Superintendent. Doubt it though, it's not modern practice.'

'It was thought Sally became depressed because she had been dropped by a boyfriend. Have you any idea who this man might have been?'

'I couldn't even guess.'

Hallows began to shift his feet as a prelude to a conflict with gravity. 'Now, if you can just confirm who you met at the Leisure Centre.'

'Certainly.' The athletic Hawes was already standing in readiness to showing them out. 'I was with Dr Oliver Wyland, from the university, and Josh Elwood, the estate agent.'

Hawes's handsome face was no longer clouded as he accompanied them on to the drive. He was in the present again: his dark eyes regarded the departing detectives with the easy assurance of the successful man fronting his achievements.

Hawes watched the police officers' retreating car. When it had shrunk to the size of a toy he turned on his heel and went to find Anne.

She was tidying away equipment and he paused unheard in the treatment room doorway for the pleasure of watching her. Her shoulder length hair was more honey-blond than brown and still stranded with gold from the summer's sun. She equalled him in height, was slim, almost angular but undeniably feminine with a very gentle grace that their strenuous work had not coarsened.

She tossed a folded blanket on to the couch, then stretched languidly, pushing with feline suppleness towards the ceiling.

A frisson of pleasure rushed down Keith Hawes's spine. He spoke softly: 'Hi.' And his voice brought her twirling around.

'And how long have you been there? You could have helped,' she accused mirthfully. 'Ready to go home? We have a party to give.'

'And it'll be talked about for years.' His smile gave way to a thoughtful pout. 'Anne, nothing to worry about but the police have been here, asking questions about Gina and Sally Webber. Something new has come up.' He kept back the fact of the body, not so much to oblige Hallows's wish as out of care of Anne's sensitivity.

'Oh, *no*.' She slammed her fists together. 'I *won't* have you put on the rack again.'

'Hey, steady, darling. Don't be needled for me. I'm not bothered by their questions.'

'It's so unkind. I won't have you badgered.'

'Shhh.' He brought her forward into his arms. 'Smile on them, woman-mine. They're only doing their job.'

'I don't know how you had the audacity to call at the Fitness Centre. I'm sure only lissom creatures go there, Mike,' his wife teased.

Hallows had not told Isla why he had called, nor would she ask, but he had described the place for her entertainment while they ate their evening meal. He laughed. 'I deny that I'm fat. Well-covered, maybe. And it's the bad-back brigade who attend there principally, and they come in all shapes and sizes.'

'Even so, I'm sure they had you marked down for some suitable exercise regime as soon as you crossed the threshold.' Isla hooked a wave of teak-brown hair behind her ear, then passed him more broccoli.

'Nobody gets me stripping to my shorts except you.' His dark eyes twinkled, and then became serious at a new thought. 'Lareine.'

'Mmm, lovely. Is that telling me I have to run away and slip into something more comfortable?'

The eyes twinkled again momentarily. 'Later.'

'So what did you want to ask me? I recognize question time.'

'What does wearing Lareine tell you about a young woman?'

'She's wealthy and can afford to wear it all the time. She's frugal and would sooner penny-pinch over other things in order to have something exquisite always against her skin. She's been treated by her man and wears it whenever they are going to meet. Do I keep going?'

'No.' He smiled thanks. 'That's fine.'

Ferret ran a hot, scented bath. Abbots Hill was going to be forgotten for a while. She had given herself nearly two hours to work some sort of personal transformation. Trousers and flat shoes could take a rest: she was going to shock her body by wearing a dress and vampish heels this evening.

Relaxed and distanced from work, she could giggle at the possibility of startling Oliver Wyland too.

She was ready when he called.

She released the outer security door, opened her front door and listened to his light, rapidly approaching feet on the stairs.

Watching for the shock in his eyes, she saw it and gave him a full, slow twirl. 'Thought I'd get into the little black number,' she said casually, 'since you're wearing a DJ. Will it do?' It was an artless question said in fun.

'Oh, I need another twirl to be certain.' He chuckled and followed her into her sitting room.

She had accepted that Wyland was lean, but this formal gear had accentuated his angular tallness. He could almost make Hallows seem short. Beside him, she thought ruefully, she would look like a warning against failing to eat one's greens as a child.

He circled his finger and she turned in a slow spoof of a model.

Wyland liked such well proportioned slightness. Ferret's straight dress was full length, but there was no mystery concerning her legs. As she revolved, a high slit betrayed a good measure of shapely thigh clad in chic, opaque black tights. A soft draped neckline revealed a slender neck and good shoulders. She wore no jewellery other than a pair of gold and pearl drop ear-rings. Everything was understated, faultless.

'You'll pass in the crowd,' he said wickedly.

'That's a comfort. I hope there'll be enough loaves and fishes to feed us all, I haven't eaten for hours. Oh, don't introduce me as a policewoman. People start treating me as if I've got three heads.'

'Well, if you have, you'll reap a social advantage: you'll be able to eat, drink and talk, and all at the same time.'

A broad gravel drive flanked at its entrance by shrubs, swept in a wide curve to the long frontage of Witley House and then on to two adjoining garages. The Hawes's party was well under way when Wyland nosed his car beyond the garages on to slightly bumpier ground adjoining woodland where he calculated he would not be boxed in. Before Ferret had stepped out the purr of music, talk and bursts of laughter were clearly audible.

There was so much light escaping from the downstairs windows as well as that gleaming from the off-centre covered entrance, that she could see the details of the brick and stone building quite clearly. The tiled roof of the porch extended over a jutting window to its right and continued to the extreme corner of the creeper-clad house. The central section was built forward some ten feet giving the appearance of a wing. It rose majestically to end in its own steep gable. The ground and first floor rooms it enclosed had huge stone-framed windows with projecting keystones bearing animal masks. The other windows of rooms to the left of the wing and above the porch were wide but far less striking.

It had been a long time since Ferret had hobnobbed on this scale and it occurred to her that she might have lost the knack for inconsequential talk. She disposed of sudden nerves with a deep breath and smoothed the dress over her hips. It would be interesting to find out.

The spacious hall was thick with people, as congested as an airport terminus on a bank holiday eve. Wyland made a good pilot. He steered her into a slightly less peopled sitting room where a waitress was circulating with a tray of assorted drinks.

'Are all Helenborough here?' Ferret mouthed as he stretched for two glasses of wine.

'Could be, and I don't know half. Patients with loot, sporty types, sports coaches, people with clout.' He winked mischieviously. 'We're the misfits.' Then he spotted someone. 'Oh, lord,' he breathed and rolled his eyes upward.

Ferret turned to see a balding, spectacled, jovial gnome of a man in his late fifties homing in on them. She knew him by repute; she had seen his face in the local press and on election posters.

'Well, hello Lester,' Wyland said. 'I thought you'd be too busy to be here. Meet Liz.'

'I'm delighted to . . .' He offered a soft, moist hand and beamed. In a voice that was a trifle too high for Ferret's liking he continued: 'I wouldn't miss my new neighbours' party for the world.'

'Councillor Lester Barraclough lives next door,' Wyland explained.

'And I couldn't be better pleased the Hawes's have moved in.' Barraclough leant closer, his cherubic face suggesting confidentiality. 'The previous owner rather let the place go.'

'Wouldn't know about that,' Wyland fibbed, 'living as I do half a mile away, in the centre of the village.'

Guessing that Oliver wanted to avoid village tattle, Ferret changed location. She said: 'Helenborough must present a magnitude of problems for a councillor. What's currently most challenging for you?'

Unseen by Barraclough, Wyland beat his hand against his brow. The reason soon became clear. Barraclough rode his hobby-horse and killed support with boredom. He talked, non stop, about the need for boys' clubs and the necessity to provide a hostel for the homeless young arriving in the city every day.

With Barraclough's first long breath, Wyland engineered an escape.

'My, heavens, Liz, you won't do that again, will you?' he said as they dived into the crush of another sitting room. 'It's my opinion men talk in inverse proportion to the number of hairs on their head.'

She sipped her wine, eyed his heavy dark hair, and grinned: 'Well, if that's the case – you're wearing a wig.'

His rippling laugh had the same effect as a breathed kiss against her neck: she tingled to her toes.

While they made a reasonable success of circulating they had yet to see their hosts. 'Where are they?' Ferret asked, 'We can't keep missing them.'

For a moment Wyland appeared to enjoy a very personal joke. Then he shared it. 'They know we're well catered for, so they're not past leaving us.'

'What?' Her brow arched surprise.

'True. I know my old school chum. They'll be upstairs . . . Keith making his point felt.' He watched her eyes and saw comprehension.

'Now?' she said with startled amusement.

'When it comes to Anne, Keith's as randy as hell.'

'Please. I'm off duty.' She grinned. 'I don't want to know these details.'

'You shouldn't have asked the question then, should you? Anyway, you must have been loved to that degree.'

He was teasing and prying in one. A narrowed eye warned him off, but Wyland was not prepared to let the matter go entirely: such passion was as much true for him as for Keith Hawes or a past lover of Liz Ireton's for that matter. '*His speech is a burning fire-*' he whispered against her ear -'*With his lips he travaileth, In his heart blind desire . . .*'

She stepped back swiftly, narrowly missing spiking her heel into Josh Elwood's foot as he came up behind her. With an apology that was all laughing embarrassment she faced him and Kate.

Elwood had been soaking up the party mood like a man facing imminent drought. He knew that the first sight of Linda would bring him crashing to earth despite the conviviality around him. He dropped a smacking kiss on Ferret's cheek: 'Liz! Come with Oliver, did you? Then you deserve a break. He's a dreadful joker. If you can put up with my hobbling, let's trek to the dining room and inspect the grub.'

'Food . . .' She glanced back at Wyland. 'Why didn't you suggest that?'

'Didn't realize you were such a gannet,' he called after her.

They were watched for some minutes, before Kate turned to her ex-husband, 'An attractive woman. You're a dark horse, Oliver.'

'More impetuous, I think.' He forestalled her question. 'No, we're not an item – yet.'

'Then I'll hope. Shall we eat too, Liz is not the only one who's hungry?' She made a move towards the rear of the house. 'Hear the music?' she said over her shoulder. 'After we've eaten, I might let you have one dance with me.' She pointed beyond the dining room entrance. 'The music, if you haven't already discovered, is coming from over there. The parquet floor in the oh-so-posh conservatory is where we're meant to shuffle.'

'Only one dance, when Josh is out of action?' he said, resting his arm around her shoulders.

'One,' she repeated. 'You came with Liz.'

Like the furnishings Ferret could glimpse between milling bodies, the food was sumptuous. 'This is serious eating,' she said, and juggled plate and glass to lick crab sauce from her finger.

Elwood smiled equal appreciation. 'When Keith and Anne throw a party, they don't spare the pennies. What do you fancy now? I don't think I can resist a chocolate crème brulée.'

'That's a spoon job. We'll have to sit somewhere, but perhaps your leg is already telling you that.'

'It does ache a bit. Let's take a pud and cheese, and look for a perch.'

He seemed to know where he was going. Shadowing him, she found they had arrived in the Victorian conservatory. She looked up and gasped, the glass vaulting was so high, trees could have grown here with complete ease.

Josh Elwood was making for a wrought-iron staircase at one side which curved to ventilators in the roof.

'Perch, indeed.' She chuckled. 'Good place for a bird's eye view.' She went ahead. Halting half way, she sat and watched Josh settle with obvious relief two steps below.

They had been there only a few minutes when Keith and Anne Hawes were suddenly amongst them, effervescent and chivvying everyone to make the most of the music.

'It'll have to be another time, Liz.' Elwood shifted slightly so that he could see her as well as the small dance square.

'I'll hold you to it.'

The music was provided by four players tucked amongst lush plants in a corner. Keith Hawes had taken the floor with Anne. Ferret watched Anne and sighed: what luck to be born with poise. The two moved in perfect harmony; stepped and turned to present-day, middle-of-the-road tunes. It was all very Rogers and Astaire, she thought, charming and unreal. Partying on this scale must cost a bomb.

She caught sight of Oliver and Kate. As they skirted the floor the music ended. Their hosts, parting with the intention of bringing others out to dance, claimed the two.

Ferret finished her cheese and contentedly tapped her feet.

Josh Elwood was similarly affected by the rhythm, his hand rapping his thigh as he gazed down on the dancers.

His sudden stillness made Ferret look at him. Seeing his face become unexpectedly stern, she followed his eye.

He was staring at Linda Thorne. Sheathed in dark emerald, she was standing at the edge of the dance floor surrounded by guests in dinner jackets. She was as obvious as a lit gem stone on black velvet

Glancing back at Elwood, Ferret saw all expression wiped away. She recognized a direct effort to cover up and was awhirr with curiousity. She looked at Linda again.

The colour she wore enhanced the brilliance of her hair. This evening she dazzled; this evening she blazed, paling all other women who dared to stand near.

The music was indicating a change of partner and Oliver Wyland took Kate while Anne, in an elegant, beautifully drapped ivory silk, was instantly claimed by another of her guests. Keith Hawes, looking to the edge of the floor, could not fail to see Linda. He led her forward.

From her sweeping viewpoint, Ferret saw Linda Thorne move sensuously into Keith Hawes's arms. The music ran its course, ended, began again and Linda was still with him. Anne had not taken a new partner. She had stepped to the side of the floor.

Ferret felt a slight movement close to her legs as Josh Elwood fidgetted. With something of the spy's excitement, she realized he was trying discreetly to catch Oliver's eye as he talked with Kate at the foot of their stairs.

Oliver looked up. Immediately he followed Elwood's silent instruction to look at Anne, as Ferret did. Anne might have been made from marble. She watched her husband with the stillness of the sphinx.

Wyland acted. A nod to Elwood, a word to Kate and he slipped in amongst the dancers. As Kate climbed the stairs to join Josh, Oliver Wyland cut in on Keith. With easy charm, he took possession of Linda. Keith immediately stepped to the edge of the floor and brought Anne into his arms. She became pliant, and danced.

When the music next changed, Anne and Keith Hawes moved away to speak with other guests elsewhere in the house.

Wyland, having paired Linda with Barraclough, climbed partway to reach for Ferret's hand. 'Enough idling,' he said and brought her on to the floor.

'What was all that with you, Josh and Anne?' she asked as she matched her feet to his.

'Friendship, that's all.' He spun her before she could ask more.

It was none of her business and she let it drop.

The music had settled into a slower beat and they danced closely for half-an-hour, before she asked to be driven home. 'I'm a working girl,' she reminded him.

'So you are, Chief Inspector.' He grinned. 'I'd almost forgotten.'

'Well, Oliver Wyland, I advise you to keep that in mind when we reach Quay House. My word is law, when I offer you *only* coffee.

PART TWO

Chapter 1

Hallows had been standing. Now he made space for himself on one edge of his desk, then half sat and half leaned against it. Roy Kennet had propped himself against a filing cabinet with most of his weight taken on one leg while the other foot made an occasional tap at the carpet. Ferret had sat on a hard chair, tucked her feet underneath and eased off her shoes. Rob Curtis, looking as usual like a greyhound watching for the hare, stood against rather than rested into the closed door at his back.

It was still early in the working day but they had been talking for a good hour.

'Right, then I'll summarize.' Hallows took a deep breath, and began:

'Keith Hawes had to be DI Merrison's prime suspect when Gina Hawes was identified as one of the victims in the Briers Way fire. He interviewed him on a number of occasions and, as we've seen from Hawes's statements, his story never wavered. Merrison talked to Oliver Wyland and Josh Elwood at least three times and they were adamant that Hawes was at the Leisure Centre with them at the time of the murders, and when the fire must have been set. Merrison was entirely satisfied that he had heard the truth. From there he looked to Sally. From what he had learned of her, he considered it was not beyond a reasonable possibility that she could have killed Gina Hawes and Carol Reynolds.

'Now we have *Vicky*. From what we know: height, colouring, age, blood group, there is a strong possibility that *Vicky* is in fact Sally Webber. What motive brought about her death? That I'll come to in a minute. Why was she decapitated and why was she left in that house – for we doubt that she died there? If Bisset had nothing to do with her killing, and we all think it's safe to presume he did not, then we look at Rob's suggestion of the other day. It was simply a convenient place to leave her body. The murderer needed to get rid of the body and he knew Bisset did not use the upstairs of his house. If he satisfied himself that Bisset was in his sitting room, he could have entered through the front door and started up the stairs unseen. We know that Bisset didn't lock his front door until he was going to bed. We've checked with the medical people who attended him and they say he was in the habit of turning in around ten-thirty. Sally's body had to have been placed in the cupboard before then. Why was her head removed? Possibly to slow identification. Possibly because a headless body is less heavy to move. And move from where, and by what means? Roy is continuing to investigate the other houses in Victoria Crescent.

'While Hawes had knowledge of Bisset's circumstances, he couldn't have killed Sally for the same reason that he couldn't have murdered Gina. He was with other people until after the time Bisset would have locked his door and gone to bed.

'Nor can we find a motive for his killing Sally. From every source, Merrison established that Hawes was devoted to his wife with no evidence remotely suggesting he might have been seeing another woman.

'Now we come down to the fact that *Vicky* was pregnant. In Merrison's case report, we've read that friends of Sally's presumed she was pregnant. The pregnancy is of considerable significance. Firstly, it ties *Vicky* and Sally together and, secondly, it gives us a motive for her murder.

'We've said: suppose Sally's lover, having dropped her, then learned not only that Sally was pregnant, but also that she intended to have his baby. Would he have seen this as posing a threat? Was he married? Did he have a reputation to protect?

'A knife was used on Sally. A knife was used on Gina and Carol. Did one person kill all three women? If not, can we believe in coincidental murders? We've argued and we're undecided. There's no clear motive for his wanting Gina and Carol dead. If he had intended three to die, why not leave three to the flames.

'Now, moving on, Sally was last seen during the mid-evening, walking alone beside the Nean. Was she on the way to meet her killer? Keep in mind she was wearing Lareine underwear. Was she dressed to meet a lover? Remembering that Gina was calling at Briers Way with the express purpose of seeing Sally, it seems odd that she wasn't there awaiting her arrival. Was she persuaded to leave the house beforehand by a letter or phone call? Or was it more simple than that, did she resent Gina Hawes's proposed visit and just duck out of the house before Gina arrived?

'I come now to the present day. Huey Alcott was supplied with alcohol and he died in the house where *Vicky*'s body had been left. Whether these two facts have any bearing on the *Vicky* case we have yet to see.

'While *Vicky* was discovered in Jacob Bisset's house we don't think he's involved. Bisset, however, is not appearing whiter-than-white. As Liz investigates, he might well consider this macabre event a gross misfortune.

'We need to find Sally's brother, Richard Webber, to match his DNA against *Vicky*'s.

'I'd like to talk to those friends Sally had while she was a student. They might speak more freely now.

'Liz has confirmed that Hawes, Elwood and Wyland are close friends, but there is little to be gained now, I think, in re-interviewing Elwood and Wyland. Merrison did an efficient job.'

Recognizing Hallows was coming to a close, the three listening shifted position.

'Liz-' Hallows saw Ferret grimace as she pushed her feet into her shoes. Tired? Swollen? He curbed curiosity -'stick with Bisset. We'll look after the *Vicky* side of things.'

Elwood did not arrive at Earle's until mid-morning.

'Linda. My room.' he ordered from the passage.

She rose without hurry.

'What the hell were you playing at last night?' he snapped as she closed his door.

'Playing?' Her smile mocked.

'You were giving Keith the come-on.'

'It amused him. It amused us both.'

'His wife didn't find it entertaining.'

'If insecurity is her problem, then she must learn to live with it.'

He steepled his fingers and gave her stony consideration. 'Linda . . . keep away from Keith and Anne.'

'A threat, Josh? Are you warning me off?'

He leaned forward: 'It's advice you would be wise to take.'

*

Through her open door, Ferret heard the sharp military click of Scott's feet. He swung into her room with the precision and purpose of a determined hippo.

'News of Stan Parkin?' she asked.

'He's still unconscious.'

She pouted sympathy: 'He might be slippery as an eel, but . . .' Scott was so unhandsome with his thick bull-neck and harsh features, but she saw nothing of these, only a slight smile of triumph as he flapped a computer print-out in her direction.

'Bisset volunteered his fingerprints,' he told her. 'No bother. Said nothing other than asking if our requiring them was down to you.'

'I presume my name didn't bring him joy.'

'Mouth curled.'

'Mmm.' She could visualize Bisset's expression; the loathing in his soulless, piercing eyes.

Scott recited: 'Jacob Bisset, otherwise known as Franklin Noyle . . .'

Franklin Noyle had trained as a singer and had toured with a number of opera companies in the UK and abroad. For reasons not specified on the record sheets, work in these companies had dried up, forcing him to seek alternative employment. He had combined giving private music lessons with peripatetic teaching for his local education authority. He had been employed at St Joseph's, West Hillington. He was discovered, charged and found guilty of sexual acts with a number of the older pupils.

'Went down for ten years – discharged fourteen years ago.' Scott looked up.

'Thanks.' She wandered to the window where her warm breath misted a small circle on the glass. She looked at it – drew a V with her finger. V for violation. Then scrubbed it out in a rage of grief and hate. 'So he acquired a new identity.'

'He needed it to live an untroubled life. He'd got enough other problems by then. His osteoporosis started soon after he was banged up. He may have been crippled, but people with youngsters would still regard him as a threat.'

She turned on him fiercely: 'I do know, Scotty.'

'Sorry, guv.'

She shook her head dismissively. 'How was the change of ID brought off?'

'The probation service were the chief movers. They geared up the DSS who were obliging once they knew how ill he was and that a friend of Bisset's was prepared to buy a house for him – 6 Victoria Crescent – and play guardian.'

'His name?'

'No details anywhere unless you believe he's John Smith, as noted on the purchase details of the house.'

'You're joking!'

'It's true. Cheques were paid from a Lloyd's account under the name of John J.J. Smith. The account was opened with deposits of cash six months before Bisset came out of prison and was closed when he had been living in Victoria Crescent for a couple of months.' He passed her a file clutched under his arm.

With a wet finger she spun pages. There had to have been an address for the bank to use.

There was. For the time the account was open, Smith had rented an attic flat in a private house. But the elderly owner had long since died. 'Lucky, faceless, John,' she muttered. 'But perhaps he's not quite so faceless.'

'The tall man?' Scott suggested.

'It's as good a bet as any other.' She rubbed her hands together with sudden vigour. 'If he's been able to call on Bisset so regularly, he could live reasonably near. We've got our artist's impression, let's do the rounds. GPs, shops, postmen . . .'

The house, that was now home to the Fitness Centre, could be seen clearly from the road. It was square and of perfectly balanced proportions. Its portico had a pair of columns set *in antis* to the advantage of its south-easterly facing front. On a fine day, while the door became a pool of shadow, the fresh cream stucco gleamed in the bright light. Nine windows looked towards the road, five on the first floor and two on either side of the front door, each elegantly glazed and framed by eared architraves. No climbing wisteria had been encouraged to grow, which was a horticultural kindness since the eaves of the low pitched slate roof were excessively wide, creating an area of near drought at the foot of the walls.

Dividing the house from the public footpath was a drive wide enough to remain uncrowded even with a good scattering of parked cars, and a sizeable semicircle of weed-free verdant grass.

Linda Thorne parked beneath the bare boughs of one of the many Japanese cherry trees lining the moderately busy road, her car inconspicuous amongst others, and prepared to wait. She was happy, with not an atom of indecision in her body. She knew that Anne Hawes took some of her lunch hours in town, shopping. When she did so, Keith ate out.

She saw Anne walk briskly to her Metro, toss a shopping bag into the back and then drive off. Ten minutes later, Keith Hawes emerged.

She let his Rover join the sporadic stream of traffic, then eased out, content to follow three cars behind.

Hawes was heading in an easterly direction from the city. There was no urban sprawl here. Large houses enjoyed isolation, separated by huge, mature, ornamental gardens.

She now guessed where he planned to eat. The Nean, with the Mill Restaurant on its southern bank, was very near. On this stretch of clear deep water swans dabbled and glided. Diners could imagine they were in the heart of pastoral England as they ate well but not at excessive expense.

Hawes indicated left and entered the Mill's grounds. Linda drove on, while calculating a time that should divide them. She turned, and parked her car some distance from his.

The single story restaurant had been built in harmony with the disused mill it abutted, brickwork and timber suggesting romantic decay.

Linda entered through glass doors, into an exceptionally spacious lobby. Ahead on her right was the bar and to her left lay the restaurant, bright with polished glass and crisp white linen.

Keith Hawes, choosing vegetables, had failed to see her approach. It was the pleasant timbre of her voice that made him look up.

'Keith! What a surprise. Eating alone? May I join you?'

'Linda – well, well.' He smiled. 'Please do.' And with a nod to the waiter, he had her chair pulled out and a second menu brought.

She read quickly, declining a first course, then glanced around. Most tables were occupied. She wondered how many here recognized Keith. 'There's a thank you letter on its way,' she said, fixing him with amused and intensely green eyes: 'Your party was terrific.'

'I'm relieved it was hitch free – not always the case.' He chuckled, then entertained her with tales of past disasters until his curried almond soup arrived, when he paused to accept a roll.

He was giving the impression they had done this before. Linda was not surprised, his manner was so easygoing but, none the less, it suited her purpose well. Beyond this, there was pleasure in being with him, he was puckishly amusing: she liked him a great deal.

'So which one of you has the greater organizational flair?' she asked, watching as he tucked into his soup with relish.

'I'd better say my wife since I forgot to post Josh's invitation. But of course we each have our particular talents.'

'I'm sure.' She was laughing directly at him: 'And is spilling soup one of yours?'

He glanced down abruptly, but her hand was already there with her napkin, prepared to blot his tie.

'Damn me!' He laughed. 'I'm not usually careless.'

'I'm sure,' she repeated, but with greater intimacy this time.

The album was open, resting across Bisset's knees, when the window cleaners appeared with their ladder, steps and buckets of water. As the ladder was positioned for the upper floor by one, the shorter man pulled the lower casement up a mite and called: 'Morning!' His brother was already climbing out of view and out of the conversation.

'Is it a week since you were here last?' Bisset said, but without doubt knew that it was. He shut the book, slotting its strap into the lock as he always did on closing it. He enjoyed watching these two. Their nimbleness, their strength in moving steps and ladder, their economy of action . . . so skilled, so useful. And then there was the news they brought him from outside.

'Time flies when yer busy.' A small, hard-tendoned hand reached for the top glazing bar of the lower casement. 'Got to close this for a minute. We'll have a proper chat when I've finished.'

'Good.' Bisset watched his view disappear under a soft brush full of soapy water. He waited and dwelt resentfully on other less acceptable conversations he had experienced in the last few days.

Anne had arrived home from work ahead of Keith. They frequently journeyed independently when he had a series of appointments which ran into early evening.

Having dumped her midday shopping in the kitchen, she ran upstairs to change out of formal suit and silk blouse; those smart, sober clothes she chose to wear to the Centre. She slipped into a fine-ribbed oatmeal wool sweater, corduroy slacks of a darker hue and supple casuals in navy suede. She foraged among beads in a trinket box, then changed her mind and instead clipped on small pear-drop earrings of polished wood. With her fair hair combed and shining and light make-up refreshed she portrayed what was entirely genuine for her, the lively refined wholesomeness of the country girl.

She was starting to prepare their supper when the phone rang.

Madeline Kay said: 'Anne, darling, it was a wonderful party. You do things so well. I didn't feel a bit like working today.'

Madeline, a long-standing friend, owned a boutique in the desirable Lanes area of Helenborough.

'Nor me.' Anne laughed. 'I intended to see you at midday, but I was delayed and knew you'd be shut.'

'Oooh, I'm disappointed. I'd love to tempt you into buying something wildly expensive. *Actually* I was taken out to lunch by a gorgeous man I met at your bash. You know super people, darling. We went to the Mill. Saw Keith there. Thought of suggesting we made a foursome, but my man was all for our being very tête-à-tête. Keith and his friend didn't see me.'

'Oh, Oliver.'

'No, darling, that tiny creature with the wonderful hair. Such a colour. Do you think I should go red?'

There was an unexpected silence.

Madeline waited.

'Anne?'

'Mmm?'

'You sound half gone, darling. Early night for you. Shall I dye my hair red? What do you think?'

'No!' Anne's voice cracked. 'It's not a colour I like.'

Ferret poked her nose around the Incident Room's door. Only the inspector in charge was present.

'I'm popping out. Thought I'd pick up some fish and chips at Sheer's. Want some?'

He glanced at his watch: 'Not off yet? No thanks. Scott just asked. Had some earlier.'

The phone rang. She waited only until he signalled it was nothing urgent.

The station was a cocoon of blazing lights and warmth. Outside, the chill damp air touched her face like a caress from the dead. She shivered, paused briefly by her car, then decided against picking up her raincoat. Sheer's was only around the corner, off the main road.

Weaving between early evening crowds she turned right into Lindon Street and arrived at the pedestrian crossing. Opposite was the busy shop. The crossing-light glared red. She stabbed the call button, stamped her feet against the cold and waited for green and permission to walk.

Others collected beside her at the kerb. She was ravenous and filled with outrageous envy at seeing Scott, through the plate-glass window, well advanced in the queue. If only she could catch his eye, he could buy for them both.

Scott was looking everywhere except towards her.

She stamped her feet again, but with impatience now.

The tormenting smell of hot succulent fish wafted across the busy road. It teased her nose, awakened taste buds. Her stomach rumbled unheard against the greater growl of streaming traffic.

'Scotty . . .' she mouthed in an aching, telepathic attempt to make him turn. It was futile. He was almost at the counter and his eyes were now fixed on darting, aproned assistants, scooping chips, ladling peas. And still the light showed red.

Behind her the amiable crowd thickened and pressed closer together.

Scott slid his hand into his back pocket, feeling for coins. The guy in front pulled away with an open parcel of vinegar-laced chips and Scott stepped forward.

He opened his mouth to speak, but the words froze at a prophetic noise: a piercing squeal as tyres burnt rubber.

He spun around to see a dark shape in motion, hurled high from the bumper of a cab, then plummet headlong towards the gutter.

He ran, powering towards the crossing as the green man ordered WALK!

Between the rapid ebb and flow of nursing staff and A & E's walking wounded, Hallows caught sight of Scott. He was standing close to a curtained-off cubicle like some threatening, unyielding Cerberus. He walked faster, stretching the disance between himself and Isla.

Scott had been watching for him and took two reluctant steps away from the curtain. 'She's conscious. Only out for a few minutes. Been X-rayed. Plenty of bruising but no bones broken.'

'Must be made of rubber.' Hallows glowered anxiety.

'She's waiting to be taken up to the ward. The cabby said the road was clear – next second she was in front of him.'

'Wasn't he watching the lights, for Pete's sake?'

'Swears he was.' With an apolgetic glance in Isla's direction, Scott beckoned Hallows closer and dropped his voice: 'He used the word, catapulted.'

Hallow's eyes constricted: 'He said that?'

'I haven't asked Ferret – thought that down to you.'

'Right. Good you were there. Get off now, you've done all you can.'

'In the circumstances I'd sooner not, not with that in the air.'

'Sergeant, get some rest. She'll want you thinking straight in the morning. One of ours will keep watch here.' Hallows saw Scott's body tense, his ugly mouth harden in obstinacy. He guessed how it was and said as much: 'You couldn't have prevented what happened. Stop blaming yourself. Go home. If there is any deterioration in her condition, I'll let you know.'

Waiting some way back, clutching an over-night bag she had packed in haste for Liz, Isla observed the two men. They were both stiff, adamantly rooted, will against will. Clearly Scott was wrestling with a number of anxieties, while her husband was trying hard to be patient. At last she saw Scott yield. He bade her a swift good night, his hard heels ringing along the cheerless corridor.

Hallows twitched a curtain aside and saw her.

Apart from a heavy bruise and graze above her right eye which stood out in raw relief, Ferret's features were colourless, whiter than the linen beneath her head. She appeared unreasonably small as she lay on the hospital trolley.

In that first moment, Hallows tasted a private chivalric wrath at her mistreatment on the streets of Helenborough. The reaction, he could acknowledge, placed him not far distant from Scott.

He conformed to what would be expected: 'If you think this is one way of finding my soft centre, you're mistaken,' he remarked frostily close to Ferret's ear.

She opened an eye, saw him, found the light too bright and closed it again. 'Wouldn't bother,' she mumbled. 'You haven't got one.'

Thank God! he thought with relief. He grinned but she missed seeing the unusual. 'You must have been hungry to risk jay-walking,' he continued.

'Hungry, but not pinheaded. Somebody gave me a shove. You can probably lift prints from my back.' Tentatively she opened an eye again, saw Isla and stretched her hand across the blanket to have it held supportively.

'I'm putting a PC close by.' Hallows said while secretly praising his wife. She had masked the shock of hearing Liz had been deliberately pushed.

'I want to go home,' Ferret muttered, longing for the darkness of her own room, the safe comfort of her own bed.

'You'll be here for at least twenty-four hours.'

'Can't. Haven't got a tooth brush.'

Isla gripped the small hand with its ugly scar. 'Best to stay, Liz. Wiser. I've brought a bag of bits and pieces, a nightdress, soap, you know. I'll take your clothes away for cleaning and bring them back tomorrow afternoon.'

Ferret gave up, accepting refuge in sleep.

Chapter 2

As Hallows pushed through the rear security door at Abbots Hill, Scott stepped forward.

'How long have you been here?' Hallows snapped. He had found sleep to be a restless affair. He had abandoned bed three hours ago to pursue more useful activities and it was still not yet eight. He continued walking briskly towards the lift.

Scott was momentarily defensive: 'Not long. Ferret's doing OK . . .'

'I know.'

The empty lift arrived and Scott pressed the button. 'She's had no unwelcome visitors . . .'

'I know.' Hallows watched the indicator as they rose to his floor.

'Are we releasing the low-down on Ferret, guv?'

Hallows turned sharply: 'Who's asking?'

'Duty Sergeant took a call from Dr Wyland. Personal. He hedged. The doc said he'd ring back.'

'Have him transferred to me when he does.'

The lift quivered to a halt. Hallows stepped out with Scott at his side, giving him the sense they were in a three-legged race. 'Is there something else to report or is something on your mind?'

'Both guv.'

'Come on then.'

Once in Hallows's room, an abrupt nod told Scott to start talking.

'We've got a general description of the person standing directly behind Ferret at the crossing. A clean shaven, short, weedy white guy in his early thirties. He was wearing a dark shower-proof jacket with the hood up. No idea about hair length or colour.'

It wasn't much: more than Hallows expected, less than he had hoped for. 'So go on – what's plaguing you?'

'. . . about Ferret: I think Bisset fixed it.'

'You what?'

'I've had all night to think about it.'

'Sleep would have done you more good.' Me too, Hallows thought, catching sound of his own barbed tongue. He searched Scott's face and saw he was deadly serious. 'Bisset? Why?'

'You've met him, seen how he reacts to Ferret. When that guy hates, he hates!'

'So what's new? Plenty exude loathing. Plenty spew out threats, we have it all the time.' Hallows watched Scott stiffen, aggressively impatient. The sergeant knew all this and yet, undoubtedly, he was convinced Bisset could have arranged the attack on Liz. He decided: 'Get over to Green Vale, but keep well away from Bisset. You're too keyed up. Find out who Bisset might have made contact with recently.'

There was no mist today and Scott had a clear view of Green Vale from the top of the hill where the final estate petered out. Unlike Ferret, he was indifferent to it architecturally other than thinking it looked incongruous in conjunction with so much modern housing: a Stonehenge amongst pebbles.

He stalked the corridors and found the senior nursing officer who took him to her office.

'Did Mr Bisset have any visitors yesterday?'

The heavy woman viewed Scott with cheerful, alert eyes. 'No, but I'll confirm.' She keyed in: BISSET J. then pointed to her computer screen. 'Paper records can be mislaid. See: no visitors.'

'That sort of data's only as good as the people logging in info.'

'We have terminals at every nursing station. There's never been a problem. A record is kept even if the visitor or *Mr Bisset . . .'* she stressed, '. . . decline to give a name.'

Over her shoulder he saw that the tall man's arrival had been noted.

'But if an emergency arose at the same time as a visitor arrived, making a record could be overlooked.'

The suggestion did not offend. 'You won't be happy until you've talked to everone who was here yesterday, will you? I'll give you names and addresses of staff. The nurses work shifts. Some are going to be at home.'

'Then I'll see them there. Now phone calls?'

'No residents' rooms have fixed phones. We take them a trolley as necessary. Details of numbers are recorded automatically as soon as the trolley is plugged in.' She anticipated him and indicated the screen again. 'Mr Bisset hasn't used the phone since he's been here. I presume you'll ask me about letters next. We'll if Mr Bisset wrote or received one it would be the talk of Green Vale.' She keyed in a code and the printer began to purr out staff details. 'I've never known such a solitary man.'

Scott looked at the list. People were dotted everywhere. This could take all day.

'Superintendent Hallows?' Oliver Wyland's call was transferred. 'I've been trying to get hold of Liz Ireton. Couldn't raise her at home and your duty sergeant is being very evasive.'

'At home? She's ex-directory.'

'We've . . . well, we went to a party together the night before last.'

'Oh! I see.'

Wyland heard nothing now but an extending silence. 'Have I passed *GO!* Superintendent? Can I collect information?'

Hallows wasn't sure he liked Wyland. His scowl was parental, but when he spoke he withheld very little. 'She was struck by a taxi.' He heard Wyland's gasp. 'She has mild concussion, bruises and abrasions. University Hospital will be keeping her till late afternoon. You can visit after midday.'

'Thanks.' He was gone as Kennet arrived.

'We've had a whip-round, guv. Bought flowers for Ferret. Will you deliver them?'

Hallows wondered if there was a flicker of amusement in Roy Kennet's eyes. 'If I must,' he grumbled. It was well known he disliked carrying flowers. 'When will you be through with Victoria Crescent – Monday?'

'Sooner.' Kennet's voice echoed disappointed. For all the slog, they had discovered nothing obviously sinister. There were gleanings: a host of metal objects, most rusty, which the lab would check, but he had no sense of hope that they had found a murder weapon. 'Would you tell Ferret I've got her photos of the bedrooms.'

Hallows's brow crooked interest. He beckoned for an A4 envelope Kennet held and tipped the prints on to his blotter. 'What's all this about?'

'Something about cornices. She's not confided.'

*

Unlike Hallows, the Haweses were able to sleep to a later hour.

As their paper dropped through the letter box, Anne stirred. She straightened and lay on her back, listening for other morning sounds. She was in no hurry to open her eyes, being slow about everything was part of the pleasure of Saturday.

She considered her reaction to Madeline's phone call . . . such pain.

The problem lay in her being the second wife, and perhaps the second best. Gina had been loved and Gina had died, and for her, Gina would not rest. If that marriage had failed, ending in divorce, she would have had far less of a ghost with which to contend. Doubt, suspicion, jealousy, those emotions which stemmed from her insecurity were amenable to reason, however, given time, and she was calm again when Keith arrived home.

He had sprung upstairs to change into casual clothes, placid and cheerful as usual. She followed, telling him of Madeline's call. 'One of our guests invited her to eat at the Mill. A gorgeous man; hardly Lester Barraclough. He's more Humpty-Dumpty.'

Poor Lester, they had laughed together at his expense.

'Madeline said she saw you eating lunch with Linda Thorne,' she went on as he brushed his suit jacket with attentive care before hanging it in the wardrobe.

'That's right.' He gave his trousers the same treatment. 'She came in just after I'd sat down – asked to join me.'

'Can she afford to eat at the Mill?'

'Anne, you goose.' Grinning, he pulled on Oxford-blue slacks and fastened them with a wide leather belt. 'How am I supposed to know?'

She tossed him a light-wool cable sweater he had chosen. He settled its fit, then bent to comb his hair in front of her low dressing table mirror in a wish to be tidy.

When he looked at her again he had the quirky smile of the teaser. 'Linda is not my type, woman-mine. I'm definitely not receptive. I was beguiled by you the first time we met, and I think you know I'm captive still. If Linda Thorne is on a man hunt – dreadful expression, but it will have to do – then she's wasting her efforts on me. Was Madeline trying to make something of it?'

'No. All she could do was talk about red hair.'

'Well, there's proof of a non event.' He laughed, a wonderfully open sound. 'Madeline doesn't miss a trick. If she believed Linda and I were whispering lust-ridden words over the soup, she would have said so!'

The morning drifted through another half-an-hour. Anne stretched back sensually across lace trimmed pillows, trilled softly at the wall with her fingers and then slithered out of bed. She went to the window left open a crack and slid one curtain aside before pushing it open wider. She leant far out.

There was no sun or breeze this morning. Scarcely a sound either; just the occasional chime of childrens' laughter drifted to her across light woodland from the village centre.

She turned and looked at Keith as he slept, visible in a narrow band of uninterrupted daylight.

A night's dark growth of beard had enhanced his firm, well defined features. He was good looking, but his only conceit was in what he was able to achieve for his patients.

She had met him through Oliver – so long ago – around Christmas, a few months before Gina had died. Then she and Oliver had split. She had seen nothing of Keith again until a year later, when she had been canvassed by his department at University Hospital to replace a retiring member of staff.

Meeting him afresh, she had hardly recognized him. He had become gaunt, subdued, a workaholic in his attempt to deal with the persisting nightmare of Gina's hideous death.

They had started going out together and Oliver, seeing a change for the better in his long-time friend, had dubbed her Keith's resurrection woman.

She heard him sigh contentedly in his sleep, and her pulse quickened with the pleasure of possession.

Ferret dozed fitfully during the morning. Between slides into welcome unconsciousness Bisset and his tall, white-haired friend were on her mind with a thousand accompanying questions.

The tall man had never been seen arriving at Bisset's house by car. That must mean he was local – or did it? Perhaps he had chosen to leave his car elsewhere. Why? Because, through the car, he could be traced? By whom? By the law? Why was it so important that he was not? Who did he know? How was he employed? If Bisset had been engaged in the criminal activity she suspected, was the tall man one of the principals or was he merely a link between Bisset and others?

Ferret jerked in the reflex stumble of half-sleep and startled herself into open-eyed alertness. The last question loomed large. When Bisset had decided to leave Victoria Crescent it must have meant time for tidying up, for making everything secure.

Those shadow figures involved with Bisset would feel safe with him. He was tight mouthed, tight as a drum. But what if the tall man was not made of the same stuff? He would be viewed as a risk . . .

'Christ!' From being prone, she spun into a sit. 'Hey!' she yelled through the open door of her single room.

A WPC appeared.

'Clothes! Where are they? I have to get back to Abbots Hill.'

The WPC smiled smugly. It wasn't often you could pull a CI's strings. 'I believe Mrs Hallows took your things for cleaning. Afraid you're stuck here, ma'am.'

'Damn! I'd forgotten.' The room took a sudden wobble and she clutched the bed clothes. 'And don't call me ma'am. Nobody does.' She was trapped by kindness and a horrible sudden queasiness. She lowered herself cautiously back on to the firm pillows. 'And stop grinning.'

The WPC tried. 'Superintendent Hallows rang. He'll be in shortly.'

'Shortly?' Ferret scowled with impatience and the inability to think clearly for more than two minutes in a row.

'Liz?' Hallows stood in her open doorway, uneasy and apologetic. Like all police officers, he hated hospitals. They spelt cataclysmic events. He watched her open her eyes, blink and see him.

'The crowd sent these.' As if holding a medusa, he swiftly dissociated himself from a huge spray of flowers, dropping it across her legs.

Her colleagues' warm gesture took her entirely by surprise. If her eyes hadn't infuriatingly filled she would have made fun of Hallows's relief.

Now it was she who was embarrassed. 'Shit!' she muttered and stretched for tissues.

He had not expected tears either. For much of the time he saw her as a competent officer with no distinction of gender. Now he was reminded of a valuable, feminine sensitivity, but she would be extremely pithy with him if any of this showed.

He kept to safe ground and talked shop. He told her of the description they had of the man who had pushed her. 'Not much to go on. Scott's got a bee in his bonnet – thinks Bisset had it arranged. He's at Green Vale, having a sniff. What do you reckon?'

Her mouth pinched in recollection of Bisset's heinous glare. 'He would like me injured or dead.'

'Reason?'

'There could be two. First: he dislikes women, so a policewoman is the end of the line. Second: maybe he's buying time.'

'Time for what? Getting rid of evidence? What are you chasing, Liz?'

'Guv, forget the *what* for a while – please. It's all cerebral just now. I'm worried about the tall man.'

'He's not a local in the Victoria Crescent area.'

'That fits with what I've been thinking. Will you fax his description to other nicks?'

'Sure. Now about Bisset. How's your intuition? Will he have another go at you?'

'He'll have wanted me to suffer.' Her fingertips gingerly stroked the violent coloured bruise near her eye. 'He'll be satisfied when he learns I'm detained here.'

'It's in *The Mercury*. Front page, seven lines.'

'Enough then for him to spot it.' She sagged, exhausted, into the pillows. 'Sorry . . .'

'I'll go now. Get some more sleep. If you show signs of returning to rude health, they'll throw you out this evening. Isla and I will take you back to Quay House unless you'd like to stay with us. Oh...' he mentioned it with an irritable reluctance, '. . . Dr Wyland is likely to drop by this afternoon.'

Linda Thorne, with Saturday free, visited an exclusive gentleman's outfitters in the morning and made a purchase. Back at her flat she gift-wrapped the present, slid this into a jiffy-bag and walked to the central post office where she sent it first class.

For the remainder of the day she toured furnishing shops and ate out, not returning home until mid evening.

The Laurels scarcely honoured the name home.

The horseshoe drive, bordered with overgrown shrubs and coarse grass, was rough and pot-holed. The eighty-year-old, two-storey brick house had been divided into flats of two up and two down, many years ago. The landlord did the minimum of repairs and nothing about the rising damp. The first impression of disconsolate neglect endured. The only reasons she and the other tenants continued to live here were that the rooms were spacious, the location was quiet and they could all reach work without a car.

Linda was forever decorating, but a comfortable perfection could not be maintained. Fresh wall paper peeled as soon as hung. Paint-work and polished wood developed a dull bloom before a duster was put away. To her sensitive nose, there was a persistent smell of mould. She kept the storage heaters running for most of the year, but everything she did failed to dispel it. She often feared it clung to her too.

She boiled a kettle in the rear facing kitchen whose tall window shed light on to the desolation of a decaying orchard, made coffee and took this with biscuits into the neighbouring sitting room. A small log fire burning in the iron basket of the Victorian grate would be cosy, but having toyed with the idea of lighting one she decided against it. It never drew very well. She left the three-bar electric fire in the hearth and turned on one element for some localized comfort. With warmth on her legs she sat and thumbed through the items she had taken from Earle's. She saw this theft as necessary and, much as a public executioner would view his work, she felt no shame.

Scott had been shaped to be thorough.

By mid afternoon he had interviewed everyone except a Mrs Dice. She had been away at a meeting for the major part of the day.

He was hungry, despondent and tired to the bone when he entered Green Vale in a fourth attempt to see her.

The administrative officer's door was ajar and he heard taps at a keyboard accompanied by rattling paper.

He knocked and stood wearily in the opening.

She appeared not to hear.

'Did you . . .' he began.

A sudden strong draught whipped along the corridor. Her papers lifted and she slapped a restraining hand on them. She eyed him briefly: 'Close the door and sit down.'

Scott edged into the tiny room. The only spare chair was at the corner of her desk. There was no point in pulling it away, there was nowhere for it to travel. He sat with a knee jammed against the jutting steel handle of a drawer, and waited with diminishing patience for her to pause with her accounts. Dark suit, tailored blouse, brown curly hair scooped back into a loose knot; her well shaped face was set in unyielding purpose.

Her chin came up. 'Well?' she said.

'You have a patient here, Jacob Bisset, room ten . . .'

'Ground floor, east wing.'

'That's him. I'm trying to establish if he's received any visitors. You may have been in the front hall when . . .'

She was regarding him as if he was half-witted. 'This office is far removed from the east wing and the entrance hall. I would have thought you would have noticed. I have no knowledge of visitors.' And she reached for the next account.

Sarcastic besom! He squashed his fury and said solidly: 'Even so, the question had to be asked. You might say-' he played the pedant for revenge as she noted a butcher's bill and put the paid invoice aside -'that we have to have a similar approach to what we do. Every detail, every item, however small, is important.'

She had another account in her hand. She looked at it and at him, at the fatigue that shadowed his dark eyes and the exasperation there. The cleared bill was from: F. & W. Lilly, Window Cleaners. 'Small indeed,' she said, and deliberately let it flutter. It circled towards his lap like a child's slight balsa plane. 'I'm sorry.' She smiled suddenly. It was so unexpected and so charming, he felt light headed. 'I've had a maddening day haggling with accountants. I swear they're not attached to this earth. All setbacks and frustrations.'

He could forgive. He could laugh. 'Sounds familiar.' Recovering the bill, he glanced over the details and passed it back to her. 'But that's how it goes.'

'What we need is a little cheer.' She stood up so smartly he had to yank his legs away. 'I'm going to make a pot of tea. Fancy a cup?'

'God, yes!'

Kennet had taken his tea break with the search team in the refreshments trailer left by Grandfields in Victoria Crescent. This would be the last time they would use or need the facilities. Having thanked everyone for the effort involved, Kennet crossed to the second trailer where a sergeant and a constable had begun to pack boxes with items to be sent for forensic examination.

Kennet watched over their shoulders as each specimen, numbered and in a protective plastic bag, was cross checked against the find list.

'Looks like the fruits of an archaeological dig,' he murmured.

There were broken fork tines, near toothless rakes, a piece of a Dutch hoe, several half-moon hoe blades, dining cutlery and kitchen knives, pocket knives, chisels, screwdrivers and a good number of broken hacksaw blades.

Kennet reached between the two officers for a section of a bill-hook blade that would attract keen interest. As he lifted it, he saw another plastic envelope that was so flat it appeared empty, yet it carried a number: 4/31.

'Clever things, these metal detectors,' the sergeant said.

'Yes, but what's it found?' Kennet held the envelope close to an under-powered light. Inside was a small flat triangle of metal. Three might have covered a postage stamp. '4' referred to the number of the property. '31' indicated it had been the thirty-first object recovered. It would correspond with a quadrant number on a ground plan.

'Not the foggiest.' The sergeant waited for the envelope to be passed then placed it in the box.

When Wyland arrived at the hospital, he found Ferret leaning on her window sill, looking out over a Helenborough made drab by a dull, ebbing November light.

She had been thinking that her luck was better than Stan Parkin's. He was full of tubes and still unconscious.

Wyland coughed theatrically and she turned to face him. 'Oh, very beautiful!' he said, not referring to her fetching appearance in Isla's nightdress and robe, but to the purple bruise and graze bordering her eye.

She grinned, delighted to see him. 'I thought I'd set a new trend. I'm usually behind with fashion.'

He gave her a closer inspection. 'Mmm. Bet the other guy looks worse.' Making a platform of her hand, he dropped a box of chocolates on to it.

'It was a cab I argued with, and I haven't examined it yet.' She looked at the chocolates. 'By tradition you're supposed to bring me grapes.'

'I prefer these. Open the lid and we can get started.'

She pulled off the cellophane and allowed him first choice. 'Can't wait to be out of here. Isla and Mike Hallows are giving me a lift home.'

'And are you keeping the watch-dog?' He thumbed towards the distant WPC.

'Fishing for a job?'

'Could be. There's an iron age fort my students are occupied with and I'd like to have a look tomorrow. Want to come?'

'I thought geography was your line, not history.'

'They're complementary. Well?'

'OK, providing I can be moderately lazy. I need to crank up steam for Monday.'

'Monday! You're not going back to work? Hell's grief! Hallows isn't short of henchmen.'

'Persons,' she corrected in fun, then her smile died. 'But I'll choose when I have time off, not have it dictated by some malicious baa-lamb out there on the streets.'

Chapter 3

On Monday morning Keith Hawes worked methodically through his post, leaving a small jiffy-bag until last. Breaking the seal, he tipped the contents on to his blotter.

He was staring at the elegantly wrapped package when Anne came in. 'What's that?'

'No idea. You like parcels, you can open it.' He watched amused as she unceremoniously tore off the paper.

She found a display box. The content was obvious: a tie. A very expensive silk tie. 'There's no card. Who would send you this?'

He shrugged.

'Well, it can't be a patient.' She chuckled: 'None of ours would dream of being anonymous.' She checked the label. 'It's hand made. It must have come from Beal's. I'll ring them.'

Anne sat on the corner of his desk, swung a shapely leg and dialled.

She described the tie.

To Hawes, the assistant's voice was indistinct. He could only watch her reaction. Anne became taut. Her knuckles whitened. The receiver was lowered with exaggerated care.

Leaning forward he took and enclosed her shivering fingers protectively in his. 'I'll guess . . .'

She cut in, each word clipped: 'A slight, woman – bright red hair.'

'Linda Thorne.' Briefly a visible irritation creased his eyes.

'Why?' The word choked in her throat.

'To provoke a quarrel, perhaps. Lord knows why. We'll send the tie back.'

'I'll deliver it, Keith. I'll leave it at Earle's at lunch time.' She could manage it then. She would be poised, not shaking inside as she was now.

A whoop of delight set the windows of the Incident Room rattling when Ferret entered.

She was staggered and took refuge in an insult: 'OK, you lazy lot . . .' and heard anticipated uncomplimentary responses. 'What news of my tall, elderly guy?' There was nothing and she turned to Hallows: 'Bisset was teaching at St Joseph's, West Hillington, when he was arrested. Scott's arranged a meeting with the then chairman of the governors.'

'Have you contacted Hillington's nick?'

'I've said we'll call in when we've talked with Mr Quentin Dyer.'

'Quentin? Sounds "old school".'

Hallows had earlier commiserated with Scott over his fruitless enquiries at Green Vale, but lack of progress dogged them all. Nothing useful had been learned about Alcott from local winos and dossers, and no DNA test could be run since Sally Webber's brother had not yet been traced.

He watched Liz and Scott leave, Scott looking very much the minder this morning.

With Ferret still feeling washed out, Scott took the wheel for their forty-mile drive.

Rural West Hillington and Hillington town had been divided by a congested major road until a new motorway had absorbed the traffic. Since the diversion Hillington had slipped into a kind of purposeless doze. It became lifeless at midday when other towns bustled. Putting pleasant recollections of her outing with Oliver Wyland aside, Ferret turned again to the mystery of the tall, white haired man.

Had Bisset met him in prison? No one in the prison service had come forward claiming recognition.

For the umpteenth time she looked at her copies of the drawings: full-face and profile. A man couldn't disguise his height, but . . .

'What would you do to change your appearance, Scotty?'

He glanced at her and wished she would grab some sleep. 'Simplicity's best. I'd part my hair differently. Bisset's friend is elderly, he probably normally wears glasses. He'd leave them off.' No one had described glasses. 'Likely he wears a small denture too. Once removed, the face would look more hollow. As for all that white hair . . .'

'A handy distraction. A wig then.' Immediately she spoke to Control: '. . . the drawings – less hair – glasses – face plumper under his cheek bones. Fax out soonest, including Hillington.' She slotted the ID pictures into her bag.

Scott glanced her way and frowned: 'His hair's not the only thing that's white. Why don't you get some shut-eye?'

'Are you nannying me?'

He just grinned. 'I'll wake you when we're on the outskirts of West Hillington.'

'So long as you do. I don't want to meet Quentin Dyer, rubbing sleep from my eyes.'

Quentin Dyer's sprawling post Victorian property was of no definite architectural syle. The front, south-facing mellow brick wall was finely webbed with stems of a virginia creeper to which a few crimson leaves still clung. Most lay in high russet drifts close to the front apse-like porch, where the wind and a gardener had gathered them.

Quentin Dyer's housekeeper was out and he opened the door to the detectives himself. With an air of condescending impatience he took them into his drawing room.

Ferret saw him as the epitome of the retired county man. He was erect, stiff. He wore his quietly casual clothes, once expensive and still faultless, with a dignified ease.

Glancing about, she could envy his sitting room. It was tranquil in mood, and furnished with charming pieces that had weathered family life gracefully. A four-clawed drum table had almost vanished beneath a forest of silver framed photographs.

He directed Ferret to a sofa and responded to her wish that he sit at its opposite end.

Scott became a non intrusive presence and remained standing near the door.

Dyer plucked at his trouser creases and waited for her to begin.

'You've been told we are investigating the background of a man you will have known as Franklin Noyle.'

Dyer permitted his rigid features to crease in disgust. 'Noyle besmirched the reputation of St. Joseph's. Private church schools have always been easy prey to scandal. Ours, never having been a boarding school, was not quite as vulnerable. I can't see that I can add any more to facts gathered by the police at the time.'

Ferret murmured token agreement, opened a folder and passed Dyer a full-face print of the elderly man. 'It's an artist's impression. Can you identify him? His appearance could be rather different so please look carefully.'

Dyer accepted the print with polite disinterest.

Unmistakably his eyes widened behind the polished lenses of his frameless glasses. He remained totally without movement for a good sixty seconds then, laying the picture aside, he got up and walked to the window in an act of looking out.

Ferret considered him thoughtfully. She judged he was one of those men who would communicate more readily with a stranger than family. A stranger would not require a reprise over the teacups.

She joined him, standing a little way off.

Eventually he faced her. 'His name is Devin Slade. He's less angular than in your picture and the hair is wrong.'

'But you are certain of his identity?'

'Yes. You see I have the misfortune to have him as a step-brother.' His loathing was so intense it was palpable. It forced him into silence. He worked to subdue emotion and when he resumed speaking, it was with a ram-rod detachment: 'My dislike goes back a long way. When I was ten, his widowed father married my widowed mother. Devin was already independent, working and living in Chelsea. He used to visit us here occasionally, staying for a few days. I thought it was fun having a sophisticated older brother until I was fourteen when he tried to bugger me.

'I created a ballyhoo. My stepfather, considering his second family had been betrayed, threw Devin out.

'Devin remained away from Hillington, where he now lives, until twenty-five years ago. He had a series of young male assistants, living above the shop while he, then, lived elsewhere. He was discreet, thank God.'

'Shop?'

'A photography business. Portraiture was Devin's talent. In fairness, I will say he was good – capable of holding his own with the best.'

'Why did he leave London? In comparison Hillington is a backwater.'

'I presumed there might have been some trouble.'

She nodded and let him continue.

'In this small town he had to diversify: snap weddings, presentations, fêtes and fairs, school photographs . . .' He met Ferret's eyes. 'He was called to St Joseph's and so encountered Franklin Noyle.'

Dyer struggled to remain disengaged from Devin Slade's history. He paused, his nostrils flaring at something wholly offensive. 'He fell in love with Noyle,' he said at last, as if spitting dirt. 'The possibility had not occurred to me. I'm not sensitive to these things. Perhaps I should have taken note of an overheard remark. A parent was referring to Noyle. She described him being as beautiful as Michelangelo's David.'

Ferret felt compelled to ask: 'And in manner, what was Noyle like?'

Dyer regarded her with some surprise. 'Cordial. Refined. Staff thought him decent, hence the shock when he was caught in a state of undress with one of the boys; this followed by subsequent revelations from others.'

'Did your step-brother cut the friendship when Noyle was imprisoned?'

'Ostensibly.'

He evaded explanations, saying instead that there had been no young men since Noyle. He had employed a woman to assist with the business, Libby Stratton. When Devin retired some years ago, Libby took total responsibility. 'He lives quietly in the upstairs flat,' he added.

She pressed him: 'Why, ostensibly?'

Dyer's skin took on a greenish tinge. 'Franklin Noyle had been in prison about a month when Devin called here. Fortunately the family were out. He started sobbing, bleating about his love and how could he live without Frank? So repugnant! Such whining obsession: it was perfectly odious. In the end I sent him packing.'

For the first time Scott spoke. 'Did he visit Noyle in prison?'

'No idea. Since that day we've not conversed.'

Scott continued: 'These are difficult times. Does the business pay its way?'

'I've never heard of Libby Stratton complaining. I would have: town's gossipy.' He stepped away from the window abruptly, intimating dismissal. 'I don't believe I can assist you further.'

Ferret was satisfied. She scooped up her bag and the folder. 'We'll need Mr Slade's address.'

'ViewPoint – at the centre of the High Street.'

Behind them the front door snapped shut.

'Photography!' Scott growled, marching to their car. 'Are you thinking what I am?'

'More than likely.' Suddenly she felt shrivelled with cold and she huddled deep into her coat. 'Hillington nick, smartish. Their DI will want to be in on our interview with Slade.'

He turned on to the main road and keeping close to the limit arrived at the roundabout at the foot of a steep hill. They bore right while the High Street rose away to the left. It was virtually empty. Hillington's shops had closed for lunch.

Ferret wanted food now, for comfort, not to slake an appetite.

Hillington's police station, hiding behind a screen of terraced houses, was so cubic it could have been made from Lego. Not so its senior DI. Don Turley was markedly cylindrical with sepulchral features which belied a genial disposition.

He strolled them to the first floor of the small station, their feet sounding monstrously noisy in the naked stairwell. 'Your second lot of drawings came through about twenty minutes ago. Recognized him: Devin Slade. What's he been up to then?' Turley had halted by his office. 'We've had no bother. He's so bloody quiet he could be dead.'

'Dead, is what's worrying me.' Ferret fingered her bruise now in transition from purple to yellow. 'No accident. I'm concerned for Slade's safety. I need him watched – discreetly.'

'I've already posted a DC in the High Street.' He shifted his weight with something else on his mind. 'Have you eaten?'

'No, no time.'

'So brief me while you do.' With unexpected speed Turley moved off down the echoing corridor, turning into a compact kitchen where stacked slices of bread were ready for toasting. He pointed Scott in the direction of tins of baked beans and saucepans and left him to it.

Ferret, feeling less hunched but not yet prepared to cast her coat, sat beside Turley at a pine table already laid with cutlery. She repeated what they had learned from Quentin Dyer.

'And Slade's kept up with Noyle – your Jacob Bisset?' Turley spun a knife absently with his finger. 'They could be just two consenting adults.'

'They could be, but not in Bisset's upstairs bedroom. He's crippled with osteoporosis. A lad in tears was seen running from the house.'

'And Slade's a photographer of some skill. Niffs, doesn't it? Ah!' Scott pushed an overloaded plate in his direction. 'Thanks. Missed breakfast. So when we call on Slade, you'd like the green light to search.'

'Right.' Ferret eyed her beans on toast. Comfort food was what she had needed and this would do very well. She had eaten over half when a bellow for Turley rang along the corridor. He leapt up with Ferret reflexly following.

'Fire!' She heard beyond Turley's bulk in the doorway. 'ViewPoint. Brigade's on its way.'

The shops in Hillington's High Street had developed piecemeal over the years. Their plate glass frontages varied as much as the goods they sold, but they all had in common their narrowness and height. The properties were three or four storeys tall.

The detectives saw a dense pall of smoke creeping towards them over the irregular roof lines of the shops to the left as their cars raced towards the lower end of the street.

Fire officers swarmed around two engines in attendance. Already fat, hard hoses snaked across the pavement wetting blackly with water spillage. Jets streamed through the ground, first and second floor windows. Steam and smoke poured in a fog from every opening. Thick noxious smoke belched like a satanic cloud from the uppermost third floor to where an extending ladder was stretched.

Weighted under breathing apparatus, a fireman climbed. He vanished quickly into the dark, stinking, whirling vapour that vented from every floor.

'Slade?' Turley shouted.

Turley's DC hurried forward. 'Libby Stratton said he was in his flat when she locked the shop at lunch time.' He pointed at the smoke. 'Toxic as hell!'

'Libby Stratton-' Ferret pushed in -'is she all right?'

'Shocked to find the shop well alight. There's only one set of stairs. Slade has to be in there.'

'Where is she?' Scott asked. The DC pointed. Across the traffic-free road a smart, silver-haired woman gazed up, looking stricken. 'I'll talk to her.' He encouraged her into a wool shop where there was a chair.

Ferret's heart thudded with the adrenalin rush of anxiety. Slade must survive; she had to speak to him. As an ambulance backed closer, she rushed to wait by its open rear doors.

A shout. She squinted up – saw nothing but the vanishing ladder while flittering cinders pricked her skin, painful as hot needles. Then, like an emerging prophet, the fireman appeared out of the soot-laden cloud with an inert figure hanging across his back.

The paramedics reached up and began pumping oxygen into the smoke-stained flaccid mouth before the victim was released and lifted swiftly into the ambulance. As Ferret sprang after them she heard him groan.

She peered down: saw through the grime this was Slade. His reddened watering eyes stared back at her with a grasp of what was happening.

'Police?' he mouthed silently.

'Yes. Who started the fire?'

Through the clear face mask his smoke-stained lips moved feebly. 'Li . . .'

'Libby? Libby Stratton's quite safe,' she assured him. 'Devin, who wanted you out of the way?'

His eyes drifted. His mouth moved again, slackly . . . hardly at all. And he slipped into unconsciousness.

Ferret watched the ambulance pull away.

Someone joined her and she turned to face Turley. 'Any objections if I follow?'

'No, but keep me up to date.'

'You will go over Slade's place with a fine-tooth comb?'

'You can believe it, but with the extent of the fire damage, unless there's stuff on the top floor, don't count your luck we'll find any still photographs, obscene or otherwise. Same will apply to videos, of course.' Half watching the firemen reeling in their hoses he failed to see her expression change. A whispered expletive brought him spinning around. 'What's up?'

'Videos! Videos – that's where the money is!' She could scream; she was so bitter at her own blinkered vision. 'A studio. Lights bright enough to show up cracks at the bedroom curtains . . .'

'If this turns out as you think, you won't be the only one kicking ass!' Turley muttered. 'We'll look sap-headed if Slade's been processing porn here for years.' He stuffed angry hands into pockets. 'So who's doing the marketing? Who's the mail man with a loaded disc of addresses? Who's holding the purse? Is he going to be my collar or yours?'

'No idea. Just hope Slade can talk.' Ferret stepped towards Scott's waiting car. 'Let Quentin Dyer know about Slade, he might want to visit.' She wouldn't have rated it likely, however. She couldn't see Dyer finding a crumb of compasssion.

Scott cleared the roundabout then spoke of Libby Stratton.

'She locked the shop at one. Slade was in his private rooms on the second and third floors. He had his own darkroom on the first floor. She said she hadn't heard him use it recently. With only one flight of stairs she knew he'd be trapped up there. Turley's DC discovered the blaze at twenty past one.'

'Did Libby have any idea how it started?'

'No. Couldn't stomach it might have been deliberate. Said Slade didn't have any enemies – was a lovely man – honest as they came.' He heard her sigh and glanced at her. She looked pinched and was very pale again. He took a guess: 'Repetitive, isn't it? A & E yet again.'

'So right. Stan Parkin, me, now Slade.'

She waylaid the registrar.

'He's very weak but stable,' he answered. 'He has lung damage typical of smoke inhalation. He also has age related problems: tired heart, poor circulation.'

'Can I talk to him?'

'Only for a few minutes. He might end the interview himself: he's slipping in and out of consciousness.'

Ferret faced a shuddering reminder that a similar cubicle to Slade's housed her on Friday. She made a deliberate effort to ignore wires and meters and all the other resusc. gear. She focused on Devin Slade's face as Scott pushed a chair under her.

Slade's mouth gaped beneath the oxygen mask. His thin hair was rumpled. Wisps lay across the pillow in fine spikes. His face, cleaned of soot, resembled old white tissue paper. Only one thing surprised Ferret as she bent close. There were tears in his eyes and on his cheeks.

'You'll be all right,' she encouraged.

'No . . . I've had enough.'

'Do you remember me?' His head dipped in a token nod. 'I need to ask you questions about your part at Jacob Bisset's house. You took photographs of . . .?'

He began to wheeze out words that went beyond anticipation:

'Helenborough's sweet young things. God's beautiful . . . creatures.' His speech came chequered with gasping breaths. 'Maturing boys have such . . . fine bodies-' a reflective smile wandered across his face – 'wonderful skin quality for black . . . and white film.' He paused to suck deeply at the gas. 'Always a challenge to do them justice.'

'And videos? Did you make those at Victoria Crescent?' God alone knew how she hoped he would deny it; a denial that was the truth.

'They're not art.'

Her stomach turned.

For all his breathlessness, he was clearly insulted.

'If not your work, who made them then?'

'Frank liked to pass the time – amuse himself.'

'You mean Bisset. How?'

'Remote control. Easy.' Again the pause, again the concentration, the struggle. 'He was cheerful when he was busy, like he used to be . . . like the dear boy used to be.' Suddenly he began to cough, a hideous squeaking, rasping sound, and instantly a nurse appeared.

Ferret skipped out of the way, barging against Scott as the nurse used a sucker to clear Slade's throat. She felt him against her back, rock hard, reassuring. She stayed put, trying to leach his strength until the nurse left.

She bent close to Slade again. 'Who was commissioning you and Bisset? Who was buying?'

To her astonishment, Slade looked as though he was going to laugh.

'What's funny?' she asked.

'Images. Babies to adults. How we grow. How we differ.'

'Who? Give me a name. We'll keep a watch. He can't harm you.'

'A paragon. A putto.' He smiled at his own obstructiveness.

'Devin!' No space here for formalities. 'Don't hold back now.'

'You know what you know, there's no proof. The rest . . . I shall keep.'

Every word had its price. He laboured for air. He looked toward the ceiling, tearful again.

'Why cry? Do you regret what you've done?'

'I regret time stolen.' As his mourning eyes returned to hers, his speech became punctuated with huge exaggerated breaths. 'Frank . . . in prison . . . kept from me. Lonely . . . so lonely.' While every gasp for air was a harrowing effort, the wish to speak drove him on. 'But, believe me . . . you're a loser . . . if you never . . . experience . . . an absolute . . . affinity with . . .'

She was frightened for him. 'Take it easy.' Though what he had admitted was odious, she couldn't be party to this struggle. 'We'll return tomorrow. You'll feel better then.'

Ghastly noises were coming from his chest again.

The nurse entered ready to chase the officers away.

They walked in silence to the A & E's exit.

'You were standing on my foot,' Scott accused as they pushed out into an early dusk. 'Still, you don't weigh more than twopence-o'-nothing.' He raised a quizzing brow: 'Want to talk about him?'

'When we've stopped at a roadside and bought a cuppa.'

'Suits me,' he said cheerfully, unlocking the car's doors.

She settled into the passenger seat, and fastened her belt. Strange that such humdrum actions could be soothing.

It was a rum world, she thought, when an elderly, porno-peddling sodomite tried to teach her about love.

At the time Scott and Ferret had met Quentin Dyer, a Mrs Jenny Walker had taken a seat in Hallows's office.

'I was fond of Sally-' she told Hallows -'the sister I never had. I've grieved for ten years, not understanding how, but knowing she must be dead. I'm so glad you've opened the case again. We shared a room in residence at Helenhall for four terms. How can I help?'

'I'd like to get to know Sally.' His heavy features softened encouraging openness. 'Was her move to Briers Way a sudden idea?'

'She'd been fidgety for a while. I think she wanted to get away from the claustrophobia of living amongst so many. It was a beehive environment. It doesn't suit all.'

'There would have been a greater freedom too, in meeting a man-friend,' he suggested.

'True. But I can't tell you any more about Sally's guy, or guys, at the time she vanished than I told Detective Inspector Merrison. Sally was very secretive over who she dated.'

He produced the photograph from Sally's file that had particularly interested him. 'Is this a good likeness of Sally?'

Jenny sighed deeply in recollection. 'I took this. But she was prettier in a way that's difficult to describe. I suppose I'm thinking of her intelligence, her kind and lively spirit. We enrolled in a host of societies like everyone does.' Her smile was brief and sparkling. 'Helped Patronus with fund raising. Did all the usual student things.'

Hallows had no difficulty imagining Sally and Jenny as a happy, effervescent, compatible pair.

Jenny breezed on: 'If it happened, we were there. Used to swop clothes to ring the changes.' She touched the photo lying between them. 'Sally was rather bigger than me. This was my Laura Ashley dress. A skin-fit on Sally as you can see.' She pointed to little puckers where the fastening buttons of the bodice strained. 'A cause for laughter: we laughed at so many things.'

'Familiar, as you were, with each other's wardrobes, can you recall Sally having a taste for luxurious underwear? Did she receive presents? I was thinking of Lareine.'

Jenny's fine bow lips shaped a small *moue*. 'Lareine? No. But I can't answer for what she might have received after she moved to Briers Way.'

'I understand. It was reported that her work dropped off, that she was depressed through a failed love affair. Is that true?'

'She did get rather low, but I've no idea if it was because she'd split from her current man or because she was so fed up with living in. I thought she seemed brighter after moving.'

'But if that was generally obvious, why did Mrs Hawes arrange to visit her?'

She looked at him thoughtfully. He probed in an aura of friendship: there was nothing forceful in his manner, not what one might associate with such a big man, but then she was helping him. She wasn't guardian of a guilty secret. Perhaps, if he was investigating her, then she would have a sense of power, of intimidation even. The possibility interested her, but she wouldn't care to put it to the test . . . no.

She answered him: 'Perhaps her tutor was tunnel-visioned-' her brow crooked cynically -'slower to notice than I was. Perhaps Gina Hawes thought something of a matriarchal chat was in order since Sally was living off campus. I doubt there's anything cut-and-dried in college records to help you answer that one. Anything to do with a student's psyche was known to throw them.'

She was correct, though nothing about Hallow's face confirmed this. Merrison had had all pertinent documents copied. Anxieties and suggestions had been expressed on paper with deplorable vagueness. He moved on: 'Campus talk implied that Sally was pregnant. How would she have handled a pregnancy?'

She sniffed dismissively. 'Well, she wouldn't have jumped in the Nean. Personally, I can't believe it. I think she would have told me, but then, maybe-' she shrugged -'I flatter myself. As to her having killed Gina and Carol, I agreed with her brother, Richard. We thought Inspector Merrison's suggestion ludicrous.'

'Do you know where Richard Webber can be found?'

'I think he moved north.'

Hallows wound up the interview.

Left briefly alone, his mind rested on Sally's brother. Webber was a common name. A detective with Greater Manchester had phoned. They had traced a couple of possibles. He'd come back later.

It was hard to believe that Dr Joan Adams, headmistress of Helenborough High, had been at Helenhall University with Sally Webber and Jenny. She was older, but appeared far more so than her years. Her white hair, angularly cut only enhanced the sharp geometry of her features. Her expression was austere.

She was saying to Hallows: 'Sally and I weren't doing the same degree course. She was sciences, not my thing at all.' She smiled suddenly, and for a moment the unflattering years dropped away like a curtain. Revealed was an immense good-heartedness. 'Sally and I met when we joined the archaeological society which is affiliated to Helenborough's County Museum.'

'Meaning townspeople, lecturers and students are involved together.'

'Quite so. At that time, there were a number of nearby sites under investigation. Plenty for us to do.'

He glanced to where Curtis sat making notes and saw his veiled grin. Her primness tickled him and pleased Hallows, who could believe she was entirely truthful. 'So you used to go on digs together?'

'Much of the time, yes.'

'Much of the time?' He was intrigued.

'Oh, sometimes Sally didn't appear as we had arranged.'

'She'd cancel?'

'No. She said she had forgotten which particular dig and had mistakenly joined another group. Full of apologies.'

'She forgot?' he asked abruptly. 'Was that likely?'

'Most students over-stretch their time. Always dashing from one activity to another. When Sally owned to some confusion I accepted it.'

'And now, in retrospect, what do you think?'

Again the smile flittered across her face. 'I think she preferred to be with someone else other than me.' She held up her hand stonewalling a question. 'I have absolutely no idea who he was. Most young women talk of their crushes. Sally never once mentioned a name.'

'Interesting, this secrecy, don't you think?'

'Yes, something I have dallied with. Being somewhat of an innocent in these matters, my only conclusion has been that he was married.'

'It's a possibility,' Hallows owned, while thinking of other reasons, and he moved on to ask about the rumoured pregnancy.

'Maybe she was, but I think not. Sally was most practical, even given the immediacy of passion.'

Hallows, for a minute, had a hard job not to smile himself. It was the phrasing, so maiden-auntish. 'And the possibility of suicide?'

She drew herself up, tut-tutting. 'Suicide: never. *Or* to murder. Both were macabre ideas and utter nonsense.'

As the Guildhall clock in Helenborough chimed one – the time that Libby Stratton was closing ViewPoint miles away at Hillington – Anne Hawes walked into Earle's. She appeared strikingly smart and self-possessed.

'Can I help you?' A sales clerk hurrying forward failed to notice the tension in her eyes.

'Yes. I'd like to speak with Miss Thorne.'

'I'm afraid you've just missed her. She's left for lunch.'

'Oh!' Anne twisted away from scrutiny; her face was readable. Relief and vexation were written large. She wanted the business of the tie out with Linda Thorne, but not with heated words. She sought only a civilized exchange. In the pause that marked indecision she was aware again of the exaggerated thudding of her heart. It had beaten a tempo to her dreads all morning.

But she would finish what she had started in coming here.

She turned back abruptly. 'May I have paper and an envelope? I'll leave a message.'

She wrote briefly and quickly, slid the envelope into the jiffy-bag containing the tie and asked that it be placed on Linda's desk. Immediately she escaped on to the street.

She knew she had looked cool. If only she could feel confident detachment. Damn the woman for stirring so much agony.

Linda saw and recognized the plump package. She was not in the least surprised and, with amused curiosity, she tipped the contents out and took up the note.

Dear Miss Thorne,

Thank you for the tie, which you will find enclosed. We would prefer it if you did not send gifts. They are not merited.

Sincerely, Anne Hawes.

Linda became thoughtful. So Anne had called in person. That showed an unexpected control so, perhaps, after all, Anne had the fibre to be calculating. None the less, in this particular war of attrition, she had scored some further useful points.

Having crumpled the letter and thrown it away, she dropped the tie into a desk drawer and moved on. She felt the excitement of the angler after another fish. A small fish, admittedly, but with her larder empty, all scraps were attractive.

After work she would visit the Mitre. Among the thronging academics she would most likely run into Oliver Wyland.

Her intercom buzzed. Josh Elwood asked coldly: 'I presume you haven't changed your mind over an apartment at Shillington Court?'

'Of course not, Josh,' she said brightly.

'Then you'd better come in here. There are papers for you to sign.'

On their return journey from Hillington, Scott took a link-road from the motorway and found a transport cafe. At late afternoon they were the only two customers. Over a mug of steaming tea and a fat Chelsea bun each, they had moved from Slade's admissions to discussing the fire at ViewPoint.

Scott said: 'There had to have been more than one source, it got going so quickly. Was the intention to kill Slade or destroy evidence?'

Ferret shrugged: she was feeling as lively as a pinball machine with a duff fuse.

He looked at her narrowly. 'Maybe not such a good idea to talk any more. I'll drop you off at Quay House. Bring you in some food. You can get to bed early.'

She glared: 'That's enough, *mother*. Anyway, my car's at Abbots Hill. What's more, I want to tell Bisset, today, what his past lover had to say. We'll drive straight there. Slade inferred Bisset is heir to pride. He might like to boast and fill in some of the gaps Slade left open. After that I must put Roy Kennet in the picture.'

'Bisset won't talk lovers to you, though he'll enjoy looking at your shiner.'

She knew it, but it galled keeping back. 'I'll stay in the car. Play him carefully. No accusations relating to me. Stick with videos and how it was worked at number 6.'

Ladling out instructions! He eyed her across tea strong enough to support a spoon. Her obstinate, sensitive face had less colour than their white mugs. 'Yes, mother,' he answered and grinned disrespectfully.

'Roy!'

Kennet halted, as he climbed the stairs at Abbots Hill. Leaning back against the metal hand rail, he watched Ferret toiling up.

'You look bushed,' he said.

'Don't you start. That conduit that ran from Bisset's sitting room to the bedroom – I've got the answer. It carried cables for working remote controlled camaras and a lighting set-up. Bisset wasn't just spying on tricks going on upstairs, he was filming them. He bragged to Scott about his competency. Makes me want to puke!'

'Who posed? Who bought? Who distributed?'

'He's not dishing out cake as well as bread. He's confident we'll find no proof but as to names – nothing. He'll relish his secrets.'

Kennet offered a commiserating grunt: Bisset's muteness left her sieving through sewage. 'A builder came in: Reg Falder, asking was there any news of Martin?'

'Poor man.' Her mouth crescented sympathy. 'Zilch. I'll give him a ring.'

Oliver Wyland pushed through the door of the Mitre and faced a crush of councillors and lobbyists. He eased between tight knots of people and made for the bar where Neville Howard sat sipping a gin and tonic.

'Gather there's a council meeting this evening,' Wyland said.

'Makes me think of plea bargaining. Is this a flying visit, Oliver, or can you eat with me?'

Wyland had plans elsewhere. 'I'm only in for a half of Ruff's.'

He had just given his order when he caught a glimpse of fiery hair reflected in the mirror behind the spirits optics. He turned: 'Linda, nice surprise, don't usually see you here. Good party, wasn't it?'

'Lovely.' Her smile travelled to Howard.

'Meet Anne's father . . .'

Howard offered a drink and his face lit when she accepted.

Wyland was puzzled by her appearance at the Mitre, but asking her to salve his curiosity had to be postponed. Dr Duncan Milo was homing in on them. Milo, true to form, was sniffing out a match.

'No hard feelings, Oliver,' Milo was saying, 'over our scrabble for research money?'

Wyland replied lazily: 'No, no. So long as it's a fair race – mmm?'

The jab hurt. Milo's quick piggy eyes darkened. He turned to Linda: 'Are you eating here?'

Linda could recognize a rapacious snooper. If she needed him, however, she could talk to him any time. 'No, I've just popped in.'

Milo felt himself being squeezed out. 'Me, too,' he said and, with a flourish of his drink to her, left.

Howard leant forward: 'Linda, will you change your mind about dinner, if you don't mind an old man's company, that is?'

She looked into the alert yet fading eyes and appreciated she could relax with him. 'Thank you, I'd like that.'

He smiled total pleasure. 'Good. Then I'll nip off and reserve a table.'

Wyland watched him enter the dining room. 'He's lonely.'

'I recognize that,' she said. 'It's a common condition.'

The sudden tension in her voice made him realize she referred to herself, yet it was hard to accept she had no one, but he could hardly ask. Instead he returned to an earlier question. 'Why did you come to the Mitre this evening?'

'Since it's not a haunt of mine? To see you.' Her smile teased. 'But I'll tell you why another time,' she added, spotting Howard returning.

Wyland swirled his glass and downed the small remainder. 'To another time, then,' he said and moved away.

He had to shoulder through the politicking crowd again to reach the door. On the point of pulling it open he saw a hand waved from a distance. Wyland acknowledged it. Lester Barraclough was talking with Charles Saville and presumably trading favours.

Josh Elwood hoped the phone call Kate was answering would not be for him. He was well settled into his favourite armchair, a glass of whisky in his hand and his injured leg raised and comfortable.

She covered the mouthpiece and beckoned.

'Sod!' He heaved himself upright and thought seriously about buying a cordless.

'It's Charles.' She passed the receiver, blew a kiss and left him.

Saville was brief and to the point. 'I've been with Barraclough at the Mitre. Linda Thorne arrived. She had the look of wish-fulfilment when she saw Oliver Wyland at the bar.' Elwood groaned. 'Quite! I don't know what she might have on Wyland, presumably you do, but now she's got a taste for blackmail. . . . You'd better think about warning him.'

Turning into the forecourt of Quay House, Ferret's heart gave a leap of fright. Then she realized the Citroën parked close to her front door belonged to Oliver. Convinced though she and Hallows were that a watch over her was unnecessary, it was difficult to switch off being jumpy.

'You keep dreadful hours,' he called, unfolding himself from his car. 'I nearly gave up and left you a note.'

'You should have. I'm too tired and hungry to be sociable.'

'Ah! Then perhaps I've brought a suitable remedy.' He raised a carrier bag. 'Food. All it needs is a quick blast in the microwave.'

She came close and eyed the bag: *Peking House. Chinese Take-Away*. 'You do know how to get round a copper. You can come in, but for only the length of time it takes us to eat. A deal?'

'A promise.'

They sat facing each other, a heap of cutlery between them. Ferret chose a fork. She was too hungry to be dainty with chop sticks.

'I was going to ask you out.' From his back pocket he took a folded advertising bill. He smoothed it out on the table and passed it to her. 'Jazz week at the university; different nights for different tastes. Which evening do you fancy?'

'Oh! Tomorrow or Wednesday, but I can't guarantee to be free.'

'Understood. It's not a problem. I can pass the tickets on.'

He began stacking the empty dishes. She took them and pushed a bowl of fruit in his direction. Taking an apple, he followed her into the kitchen where she was filling a kettle. He bounced the apple in his hand and looked at her thoughtfully. 'You've been wearing a continuous frown. Headache or a brute of a day?'

'Something of both.' She leant back against the sink and watched the apple leaving and landing in his long, thin fingers. 'I've been paddling in filth for hours. Sometimes it gets right under your skin. It taints. It constricts your view of life. Going out tomorrow will be good – curative, like sloughing.' For a moment she was able to grin: 'Apples and snakes.'

'A potent mix.' He was unexpectedly serious. He laid the apple aside and very gently stroked the bruise on her face. 'Am I allowed a coffee or do I leave now?'

'Coffee's permitted.'

He hooked a finger under her chin. It really was time he kissed her.

*

An hour later, when she was alone and nodding off in front of the TV, Ferret was jolted back to reality by her phone's insistent ring. She killed the programme's sound, then hauled herself free of her favourite armchair.

Turley had chased her to ground.

'Thought you'd want to hear soonest,' he said. 'Devin Slade died half an hour ago.'

'Sod!'

'You said it. Fell of the perch without another song. We're still chasing witnesses who might have seen how the fire was started. My DC found it roaring at thirteen-twenty. The FI officer says there were four sources. Four shows bloody determination. The largest was on the stairs just below the entrance to Slade's flat.'

'Somebody must have noticed something. There's no rear access.'

'In Hillington's High Street . . .' He laughed humourlessly. 'I'm doing like the quote says: *nursing the unconquerable hope*. SOCO tried making a comb of the debris this afternoon, but there were too many hot spots. I'll be in touch. Cheers.'

Chapter 4

Elwood had slept badly. If he had not been such a magpie, there would have been no threat to Oliver. A photograph, taken in fun years ago, kept against Oliver's wishes out of sentiment. What folly!

When he was told, he would go spare.

The university had rules, archaic maybe, but they clung to them as vigorously as a nun guarded her virginity. An infringement would not be regarded as any less a sin by reason of a lapse of ten years. Lecturers did not go out with students, and Oliver had, and on numerous occasions before his marriage to Kate.

If Linda made known this information, Oliver would not only lose the research funding he needed, he could very probably be out of a job as well.

There was a long neglected stand of hazel between the Haweses property and Lester Barraclough's. It was a wilderness that made it very difficult to reach the near-derelict stables on their land. Anne fancied bringing the building into good repair. As a girl she had ridden and she had a strong hankering to own a horse again.

'I suppose the hazel should be coppiced,' Hawes was saying over their mid morning coffee. 'We could ask the landlord at the Latimer, he's bound to know someone local who would do it. We could eat there this evening.'

'Good idea. Shall we ask Oliver to join us?' She filled the delicate china cups, passed him his and then took up her own. 'You can persuade him to take part in the next Patronus play. Charley's Aunt raised such a lot of money, and despite his grumbling, he did find the time.'

'I'll give him a ring.' Hawes pursed his lips thoughtfully. 'About Barraclough – I ought to have a word out of courtesy. If we do cut back the hazel, he'll lose some of his privacy until new growth breaks.'

'I'm sure Lester will be in favour. He keeps going on about our making everything ship-shape at Witley House. How he can talk!' She began to giggle: 'Don't tell me – that's why he's never been proposed for Patronus.' And her coffee slopped into the saucer. 'A natural for filibustering. Oh, poor Lester,' she added with a show of genuine kindness. 'But I don't suppose he'd have the time anyway, not with so many committees. Just as well he has only himself to please.'

Lester Barraclough was indeed busy. He and nine fellow councillors had elected to view a number of local nursing homes for the purpose of familiarizing themselves with good working principles.

Green Vale had won many awards for excellence and early on Tuesday afternoon their cars, in convoy like some presidential showing of face, rolled into the car park of the nursing home.

After being greeted and having a general discussion with the management, they split up into pairs to see for themselves exactly how theory and practice met. Tea was to be provided at the conclusion of their tour.

Barraclough was making his round with an equally ample figure, Councillor Marie Wyatt. She was a forceful personality who could match Barraclough in words. Both asked a volume of questions of the anxious nurse detailed to conduct them.

'You've been very helpful,' Marie told her at the tour's end and then patted the young woman's arm warmly, taking her by surprise. 'I'm sure your patients aren't nearly as much trouble as we've been.'

The nurse relaxed. 'Not at all. I'm pleased to have taken you round. Is there anything else I can show you?'

'Yes, my dear-' Marie smiled -'The Ladies.' She turned to Barraclough. 'I'll meet you at tea, Lester.'

The nurse, anticipating he might also have a need, pointed to the Gents in the opposite direction.

At the same time Barraclough had entered Green Vale, Linda Thorne waylaid a student in the handsome ashlar-fronted building that housed the geography department at Helenhall, and asked where she might find Dr Wyland.

The young man, wearing an ancient flak jacket over flapping shirt and slit jeans, sized her up in her stylish suit and then awarded her a happy, lecherous grin.

'He's probably in his study. That's in Anselm House.' He thumbed in the direct of a window. Seen through it was a six floored, featureless concrete edifice, streaked with crusts of dribbled lime. He laughed at her grimace. 'More Euro Economy Modern than English Perpendicular.'

'It's not so much the design: I hate concrete. It won't age gracefully.'

Indulging in a little jokey flirtatious patter he took her as far as the lifts in the new building. It amused her, this stretching of wings with an older woman.

He saw her enter: 'Second floor – name's on the door.'

Wyland's corridor could have been lifted from a two-star hotel: low illumination, buff-and-green carpet, beige-painted walls and a scatter of mass-produced mediocre prints. His room was close to the far end near a flight of stairs.

She knocked, heard him shout: 'Come.' and walked in.

As she did so, Duncan Milo arrived at the top of the stairs. He watched her disappear, then paused briefly outside the door.

Linda found Wyland sprawled in his chair, his feet resting on his desk. He was eating from a pack of sandwiches.

Instantly, in surprise, he swung his legs down. 'I thought you were one of my students. They're used to my snatched breaks.' Waving a sandwich, he said: 'Do you mind if I go on eating? I'm running tight on time.'

'Please do.' She strolled to the window behind him and looked out. Shrubs, grass and flower beds wore a winter dejection she was far from feeling. 'I won't keep you long.'

'Has Josh been trying to contact me?' He picked a crumb of cheese from his navy sweat-shirt. 'I've been in a lecture theatre for much of the morning.'

She collected a chair and carried it back to the window. He would be forced to look this way and the light would show up his every expression. 'This is personal,' she said and took a photocopy of a photograph from her bag. It was not particularly good, but the subject matter was clear enough.

His eyebrow crooked curiosity as she passed it to him.

To her surprise Wyland's face remained bland. For a moment Linda wondered if she was on a fool's mission, then her confidence returned. 'A happy couple. What were they doing? They look rather shame-faced, but perhaps that detail is not as sharp as in the original . . . which I have. On the back of the original are written two names: Oliver and Sally.'

His face continued to register nothing. Only his eyes changed. They darkened to the depth of jet.

'I've been running through the press archives. Some names stick in the mind, you see. I'm now certain this Sally is Sally Webber.'

She still saw no reaction: he might have been a photograph too, a feelingless two-dimensional figure.

'Did the police know you knew her?' she continued unperturbed. 'It goes without saying, you would have kept the fact from the university authorities. She was a student, after all.'

He moved fractionally. He touched a dry lip with his tongue, then spoke as casually as if asking the time: 'What do you want, Linda?'

'Oh, nothing very much. You can buy me dinner one evening at the Mitre and I'll tell you. I'll give you a ring.'

Exactly then the telephone on his desk sounded noisily, making them both start a little.

He reached for it. His said, with the customary rush of friendship: 'Keith. Hi! Dinner with you at the Latimer this evening? Great idea but it's likely I'm committed elsewhere. Sure,' he agreed to a new proposal. 'Sounds like old times . . . talk details later.'

Linda watched him hang up unhurriedly. 'Finish your lunch, Oliver.' She stood, her easiness suggesting the room was hers rather than his. 'And enjoy the prospect of our future meeting.'

When she had left, he stared fixedly at the closed door for a good five minutes.

Was it always the same? he thought, the deadening effect of shock. One seemed to act in a reflex way. He could believe he had said goodbye to her coolly, with a card-sharp's smile.

But the thaw was setting in.

He rang Josh Elwood in a white fury, learned that Josh was out and had to chew on anger unshared.

Linda Thorne returned to Earle's in an elated frame of mind, confident Oliver Wyland would pay for silence. Luck had played a part too, in timing Keith Hawes's call so that she would hear it.

She rang the Latimer at Roxleigh and learned the time he had booked to eat.

Keith Hawes and Anne: an interesting couple. Was such adulation normal? Who else, of all the people she had ever met, would invite guests to a house-warming and then tiptoe away to make love?

When she had arrived at the party she took her coat upstairs to a room off a half landing. Being alone, she had delayed going down, instead she had wandered up to a lesser-lit second landing in order to explore.

She found a woman's dressing room, idly touched and stroked ornaments and pretty furniture there, then pushed open a communicating door a crack. She saw them reflected in a cheval mirror. Decency dictated she should go, but she had lingered, held by a curiosity that was detached from the voyeuristic. They were naked, lying head to tail on the bed. Anne was fondling him, while he worshipped intimately with kisses, licks and caresses.

She had felt weak, wet with envy and desire for Josh. Creeping away, she had sat on a dark stair, waiting for the agony to pass. If only . . .

But that affection must die!

With an abrupt movement, she bent down to the desk drawer where the tie lay. She shook it from its box, walked to her notice board and pinned it there. You took consolation where you could, and there was a mite of comfort in knowing she had several men by the throat.

Linda arrived at the Latimer half an hour before Keith and Anne Hawes were due. She ordered a bar meal and chose a table not in their immediate vision.

Anne was the first to enter, with Hawes a step behind. Without a glance in her direction, they strolled to the farther end of the exceptionally long room and selected a table near a brightly burning log fire.

Taking supreme pleasure in playing a solo game, Linda fixed Anne with her green eyes and waited. She saw their order taken and the first, and then the second course brought. She knew that in time she could compel Anne to look her way.

As if hearing her name, Anne turned her head sharply.

The abrupt move made Hawes forget his roast duck and look up. He saw Anne's expression freeze. He searched for cause and spotted Linda.

Linda's attention remained with Anne. She offered her a warm nod. Anne had to be in some distress since Keith was placing a reassuring hand over hers.

Her game over for this evening, Linda collected her bag then walked casually in the Haweses direction.

'Passing ships-' she smiled -'I'm just off. Delicious food. I hope you're enjoying your meal.'

'Do you make a habit of eating here?' Anne asked stiffly.

'No, this is the first time.' Linda's eyes went to Keith. 'But perhaps I should.'

Ferret had managed to keep Tuesday evening free for Oliver Wyland.

She told him she felt far less burned out than on the previous day. In fact, when he collected her from Quay House, she was quite perky.

There was no tension about Wyland.

He was not a man to sustain a rage. It had given way to much thoughtfulness several hours before he met Ferret. Nothing should be done in haste, he had to plan where he was going, and feeling time was in his favour, he was able to put aside anxieties and enjoy his evening.

The trad-jazz session at Helenhall ended to noisy, euphoric applause. They made a quick exit, escaping boisterous youthful enthusiasm for the relative quiet of the courtyard outside.

'Like it?' he asked unnecessarily. He had been only too aware of how the music had reached her. Jammed against his side on seats too closely packed together, he had felt her sway and flex according to the beat, and seen her face alight with pleasure.

He was on cloud nine himself.

'It was terrific!' she said. And she spun around, her arms held high, cutting the cold damp air in exultation. Above her, she could find no stars. No moon either. It was an intensely black night, one where evil could roam freely, but not one that could oppress their spirits.

'A drink at the Mitre ... or at my place?' Nuances in his voice conveyed that he had more than a drink in mind.

'Coffee, at mine,' she replied without giving or dashing hope.

'*His speech is a burning fire* ... Mine can be, if you let me get close enough.'

In the lowest of light on her balcony, Ferret could make out Oliver Wyland's brow lift encouragingly.

He turned from her and leaned with a gracious ease over the railing. Below, the river ran inkily to the sea, visible only where the occasional band of light escaped from neighbouring windows and danced across the surface of the water: a Midas touch which brought an hypnotic, shimmering brilliance, gleaming in the darkness, with the power to bewitch if one was susceptible.

'You quoted the same piece at Keith Hawes's party.' She chuckled and rested against the iron railings some distance from him.

'*With his lips he travaileth* . . . Keith doesn't have sole claim to passion. Why are we yards apart, Liz?'

'Feet,' she corrected, 'but probably we should be talking metric.'

'Sod metric!' He laughed. '*In his heart is a blind desire* . . . ' He stretched out an arm and pulled her against him. 'As you can tell.'

Chapter 5

Nobody had made love to Ferret since she and Mac had parted. When sober, he had been a wonderfully considerate lover. Oliver Wyland too, was sensitive to her needs. He climaxed before her, but brought her on, making her gasp at a pleasure almost forgotten.

In the early hours, as rain dashed against the windows, Wyland awoke with a renewed libidinous urge. He had been dreaming – whirling and weightless with her, bound close in the arms of his love – and had to fulfil the sensual gratification the dream had begun. In the blackness of the room, he rolled towards Ferret, found her and began to kiss her neck, then her small firm breasts.

She stirred and sleepily recognizing each voluptuous touch, contentedly surrendered to each caress. She grew hungry for him, welcomed him, was as much afire as he, and came, seconds in advance of him, in pulses of violent ecstatic joy.

'Dear life!' he exclaimed. 'Dear heaven!' Reality and dream merged. In rapturous orgasmic release it brought him gasping: 'Kate! Darling, darling, Kate!'

Ferret froze, then in a rush of anger, pulled herself away. 'You *bastard!* I don't stand proxy for anyone.' Her hand darted out for the bedside light. 'Look!' she shouted in the sudden brilliance: 'This is me! This is *Liz!* '

'Liz, I'm . . .'

She was out of the bed, running for the door. 'I'm taking a shower. Make sure you've gone when I get back.'

She hadn't heard the front door close.

She stood in the centre of the bedroom, looking at the tumbled bed. She hurt: every nerve that Mac had scraped raw, screamed out again. She snatched up her pillow, tugged a blanket from a drawer and stumbled into the sitting room. She poured a whisky, drank it straight off then flung herself and the bedding on to the sofa. If she could manage to sleep at all it had to be here.

The phone woke her.

After two hours of tears and tossing, Ferret had eventually dozed.

She was pleased to wake. She was stiff and the dream had been unpleasant.

'Guv! Duty sergeant here. Sorry about the early call.'

''sOK. Trouble?' She reached out to pull back a curtain. The first crack of daylight showed in the eastern sky.

'Message from DS Scott. Green Vale. Suspicious death. Jacob Bisset. Police doc's there and SOCO are on their way.'

'What? Bisset, did you say?'

'Right. What'll be your ETA?'

She squinted, trying to focus through puffy eyes at the carriage clock next to the Jane Austens on the book shelf. 'Twenty-five minutes from now.'

'Noted.'

She walked into the bathroom and plunged her face into cold water.

Scott had not stopped to shave. He met her in the corridor outside Bisset's room, scratching a chin black with a good growth of stubble.

'You look gruesome,' Ferret said.

'Thanks.' He noted her red-rimmed eyes, but that could be down to fatigue. 'And you resemble a seen-it-all battlefield waif,' he returned amiably.

'Battlefield's right,' she muttered. 'Who found him?'

'A night-nurse, shortly before the shift changed. He was on the floor, a pillow over his face. She didn't touch anything other than to check for life signs. The senior nursing officer rang us, sealed the room and then contacted the senior management exec. Doc's confirmed Bisset was smothered: petechial haemorrhaging around the mouth. First look – he reckons death to have occurred shortly before midnight. Rigor's apparent in the jaw. He'll complete temperature checks when you've had a squint at the way he's lying.'

They entered the room brilliant with spotlights as SOCO, fingerprint officers, and video and stills photographers worked.

She squinted in the sudden glare and couldn't help enjoying the present irony. Bisset, who had professed a preference for being alone, had a great deal of company this morning.

While the pillow had been removed, Bisset was lying as originally found, his limbs at strange angles as if a child had assembled him from a kit of parts. She stepped forward noting the state of his clothes. His deep blue pyjamas were twisted about his body, rucked up, clinging in concertina wrinkles to his knees and elbows. An expanse of flesh was exposed: toneless, with the look of old polished ivory.

'He must have kicked and thrashed about,' she said. 'No mean feat, having in mind his poor physical condition.' She moved out of the way. In the cause of protecting evidence an officer sealed Bisset's hands in plastic bags.

He pointed to Bisset's nails: 'Blood here. Could be tissue as well.'

Ed Browne, the senior officer present, interrupted what he was doing and came forward. He must have noticed her red eyes, but his gaze remained direct and impersonal. He said crisply: 'Pressure marks on the pillow showed two people involved. We've got photos of the impressions.' He pointed to Bisset's emergency call-button. It was dangling just above the floor close to the wall, and far out of Bisset's reach. 'They moved it. No prints.'

'Thanks.' She and Scott approached the bed. Sheets and blankets were in wild disorder, dragged towards the side where Bisset had ended on the floor. 'Why haul him out of bed to smother him?' she said. 'Doesn't make sense. He must have been asleep when they arrived, or he would have hit the button. Murder can't have been the reason for their visit.'

'So they were searching for something.' Scott glanced around. 'But nothing else appears disturbed.'

The emergency button continued to interest her. 'Did they move it before he opened his eyes, or in a rush as he woke? If the latter, they must have been right beside the bed . . .'

'. . . looking for something. But what?' He glanced towards Browne who was crouched down near the second window. 'While you talk to Ed, I'll find the nurse who was the last to see him alive.'

She nodded. 'Tell the doc he can finish his checks.'

Even while wearing protective overshoes, she was careful where she walked. Footprints didn't have to be visible to be there. She made her way towards the window Bisset had favoured. His chair was in exactly the same place.

She looked from it, back to the thin pathetic body. Wheels began to turn. At every interview Bisset's hands were fanned over a weighty album. An album . . .

Browne cut in: 'You'll like this, Ferret.' He rose, pointed, and left her to look for herself. 'Could help with timing.'

Beneath the wide open sash window the carpet was dark from being sodden. She checked the curtains. Over their lower length, the linings were equally wet. She scrutinized the sill. There was no mud, not a speck, nor on the carpet, yet – she peered out – there was a miry, empty, flower bed that would have transferred soil to shoes.

She indicated outside: 'Time for a walk.'

'Torch!' Browne called to a colleague and was passed a powerful flashlight.

While it was now dry with daylight reasonably advanced, there was not sufficient natural light for their inspection.

They were discussing the tall sliding windows when they left the building. 'Have the locking-bolts on the butting-rails of the sash windows been checked for prints yet?' she asked.

'Yes. Too clean to be true.' They had turned towards the east wing and were walking around the building on a wide path that separated flower bed from lawn. 'I know it didn't rain until around two, but the ground must have been far from dry before then. It's November, damn it. Something should have transferred from their shoes.'

'Perhaps they took them off.'

He glanced at her sharply. 'Cheeky devils!'

While SOCO had already checked the ground out here, she kept alert for anything significant.

He was panning the strong light over the empty dug flower bed as they progressed to Bisset's room. In a wall-to-path rectangle beneath each window were a score of foot prints together with a series of evenly spaced, narrow slots. Every depression was a pool of brown opaque water.

'Stepladder holes,' she said at once. 'A window cleaner's calling card. The gardener here must curse them.'

The soil outside Bisset's window was no less cratered. Browne grumbled: 'Making casts here won't be a quick job.'

'We'll need prints from beneath other windows.'

He sniffed good naturedly: 'To eliminate the window cleaners. I had a horrible feeling you'd say that.' He directed the torch beam over the exterior surface of the sill. 'No footprints on there, either.'

She looked at the height of the lower sash. To open the window by its top edge, you would have to stand on the sill in order to reach and lift. 'We'll have to check the counter-weight of the sash – see if it runs up easily while lifting from the lower glazing bars.'

'Right.'

Through the window she saw the police doctor bending down to complete his examination of Bisset. It was something she would be pleased to miss and she walked back unhurriedly behind Browne.

Scott was waiting for her in the entrance hall. Beside him stood a tiny, whey-faced nurse. He said: 'Nurse Hammond's on nights. She tucked Jacob Bisset up last night and found him this morning.'

Ferret grimaced sympathy: 'A nasty shock for you. Sorry we've had to keep you from your bed. Let's sit to talk.'

There were chairs to hand. The nurse thankfully dropped into one and clutched her arms in a nervous hug.

'How did you get on with Jacob Bisset?'

'I didn't like him, but it made no difference to my nursing. I'm professional.' She showed a moment of hauteur. 'He was always so grumpy, an ingrained act probably, a means of keeping people at a distance. We all erect barriers when we're hurt. Hurt mentally, for most of us. Physically as well, for him, through his crippling condition.'

Time paused for Ferret. Painful memories of last night rushed upon her, unbidden and uncensored. Her mind vaulted all tender stages to relive nothing but humiliation. Damn. Oh damn Oliver!

She clutched at the present. 'What routine brought Mr Bisset's day to a close?'

'He had a hot drink, then I got him to bed at ten-thirty. As usual he had that heavy album beside him.'

Ferret glanced back to Scott. His right eyelid dropped a mite. So he was thinking as she was. 'Did you ever see inside this album?'

The nurse laughed scornfully. 'No! He closed the strap.'

From the corner of her eye Ferret saw Scott head towards Bisset's room.

She said: 'Are the windows left open at night?'

'Only in summer if it's stiflingly hot. There are special locks which allow a slight air gap. The management are strict on security.'

'So you checked the normal locks were fastened before you left Mr Bisset?'

'Not me personally. At this time of year the nurse dealing with teas locks them when she draws the curtains. The windows must have been locked . . .' An agonizing wave of doubt crossed her face. 'They couldn't have been open. There was a slight wind: I would have seen the curtains billow.'

The work roster would say who served Bisset tea. Ferret moved the nurse on from this new worry. She pointed to a duty post, a glass-fronted bay near Bisset's room. 'Could you miss a bleep from a call-button?'

'No chance. It's shrill. Anyway, it triggers the room number to flash on a monitor. They stay up until we cancel.'

Ferret nodded. 'So let's talk about visitors. Could anyone have reached Mr Bisset's room without you noticing?'

'Quite impossible. Anyone walking down the corridors after ten-thirty will trigger the in-house security lights. They're very bright.'

The nurse was drooping wretchedly from want of sleep. She looked more and more strained. 'I've nearly done,' Ferret said. 'Did you hear anything? A cry perhaps?'

'Nothing.' The tired nurse's voice cracked. Exhaustion and shock had a price. She teetered close to tears. 'It was a night like any other.'

Hallows was kept waiting by Liz Ireton. She had dashed from the nursing home to see Stan Parkin who had regained consciouness.

The big man rested his fingers on a high glazing bar of his window and looked down on to Peel Square. The people there were driven by purpose. They hurried in the early-morning: at duty or play, they were very much alive.

Killings were infrequent events in Helenborough and now, like spots, there were a cluster with Jacob Bisset as the latest.

He reviewed the mounting score and order of precedence. Discovering who had benefited from Huey Alcott's death looked impossible to solve. *Vicky*, poor mutilated *Vicky*, had been dead for such a length of time, there no longer existed an extreme urgency over solving the crime. Bisset, now, would take first call on their limited resources.

Yet, while this was decided, Hallows's mind was fixed on the past. *Vicky* . . . After ten years it could be argued that there was no likely risk of her killer striking again, but Hallows was not so sanguine. Her death had not been the result of sudden passion, an impetuous act. It had been planned, and if an individual had planned a death once, and with apparent success, there was always the possibility he would do so again. Premeditated murder: the ultimate solution to a problem.

His ears pricked. He heard the tap of Liz Ireton's quick feet echoing along the stark corridor. Pulling out his chair, he sat down heavily.

'Scott's attending the post-mortem on Bisset,' she said, bursting in. 'There were two people involved – don't think more. I don't believe murder was on the agenda. They wanted his album. That's the only item missing.'

She had to be tired but she made no move towards a chair. He asked: 'Do you see a link between this death and the fire at Slade's shop?'

She had started quartering his carpet with quick irregular steps. 'Too much of a coincidence to think otherwise. They'll be carrying scratches; Bisset drew blood. Useful for a DNA match when we find these guys.'

He watched so much unexpected restlessness uneasily. A surfeit of adrenalin, he thought, but what had set it rushing?

'There's some uncertainty-' she was saying -'about who drew Bisset's curtains at dusk yesterday afternoon. It's tough on the staff.' She sighed sympathy and slowed down briefly. 'Yesterday, Green Vale were riding high after a successful visit from local councillors. It'll be a different story today; many patients will want to transfer elsewhere.'

'DI Turley rang.' This news brought her to a halt. He was grateful. He felt he was conversing with a pendulum. 'He's cock-a-hoop. He has something and hopes to be with us this morning.'

'He didn't say what, exactly?' Her feet began to shift restlessly again.

It irritated him, no matter the reason. He was strongly tempted to bark at her to stand still, but instead he asked quietly: 'This album of Bisset's – I presume it's full of hard-porn material?'

'Has to be.' Suddenly she subsided on to the nearest chair. It was as if her own weight was too heavy to bear. She looked dreadful, pale as bleached almonds. Her fine grey eyes receded into dark hollows. 'I spoke with Stan Parkin . . .' The sentence hung.

Her closed face was reminiscent of a death mask, and Hallows realized she was angry, so angry every fibre roared with pain.

He left her, strode down the corridor, shot coins into a dispenser and took back a cup of hot, dark tea. He passed it to her, then closed his door. 'Drink!' he ordered, then perched on a free patch of desk.

She sipped.

He said nothing more until the tea was gone. 'So what's wound you up?'

'Finding what I had feared most: that two and two make four. Stan Parkin can't remember anything of being beaten, but the reason is down to Bisset's trunk which was locked when Stan took it from Bisset's house.'

'A Pandora's box.'

'Would be, to mistrusting minds like ours. More a Klondyke in Stan's view. He had it open in no time. It was full of sado-masochistic stuff: leather straps, masks, chains – all the bondage gear, and a goad, sharp as a cactus spine. Since money alone motivates Stan, he acted true to form and hid the gear while he wondered how he could use it to raise some readies. He described a recess behind panelling near the vestry. Ed Browne met me at the warehouse and we found it. The space is clean. I believe Stan was beaten into saying where the stuff was hidden.'

'Why such a beating? He's not the stiff-lipped heroic type.'

'No, but he's obstinate and calculating. Perhaps he hinted at blackmail and his visitors chose to frighten him off. I think the row Devin Slade had with Bisset is connected: something had not been done. I can't see Slade as directly involved but I do think he told someone else. It was that someone else who arranged for Stan Parkin to be attended to and the gear removed.'

'And arranged Slade's death as well? If Slade was a middleman you have an immediate motive for the fire at ViewPoint.'

'Slade loved Bisset and then, as a genius would, he loved his camera. That goad . . . I'm certain Slade wouldn't have touched a goad. Someone else took pleasure from using it. Someone else was in control of the whole set up. He arranged for juveniles to be coaxed into visiting Victoria Crescent – boys, guv, boys.' Abruptly she sprang from the chair.

At the window she glared down at milling pedestrians and seething traffic. 'Out there is a Mr Fix-it. Turley wants him, but-' Her fists clenched. The knuckles blanched. -'by God! I want him more. This creature must have been overjoyed when Bisset chose to join in, filming his nasties. What a profitable line,' she snarled and dashed spittle from a taut, bloodless mouth. There was a long pause and when she spoke again control was almost complete. 'I have to catch this man, guv. I have to find the mailing list he must be holding. The fruits of Bisset's and Slade's labours will be all over the country, with degenerates slobbering over what the post has brought them.'

She turned her back on the city. 'Youths. Homeless boys: all mouth and innocence. They were probably partially drugged. Bisset's radio was sometimes exceptionally loud. Did it drown shouts of protest or pain? We've had no complaints from these kids, have we? Why not? Because they were frightened witless!' She struck a solitary angry tear from her cheek. 'Helenborough is awash with penniless, vagabond young, ripe for taking and using.'

He had listened and watched. If he had needed any confirmation of her commitment he had received it. She was driven, yes, but fervour was tempered with compassion. He could also see her vulnerablity in this. Whatever the outcome of the case, it would leave her marked: empathy was both a strength and a weakness. All he said, however, was: 'With news now out that Bisset and Slade are dead, some of those teenagers might be prepared to talk. Time to get on to the streets.'

'That was my view, too.'

'And Liz-' she was already opening his door -'fright's not the only emotion to bind a person to silence.'

'I know, that's what chews me up most when I think of the bedroom at Victoria Crescent. All those guiltless young men, each nursing an overpowering shame.'

Extreme remorse was a new experience for Oliver Wyland.

Thankful to be undisturbed in his study at Helenhall, he yet again reflected on the sin he had committed. There could be very little worse to offend a woman and he was mortified to have caused distress. Was he really still so infatuated with Kate that he had no room for another woman in his life? No! He was very fond of her. He wanted her above all things to be happy with Josh. But he knew with certainty today, that he was no longer a moon to her earth, unlike Keith whose focus on Anne was absolute.

But how to make amends? Liz would slam down the receiver if he rang her. He could send flowers. She would probably stamp on them, but at least she'd know he was repentant.

He snatched up his coat. There was a florist's just off campus.

DI Turley arrived at Abbots Hill carrying a buff cardboard folder and a large and heavy, black plastic bag.

Ferret took him up to Hallows's floor in the small, complaining lift. 'I usually walk,' she said, eyeing the bag. 'It keeps the junk-food from settling on my hips.'

More stomach than hips himself, Turley chuckled.

In Hallows's room, Turley became the focus, circled by Ferret, the superintendent, Kennet, Curtis and Scott.

He began: 'SOCO are still on the premises sifting ash, but this is how it goes so far. Everything on the ground and first floor at ViewPoint was wiped out. The fire had penetrated into the second floor. Only a few solid pieces of furniture there were recognizable – a table, a sideboard. Smoke damage was intense. The third floor, from where Slade was rescued, was badly smoke damaged too, but the bedroom furniture, while scorched, was still whole. In a wardrobe we found this.' He plunged his hand into the plastic bag and tugged out an old, very worn, brown-leather briefcase. It was of a traditional style fastened with a central lock and two straps. It stank of smoke. 'The key was on Slade's person with those for the shop.' Taking a clear plastic envelope from his pocket, he tipped the tiny key into Hallows's hand.

Without speaking, Hallows unlocked the case and began to slide the contents on to his cleared desk. Two video cassettes emerged first, numbered 551 and 552. He caught Liz Ireton's eye. Were these originals, numbered before editing and copying? Were there over five hundred different tapes in circulation? She had lost some colour, obviously stunned by the same depressing thought. Following the videos was a deep A4 box. He hesitated and then eased off the lid.

Slade had spoken of art. Certainly the photography was superb but, in the minds of the officers facing four hundred or so black-and-white prints, they were looking at a gross betrayal of a remarkable skill. Fifteen, sixteen, seventeen year-old boys in poses that were extreme – far beyond the suggestive. The bondage gear Stan Parkin had described had been put to use. Some boys were manacled to the floor by wrists and ankles.

Like the others, Ferret had taken a handful of prints and was going through them with the rapidity of dealing cards. Suspicion and truth met. Half of those involved looked terrified. She halted, stared hard at one print, then passed it to Hallows. 'There's a glimpse of the goad.'

With a fierce, private resentment he looked from it to the alarmed, dilated eyes of the youth. He turned the photo over. There was a number, nothing more. 'Pity it's not dated.' He nodded for Curtis to return the prints to the box.

'Indirectly they are,' Turley said, pointing to a final item in the case.

It was exceptionally heavy for its size and required a tug from Hallows. He had in his hand a deep ring file that held partitioned, clear, plastic sleeves. It stored Slade's 35mm negatives: ten short strips to a page, each numbered and dated. If he wanted dates, providing the negative was here, he was home-and-dry. 'Have you counted these?' he asked Turley.

'Yes. Hold your breath, sir. You've got eight thousand individual negatives there.'

Kennet let out a long-low whistle. 'Slade was a methodical man.'

'A professional,' Hallows responded drily. 'Let's hope it now works to our advantage.' He looked to Liz, this was her case.

She said to Turley, 'Let's go back to the beginning. Any progress on who started the fire?'

'We've nothing solid. As you're aware, Hillington High Street empties between one and two. A blue van was seen parked a few doors up from the shop ten minutes before closing time. On the opposite side of the street some blokes were cleaning a butcher's window. While they were seen before one, no one noticed if they knocked off for lunch. We haven't tracked down the owner of the van, it might have been theirs. They weren't the butcher's regulars, but with the glass mucky, he was pleased to have them do it. He paid them before he closed. No window cleaners on my patch match their description: light build, thirties, mousy hair, likely to be brothers.'

There was an intruding cough.

Everyone turned to Scott. He was not noted for registering excitement, but he was shifting his weight like a nipper wanting to pee.

Ferret's sharp nod set him off.

'Two brothers are contracted to clean for Green Vale. I've been looking into them – they drive a blue van. As you'd expect, their footprints are all over the ground outside the nursing home's windows. They wouldn't need to worry about our finding matching mud on their shoes from outside Bisset's room. They could have left them off before sliding inside. They're smallish blokes and fit the Hillington descriptions.'

'And what names do these clever monkeys go by?' Hallows asked.

'Frank and William Lilly . . .'

'Oh!'

Everyone turned as Ferret punched angry fists together. 'Slade told me – well, he tried. I thought he was speaking of Libby Stratton.'

'So we build on what we've got,' Hallows said. 'How are you intending to play it?'

'Sprats to catch a mackerel. We'll watch them.'

The mirror told her she was perfectly groomed. While her confidence was high, Linda Thorne was pleased to have this extra reassurance. She left Earle's and drove to the Mill Restaurant. She had confirmed earlier that Keith Hawes was booked there for lunch.

She bought a spritzer and carried it to where she could watch the entrance without being immediately seen.

Games earnestly played brought the pulse racing: hers was no exception. She looked around. How many people here knew Keith by sight? She guesed it would be quite a few. Her eyes moved back to the entrance: Keith Hawes had a reputation for being punctual.

She glimpsed him through the glass before the doors began to revolve.

He was half-way to the dining room when she materialized in front of him.

'Keith!' Her voice sparkled and carried, as her hands went out to take his. Heads turned. 'I was beginning to worry, but I know you're so good about time.' And she kissed him full on the lips.

'What . . .!' he began, but got no further.

Linda laid a finger across his mouth, while laughing up at him as a lover might. 'Sssh,' she cooed. 'I just wanted to show you there are no hard feelings over the return of the tie.'

He stepped away from her but she linked her arm possessively through his.

He looked down at lively features and left her arm where it was for the moment. 'You do keep popping up, don't you?' he remarked with a quiet patience. 'So what do you want?'

'Perhaps I have a school-girl crush. You must have lunch with me today.'

'Definitely not.'

'Oooh!' She gave a pretty tinkling laugh and then pouted, and again eyes glanced in her direction. 'You don't expect me to eat alone?'

He considered her thoughtfully. 'No, I can see there's a risk if you're seated on the other side of the dining room since your behaviour is somewhat unpredictable. You can be my guest and at the same time consider the fact that I probably won't be eating here again.' He disentangled their arms and ushered her ahead of him through the glass doors.

As he signalled two, to the head waiter, she was teasing: 'What? Will you be pushing a trolley around Sainsbury's with Anne?'

Chairs were pulled out for them. 'I'm coming around to believing that might be quite attractive,' he replied with a small grin.

The waiter hovered and they ordered.

From the corner of her eye, Linda saw a woman at a far table changing chairs. They were now in her direct view. If Keith was conscious that they were being watched, he gave no indication. He appeared relaxed as she bubbled with a schemer's exhilaration.

As the waiter disappeared he said with wry humour: 'Not soup today, I think. Now . . . what shall we talk about?'

'I could tell you how I intend to furnish my new apartment at Shillington Court. And you could tell me about Patronus. Is it true you're doing another play?'

He smiled readily. 'We're well into rehearsal, yes: *The Importance of Being Earnest*. But, as with all these ventures, we've hit a bit of a snag. The guy playing Jack Worthing has injured his back.'

'I thought-' she giggled softly -'you were good at mending people.'

He was highly amused and laughed quietly. Eyes slid in their direction, engaged by their bonhomie. He replied: 'Impossibilities I can attend to – miracles take rather longer than we have time for. I intend to persuade Oliver Wyland to step into the breach.'

'He'll do well. I remember him in *Charley's Aunt*.' She added mischievously, 'I suppose all the women's parts have been taken.'

'I'm afraid you're out of luck there, Linda. Students from Helenhall like to be involved.'

'What a pity.' Her laughter glittered. 'Though I can't see a twenty-year-old doing justice to Lady Bracknell.'

'That was the director's opinion.'

'So do I know the person who's playing the formidable Bracknell?'

'Yes, you are acquainted. He's giving you lunch.'

As a trencherman, Turley appreciated the food Ferret bought them at the Dog and Duck. After seeing him leave for Hillington, she burnt off fish pie and three veg by walking rapidly to Earle's. As agent for the Grandfield Development Company, Josh Elwood had dealt with Victoria Crescent and called on Jacob Bisset. He might have met Slade, or noticed something.

She waved to Linda on her way to Elwood's office and wondered, with slight curiosity, why there was a tie pinned to her notice-board.

Concluding a phone call with Keith Hawes, Elwood beckoned her in.

Ferret closed the door. 'Business. My kind this time,' she said.

'Oh?' Realizing he was sounding preoccupied, he pulled himself up: 'Am I helping with inquiries?'

'Haven't you heard the news, seen today's mid-day papers?'

'No. I've had a rush job. Been shut in this office since eight this morning.'

'There was a murder last night at Green Vale: Jacob Bisset.'

'Good lord!'

'So you see why I'm here. Think back to Victoria Crescent, Josh. Did he ever have company when you called?'

Elwood pulled his hand back over his hair in an odd freeing gesture. 'Like who?' he said.

'You're supposed to be helping, not asking me questions.'

He shrugged amiability. 'I met no one. I used to knock and walk in: not a soul there. Not surprising, he only ever snarled.'

'Did you always knock?'

'I'm a polite chap, Liz,' he protested lightheartedly.

'So what was he doing? How did he fight boredom?'

'Sometimes the TV was on. More often the radio . . . a background purr as he read.'

'Read what?'

'In particular? I don't know-' he pulled an ear lobe thoughtfully - 'papers, magazines. Honestly, Liz, I really can't remember.'

'Did you ever find him looking at a photographic album, a thick book, leather bound.' Her hands shaped the size.

'No, I can't think I did.'

She watched his pale blue eyes with their beautiful lashes and wondered if there was a defensiveness there.

Linda had bought the noon issue of the Mercury on her return from lunch. Jacob Bisset's death did not disturb her. She knew Josh would soon realize it would make no difference to their arrangement over Shillington Court. In fact the threat had been bolstered. While she had suggested she could go to the police, now they were actively looking for information.

The intercom buzzed and she picked up documents she had been checking and took them to him. He looked tense, a fact she noted with a mixture of sorrow and satisfaction.

'I've made pencil notes in the margins where there are queries.' She passed the close-typed pages to him, then added: 'Nasty bruise DCI Ireton has on her face . . .'

His head lifted abruptly: 'You spoke to her?'

'Not today.' He visibly relaxed. 'I presume she's interested in Jacob Bisset. I've just read the paper.'

'Don't feel too secure, Linda,' he said with quiet emphasis.

'It's about time I did, Josh. I've turned thirty.'

'I hear you went to the Mill for lunch. I'm probably being obtuse, but what was the point of your one scene drama?'

'I'm surprised you don't see.' She went on with an elder's patience: 'What do you prefer, Josh, conflict or peace?'

'Peace, of course.'

'And you're not alone. It can be won, or it can be *bought*.'

Scott, with other officers, had already left to talk with Helenborough's homeless juveniles when Ferret returned to Abbots Hill. He had had faces enlarged from the most recent negatives taken by Slade. He hoped that lads confronting their own picture might be more prepared to talk, and particularly if there was an offer of a night in the warm with a free hot meal thrown in. Scott had organized things with Social.

Ferret ran up stairs, dragging off her gloves and rubbing the tip of her chilled nose. A dozen delicate-pink roses were waiting on her desk. Seeing them, she pulled up abruptly, then circled them like a wary cat. Opening the accompanying card, she read: *Contrite!*

She ripped it into shreds, then lifted the flowers and from a height, dropped them into the waste bin.

Curtis saw as he passed her doorway. 'You can't do that!' He was outraged. 'They must have cost an arm.'

'So give them to your latest.'

He wouldn't, of course. Second-hand flowers didn't conform to Curtis's principles. She turned away and stared out of the window at a darkness that never wholly took possession of the city.

Damn Oliver Wyland! Damn him. Flowers . . . Flowers . . . Oh, but why did he have to choose roses?

With a coffee forgotten and gone cold on her desk, Ferret worked on without regard for the time.

She had checked shots of the unique cornice mouldings at number 6 against Slade's photographs. Without doubt the principal bedroom had been used as a studio, and over an extensive period.

The goad appeared in very few shots but, from the turned gaze of numerous frightened eyes, it was obvious its spike was near, threatening delicate flesh.

Hallows had given her the chance to miss viewing the two videos. Unusually he had suggested the time she might like to visit Earle's and recognizing he was offering an escape route, she took it. He would pass on stills of evidence he thought important.

She was boxing up Slade's photographs when Hallows appeared. He sank on to a chair leadenly and stretched his legs.

'It's late, Liz. You should be at home.'

She was about to suggest the same advice could be applied to himself, when one photograph fluttered away towards Hallows's feet. He bent and picked it up, looked at it expressionlessly then handed it back. A youth was fixed in a contorted posture, a pose favoured by Slade. It gave the illusion the lad was padding up a vertical pane of glass. Hands, feet and genitals were closest to the lens.

She caught his eye and saw the reflection of her own disgust. That was why, she realized, he was still at Abbots Hill. He wanted to work out some of the taint here, not carry it home undiluted to Isla.

'The nurses at Green Vale-' her diversion was intentional -'I'm quite sure they're not covering up for one another over who failed to lock the window or who drew the curtains. Bisset had no visitors. The councillors making a tour were steered clear of him.'

'So could it have been Bisset who pulled the curtains?'

'No. The medical staff are confident he wouldn't have had the strength. They're long and very heavy. The fact of their being wet supports the time of death suggested by the pathologist. We know when it rained last night. It was heavy but didn't last for long. We know Bisset was alive at ten-thirty: the window had to have been closed then, there was no draught moving the curtains. And he died before it rained. The murderers left the window open allowing the downpour to soak the curtains and the carpet beneath the sill.' She paused, her mouth curling cynically. 'What's the odds the Lilly brothers have proof they were playing cards until after that time?'

'I don't bet on certainties. What have they been doing since you started surveillance?'

'Earning an honest penny, cleaning windows. Last report said: home, then to the Blue Cow, their regular pub.'

*

Oliver Wyland eased through a small crowd at the Mitre with the expectation of seeing Neville Howard at his usual place by the bar. Instead, with gut-jerking shock, he saw Linda Thorne in head-to-head conversation with gabby Duncan Milo.

What a devil's cocktail they made. The only way to shut Milo's mouth was to join them. He edged in: 'Am I intruding?'

Linda smiled. 'Not at all. Dr Milo says he can't stay and I do dislike drinking on my own.'

Wyland ordered his Ruff's. 'What's dragging you away, Duncan?' he asked with perverse pleasure. While so interested in other people's affairs, Milo was very private about his own. For all Wyland knew he might have a fancy for rent-boys or be a cross-dresser.

Wyland got satisfaction.

Milo's nostrils flared. 'Work,' he said and left them.

Linda laughed softly. 'Such obvious dislike between you two, Oliver. What fun.'

Contempt, of self, is a cold companion. He had been sharp all day. 'You have an odd sense of humour.'

'You're very grumpy. Did our little talk give you a sleepless night?'

He gave her the opportunity to stare at his back. He leant against the bar and tasted his beer. Strangely, his cataclysmic night with Liz had done some good. He had been able to make an objective decision about Linda. He took another deep, cool sip and turned back to her. 'Well? I can't think that this is a social meeting.'

'Quite right. You can buy us a bar snack. We'll order and then sit over there.' She pointed to a vacated corner table.

'Since you appear to have thought through the evening, I presume you've already decided what you want to eat.'

His tone amused her – so acid. 'True. I'll have a ham and cheese stuffed aubergine with a green salad.'

'You'll have to wait a while for that.'

'We're in no hurry.' She left him to make his own choice and carried her glass of red wine to the empty table.

He wanted nothing to eat, but he ordered an omlette; it would be something with which to toy.

'Would you like to know what Duncan Milo was confiding to me?' she asked when he joined her.

'Not especially.' A lie. He hoped his eyes did not betray him.

'As a physiologist, I think he flatters himself he has a professional curiosity concerning your libido.'

Wyland heard his own laughter. It had a very earthy, tension-free ring.

She continued blithely, 'He was chatting about ten years ago. The constant flow of women students to your lectures, and to your tutorials in Anselm House. Then he mentioned names. He said that while you were seen around with Anne Howard – Mrs Keith Hawes now – you were conducting an affair with Gina Hawes.'

'Does he?' He gave a quirky smile. 'Keith would think that very funny. He believes I have some integrity, you see. . . . not the way I would treat my best friend. But anyhow-' the smile was there again -'Gina was quite a prude, you know. Tin knickers. Sex was something you had with your husband on a Friday night. She would have considered a party kiss from me, or any other guy, very suspect.'

She eyed him thoughtfully across her glass. 'I don't think I believe you. Of course this thing with Gina would have been at the same time you were having a fling with Sally. What energy, Dr Wyland. You're reputed to have changed since you married. I suppose an interval of ten years will see a slow down in a man's vigour.' The goad invited a denial.

He kept his mouth firmly closed. She would drop that line of conversation if he was mute. Their food arrived. He reached for the remainder of his beer as she settled a napkin across her lap. Anytime the business of the evening would begin.

She confronted the matter of money as she made the first cut into her aubergine. 'In order to keep our arrangement uncomplicated, I'll expect payments to be made to coincide with the end of each academic term. I think a tenth of your annual salary is very reasonable. It shows a remarkable lack of avarice on my part.'

His expression was unrevealing.

'We could meet here on the Thursday before Christmas. My first payment will make a lovely seasonal treat.'

He put his knife and fork together and pushed his half eaten omelette away.

'Not hungry?' There was a triumphal glint in her eye.

'Not interested. I'll not be shackled, Linda. I'll agree to one payment, a round thousand, in exchange for the print and the certainty that you haven't had it copied, and that's all. Be convinced of that.' He eased his long legs from beneath the table. 'Be absolutely convinced.'

She watched him rise, unconcerned. 'Why should I be?'

'Out of caution's sake.' He bent close to her ear. 'Blackmail is a risky business.'

It was not only cold but a damp evening when Wyland left the Mitre. It had driven people indoors. He had the dark, lamp-lit streets virtually to himself which suited him. He wanted to stroll and think, and the fact that the moisture laden air could wet as thoroughly as a downpour was of no interest or consequence to him.

He crossed through the Lanes, the most ancient part of the city, downhill towards the river and, arriving at Canongate Bridge, leant over the stone parapet. The Nean, high with autumnal rain, was running fast between the arches. There was no sense of tranquillity below him, no sense of repose that he knew could accompany the sluggishness following a period of drought. Now, an orange glow reflected from a nearby street lamp was breaking into hostile shimmering shards.

The river kept secrets, not answers. He turned away, walking in the direction of Abbots Hill, that Odeonesque building which monopolised the major part of the upper side of Peel Square. Once the city's central police station had occupied just the corner site of the angular Art Deco block of offices, but time and need had moved on since the thirties. Now the entire building provided for the demands of Helenborough's Police HQ.

He stood on the empty pavement, looking up at the continuing bright, uncovered windows. Was she there or at home? She must have cooled off a little. An apology should be made in person, and if she would give him space to speak, he would attempt to do so.

He entered the front reception lobby.

'DCI Ireton?' The desk sergeant repeated. 'I'll try her number, Dr Wyland.' He disappeared and was back in seconds. 'Sorry, she's not available.'

Out on the street again Wyland turned towards Helenhall to collect his car. An impasse – well, for now, anyway.

Which of them would have the greatest stamina over this when, undoubtedly, attraction was mutual; which the greatest degree of obstinacy? He saw the truth clearly. They were equally matched. Well, she had better beware. He was about to mount a campaign of attrition.

Even with this resolve, he didn't walk faster. He remained entirely detached from the weather and the worsening effect it was having on him.

Wyland's saturated hair clung to his head as if tarred. Droplets of water trickled over his face and down his neck. Long before he reached his car, the fabric of his shirt and the lining of his coat were as wet as if he had been wearing no coat at all.

Where she could, Anne Hawes touched fifty as she raced through the narrow back roads of Helenborough. Her mind rushed ahead of her to the unpretentious house with its comfortable furnishings left as her mother had lovingly arranged them so many years ago. She knew there she would always find an inexpressible peace.

Two long rectangles of light from the downstairs sitting room window suddenly died as she swerved into the short drive. They had been a welcoming, desperately needed comfort. She sprang from the car and ran to the front door.

It opened before she reached it, with Neville Howard on the point of leaving for the Mitre.

He was startled to see her and in such an obvious fluster. 'My God, Anne! Whatever is the matter?'

She was trembling, too wound up to speak. She stumbled through her father's hall into the sitting room where a coal fire burned behind an old, tall nursery guard. As she pressed her back against it to absorb some heat, he turned on the light.

Tossing his topcoat aside, he looked at her critically. She had been crying: her mascara had smudged. The streaks reminded him, with a pang, of her attempts at drawing with charcoal as a child.

Howard poured them a nip of whisky each and, endeavouring to be patient, saw her carry the heavy glass to bloodless lips.

She sniffed, 'I expect I look a mess,' and turned towards the fire, willing its heat to drive out her shivers.

Conscious of the inquisitional effect of the overhead light, he turned on softer lamps instead. 'So what's this all about?' he asked unable to contain himself any longer.

'I didn't work this afternoon. I was at home baking – doing the usual things. The house was peaceful until around five, then the phone started ringing. Word upon word. Keith's seeing another woman.'

'Anne! That's rubbish! Even to the least sensitive of beings it's obvious he worships you.'

'Pa, they were at the Mill. They kissed and held arms. Had lunch together.'

'Sounds utter bunkum,' he snapped. 'Hardly has the ring of a clandestine affair. You spoke to Keith?'

'As soon as he stepped in the door.'

'And what did he say?'

'That she was simply striking a pose.'

'And knowing you, you'd worked yourself into a high state of agitation by then and wouldn't listen. Really! Why will you torture yourself?'

'Doubt's the very devil.'

'It is for you when you get too hot to apply reason. Keith's far too placid. He should storm once in a while to bring you down to earth.'

Her light-brown eyes, memorable, beautiful, filled with tears again.

Why was she so cursed? he thought, to be so damnably sensitive. 'So he did react.' Howard concluded and reached for her with an exasperated sigh: 'Oh, come here.'

She leant into him, snuffled, pulled a crisp handkerchief from the top pocket of his jacket and blew her nose.

She was saying from under his chin: 'I was going on and on and on and suddenly he went white and sort of stiffened. I thought for a moment he might slap me.'

Howard snorted disbelief. 'He wouldn't.

'I know.'

'But you took off anyway. He's probably worried to death, thinking of you driving in such a state. If you love him . . .'

'Of course I love him.'

'Then ring him. I'll make us a scratch meal while you tell him you're safe.'

'Oh-' he said, on his way to the kitchen -'who was the minx, playing to the crowd at the Mill?'

'Linda Thorne. She has the most incredible . . .'

'. . . red hair. Yes, I know. She's doing the rounds, my dear. She had dinner with me at the Mitre, yesterday.'

Ferret had been in her flat only a short while when the security buzzer sounded for the main outer door. She pulled back a curtain. Below, parked in a pool of lamp light was a familiar Citroën. Her heart lurched. She stood stock still. The buzzer sounded again – and again.

His finger might have been stuck to the wretched thing. She lifted the receiver and dictated icily: 'Go away, Oliver.' and hung up.

He was not to be put off. The buzzer vocalized tunelessly.

She snatched at the handset. 'Oliver! Stop that bloody noise!'

'No! Let me come up. I want to exchange at least a sentence at closer range.'

'You said too damned much last night.' She slammed down the handset. 'Duplicitous jerk, you've cracked my wretched heart!'

The buzzer squawked without pause.

Pulse roaring, she seized the handset. 'Grief, you're persistent!' Capitulating, she released the lock on the outer door, rocked nervously on her toes, then ran to the flat's front door and slid the chain across. She hesitated, opened it a span and heard his feet springing up the stairs to her landing.

He didn't jam his foot in the gap. Instead he pushed his right hand through. He was holding a letter.

She flattened herself far away against the hinge-side wall in the improbable event that those long thin fingers, ornamented by a small signet ring, could make a snatch for her. Thank God, it was impossible for him to see her . . . to see in her eyes exactly how it was.

She said dryly: 'You're taking a risk, Oliver. If I throw my weight at this door I could chop off your fornicating mitt!'

'Do it then. Then you can have hand and letter.' He flapped it.

She said nothing: did nothing.

'Liz?'

Those beautiful long fingers waved the letter again and she heard him sigh.

'Liz, I know I deserve what you're dishing out, but give me a small break, read it before you tear it up.' The letter fluttered to the floor. The hand was withdrawn, and she listened to him descend the stairs two at a time. The outer door opened, then clicked shut.

She slammed her front door, flicked off lights as she raced to the window. She watched him walk to his car, turn and look up. Confident she was unseen, she gazed at the indistinct details of his raised face. He folded himself into the car and drove off, swallowed up by the purring traffic-filled night. She moved back into the room feeling bitter and hideously lonely.

Ferret propped the letter against a jug on her kitchen table. It had been a particularly long and repugnant day. Now was not the best time to give Oliver fair consideration.

Sixteen-year-old Danny Hammond trudged beside Scott into Abbots Hill.

The sergeant glanced at the lad. In the station light, he looked wizened from the insinuating cold and lack of good food. 'Three teas,' he said to a constable, then nodded for Alan White, the waiting Social Services officer, to follow. He led the way to a sparsely furnished interview room.

'Is this where ye're going to interrogate me, then?' The scrawny lad acted bravado, but a different story quivered on his tongue.

Scott pulled chairs from a table and motioned Danny to sit. 'Young persons of fourteen, fifteen and sixteen are not interrogated,' he said solemnly 'Juveniles – which is what you are, unless you celebrate a seventeenth birthday during the course of the night, when we could have a bit of a party – are interviewed.' He indicated Alan White, a slender young man in his mid twenties, dressed casually in jeans, trainers and a roll-neck sweater. 'Mr White is here to see fair play. It's his job to look after you, your interests – not mine.'

White explained the method of recording the interview and that afterwards he would take him to comfortable accommodation for the night.

Danny heard him but he was more intent on watching the door. His eyes darted to the tray as the tea arrived.

'What, no biscuits? I only come for the biscuits.' He clamped his filthy hands around an offered cup. The heat of it, in sharp contrast to himself, brought out a violent shiver.

Scott leant across the table. 'When did you last eat?'

The lad looked at his tea, slurped some and thought about an answer. 'Yesterday morning,' he said.

Scott and White exchanged glances.

Scott rose. 'I'll organize some grub for you now and while it's coming we'll just do some light talking. I'll take a written statement in the morning after which you can have a slap-up breakfast. Do we have a deal?'

Since Danny's stomach griped painfully, swift agreement was reached.

With soup sent for and anything else not likely to upset a deprived stomach, Scott got under way. 'Now let's talk first about 6 Victoria Crescent. Slade, the man who took your photographs is dead, as I told you, and so is the man who lived downstairs . . .'

'The cripple?' The words shot out.

While Danny Hammond had seen it splashed across the *Mercury*, had heard it from this brawny copper when he had been found squatting in a doorway, and now again here from the same copper, having lived under a threat for over a year, he needed repeated confirmation.

Chapter 6

The youth looked considerably improved when the three met again, less pinched and very clean with the suggestion of a gentle male beauty that would have appealed to Devin Slade.

During the earlier interview he had told Scott and White that in October of the previous year, after yet another violent row with his dad, he took off, hitching a lift to Helenborough. He had been dropped at the bus station with little money in his pocket and unsure what to do next. He was mooching around when a small guy asked if he was looking for work. Danny, with barely enough money for a meal, was willing to listen. The small man bought them a burger and chips and while they ate, it was suggested that Danny might help out a photographer he knew. Danny's need for cash overruled caution. He went with him to 6 Victoria Crescent where he was left on the doorstep.

A white haired man showed him into a sitting room and introduced him to the cripple. He had been offered a Coke and shown a fashion magazine with guys wearing trendy gear which the white haired man said had been taken by him.

Scott had asked: 'Did you believe him?'

'Didn't see why not . . . though it was difficult to think, me head felt funny.'

'In what way, funny?'

'I don't know. A bit like when I was coming round from having me appendix out.'

'Did the cripple join in this conversation?'

'Nah. He sat looking at telly. The white haired guy said he'd show me the studio. I . . .' His brow furrowed in troubled recollection.

'Yes?'

'I think he had to help me upstairs.' There was a new note in the youth's voice. A resistance.

Scott's eyes had met White's. White signalled caution.

Scott approached the nub more slowly. 'Tell me about the studio.'

'Looked real pro. Plenty of lights, reflectors, cameras on tripods. Think the white haired bloke was worried about his stuff getting damaged as I felt wobbly – told me to sit down – said I might feel better if I took off my jacket. He helped me wiv it and . . .'

Abruptly Danny Hammond's mouth had closed. He wore the vulnerability and petulance of a small child.

'Dan, come on,' Scott coaxed. 'We've seen the photo's. You weren't the only . . .'

The youth turned pleadingly to White.

White nodded understanding: 'We've been at it a long time. I suggest we all get some sleep.'

And so the session had ended.

Now, after running over what had already been learned, Scott returned to the matter Danny had wanted to dodge.

'You felt groggy: light headed and hot perhaps, and it seemed reasonable to be helped off with your clothes. Am I right?'

'Yeh.' Danny looked at his sweating hands and rubbed them hard across his ragged denim knees. Details he had tried strenuously to forget began to gush up uncontrollably. Sensations, fears, burst forward in his mind. He shuddered so violently the table shook and water slopped from glasses.

White bent protectively towards him. 'It's all right, Dan. Take it easy. We can help, I promise we can help.'

It had been anticipated where the interview could lead. Rape counselling had been discussed.

Danny was persuaded to speak again. After a drip-drip of information, he plunged into gabbled details.

As suddenly he stopped, drew a mighty breath then toppled into wracking sobs.

Scott's voice soothed as he consoled, 'Dan, it was out of your control.' He pushed tissues in the lad's direction. 'This other man – you said he arrived after the photography session had begun. Can you describe him?'

' 'course not, I had a blindfold on.'

'Could it have been the man who brought you to the house?'

'Can't say.'

'Think. You felt his weight against you.'

The youth shuddered. 'He was – he was heavier.' With a leap that took both men by surprise, Dan sprang up, sending his chair crashing against the wall. 'I don't want to say no more!'

White too, jumped up warningly: 'That's enough, sergeant!'

'OK.' Scott's manner visibly eased. He pushed himself lazily back from the table: a very casual unintimidating action. 'You've done well, Dan. Let's go and find that breakfast. Sausage, bacon, the lot. You can eat while your statement's being typed.'

Dan looked at him from wild eyes.

'Breakfast . . .' Scott repeated quietly. 'Best meal of the day, lad.'

No one moved.

From some way off came the sound of a door banging.

Slowly the youth wound down. His mind turned to the promised meal. 'I like spaghetti wiv me bacon: the rings.'

'I'll check it out. Oh, Dan-' Scott had his hand on the door -'why didn't you tell someone?'

'The crippled bloke . . . He said if I did, I'd end up in the Nean. I believed him.'

Morning had advanced very little when Scott dropped four statements on Ferret's desk.

'We got lucky,' he said. 'All tell the same story. I didn't call you in. Thought they'd funk it with a woman present.'

It was a valid point, but he could still be clucking around her. She scowled into his amiable ugly face and then began reading.

'They're so young, too young,' she said, clawing hair back from a worried brow. 'If we ever get this to court, we need an older witness. Someone photographed some years ago who can view what happened with an adult eye.'

'Someone who's come to terms with what happened.'

She gave a disparaging snort. 'I can't imagine anyone becoming reconciled to that kind of experience. Bisset's enterprise was running for at least ten years. Ten years! Think how many mentally crippled young men there must be around, all trying to forget, all trying to live normal lives.'

After a gruelling night he wanted to be optimistic. 'Some guy might come forward.'

'Can you see any guy out there with that kind of courage? And where might he be now?' she snapped. 'After being violated he probably upped and ran. Living in Portree or John O' Groats, I wouldn't wonder.'

He rocked serenely on his feet and said nothing.

'Well? Got a bright suggestion? Do we advertize? "All men buggered in the last decade at 6 Victoria Crescent, please apply . . ." '

'I'll get us a coffee.'

'Hell keep the coffee.'

'See the bruise is improving,' he remarked casually. 'Pity about the mood.'

'Oh, shut-up, Scotty. I'm depressed. There's a man, living in or around Helenborough, a sodomite who's made big bucks peddling filth and I don't have any confidence we'll ever get him.'

'You're most likely right, but let's go for a long shot. I'll circulate a few faces from Slade's collection taken four, five, six years back. Doctors, Sally Army, UB offices: someone might come up with a name and address.'

She looked at him hard, shrewdly, before her mouth hinted peace. 'You'd better sit down, Scotty. Preserve some shoe leather. *I'll* get the coffees.'

On the floor above, Roy Kennet walked briskly into Hallows's room. There was something of the smug schoolboy about his expression: as if he had won the senior maths prize.

'Turning over all the gardens in Victoria Crescent has been justified, guv.' He watched Hallows counter-flex the reader's hump out of his back. 'The lab. results.' He produced three photographs from a folder and laid them side by side in front of the big man. 'Actual size . . .' he pointed at an image of a flat triangle of metal smaller than his smallest finger-nail. 'First enlargement . . .' A large stain became apparent. 'And second at greater magnification.'

Hallows compared them, shuffling the prints from one hand to the other. 'Is this a party game?' he said mildly. 'Am I allowed to guess what I'm looking at?'

Kennet nodded.

'What you have here is a broken piece of a scalpel blade.' Hallows had seen his brother-in-law using them often enough.

'Right. A metal detector turned it up in the greenhouse at number 4.'

Hallows scrutinized the first enlargement. 'Then is this rust staining or something more significant?'

'It's blood.'

'So I'll offer a damp squib. The blade broke and nicked a finger while being used to take cuttings?'

'That was my first thought except we know from the owners, going back fourteen years, that none of them went in for clever gardening. Mr Keech used the greenhouse to store his toddlers' tricycles. Mr Hawes's wife grew a few tomatoes, he said. And the Brands, the last family to move out, kept their sun-loungers in it for the winter.'

'Has the blood denatured from contact with the soil?'

'No, thanks to the dry conditions. It's group O Rh positive, the most common.'

'So we don't get too excited.'

'No, guv, except that I did some checking. The Keeches are As and ABs, Keith Hawes is A, and the Brands are A and O Rh negative. Sally Webber and Gina Hawes were both O Rh positive.'

'Which brings us back to Gina Hawes trimming her tomatoes – or whatever you do with them – and cutting herself.'

'Perhaps. I've ordered a DNA test on the sample. And while they're at it, I've asked for a match against *Vicky*.'

'From nothing, it's suddenly all happening.' A touch of excitement coloured Hallows's voice. 'Sally's brother's been found. When he arrives there'll be another DNA test for the lab.'

Lester Barraclough peered through his reflection in Earle's window, screwing up his eyes to see between columns of revolving photographs of properties for sale. He was looking for Linda Thorne.

He stepped inside: 'Is Miss Thorne about?' A sales woman went to find her.

'Lester?' Linda, smiling, dismissed his surname, presuming on their acquaintance so recently made. 'What can I do for you?'

'Any chance of a private word?' His small eyes flickered in the direction of her colleagues.

She nodded and he followed her to her office.

'I've come to ask a favour-' he pushed the door closed -'I'm hoping you'll be free between six-thirty and eight this evening. There's a council cocktail thing and I'd like a charming lady to accompany me. Not married, you see.'

'I remember.' She felt flattered. 'I'd be really delighted.'

'Ah, splendid.' His round cheeks dimpled. 'Where do you live? I'll pick you up?'

'Opposite the Leisure Centre. An apartment at The Laurels. A crumbling heap, but I'm moving out soon, thank heavens.'

'A horse-shoe drive. I know it. Six-ten be all right?'

'I'll be ready. What's the occasion?'

'A spot of palm-squeezing,' he said spiritedly. 'We want money – nothing new in that – this is for a hostel for the youngsters sleeping rough.' Suddenly he spotted the tie pinned to her notice board. The sight of it tickled him, he beamed. 'A past conquest?'

She chuckled: a pretty sound, he thought.

'Not a trophy,' she assured him. 'More a tease.'

Anne Hawes saw her patient to his car, then returned to run up the wide sweeping stairs of the Fitness Centre to their small private sitting room on the first floor. With its vases of flowers, its apricot-painted walls and complementary pastel furnishings, it gave the sense of a tranquil garden come in doors. With Keith not yet arrived for coffee, she walked to a pretty little Hepplewhite bow-fronted sideboard and reached for the phone.

'Pa?' Anne heard her father's yawn. 'You've been dozing over your morning paper!' she accused with a laugh, and then went on, 'After creating such a to-do yesterday, I think I should make amends. I'd like to meet you at the Mitre this evening-' she heard him begin to murmur delight -'providing dinner is my treat.'

He was old-school and began to protest.

'No, Pa! Unless you agree, I'll go with Keith to the Leisure Centre and watch him playing squash with Oliver.'

'Conditions? Oh. Well, yes then.'

'Good. Keith will drop me off about seven. He'll join us sometime after nine.'

'Will we wait dinner?'

'Heavens, no, Pa, I'll be far too hungry. When he, Oliver and Josh want something, they'll decide where to eat.'

Ferret had read Oliver Wyland's letter once, and put it in her handbag. Now, in a lull near to lunch she read it again.

Liz, however it sounded, I do care for you. I slept around before my marriage to Kate, but not since its break-up. We can't control what we dream. You were wonderful . . . perhaps that's why I dreamt of Kate . . . you conjured up a past happiness . . .

'So I'm getting the blame,' she muttered.

I can't be more abject, more sincere in my apology. You're a great person to be with. Witty, droll, considerate, an enthusiastic liver of life . . .

'Sounds like a reference for a house-mother,' she growled.

And you're fair...

Rat!

So, give us another chance. From scratch, nothing rushed: a drink, a meal, a doorstep farewell. What do you say, Liz? Oliver.

She sighed. Did she really want to step on the emotional switchback again?

The appearance of Curtis forestalled an answer.

'Ferret. Reg Falder's in reception. Can you give him five minutes?'

'Sure.' But her heart sank. She could offer little hope of news of his son.

He was standing in a corner, looking embarrassed, dressed in his working clothes. 'I'm not expecting anything,' he said quickly. 'You made it clear how difficult tracing Martin would be. Only something occurred to me. Something I hadn't thought important, but if he's been ill or in hospital . . .' The image distressed and he rushed on, 'Well, someone might have noticed. When he was three, he cut his left foot on a piece of glass. He has a scar. It goes from his big toe to his heel. A thick white thing.'

She raised her right hand, back uppermost: 'Like this?'

'Yes, just like that. It was thinking about my Rosie and you made me remember. Will it do any good?'

'It might Reg. It just might.'

*

Ferret tore up stairs, an idea exploding in her mind. From the landing she saw Curtis at a distance.

'Rob!' Her voice ricocheted along the bare, fluorescent lit corridor.

He walked back to meet her.

'Can you spare half an hour? I want help going through those sod-awful photographs of Slade's.'

'Got a lead?'

'Could be. Five years ago, Reg Falder's sixteen-year-old son went into Helenborough to meet friends and never returned. We asked questions but got nowhere. The lad was happy. No rows at home. There's no question of him being dead. He's sent Christmas cards for the last four years.'

'So you think he was talked into visiting Victoria Crescent, couldn't handle what happened and did a runner.'

'It's a possibility, isn't it?' She unlocked the cupboard where the prints had been placed. 'Reg says Martin has a heavy scar down the sole of his left foot.'

They hunted in silence, the photographs making a soft flick as each passed from hand to growing stacks that were beginning to smother the desk.

'Got him!' Curtis yelled.

'Let me see!' Hands and feet padding up imaginary glass. She slapped a sheet of paper across the image of the naked figure except for the foot. The scar, snaking from toe to heel, was so clearly lit the print might have been used for a medical journal. 'That has got to be unique,' she said quietly, daunted suddenly by good fortune. 'This must be Martin.'

She slid the paper away to show the less sharply focused teenager's face and shoulders. His eyes, tense, fearful, were staring to his left. Like some of the other boys photographed, he was wearing an item of jewellery. 'Rob . . . there's something odd about the gold chain around his neck?'

He took the print, turned on her desk lamp and looked at it under the sharp light. 'Bloody hell . . .' he breathed disgust. 'It's covering a thin wire. How many volts does it take to make you toe the line?'

She moved to the window, pressed her forehead against the cold glass and closed her eyes. Slowly, very slowly, the nausea receded.

'There's no way I can show that photograph to Reg Falder.' She turned around. 'He'll go absolutely spare. Not only is it an obscene pose but the boy's petrified.'

'But the lad's not been blindfolded, Ferret. If somebody else is in the room besides Slade, we've got him. Our lad's twenty-one now. An adult. He must be responsible: he must talk. Get confirmation that this is Martin Falder, then we can find him.'

'But *not* with that print.' She silenced him: 'No! I'll get confirmation, but not that way.'

'Josh?' Linda passed Elwood his letters for signing. 'I'd like to leave a little earlier this evening. Is there anything urgent before I go?'

'No.' He rested his chin on interlocked fingers and regarded her pensively. 'Not contemplating being an irritant to my friends this evening? If so you'll be out of luck. We're all out together.'

'They can feel safe, I've been invited to a council drinks party.' Her green eyes teased: 'Stop carrying your friend's problems. Oliver and Keith are perfectly capable of looking after themselves. While I raided your cupboard, their anxiety is all of their own making.'

'*My* cupboard, yes.' He stamped to his feet only to gasp as an excruciating pain shot through his leg. 'Ye gods!' He snatched for support, his fingers blanching as he gripped his chair. Collecting his breath, he bent to rub the muscle.

'I could do that,' she said quietly.

Seething, he looked up, searching for mockery, but found none. Instead he met the unexpected: compassion.

'You've been awfully blind, Josh, I've loved you for years. But I've accepted you're never going to be available. My treatment for a broken heart is Shillington Court with no financial anxiety.'

Elwood straightened up, his mouth slack with surprise.

'Linda-' in kindness his hand reached for hers -'not blackmail,' he urged gently. 'There has to be another way.'

'Too late, Josh.' And she moved from him and closed his door.

It was his anxious and profoundly tired blue eyes that Hallows first noted. He welcomed Richard Webber with a swift open hand and offered him a chair. 'This has to be upsetting.'

'It's not knowing; never having answers. That's the worst of it.' Webber's unsteady fingers pressed back thick greying hair. 'How certain can you be that the body you've found is my sister's?'

'Height, age, colour, blood group, all match Sally. But I can't be certain, not until we've run a digital DNA profile.'

'And how long will we have to wait for the result?'

'With the digital system, only a few days.'

'I see.' Webber exhaled tension through pursed lips. 'Now I'm not sure whether I want it to be Sally or not? Thinking of her as a murder victim is a dreadful thing to bear. You'll have some questions . . .'

'Just one or two, before you part with a drop of blood. Did Sally ever speak of her men friends?'

'No. She was very private over her guys.'

'Do you know why she chose to move off campus and into Briers Way?'

'She said she felt stifled there. No other reason.' He looked at Hallows and anticipated his next question. 'The rumour . . . Obviously accidents do happen, but I find it hard to believe Sally was expecting a baby.' He studied Hallows with a new awareness. 'Was the body . . . was she pregnant?'

'Yes. Ten weeks.'

'Oh, lord.' Deeply upset, he clamped his hands together. 'Two deaths at a single stroke.'

Ferret had learned that Reg Falder was working at Brooke House on the Roxleigh road.

The isolated three-story brick mansion rose squarely amid neglected lawns from a strong moulded stone base. Except for fluted stone surrounds to elegantly glazed windows, the walls were unadorned, terminating in modillioned eaves that were constructed in the local style, very wide. Its low pitched roof was dressed with Westmorland slate pierced by five dormer windows which offered magnificent views over a rural landscape.

From an inescapable air of neglect, it was clear the property had been empty for a long time.

With daylight slipping away, Ferret walked cautiously between stacked building materials, skips heaped with scrap, and under scaffolding that boxed in the portico with its two Corinthian columns. In the wide hall, flaking plaster and accumulated filth softened her tread.

'Reg,' she yelled above the din of hammering. 'Reg Falder.'

'Up here.' His voice echoed down the wide stairwell.

She found him on the uppermost floor before the roof space. He was replastering a wall where a fireplace had been removed. 'You're a man of all trades,' she said.

He grinned but kept working. 'Need to be when you have a small business. I've teamed up with Joe Grant's firm for this job. We're converting the house into flats.'

'Not filling in all the fireplaces, are you?'

'No, only those in the bedrooms – cuts down on draughts. He darted a questioning glance over his shoulder. 'But this can't be a social call.'

'I've been thinking about Martin.'

He continued to skim the plaster. 'Yes?'

'He'll have changed – matured. Did he take after any relatives of yours?'

'My brother, Tom. Martin was very like him.'

'Good. I want to borrow photographs of your brother in his twenties, and of Martin at sixteen. Our photographic department can create a picture that could be Martin now.'

He paused. 'Will it really help?'

She shrugged noncommittally: 'It's worth a shot.'

Close to mid evening the flow of traffic passing the Leisure Centre had become sporadic. The dark monolith of the Centre behind its wide front of ornamental trees and neat lawn loomed up on Lester Barraclough's near-side. He slowed in preparation to turning right into the left arm of The Laurel's drive. He glanced at Linda, her face illuminated by the glare of an oncoming car.

'I'd say it was quite a successful evening. I think we may have got the hostel project out of stall.'

'Everybody did part sounding genuinely keen,' she said. 'And after all, we all want somewhere comfortable to lay our heads.'

There was a gap in the advancing traffic and he swung right, turning into the poorly lit drive.

'And with comfort in mind,' she continued, 'I'm not going to invite you in for coffee, not to this flat. Wait until I've moved into Shillington Court; you'll be one of the first to be invited.'

He dimpled with pleasure. 'I shall look forward to it.' The approach to the front door was riddled with pot-holes as prolific as daisies in grass. He advanced at a trickle: 'Good choice – Shillington Court. It's a fine house.' He cut the engine, stopping close to the open, jutting porch. 'If I wasn't happy at Roxleigh, I'd consider moving there myself.'

'You're a neighbour of Keith Hawes?'

'I own the only other property in the lane. Mine's much smaller, and older. Sweetie-box stuff.' He chuckled like a boy. 'Thatch and lots of timber. Fortunately, with a front hedge of evergreen trees, the summer tourists miss me.' His hand moved to his door.

'No, Lester, stay put.' She smiled. 'And thanks for an interesting evening.'

'My pleasure entirely. You have your key?'

'Yes, but I can always buzz my neighbour, David Foss, to release the lock.'

He watched until she had closed the front door behind her, then moved off along the second rutted arm of the drive to the road. A spattering of cars were coming from his right and he waited for a reasonable space.

There was a gap. Preparing to accelerate, he glimpsed a woman making a dash from the Leisure Centre side of the road. She had reached the pavement by the other entrance to The Laurels as he pulled away.

In the Leisure Centre, the glass dome above the two pools reflected loud happy sounds from a vast number of voices.

Like a dolphin surfacing from fathoms deep, Hawes burst up in a sheet of spray in front of the other two, bringing Wyland and Elwood to a halt and treading water.

'Well-' he was exuberant -'how many lengths have you managed?'

'Lost count.' Elwood grimaced at so much enduring energy.

'Me too. Spent all my time avoiding collisions. I forgot it was the cheap night for the under twenties. All of Helenborough must be here.'

'Bet they've cleaned out the snack bars.' Wyland had eaten nothing since one and was ravenous. 'I suggest we go straight down to the Mitre. I could murder a steak.'

PART THREE

Chapter 1

David Foss opened his front door onto the communal hall expecting to see his morning paper lying close by. Linda usually dropped it there when she collected hers from the outside letter boxes. Disappointed, he showered and dressed.

With his paper still missing, he stepped outside and pulled both jutting papers from their boxes. He shied his into his flat before knocking at Linda's door.

'You're going to be late. I'm making coffee, do you want a cup?' He fidgetted, tapping her paper against his thigh. 'Linda! Wakey-wakey!'

Nothing.

'Linda!'

Upstairs a door opened and then closed again, leaving a heavier quiet settling around him.

He was a little worried, and angry at being worried. 'God, woman, I haven't got time to mess about.'

Nothing. Silence, like a malevolent fog, seemed to creep from behind the door.

She could be ill, he thought suddenly. Darting through his own sitting room, he yanked up the sash window, sprang through and ran over gravel and rotting leaves to hers. The curtains were closed. He hurried to her kitchen window, flattened his nose against it and peered through. No sign of breakfast in the making. No sign of Linda.

Foss rapped the glass with a hard knuckle. *'Linda!'* His voice, raw now with anxiety, carried upward and a man's head emerged from the kitchen above.

'What's up?'

'Can't rouse Linda.'

'Perhaps she's already left.'

'No. Her paper was still in the box.' Foss had decided. 'Throw me down something heavy.'

'What?'

'Oh, for Christ's sake, Hal, come on.'

Seconds later a rolling pin thudded at his feet. His heart thumping against his ribs, Foss hoisted himself on to the sloping sill and hit the glass once near the catch. The end of the pin went through, scattering jagged fragments across the polished tiled floor. Reaching in cautiously, he released the lock and heaved the window upward. Yelling her name, he stepped inside.

The sitting room was not totally dark. Soft daylight passed through the curtains. He could see her well enough as he came to a halt in the doorway.

She was tied hand and foot to a dining chair. Over her head was a clear plastic bag, secured at her neck by a circle of twine.

Kennet had received the shout.

When Hallows and Curtis entered the shared hallway, SOCO were well forward in checking Linda Thorne's flat. They had gridded the room with ribbon and were mapping the location of every item.

Hallows heard a broken murmur of voices through her open front door, muted and indistinct as a deaf man would hear. Dispirited, saddened, he would like to have turned on his heel. Too many deaths – every one too many – and each corpse owed justice. What a responsibility the dead heaped on them.

'We had to move her. Photographs will show you the position we found her in,' Kennet said, coming out to meet them. 'From the degree of rigor mortis, rectal temperature and hypostasis, the doc estimates death to have occurred between seven-thirty and nine-thirty yesterday evening. He's organizing an eye potassium test to try to be more precise. The place isn't topsy-turvy – doesn't appear to be the work of a thief. The grate's interesting. There's a mound of paper ash, but not totally combusted. SOCO are ready to remove it, layer by layer, when you've had a look.'

Hallows walked through to Linda's sitting room. It was large and high-ceilinged, its walls papered in a delicate olive-green stripe. The curtains of a darker hue, had been drawn back, revealing a long sash window through which could be seen a gnarled apple tree and a tangle of dead grass and weed. Bright throws and cushions made comfortable three sagging armchairs and a life-weary sofa. Pots of assorted flowers and a vase of freesias proclaimed a female owner, but now their perfume seemed overbearing in the presence of death.

Despite warmth issuing from a storage heater, there was a pervading sense of damp. He realized she had been generous with the polish in her attempts to overcome it. The furniture gleamed.

The chair, to which she had been tied, remained, as discovered, at the centre of the room. It faced the deep iron basket of a Victorian fire grate.

They had lifted her free for the doctor to complete his checks. Now the stylishly dressed, dainty woman, was lying on her side, but in the posture she had assumed when seated. The ropes had been cut once to release her, but otherwise remained intact around her wrists and ankles. Both upper and lower limbs were enclosed in polythene bags to protect against contamination. The sight of Linda's head and her mass of red hair forced into a clear airtight bag which trickled with water like dew, a relic of exhaled air, seemed a profanity to Hallows. The hair was flattened against her scalp, wet in places, without beauty, without vitality. It made him angry, more than the death itself. It was as if the treatment was a deliberate insult to what had been outwardly best.

He bent nearer. Her eyes were half closed as if she were overcome by a pleasant sleep. They lied, he thought. She must have sucked her guts out, trying to drag in fresh air. Her lips had been prevented from opening in a scream. A thin butterfly of elastoplast bound them together.

There was nothing unusual about the twine or the knot that had been used to fasten it. Nor had it been secured any more tightly than was necessary to hold the bag in place.

He straightened up. 'Relatives?' he asked.

'No one as far as I've been able to discover.' Kennet's sigh spoke reams. Who would mourn, who would weep? It made him acutely aware of his own position. He had a father, however, but Time was a reaper.

Hallows gave his attention to the fireplace. An electric fire had been moved to one side of the attractive Delft-tiled hearth. The fire hood was a pretty thing, so suited to a woman's room. Raised blooms, stems and leaves of honeysuckle twirled and twined over its surface, an exuberant display which umbrellaed a mound of suspect burnt paper.

The electric fire: had Linda or her killer moved it? Was she responsible for burning paper or was this the murderer's inefficient conflagration? Presumably the chimney had produced insufficient draught.

'Well?' He turned to let his sergeant loose. Curtis was never short of an opinion.

'Our killer lit it.' Curtis was adamant. 'Burnt paper and blackmail – situation close as Siamese twins. He, or she, put a match to it, but had to leave before making sure it had burnt right through.'

Ghosts of pages, ash shapes with shadow words, lay in random layers. The colourless form of Earle, Elwood and Davis, written as a business heading, was quite distinct on the top sheet.

'Earle's?' Hallows glanced back at Kennet.

'She worked for Elwood.'

The big man peered deeper. There was something he could see which remained partly undamaged. A thicker paper. Watched by a photographer and forensic conservation officer, Hallows held his breath and bent much closer. It was a portion of a photograph. He moved away again unhurriedly to avoid all chance of the insubstantial evidence being sent on a flutter of total destruction.

'I want an enlargement of that-' he pointed towards the photograph -'and as soon as possible.'

As Hallows went over the contents of her bag, Curtis picked his way towards the kitchen. The window had been closed but shards of glass remained where they had fallen on the shining floor.

He soon decided Linda had not cared for cooking. There was a gleaming, stain-free double ring and grill, no oven but a microwave. Pots and pans were at a minimum. There were a few tins stacked in military rows: soup, meat, fish, fruit and two ready-chill meals in the fridge together with fruit juice, eggs and milk.

One cupboard under the sink held potatoes, another cleaning gear. Soap powder, liquid detergent, conditioner, half a bottle of disinfectant, precisely folded dusters, an almost empty tin of furniture wax, a full aerosol of oven cleaner, shoe polishes, dustpan and brush. Curtis retreated. Her place was spotless – and he thought he was tidy.

'Not much fresh food around,' he told Hallows. 'She must have eaten out quite a bit. Where now?'

A short discussion with Kennet had decided it: 'Earle's.'

At eight o'clock at Roxleigh, Harry Lipton dismounted from his bicycle, pulled his trouser bottoms free from the elasticated tops of his socks and wheeled it in the direction of Keith Hawes's two-doored double garage. At the same time, Hawes emerged from the house, unlocked both doors and let Lipton prop his bike against one wall and collect his chain saw and other tools left there in safety over night. There was space since Anne's car had been parked on the drive. Lipton had begun work on the copse the day before.

Barraclough had made no objection. His only request was that a narrow strip of hazel be left growing at the boundary of the two properties.

Lipton had started by clearing the ground around the small derelict stables. The sad, ivy-clad building was denuded in places of tiles. Those that remained, shielding the clutter inside from the worst of the weather, were dressed in silver-grey lichen. Its brickwork, where visible between so much abundant leaf, cried out to be repointed. And the heavy divided door, secured by an iron bar, had lost all signs of paint.

A stack of good felled timber was already growing, and the useless thinnings and bramble were being burnt on a bonfire as he worked.

Hawes left him to it, disappearing indoors to finish his breakfast.

Half an hour later, husband and wife came out of the house together. Anne took her own car, intending to shop before going to the Fitness Centre. Hawes reversed his car from the garage, relocked his door and left the keys by the bike. Lipton would lock the other at the end of the day and drop them through the letter box. This done, he looked to where Lipton was busy with his saw. He was some distance from the bonfire which was leaping quite high with flame.

Hawes walked to it, gave it a prod or two, made sure everything was safe and then left for work.

At Abbots Hill, Scott and Ferret studied a timetable showing the activities of the Lilly brothers.

On the previous morning they had cleaned windows in an older residential quarter of Helenborough. Midday they had visited Kempe's, a betting shop on the Roxleigh side of the city. In the afternoon they had driven to Roxleigh, concentrated on properties near the church, including Oliver Wyland's cottage and then moved on to Witley Lane, working on Keith Hawes's property and then on Lester Barraclough's. The evening had been divided between home and the pub.

'What do you reckon?' Scott's freshly shaven chin itched and received a scratch. 'Window cleaning's not a bad cover for delivering videos, so are they shifting stuff under our noses or has the business ground to a halt?'

'If they hire, not sell, it'll keep rolling. They could be trading while we watch. Videos aren't big. They could be carried in a bucket, hidden beneath a chamois leather.'

'What about the cash? They have to off-load it. No stack of notes were slipped at the pub last night.'

'What about here?' Her neat oval fingernail drew a line under Kempe's.

'Made for it.'

'Let's put a DC in there.'

'Got just the man-' Scott's mean features crumpled in a laugh -'Frank Steed fancies he knows a good runner!'

'Spare me the jokes.' She grinned.

Her internal phone rang and he passed the receiver.

'Reg Falder has the photos. Brief Steed,' she said and headed for the stairs.

Hurrying forward as she pushed through the security door, Falder pressed a lightly filled, brown paper bag into her hands.

'Don't get high on hope, Reg,' she warned.

'I'll handle it.'

She watched him shift uneasily, shuffling his paint-stained booted feet. 'Are you off to Brooke House now?'

'No, later. Going to Roxleigh first. Councillor Barraclough has damp coming in. I said I'd have a look – give him a quote.' He backed towards the entrance, a shy smile enlivening melancholy features: 'Ta, Miss Ireton.'

Kennet had had a constable posted outside Earle's to prevent admittance to the staff.

The journey there had allowed Hallows time to ruminate over blackmail in general and Linda Thorne in particular. If she was guilty, who and how many would be glad that she was dead? Someone in a photograph? Someone connected with the estate agent's? Who else?

Elwood was waiting, looking thunderous at being kept out of his own premises unexplained. While Curtis had all the clerical and sales staff gather in the front office, Hallows walked with Elwood to his room. He waited until Elwood was seated before enlightening him of Linda's death.

'What . . .?' Josh Elwood's mouth gaped. 'I can't believe this.' Horrified, he sagged back in his chair. '. . . I just can't.'

Hallows listened to himself saying what was always said. The words sounded so thin, so ineffectual, but what else could one say to console?

He paused, letting Elwood find second wind. 'I have to go through Miss Thorne's desk, then we'll talk. I must ask you to stay here and not to use the phone until I give you the all clear.'

'Why ever not?'

'It's normal procedure,' Hallows parried. 'I presume you have a kitchen on the premises. I'll suggest one of your staff makes you all tea.'

'Very curious.' Curtis walked directly to the tie hanging like an abandoned pennant in Linda's office and peered at it closely. 'Cost a bob or two. Doesn't appear to have been worn, so she didn't snitch it as a reminder of a bedroom tryst.'

Hallows, bracing himself for the necessary and distasteful act of prying, pulled Linda's chair out and sat down. 'Tryst or not, why would a woman pin up a man's tie in full view of everyone passing by?'

'Take your pick, guv: she's got him, she's dumped him or she's nettling him.' Curtis oozed disapproval. 'I'll bag it.' And he enclosed it in a plastic evidence envelope.

The furnishings of the small room were entirely functional: desk, stationary cupboard, filing cabinet, computer terminal, keyboard, waste paper bin, adjustable swivel chair. It could have been any office anywhere except for Linda Thorne's hallmark: order and neatness.

She had unwittingly insured that Hallows's search through her desk would be entirely straightforward. He found nothing thought provoking until he arrived at the last and lowest drawer. It was one she had clearly designated for her personal use. It contained a silk scarf, two packs of tights – one pair black, one taupe – perfume, make-up, pearl drop earrings: items a woman might need if asked out unexpectedly.

Beneath these lay an orange folder. It felt heavy.

Curtis, who had made an unrewarding journey through her store of files wandered across to stand beside Hallows. He watched expectantly, as the contents were pulled out. On top was a brochure. 'Shillington Court,' he read aloud. 'They've aerial shots displayed in the front office.'

'I noticed.' Lifting the cover, Hallows found a formal agreement to the sale of apartment 3 to a Miss L. Thorne. Occupation to be in four weeks time.

'Tell me another!' Muttering disbelief, Curtis was gone, returning in seconds with a price list. 'They cost a bundle, and her choice was not the cheapest. It's an option: she could have been sleeping with money.'

Hallows, turning papers, said nothing. She had been shopping, ordering carpets, curtains, furniture. Insurance had been arranged. There was a letter, ready for posting, giving notice that she would be quitting The Laurels.

Given this much, Hallows was looking for more. Not finding it induced a grunt. There was no communication with a building society, no mortgage mentioned, no figure named as an advance, nothing that revealed her financial arrangements. He leant back in the chair and plucked at his lower lip thoughtfully. 'Since she was so precise, I'd have expected everything relating to the purchase to be here. Financial details could have been removed from the folder already, of course.' He awaited the foreseen reply.

'Why take only those? Simpler to shred the lot.'

'Quite. Which leaves us with the thought that someone was prevailed upon to take charge of the purse.'

Leaning across Hallows, Curtis tapped a signature confirming the sale. 'Him, most likely: Josh Elwood.'

Linda's phone rang.

The call was for Hallows from Kennet: 'David Foss saw Linda leaving The Laurels around ten past six yesterday evening with Councillor Barraclough. Foss didn't hear her return, but her TV was irritatingly high for a short while. Went off at eight-forty.'

Hanging up, Hallows passed on the news.

'Barraclough?' Curtis sniffed disgust: 'He's all piss and wind.'

'May I . . .?' Hallows seated himself so close to Elwood that Elwood must have had to resist an immediate urge to move back from the dividing desk.

Elwood assigned a curious glance to Curtis. He was closing the office door and taking out his notebook.

'Do you know what Miss Thorne's plans were for yesterday evening?' Hallows began.

'Only that she had been invited to some sort of council junketing.'

'She was accompanying Councillor Lester Barraclough, I believe.'

'Was she?' Elwood's face furrowed surprise.

'Did she often accompany him?'

'Don't think so. I thought they met only recently at a party given by his neighbours, Anne and Keith Hawes.'

'Who else was she seeing? Was there a lover?'

Elwood shrugged: 'No idea. The sales staff might know.'

Watching Elwood keenly without appearing to do so, Hallows changed topic: 'We found a folder relating to the purchase of an apartment at Shillington Court together with your signature. How could Miss Thorne afford to buy there?'

Elwood made a show of frankness: 'At Grandfield's asking price, she couldn't, of course. But you must understand that Linda was a much valued member of staff and when she expressed a wish to move to Shillington Court I offered to negotiate a special price with Charles Saville, the chief executive for the development. This firm has served his company well and I thought a favour was due. Saville showed his appreciation by agreeing.'

As if pre-arranged, though it was born out of long familiarity, Hallows prepared for Curtis to pop into the conversation. Sure enough, Curtis said: 'So how much, exactly, was Miss Thorne going to have to find?'

Elwood hesitated only slightly. 'Three fifths of the asking price.'

'Very generous,' Hallows said smoothly, 'and how was the mortgage to be arranged?' With interest, he saw a slight colour tracking up Elwood's neck and jaw. Fair skinned people operated at a disadvantage.

Whether from unease or guilt, a blush was a useful indicator to the watchful.

'There was no mortgage.' Elwood was forthright. To the less attentive it would have masked that signal of disquiet. 'Linda was to have a direct, interest-free loan from this firm. I was standing as guarantor. She was arranging a direct debit mandate with her bank for the monthly repayments.'

Hallows paused, thought, pouted: 'Weren't you taking a risk? She might have left the firm. While you had the task of training someone new, she would be sitting pretty elsewhere.'

'I didn't think it likely.'

Hallows was silent: thoughtful again.

Few sounds from the street disturbed Elwood's office.

The interval provided space where a worried mind could amplify every possible error of judgement.

Hallows resumed: 'I've not encountered such an unusual level of benefaction before. You can appreciate how I must look at this in view of her sudden death.'

Elwood shifted in his chair. 'No?'

Hallows adopted a confidential tone. 'Well, with so much money involved, Miss Thorne's dying could be seen as an advantage to you and Mr Saville, should you have wanted to be free of the arrangement. With the status quo restored, Mr Saville could anticipate the full asking price for his apartment, while your capital would be left in place to earn interest, presuming you have it wisely invested.'

Elwood's back stiffened with protest. 'I find that viewpoint totally offensive. I deplore Linda's death.'

Deplore: Hallows wondered what Curtis would make of the word. Pretentious, perhaps . . . in fact a pretence? Was Elwood's sorrow a fiction?

With that blush in mind, Hallows continued down the same road. He asked placidly: 'So was her worth reflected in her pay?'

Again he saw the traitorous rise of colour along Elwood's jaw, but Elwood's speech betrayed no discomfort.

'Of course,' Elwood said. 'Miss Rowe can give you salary details.'

Hallows changed course: 'Mr Elwood . . . the tie that was hanging up in Miss Thorne's room. What can you tell me about it?'

Elwood's tone suggested tolerant amusement: 'Nothing at all.'

'So you don't know who owned it, or who it was intended for?'

'I have absolutely no idea.'

Appearing satisfied, Hallows left the routine questions to Curtis.

'Just to keep things tidy, sir, where were you between seven and ten last night?'

Almost imperceptably, Elwood's back softened against his chair. 'At seven I drove from home to the Leisure Centre.'

'Opposite The Laurels.'

'Some little distance away but, yes. I met friends, Keith Hawes and Oliver Wyland, and watched them play squash for half an hour. They showered and then we all migrated to the pool. We power swam for forty minutes.'

'Power swam? What's that, sir?'

'Oh, the idea is that you get your head down and go like crazy.'

Curtis, who was not a fan of water sports, grimaced. He had times pinpointed, then let Elwood continue.

'After which we drove to the Mitre and met Keith's wife and her father. We parted at about ten-thirty.'

'Fine, sir. I'd like you to write those few details down for us. One last point. Where do you keep sensitive business documents?'

Elwood pointed to the locked metal cupboard.

'And the keys, sir?'

Automatically Elwood stretched his hand to the right of his desk. As his fingers closed on nothing, colour scorched his neck.

They were resting on top of the filing cabinet.

Hallows found the detectives mustered in the Incident Room were unusually mute when he arrived. They were reeling at this new death and the further pressures they faced; their numbers would not be increased.

He conferred with Roy Kennet. Kennet was saying:

'No one living at The Laurels is in the frame. No opportunity except for David Foss, but he's not a fool. This was a planned crime. If he had needed to burn papers he wouldn't have used Linda Thorne's grate. The same argument could apply to Barraclough, of course. No, she saw no danger and let someone in and that someone was in a hell of a hurry.'

Focusing on timing, Hallows ran through the sequence of what could have occurred: 'He, or she, tied her up, turned the TV high to drown any yells, threatened her and was directed to the papers. This person sealed her mouth with plaster, lit the papers and while they got going, secured the bag over her head. How long would you estimate that to have taken?'

'From entering, twenty minutes? The council beano didn't last long. Barraclough has to be interviewed. Shall I see him or . . .? Kennet let the sentence hang and hoped. He was no prima donna, he needed active help from all ranks. However, while he wanted Hallows in with the foot soldiers, he accepted they could cross swords. Each had his own way of doing things.

'I will,' Hallows said immediately. Others would check out Elwood's statement.

Barraclough's property was so well screened by trees that Curtis almost overshot the entrance. He backed up, reversed into the drive and parked alongside a builder's van.

The timber-framed cottage was tiny, and painted according to fashion, black against white. There was a window on either side of the ornately hinged front door and a matching pair above like shining eyes beneath thick brows of thatch.

While Hallows and Curtis shuffled their feet waiting for a response to their knock, a chain saw buzzed nearby. Its drone was interspersed with the crack of timber. The Haweses house was just visible to the policemen through slender trees. Nearer to them, and clearer, was a dilapidated stables. Between these two a wisp of smoke curled up to merge with a slate-grey sky.

The sound of muffled voices accompanied the click of the latch. As the door swung wide, Reg Falder stepped out, leaving Barraclough in the hall. He nodded to Barraclough's visitors while continuing their conversation:

'I should be able to fit you in tomorrow or the day after. You'll need to clear the room, plastering's messy.' He walked towards his van. 'Do you want a written estimate?' he called back.

A smile bloomed on Barraclough's round face. 'No, I know you're fair.'

Barraclough had met Hallows before and immediately took his visitors inside. They arrived in a tidy and very warm, oak-beamed sitting room. Logs crackled in a wide hearth.

Unlike Linda's room, there were no plants here, no flowered fabrics, few cushions and the dark leather settee and fire-side chairs were for sitting on, not curling into. Opposite the fireplace stood a long-case clock marking time with a contented tick. Near by was a bookcase partially filled with works of reference.

Hallows was being careful where to stand. The major beams were so low they might easily part his hair. He said:

'I understand you took Miss Linda Thorne out after work yesterday. I'm afraid we've brought you bad news, Mr Barraclough. Miss Thorne died during the evening. She was murdered.'

Barraclough deflated like a burst balloon and dropped on to a chair. 'Oh, my!' he muttered.

To remove himself from danger, Hallows sat down uninvited. 'I need to know the times you arrived and left The Laurels, sir.'

'Yes, yes, I understand.'

Curtis cast a critical eye over the clearly shocked councillor. Prejudice wouldn't be denied. He was reminded of Toad, a collapsed Toad.

Barraclough collected his thoughts. He remembered seeing Linda's neighbour, David Foss, on their way out.

'And when you returned with Miss Thorne?' Hallows asked.

'No one I knew. I left Linda and drove to Roxleigh. Stopped at the Latimer and had a meal. These nibbly bits you have at council gatherings aren't very sustaining.'

The journey time and the time he said he entered the inn would be checked. Hallows knew that if he had, as he stated, entered the Latimer close to eight-forty he was in the clear. That was the time Linda's TV had ceased its noise.

Hallows returned to a point: 'You said when you returned with Miss Thorne you saw no one you knew. So you did see someone?'

'Yes, but far from clearly. As I was waiting to enter the main road, a woman crossed from the direction of the Leisure Centre. She was by The Laurels's drive when I joined the traffic.' He said with sudden energy: 'She might have seen someone.'

'Indeed. Can you make a stab at a description?'

Barraclough puffed out his Bunter cheeks thoughtfully: 'Oh . . . headscarf. Raincoat, I think, with the collar turned up. No recollection of the colour. As to build?' He raised his hands in a gesture of hopelessness. 'Average, I suppose.'

'Did you notice any cars parked close to The Laurels?'

'No, none.' The councillor sighed: 'Poor Linda . . .'

Barraclough watched them leave, then returned to his sitting room and poured himself a large malt whisky. Linda had been a find – useful to have a woman pleased to accompany one – damned bad luck she'd died. Just as well he'd had a meal at the Latimer, could have been awkward.

He stood with his back to the fire, feeling the flickering pattern of heat on his thighs, sipped his drink and moved beyond Linda to the building problem he faced.

When his malt was finished he walked swiftly to the phone.

'Lester!' Hawes said. 'What can I do for you? Not being troubled by our man's bonfire, are you?'

'Not at all. Actually, I'd like to beg a small favour. I need to empty my television room – got a builder coming in – he's promised to make a mess.' Barraclough's abrupt high laugh trilled uncomfortably in Hawes's ear. 'I thought if I could store my conservatory furniture in your stables, I could transfer the more sensitive furniture to the conservatory. It will only be for a short while. Am I imposing too much on your good nature?'

'You're welcome to use the building, Lester, but its damp and there's not much room. The previous owner left it full of bulky junk: three-legged tables, hat-stands, wardrobes without doors . . .'

'I'm most grateful.'

'Not at all. Better mention what's going on to our man, though. You know Harry Lipton, of course – fellow villager.'

Lipton used the chain saw to create an adequate pathway from Barraclough's boundary to the stable and then gave a hand, moving the light rattan furniture.

Barraclough returned indoors: one problem was resolved.

All the scene-of-crime prints taken at Linda Thorne's flat were sent to the incident room, but those of the material lifted from the grate were delivered directly to Hallows by messenger.

Every case needed an early break and Hallows hoped, with a sense of excited expectancy, this would be it.

As well as an enlargement of the fire-damaged snap there were first-stage prints taken as the layers of ash had been painstakingly removed from the fire-basket.

He concentrated on the snap.

The fire had consumed the upper two-thirds of the image, leaving a scorched diagonal line. What remained was a triangular segment showing mid chest to knees of a man and a woman. They were standing side on, very close, suggesting they had been caught kissing. Only a portion of the woman's dress was visible but, even so, it looked familiar.

Hallows opened the file on Sally Webber, took out the photograph of Sally in the Laura Ashley dress and laid it beside the enlargement.

Fabric and style corresponded, but it was the close fit, those little puckers, which confirmed for him that Linda had been in possession of a photograph of Sally Webber.

So who was the man? He was slim and, judging by his arm, long limbed. He wore jeans and an Aran sweater and his right hand rested on the woman's hip.

The obvious conclusion was that Linda Thorne had been blackmailing him, else why would the photograph have been burnt? But what threatened from a stolen kiss? Had Linda discovered a darker secret beyond one that he had simply known Sally?

Hallows put the enlargement to one side and considered the on-scene photographs of the separate layers of ash.

The fragile papers would be treated with chemicals. Ink would gain clarity, but even without this he could make out details on one. Not only was Earle's title and logo readable but so too was a portion of Elwood's writing. He had scrawled a personal letter to Charles Saville.

Hallows felt in a top drawer and found a magnifying lens for a sharper view. With it he got the drift. Elwood was expressing a deep dislike for something he was being asked to do concerning Jacob Bisset. What had so upset Elwood: the words rang with concern?

No doubt it was this secret that was to cost the two men an expensive apartment and a sharp increase in Linda's salary.

He plucked his lip and wondered how solid an alibi Elwood and Saville had. Time would soon tell.

Hallows reached for the internal phone. 'Liz, we need to talk. Are you free?'

'In five minutes. I've just received the doctored photographs of Martin Falder. He is now a rather heavy featured young man, but passably attractive. I've decided, initially, to fax copies to police stations within a fifty miles radius of Helenborough. If Martin is missing his family, he might be living relatively close to home. What did you want to talk about? Bisset?'

'And Linda Thorne.'

'Josh Elwood's assistant – why her?'

'Haven't you heard? Hasn't it filtered through? She was found suffocated this morning.'

Her gasp hissed in his ear: 'What?'

He said: 'Kennet was called to The Laurels . . .'

'I heard about a death at The Laurels, but not who was involved. I'll be up.'

'Is Josh Elwood involved?' she said directly she turned into his room.

He nodded. 'I'm certain Linda Thorne was blackmailing Elwood and Grandfield's man, Charles Saville. He's jumpy, Liz. Very. Elwood said he was with Oliver Wyland and Keith Hawes at the time we believe Linda died.'

'And was he?' She raked hair from an anxious brow.

'We're checking. There was a heap of incompletely burnt paper in Linda Thorne's grate. Have a look at these.' He spread the prints of the ash layers in a broad fan. 'Earle's logo,' he said, tapping one.

She picked it up and squinting for a sharper focus, began to read Elwood's faint pen strokes. '. . . a personal letter to Saville about Bisset? Why personal?' she said and read on, then looked at Hallows tautly. 'Josh is really strung up.'

'Yes. There's grief there and considerable protest. What are his weak spots?'

'His family. He's a doting dad.' Her eyes widened: 'Oh!'

Hallows nodded: 'Elwood could have stumbled on activities at Victoria Crescent. Acquired evidence which Saville insisted they use.'

'And then Linda got hold of it together with this letter.'

'Must have. She'd need both. So you see why he's in the frame.'

She scowled unhappiness. 'I believed Josh Elwood could be looked on as a friend. I'll talk to him about the letter. Oh, damn Bisset and Saville.'

'Before you speak to Elwood, let's see what else turns up.'

'OK.' Despondently she picked up the enlargement of the snap. 'Another item in Linda's collection? This isn't Linda with a guy.'

'No, it's Sally Webber. I've no idea who he is.'

Ferret shifted attention to the man.

Hallows saw her tense with recognition. 'You know him?'

She ignored him, walked to the window, angled the print and peered closer. He followed.

All colour slid from her face, the fading bruise stood out stark and ugly. He wanted to bark: 'Well?' but bit his tongue. Instead he pushed the magnifying lens into her hand.

She used it, then stared out across the city. Her voice a monotone, she said: 'He knew Sally Webber, and Sally Webber vanished . . .'

'Liz . . . ?'

She faced him, feeling dead inside. 'You'll have noticed the ring on the man's little finger,' she said and dropped the print on to his broad, waiting palm. 'It's familiar. While I'm perfectly aware there must be thousands of look-alike rings being worn in the same manner in this county, there are not so many men with fingers quite as long or as bony. I think you'll find when the engraved initials are enlarged they'll read: OW.'

Hallows craggy features clouded with exasperation and concern.

'God, Liz! You do pick them,' he exploded. 'You're talking about Oliver Wyland.'

Desolation made her flare and bolt to the defensive. 'What should I do? Ask for a character reference before I go out with a man?' She stabbed at the print. 'How did Linda Thorne get hold of the snap?'

'I think from a cupboard in Elwood's room. He's not too careful with the keys.'

'And Josh Elwood and Oliver are friends . . .'

She looked sick.

He reminded her, 'Elwood's saying they were at the Leisure Centre, Liz. However,' he began to warn.

'You don't need to tell me,' she said icily. Her inclination, her wish to decide, scuppered! Out of her hands. 'Keep clear of Oliver Wyland while the investigation's under way.'

'Right.' He felt sympathy. He didn't have to be clairvoyant to see how it was.

A sharp knock on his open door had him turning from her to Scott.

'Steed's been in touch,' Scott said. 'The brothers had a phone call. A clerk at Kempe's directed Frank to a booth for punters . . .'

'Which means they weren't expecting it,' she interrupted. 'They'd have been hanging around the booth, otherwise.'

'. . . they're off, heading towards Roxleigh.'

'Roxleigh? To clean windows again?'

'Yes – interesting,' Scott agreed. 'We've got them covered.'

The Lilly brothers had been seen to turn into Councillor Barraclough's drive.

At Abbots Hill, on a wide central table beneath a bright overhead light, Scott had spread a high-scale map of Roxleigh.

What Ferret now saw confirmed her night-time single impression of Witley Lane. 'There's no place for our guys to park unseen except there.' She pointed out a bridle track opposite the Hawses' entrance. It lead from the lane to the centre of the village, where it emerged close to Oliver Wyland's cottage.

'If the wood cover's thick they'll snoop on foot,' Scott said.

With her fingers crossed, she moved on: 'When the brothers are driving back to Helenborough, have Traffic stop them. The usual reason – faulty brake light. All very low-key. A routine walk around and nose inside. Let's see if they're carrying videos.'

'I'll get on to it.'

Left alone, she didn't roll the map immediately. She followed the course of the bridle track again. In her mind's eye she could see the track opening on to the road opposite the church. A ninety degree turn and she would be looking at Curate's Cottage. Oliver's home was only a stone's toss from the track's exit. She had yet to step inside. Perhaps now she never would, however their futures evolved. And forgiveness and innocence had nothing to do with it. It was a harsh fact of life: people questioned extensively by the police during the course of a major investigation developed an antipathy to all officers.

She slotted away the map and switched off the light. Word of the Lilly brothers would come through upstairs. She bought coffee and a pack of sandwiches and carried them to her desk.

Shortly after, Hallows coincided with Roy Kennet at the doorway of the Incident Room.

'It's just through,' Kennet said and ripped open an envelope from University Hospital. He read aloud: 'The analysis of the amount of potassium contained in the fluid of the eye would suggest that Linda Thorne died between eight-twenty and nine o'clock.' Kennet declared satisfaction.

'Let's keep in mind the test is simply a guideline,' Hallows warned.

'But it does fit in with what else we're hearing.'

'True. Barraclough's statement checks out. The time he says he dropped her has to be right. Pity nobody in the flats heard her killer use the buzzer for the outer door. Just shows how loud the TV must have been for those few minutes. It stirred them all out of lethargy, but not for long enough to complain.'

'Which brings us back to the woman Barraclough saw crossing the road,' Kennet said. 'She's either directly involved, or the only witness we have so far who might have seen someone entering The Laurels. There's a description out. The Mercury and the local news are asking for motorists who were passing the Leisure Centre at around eight-twenty, to come forward.' Kennet's habitually half-closed eyes opened a moment in cynicsm. 'Trawling, isn't it? We've got nothing else to go on so far. There's no gossip about an outraged lover, no offended clients at Earle's, no colleague who hated her guts. Linda Thorne appears to have upset no one . . .'

'. . . except those she was blackmailing,' Hallows finished for him, then added to the general information: 'Charles Saville is in the clear. I've been "reliably" informed he was having dinner yesterday evening with

Grandfield's chairman at the Paragon.' It was the city's plushiest restaurant.

Kennet guessed it must have come directly from the chairman. 'Pity,' he said with quiet feeling. 'I'd like to have nailed Saville. He's an arrogant bastard.'

Hallows glanced at the clock: 'As soon as Rob Curtis gets back I'm off to talk to Dr Wyland. Elwood said they were together. Do we know for certain yet?'

Kennet felt a niggle of suspicion: a quarrel with the building bricks of rank. Hallows could be like flypaper when it came to information. Significant items homed in on him. While he shared, he had already mulled things over. It set him ahead of the field. Kennet let it go for the moment.

Statements from the Leisure Centre and the Mitre had just been logged.

Kennet received the two computer summaries from a clerk and arranged them in time sequence between himself and Hallows.

In essence: At seven-thirty Hawes and Wyland began a game of squash watched by Elwood and two others. At eight the three migrated to the competion pool via the changing rooms and showers for Wyland and Hawes to freshen up..

All this was well confirmed.

The pool's life guard knew them pretty well by sight: knew they were strong swimmers. He saw them enter the pool, then kept his eye on the youngsters who had crowded in for the evening. He saw them leave close to nine. They gave him a wave.

At the Mitre, Mrs Anne Hawes had a leisurely dinner with her father, Mr Neville Howard. Her husband, Dr Wyland and Mr Elwood were there at nine-thirty and could have arrived a few minutes earlier, there was some debate among the staff.

'So Elwood is in the clear,' Kennet said. He looked at Hallows fixedly: 'You spoke of Wyland. Have you heard something?'

Hallows didn't answer immediately. He made a mental note to have copies of the statement sheets forwarded to Liz.

'Wyland,' he said, 'had a relationship with Sally Webber. Linda knew. Remember there was a portion of a photograph in the grate.'

Raw colour flared over Kennet's cheek. 'The prints of the ash layers were sent direct to you?'

'If they hadn't been-' Hallows growled, irritated by the tone but not entirely unsympathetic to Roy Kennet's view -'we wouldn't have known about Wyland so quickly. Copies are in your tray now.'

Kennet wasn't satisfied: 'Who ID'd him?'

Hallows was damned if he'd name Liz. Who she dated was her business until it needed to be otherwise. 'Reliable recognition.' A ferocious glare dared Kennet to ask more. 'And a ring,' he added. The enlargements he had received showed the engraved OW remarkably clearly.

Kennet shut up, scowled from frustration as much as annoyance, and then said meaningfully: 'And Wyland and Elwood are buddies.'

Curtis, approaching, heard. 'And so is Hawes,' he said, breaking in. He tossed the tie in its sealed envelope down in front of them, and with a touch of a swagger gave them a history. 'According to Beal's, Helenborough's classiest gents outfitters, it was bought by a small woman last Saturday. On Monday they had an inquiry from Anne Hawes about the purchase. Red hair was mentioned. Had to be Linda Thorne. I went to Earle's. The staff described a quiet wifely indignation when Anne Hawes turned up with a package for Linda. Linda was out so she had to leave a note. A tut-tut epistle about the tie – one of them found the crumpled note in Linda's waste bin and shared it with her colleagues.' Curtis grinned smugly: 'Interesting, eh? Perhaps Anne did a short flit from the Mitre – could have been her Barraclough spotted outside the Laurels.'

Kennet and Hallows looked at each other, and in silence shared the suggestion.

'She's yours, Roy,' Hallows said, words that later Kennet would hear provocatively circling in his mind. 'Rob and I will talk to Dr Wyland.'

Curtis had learned that Dr Wyland was off campus on a Patronus matter, something to do with their next play. Patronus had rehearsal rooms in the basement of the Methodist church in Faraday Street and he drove Hallows there.

The building was exceedingly large and plain, both inside and out: more like a monument scorning the pride of adornment some said, rather than an uplifting cogent declaration of faith. Its only architectural ornamentation came from the cream and earth-brown bricks used in its construction, arranged in alternate narrow and wide bands.

It was located at the lowest corner of a steep hill. Most of the vast basement area, therefore, was not below ground. It had a street level entrance which made it independent of the church proper and consequently easy to let. Patronus had been renting the huge space for years, using two-thirds of the floor area for storing an extensive stage wardrobe department. Costumes had been acquired by Patronus over decades and were available for general hire. Theatrical companies from far afield used the facility.

When Hallows and Curtis arrived, Wyland had just finished selecting clothing suited to his part in *The Importance. . . .* Mo Fraser, in charge of wardrobe, took the items away to pack and to book them out, leaving Wyland with the policemen to talk in the scant comfort of the men's changing room.

Wyland's eyes slid from the folder Curtis was carrying to Hallows: 'So what can be so important that you pursue me down here?' he asked without requiring an answer.

Hallows nodded for Wyland to accept a chair which Curtis offered, the only one available, then he eased himself cautiously on to the edge of a table, wondering if its slender legs would take his weight.

Wyland stretched his arms lazily outwards, pushed, smiled faintly at a loud crack from his shoulders, then dropped his hands comfortably into his lap.

While observing so much casual ease, Hallows adjusted his thoughts. 'I know you'll be repeating yourself, Dr Wyland – you've seen one of my officers already – but I'd like to hear personally about the swim you took yesterday evening with Mr Elwood and Mr Hawes.'

Wyland obliged without demur. As near as he could say, they entered the water at eight-ten and power swam for forty minutes. They were showering and dressing at nine. They didn't delay, he in particular was eager to eat. They probably arrived at the Mitre around nine-twenty.

'You say you power swam: how did Mr Elwood manage with his injured leg?'

In thinking back, Wyland pinched his chin between thumb and index finger of his right hand.

Hallows had a glimpse of the signet ring.

Wyland said: 'Well, he didn't complain, but then perhaps neither of us were really pushing it.'

'So you kept pace with each other?'

'I believe so,' Wyland answered patiently.

'Then you can confirm you were within each other's sight throughout?'

The slightest of frowns creased Wyland's brow. Curtis's pen paused above the page. 'No, of course not,' Wyland said. 'If you're power swimming, you watch out for nothing but the turns. However, Josh was beside me when Keith surfaced in front of us to talk.'

'I see. You were in the competion pool, I gather.' Wyland was nodding. 'I believe that's roped off in lanes.'

'That's correct. The kids are meant to keep clear, but on their cheap nights they don't, of course. They overflow everywhere.'

'So you had to watch out for the youngsters.'

Mildly amused, Wyland shook his head: 'Had to watch? No. I watched out for neither Josh Elwood nor Helenborough's youth, Superintendent. Josh, for reasons I have already explained and, by happy chance, not the young of this city either since they kept clear of my lane and Josh's.'

'How fortunate,' Hallows observed. 'Was Mr Hawes similarly untroubled?'

Wyland considered Hallows narrowly. 'Apparently he had problems.'

'Do you recall in which lane each of you swam?'

'I was in seven. Josh was in eight. Keith took two which was mob free when we arrived.' Wyland straightened his long legs while arching either boredom or fatigue from his back. 'Does this help you?' he asked drily.

'It interests me. I know, you see, that you might have wanted Linda Thorne dead.' Hallows watched Wyland's face. His even expression told him no more than a book offering a blank dust jacket. 'Sergeant . . .' he said.

Curtis passed two photographs taken from the folder to Hallows, who offered Wyland the top print. It was the enlargement of the partially consumed snap taken from Linda Thorne's grate.

Hallows marvelled privately. Wyland's eyes gave not a flicker of recognition. He said: 'I can say with confidence, Dr Wyland, that the woman seen there is Sally Webber. Can you identify the man?'

'Hardly – since he has no head.'

'Then would you mind telling me what you see here?' Hallows offered the second enlargement and in doing so forced Wyland to stretch with his right hand.

The page was filled with the image of a ring. The shape of the engraved lozenge was clear and the initials, OW, sharp.

For a moment Wyland's mouth narrowed then he said casually: 'Since I don't believe you would indulge in forgery, I'll give praise. Clever move, Superintendent.' He passed the enlargement back, turning his hand so that Hallows had a full view of the ring. 'I'll tell you about the original photograph to save you asking. Obviously I'd rather you didn't tell the university authorities about so old an indiscretion.' He arched an eyebrow questioningly.

Hallows didn't respond immediately. Instead he risked the table's legs in search of greater comfort and slid himself further back on its top. Surely Wyland must be anxious, he reflected, but it was not apparent. Wondering what manner of man he was confronting, he said: 'I won't, Dr Wyland, unless it becomes necessary. I presume Miss Thorne's attitude favoured the reverse.'

'Yes. I offered her a straight payment in exchange for the photograph, any copies, and so on.' Wyland interlocked his fingers, looked at them vaguely and then back at Hallows. 'You'll want to know: Sally and I met on an archaeological dig. I was lecturing and working for my doctorate at the time. We were in different faculties. Wouldn't have crossed paths in a place of Helenhall's size if it hadn't been for that mutual interest. Keep in mind, there was no great difference in our ages and to make an issue of our respective roles within the university seemed perverse. It was basic attraction – we fancied each other, nothing more. We conducted a somewhat clandestine affair for about six months.'

'Who ended it?' Hallows interrupted.

'I did.' Wyland coughed, and for the first time showed feeling. It was embarrassment. 'I was seeing Anne Howard, Keith's present wife, at the same time. Needless to say, neither woman was supposed to know of the other. But Anne became suspicious – told me to choose.'

'So you dropped Sally?'

'The affair was cooling off anyway.' Wyland sighed ruminatively and returned to the photograph Linda had stolen. 'Josh had bought a new camera. He was snapping everything and everyone. Patronus members, with student support, had been carol singing around the wards at University Hospital. The students were going to return to halls of residence together, which was inconvenient since Sally and I wanted to say a swift goodbye in private. Keith guessed – offered his office. Josh caught us on film. He said he would destroy the shot and then, like a trophy hunter, kept it – the idiot.'

'Why didn't you come forward when Sally was thought to have jumped in the Nean?'

'Nothing I could have said would have clarified what might have happened to her. I hadn't seen her for about two months.'

'I'll remind you – all people at Helenhall who knew her were asked to come forward.'

'So I acted irresponsibly, I admit that. Who has the wisdom of Solomon in their twenties?'

'And let's not forget,' Hallows added factually, 'you didn't want to put your job at risk.'

Wyland sighed again. 'Sounds altogether rather contemptible, I grant you. But I was young, ambitious and in a new job that could be easily whipped away from me.' He paused, listening, then tapped a finger to his mouth. In the distance they heard Mo singing. She would be returning any time. He straightened up, his face showing a greater seriousness. 'Unless this is for public consumption, can we end now, Superintendent Hallows? Apart from Mo, I have to be back at Helenhall in twenty minutes.'

Hallows slid carefully off the table. 'We can stop, Dr Wyland, for the time being. I have other questions. I'd like to see you at Abbots Hill at the end of the day.'

Wyland pouted thoughtful acknowledgement and left them.

Absently watching as Curtis returned the prints to the folder, Hallows wondered how Liz ever knew what Wyland was thinking. He supposed she must have some idea. It was, he considered, one of the necessary ingredients for an effective relationship. His mind threw up a Curtis-like response: perhaps with her he's not covering guilt.

*

Trying not to think of Oliver Wyland, Ferret was glad to be distracted by news rung in from an officer who had been tailing the Lilly brothers.

The DC said: 'The brothers have been moving furniture out of Barraclough's cottage into his conservatory. Weren't there long. Traffic stopped their van as arranged. Bit of luck – their off-side brake light was dud. Nothing inside the van except window cleaning gear. They're now cleaning windows on the Summerside Estate.'

'Thanks.' Having hung up, she picked thoughtfully at the high neck of her sweater, then dialled an internal number.

'Scotty, fancy an outing and a little subterfuge? I think we might offer Councillor Barraclough some advice on home security.'

DCI Kennet planned to interview Keith and Anne Hawes separately and was assisted to this end since Keith was with a patient when he arrived at the Fitness Centre.

Anne was rather nonplussed by this second police visit of the day. She took him upstairs to their small private sitting room and then hesitated, standing at the room's centre, unsure of how the interview was to be conducted.

Kennet glanced around. He liked it instantly. The room was simply but comfortably furnished, decorated with a light imaginative delicacy. It offered an unmistakable sense of peace. In his job, with aspects that were repugnant and brutal, corners of serenity held a particular value. He looked at her, slim and long waisted, dressed in her professional, belted and buttoned white coat and wondered if what he was appreciating here had been all down to her.

'Please . . .' He indicated a settee. She lowered herself gracefully at one end, while he took the other. With no great difficulty he found himself smiling encouragement. 'I understand you were with your father at the Mitre yesterday evening, while Dr Wyland, Mr Elwood and your husband were at the Leisure Centre.'

'That's right. They joined us around nine-twenty.'

'They went swimming, I believe. Was this a regular thing?' He was confronted with straight-gazing eyes, large as a fawn's, deep, intelligent and . . . meltingly sensitive. Kennet had the disconcerting sensation of falling through space.

She was saying: 'Not regular, exactly, but it happens quite often and has done for years. Oliver and Keith are old school friends, you see. Josh Elwood attended the same school, but was ahead of them. Involvement with Patronus has cemented their friendship.'

'Who arranged yesterday evening's swim?' Swimming? He was swimming: well, the ground wasn't under his feet. He swore coarsely to himself: he wanted to hear its harshness, its vulgarity, its echo. He wanted to test if he was real.

She pulled thoughtfully at a fair-brown lock of hair. 'I think it must have been Keith. He wanted to see Oliver, and when Oliver couldn't join us for a meal at the Latimer, a Leisure Centre outing seemed the next best thing.'

He watched every small action intently, thought for a hard-nosed guy this was ridiculous, and recited his questions like a pre-recorded tape. 'And how long have you known Dr Wyland and Mr Elwood?' He saw the lock of hair released to nestle in a soft wave against her slender neck. He forced his eyes down to his notebook, bullied thought to concentrate on the job in hand.

There was a pause – at least, he thought there was a pause. He began to get irritable. Where was his bloody judgement? He looked at her again. Perhaps there had been no space, no hesitation after all.

She was tilting her head, clearly wondering at his choice of questions. 'Oliver introduced me to Keith, Josh, and their wives. Keith lost Gina not many months later. That was dreadful.' Not a mimicked platitude; the distress she felt settled as a truth on her face. Or so he might have once categorically stated – but now? Now he didn't trust himself. Objectivity had legged it. She went on: 'I get queasy when I think about it. I can't handle violence . . .'

Truth or lie? Where would he place his money?

'. . . no adventure films or crime fiction for me – and certainly not the action you must see.' Her smile was apologetic.

It triggered an irrational happiness. 'We all have our strengths and weaknesses,' he said cheerfully, while he couldn't think at all what his good points might be. 'I'd be useless-' he said with conviction -'a complete loss, dealing with the sick.'

Her eyes brightened, 'Oh, surely not.'

He found himself grinning and thought he must appear inane.

His mind was programmed to question, thank God! and he moved on: 'Tell me about yourself and Dr Oliver Wyland, Mrs Hawes.'

'Why?'

'I have to know about people.'

She sighed, accepting this. 'Roughly eleven years ago, I returned to Helenborough and took a physiotherapy post with the recreational sports section of the university. I met Oliver on campus. He was fun to be with.'

Kennet, with a policeman's ear despite all else, wondered if he detected some undercurrent here. He chanced a guess: 'So what went wrong?'

'It was a long time ago.'

'Please.'

'These confessions you're encouraging are not comforting. I've another fault. I'm not good at sharing. I felt sure he was seeing someone else besides me. I don't know who she was. He led me to believe the other affair was on the wane and he would end it. In retrospect, I can believe he did as he said, but at the time I was far from certain. Doubt is an evil companion, Chief Inspector. Shortly after that I walked away from Oliver, from all of them, in fact. I didn't see Keith again till I took a job in his department at the hospital a good year later.'

She had led Kennet in the perfect direction for him to introduce Linda Thorne, and it was Linda Thorne he owed a duty to, never mind that he was in some crisis of his own. He said: 'At Earle's there was a silk tie pinned to Miss Thorne's notice board.'

'Oh!' The delicate fair skin over well defined cheek bones was suddenly aflame.

'Am I right in thinking she was being a nuisance?'

She leant back into the cushions and closed her eyes. 'To think of her being murdered is odious but . . .' suddenly her striking eyes were on him: 'Right now I'm glad she's dead. *Glad!*' Such honest vehemence was like a dart. He felt it. He felt everything she was saying was the truth. And all this when training and experience told him not to be a fool. Cautioned it could all be a clever pretence, a veneer. Had wanting to believe obliterated reasoned assessment, or were they, after all, in step?

Suddenly she sprang up and walked to the cold fireplace.

He wished she hadn't. She was no longer summarized by her face, she was complete; the whole enigmatic image in the lens. An innocent or a liar? Either way, a Circe. She was as supple and delicate as the finely carved marble nymphs who danced behind her, beneath its wide mantle.

He rose, defended himself against this disconcerting witchery by being brusque: 'So tell me why.'

Folding her arms along the edge of the high mantel, she rested her head against them and spoke rapidly, if a little disjointedly, of episodes at the Mill Restaurant, at the Latimer, and of the tie.

'I presume at some stage, you and your husband had a row? Most couples would.' In conflict with himself, he struck a cynical resonant note.

'Yes.' She turned to face him, and to his shock, tears were trickling down her face.

It disturbed him profoundly, this disclosure of pain. He wanted to take refuge in Rob Curtis's often cool jaundiced view: croc's tears.

'I started it,' she continued. 'That's probably what she wanted; to cause trouble. I am so stupid. Every time she came on the scene, I rose ready as a fish for the bait. And with Keith, Keith, above all people. He cares about me, about others. About his patients and Patronus.'

The door was opening and she looked towards it. 'Keith, darling, are your ears burning? I've been singing your praises.'

Hawes came forward, smiling at first until he saw Anne's damp face. He turned sharply on Kennet: 'Have you been upsetting my wife?'

'No, he hasn't,' she insisted gently, and rested a light hand tenderly on her husband's arm. 'I'm just being me. Up and down. Being emotional over Linda again.'

The smile was back on Hawes's face as he brought her against him. 'Poor Linda. And you're a goose, woman-mine.' And he winked across her shoulder at Kennet.

Kennet privately bridled at the wink. Instinct said Anne was an honest, responsible, considerate woman, and she deserved better than a chummy signal out of her view.

Anne brought them a tray of tea and then left them. Kennet made an effort not to watch her go. She had unsettled him beyond all credibility, but he would rather have her near for all that.

Keith Hawes said, while filling their cups and placing biscuits close to Kennet's hand: 'Anne will have told you of the mischief Linda was enjoying making. Unhappiness, lack of affection, boredom, frustrated ambition, all those complex things can make us mortals behave in bizarre ways. She swept up to me at the Mill, and kissed me on the mouth in full view of everyone. Whether it was from shock or a quick fix of pleasure, she took my breath away. However, despite her games, I did feel sorry for her.'

'Even when she succeeded in upsetting your wife?' Tear-filled eyes shone in Kennet's memory.

Hawes gave a brief worldly smile: 'The thing about storms is that the following calm brings its own delight. But seriously, I thought patience was the best way of dealing with Linda. She would have soon tired of tormenting us, particularly if she found she couldn't draw blood.'

'But your wife *was* upset,' Kennet insisted.

'Yes, and she could have been again, but she would have been determined not to let Linda know.'

'It's not easy to cover up hurt.'

'True. But Anne would do her utmost to protect what is special to us.'

Could she murder, Kennet thought? Could she? 'Did you think Miss Thorne had any other motive besides wishing to annoy?'

Hawes digested this for a moment in silence. 'Well, it's possible, but just now I can't think what her goal might have been. Can you?'

Suddenly Kennet was under an intense, searching gaze. He parried. Hawes could think this through on his own. Over a second cup of tea, he heard Hawes describe yesterday spent with his friends – the swimming – meeting Anne, his *wife*, at the Mitre.

Kennet dated the interview and wished Hawes good-bye.

As he walked to his car, Keith Hawes ceased to occupy any space in Kennet's thoughts. Hawes was dropped in the Pending tray. His mind was filled with her.

His understanding of people was usually sound. But today? Which view of her was right?

He slammed his door. Oh, bloody hell!

He was furious with her – with himself – with the shock of being caught off guard. Furious at being flung up in an emotional whirlwind. Tossed off course by a woman. Not a beautiful woman, not an especially attractive woman, but a woman who left the impression, *left the impression,* he roared to himself in reminder, that she was vulnerable, of a caring and gentle nature.

Well, he'd damned well see what a lying web she was capable of weaving: even if he had to stand the staff at the Mitre on their heads to learn the truth.

He had to know the truth, not for Linda Thorne, not for Hallows and the team, but for himself. He had to know if instinct was right, though much good it would do him, she was way beyond his reach.

He touched the throttle and heard gravel spray as he pulled out into the road.

Nothing disturbed the melancholic November afternoon in Witley Lane beyond the buzz of the chain saw. A seasonal, watchful sadness pervaded the air. Lipton's bonfire blazed up occasionally, snapping with life as he added hazel trimmings, but for most of the time, only a gentle trail of fine grey smoke climbed lazily through moist, still air towards a drab sky.

Lester Barraclough's face expanded into beamed pleasure on finding Ferret on his door step. 'Keith and Anne Hawes's party, wasn't it?' he said heartily. 'Liz Ireton. You see I remember.'

'Almost right, Councillor Barraclough. But today I'm on duty. It's DCI Ireton and this is DS Scott. Can we have a quick word?'

'A police officer – well, well. Come in, come in, do.' He indicated the way to his well-ordered sitting room and followed her.

Scott gave a watchful eye to the oak beams, but his head was not at risk. Though beefy, he had not the height of Hallows.

Ferret said, 'We're making spot calls on isolated houses. A chat about security.' She ran though her patter.

Barraclough listened attentively. 'You mentioned electrical goods being a target-' he gave his high pitched chuckle, a sound as unpleasant today as Ferret recalled it from the party -'so you'll be appalled to see where my video recorder is right now.' He beckoned them through to a tiny room. It was entirely empty apart from a rolled carpet protected by a sheet of plastic.

'It should be in here, my TV room. You can see why it's been emptied.' On an outer wall was an ugly circle of dark slimy mould. 'Didn't spot the trouble until I moved some videos. Got quite a shock.'

Scott sympathized.

'I've had to put everything in the conservatory.' He walked in that direction. 'No where else, you see. Place so small. As it is, my computer room is outstandingly misnamed. It's a converted cupboard.'

They stepped out of the darker confines of the rather claustrophobic house, into the brightness of the conservatory. The semicircular glass extension jutted on to a large expanse of lawn which comfortably distanced the gloomy encircling woods.

Confusion here faced them. Armchairs, lamps and occasional tables had been dumped with no sense of order.

'Grief!' Scott said with feeling. 'Who did this? Can't be you, sir.' Barraclough's TV and video recorder nested drunkenly among a chaos of cushions and curtains. The muddle was compounded by a mass of video films left in tilting heaps.

'No, not me. My cleaning woman won't approve either, but beggars can't be choosers. Faced with an emergency, I pounced on the first help that came to mind. I chanced ringing Kempe's. My window cleaners almost live there. Don't approve myself, however . . .' He gave a resigned shrug. 'I suggested a figure and they came jolly pronto.' He pointed to the video recorder. 'I'll take your advice, move that into the house. The television can stay. It's old.'

'Good.' Ferret continued in the role assumed. She offered leaflets, and toured the remainder of the downstairs rooms discussing access and window locks.

Scott waited in the conservatory. He roamed and glanced at the occasional video title. Obviously Barraclough enjoyed old classics: *The Sound of Music, High Noon*. Not his bag, not his bag at all.

The chain saw droned nearby. Scott gazed in its direction. The roof of the neighbouring house was just visible, but the busy woodsman was quite lost behind the intervening stand of trees.

*

Control: 'Message from Oxton for Chief Inspector Ireton. Martin Falder, identified. Involved in a traffic accident. Air ambulance transferring him to University Hospital.'

Ferret's stomach turned with dismay: '. . . will attend. How bad is he?'

The voice on the car radio crackled back: '. . . a leg injury.'

As Scott swung the car out of Witley Lane, her imagination became a riot of morbid thoughts. 'By air. He must be critical.'

'Not necessarily.' He was intentionally optimistic: this case was getting personal. The Falders had got under her skin. From seeking an adult prosecution witness, she was now also involved in playing Happy Families. That worried him. It was not without risk: in all games there was always a loser. He added: 'The helicopter might have been in the area. Sending a message to his dad?'

'What! Think of the shock. I'll speak to him myself when we know how critical Martin is.' She fidgetted, looked at the speedo: 'Oh, for heaven's sake, Scotty, shift it!'

She thought about the message. 'Oxten? That's thirty miles from here: a town in the middle of nowhere.' She got back to Control. 'Do we have an address and occupation for Martin Falder?'

'Hold . . . Outdoor handyman. St Hilda's House, Woodbury.'

'St Hilda's House? What's that?

'Hold . . . A retreat run by nuns.'

'Thanks. Out. A retreat?'

'Woodbury's hardly a place at all,' Scott said. 'If memory serves it consists of a manor-cum-farmhouse and a string of six cottages. Young Falder picked the right spot for vanishing.'

The junction for the hospital came into view. He bypassed the car park and kept going. She sprang out as he slowed and ran into A & E.

She was directed towards treatment cubicles, grabbed the first person to emerge from behind curtains and flashed her ID card. She was confronting the attending casualty officer. 'Martin Falder: how serious?'

'Not in danger,' he said. 'In fact considering he took the full impact on his side of the van and so saved the nun, I think he was damned lucky.'

'Van?'

'The brakes failed. They ran into the back of an artic. carrying steel rods. One penetrated the cab and pinned his knee. He had to be cut free.

A section of metal's still there.' He saw sweat breaking out on her upper lip. 'Oh, it's not too bad. He's been X-rayed. It missed the joint. He'll be having an op later to tidy things up. Pain's well controlled. He's quite chatty.'

She raked her hair back in something of relief. 'A nun, you said. Is she all right?'

'Not a scratch.' He pointed towards a waiting room. 'Resilient old bird. She insisted on following him here. Do you want to talk to her?'

'Later. Can I talk to Martin now?'

'Sure.' He parted the curtain.

She braced herself to face wires, meters, tubes, an intimidating trolley of instruments, dressings and green surgical towels, and a patient overshadowed by all this.

Ferret's shock on seeing the young man had nothing to do with matters medical. She couldn't believe how close the fabricated photographs had come to his actual likeness. He was dark, as his father and uncle were dark, with widely spaced eyes which regarded her with wary curiosity. His mouth, partly open and relaxed at the moment, suggested pleasantness and obstinacy. While heavy boned he was not as rough hewn as Reg, with features which would invite a second interested glance. Understandably, underlying a healthy agricultural tan was an extremely greenish pallor.

'Hi, Martin,' Ferret said gently, bending forward. 'I'm told you found an unusual way to stop your van.'

'Brake fluid must have leaked.' With an unexpected jerk he lifted his head from the pillow: 'Sister Bridie! She is all right, isn't she?'

'She's fine. Martin-' she hesitated, wondering how he would react – 'I'm a police officer, but I'm not here about your crash. Your dad asked me to try and find you. He wanted to hear you were safe and well. How did you manage to hide so successfully? You've been invisible to the DSS and tax people. You're not on an electoral roll . . .'

He flinched with anxiety and she added hurriedly: 'I'm not chasing on anyone else's behalf, but names on files help us to find people. You've had two very concerned parents. They've suffered, Martin.'

His eyes misted. He looked beyond her at the ceiling.

Quietly she re-enforced the message. 'You've been missed dreadfully.

They want you to know that you're very much loved. Very, very much loved.'

He gave a single gulping sob.

It racked her: 'Oh, Martin. Everything's going to be all right. Your dad . . .'

'I can't see him!'

She had expected as much. She looked savagely at what he was coping with: the drip taking saline into his arm and the cage keeping blankets off the jutting metal rod in his leg. 'You're going to have an op. You need loving support. Let me fetch him.'

'No. He'll want to know why I ran away and I can't tell him.'

'I do understand. You see, I do know why.'

Apprehension flashed into his eyes.

She said quickly: 'I'm not going to tell your dad. That will be down to you when you're ready. Shall I give you a guarantee? I won't let him near you unless he promises not to ask questions. He'll honour a promise, won't he?'

'Yes, if he's like I remember him.'

'Good. You know the Christmas cards you've sent, they've cherished them all. Shows how they feel, doesn't it?'

She dealt more of the same. Siege tactics, but she had no qualms in compelling a surrender.

He sank deeper into the pillows, not in retreat but relaxation. 'OK, you win,' he murmured, ending barren years.

'No, you do. I'll collect him now.'

The word, now, made time suddenly important. He caught Ferret's arm. 'Sister Bridie. She has to cook dinner.'

'No problem I'll drive her back to the retreat.' It was an offer not entirely founded on goodwill. She would learn more about him from the nun.

She had joined Scott:

'Drop me at Abbots Hill, I need to pick up my car. I'll meet you back there about eight. I think it's time we pulled the Lilly brothers in, they're not taking us any where.'

'Early morning call?' He saw her nod. 'I'll get it organized.'

*

Reg Falder ran forward as her car entered his yard. He had been told simply to be ready. He thudded in beside her.

'Martin's where? Is he fit? Is he well? Where's he been? What's he been doing?'

'Reg, steady up!' It would have been impossible to tell him everything from a hospital pay phone. It was an in person job.

She chewed an anxious lip, then started with background. 'He's been working at a retreat run by nuns . . .' She waved down the first of a barrage of interruptions. 'He's been fine but – *ssh* – today when he was driving their van he – *shut up, Reg!* – was involved in a traffic accident.' She felt as much as heard his horrified gasp and rushed on: 'He's in no danger – a leg injury.' She paused, allowed him time to absorbed this, then supplied details.

With present events covered, anxiety to some extent allayed, he started down an anticipated track. 'Why did he take off four years ago? Did he say? He must have told you.'

She saw a lay-by ahead, pulled in and braked. 'Listen to me, Reg. Hear me loud and strong. You'll see Martin on one condition: I want a copper-bottomed promise you won't ask him.'

'What?' he barked incredulity.

'He's not ready to tell you. If you can't promise, I'll post a constable by his bed. Am I clear?'

His hectored eyes stared.

'Is it a deal?'

'Yes,' he said hastily, wanting to be off again.

He managed a restrained walk through A & E.

She hung back, watched him disappear into the cubicle, then went to collect the nun.

Sister Bridie had been pleased to speak of Martin on the way back to St Hilda's. She had eased her plump little body into the passenger seat, adjusted her grey calf-length habit and simple present-day wimple and launched into a stream of conversation:

'Four years ago, he arrived like a thin drowned rat. Raining it was, such rain! We took him in. Treated him like one of our guests. He wouldn't talk. Not a word about himself. A month passed. He showed no signs of moving on. Started doing little jobs: fed the chickens, took care of the goats, planted the summer crops. Lovely beans. There was winter ploughing. In the spring, planted potatoes. We grow all our own vegetables . . .'

'So you employed him?' Ferret cut in.

'No. We don't deal in money, well not in the way you do. We work and in exchange our basic needs are provided for out of the retreat's income.'

'And that suited Martin, a young, active man?'

'He seemed content. St Hilda's purse wouldn't deny him little treats.' Sister Bridie gave a soft chuckle: 'We bought doughnuts today – ate them in the van – a touch naughty, but I confess to a sweet tooth.'

In the headlights, the white board advertising the retreat shone out from a neat hedgerow.

A five-bar gate had been swung back and Ferret turned into a cobbled courtyard.

'Now you will stop for dinner,' Sister Bridie said. 'Sister Ruth will have started it. It won't take long to complete.'

Ferret was ravenous: 'I wish I could, but I have to get back, I'm expected.' She halted by an arched doorway and flicked on the car's interior light.

'Such a pity. Then you must come another time.'

In the presence of so much uncomplicated warmth, Ferret relaxed for just a moment. 'I'd like that, very much. Thanks.'

Returning to Helenborough she missed the nun's voice, the bright flow of words. She felt acutely isolated in the blackness of the car. Loneliness, like cold, was creeping into her bones. Inevitably she found herself thinking of Oliver, when the flame he had kindled, flickered. Now she didn't push thoughts of him away.

He was a far from perfect being, but . . .

That provoking poem he kept repeating echoed in her head. He had delivered three lines softly against her ear. Three lines? There had to be more. So what was the fourth?

With an urgent need to find out she cut away from Abbots Hill and headed for the Public Library. Only fifteen minutes before they closed.

She raced, soft-footed, up the central open stairway to the reference section.

Confronting a battery of books, she reached for a fat dictionary of quotations. In the index she chased "fire", found the reference, spun pages and read: *... speech ... burning fire; ... lips he travaileth; ... heart ... blind desire,*

Her eyes widened. 'Oh, God, Oliver!' Dismay was spoken aloud, bringing sharp stares.

In his eyes foreknowledge of death.

Shortly after seven, on an evening that hinted at fog, Oliver Wyland strolled into the main entrance hall of Abbots Hill police station and told the officer at the desk he was expected. As he waited he wondered what were the chances of meeting Liz Ireton.

It was Curtis who came to find him. He was led along a stark corridor to an interview room of spartan comfort. Two pairs of hard chairs faced each other across an empty table. Indicating that Wyland should take one of these, Curtis asked: 'Would you like a cup of tea, Dr Wyland?'

'Why not?' It was something with which to toy, and he stretched his legs, letting them jut from beneath the opposite chair lodged under the table.

A uniformed constable went to fetch his drink while the sergeant, with a stern glance at Wyland's projecting feet, showed him two sealed cassettes. 'Do you mind if we tape this interview?'

'No.' He shrugged indifference and watched as they were slotted into the parallel recording machine.

This done, Curtis sniffed disapproval at Wyland's jutting legs and the trapped chair.

Wyland grinned good-naturedly. He rat-tapped his feet together before targeting the sole of his right shoe. Gently the chair was propelled towards Curtis. 'There, Sergeant. Didn't mean to deprive you of a seat.'

The tea arrived seconds before Hallows.

Hallows had been sifting through statements from motorists. It was definite, a woman had dodged across the road close to The Laurels at those times that interested him. She had been wearing a lightish coloured raincoat and a head scarf but due to the orange street lighting, no one was prepared to commit themselves to exact colours. Pleas for the woman herself to come forward had yielded nothing.

Whether she had walked down the drive and rung Linda Thorne's door bell was yet to be answered, but the woman wasn't Anne Hawes. Kennet had been forthright: Mrs Anne Hawes had been seated very much in everyone's view in the restaurant. It would have been absolutely impossible for her to slip away from the Mitre unnoticed.

On confronting Wyland, Hallows offered a polite smile, then settled his solid bulk at Curtis's right. 'Sorry to keep you waiting, Dr Wyland. I hope this won't take long. We'll start with Miss Linda Thorne.'

Questions he had put in the morning were asked again. The answers were unchanged.

With his little finger, Wyland twirled his empty cup in its saucer. 'I can't see what you're gaining from all this repetition. I was at the Leisure Centre at the time that seems to be of interest to you, and not invisible.'

'The matter of invisibility is not quite true, Dr Wyland. You were seen entering the pool with your friends, and leaving it some forty minutes later, but no one is prepared to say they watched you power swimming for that length of time. And you must admit, you have a very strong motive for killing Miss Thorne. Your research funding and your job were under threat.'

Wyland smoothed his hair with a leisurely hand. 'I made her an offer. One payment, take it or leave it. She was an intelligent woman, I believe she would have taken it. She would have gained nothing by carrying tales to the university authorities. If I lost my job, there would be no income for her to tap.'

'So you intended to take a Wellingtonian course?'

'Publish and be damned? Yes. As to the swimming, Josh would have noticed if I had left the pool, as I would if he had.'

'Mr Elwood is a friend, and friends defend each other: by force, by lying, by keeping silent. While there is a strong motive for Mr Elwood wanting Miss Thorne dead, with his leg injury I can't see him having the speed to reach her flat, kill her and return, within the critical forty minutes. However, he might look to a friend in a similar predicament to rescue him. You, Dr Wyland. Not Mr Hawes. Linda Thorne had no hold over him that would convince my officers as a likely motive for murder.

She was being something of a nuisance, true, but they would take the view that Mrs and Mr Hawes would have ridden out some teasing. So, Dr Wyland, would you like to tell me the truth this time.'

'I am not lying,' Wyland said quietly. 'I remained in the pool. No excursions.'

'Why should I believe you when you lied about this?' A nod to Curtis and the enlargement of the half burnt photograph was placed in front of the lecturer.

A flicker of uneasiness crossed Wyland's eyes.

Hallows continued. 'Is it true you were Sally Webber's lover?'

'Yes.'

'And through that relationship, you could have lost your job with the university.'

'You know that.'

'And she vanished . . . conveniently.'

'Oh, for heaven's sake,' Wyland reacted with soft disparagement. 'We'd split up weeks before then.'

'Ever stay at Victoria Crescent?'

At the unexpected, a reflex frown creased Wyland's brow. He answered in a lazy drawl: 'Yes. I stopped with Keith and Gina when I was between flats.'

'When was that?'

'During the time I split with Sally.'

'And when you were seeing Anne Howard – at the Haweses home, as well as elsewhere, I presume?'

Wyland nodded.

'Did Mrs Gina Hawes speak of her neighbours? Did she talk about a cripple, Jacob Bisset?'

'The recluse? Yes.'

'She sometimes bought shopping for him. Do you recall her doing that?'

Wyland shrugged.

'Did you, Dr Wyland, ever visit Jacob Bisset's house?'

'Why on earth should I?'

'Perhaps you carried the shopping for Mrs Gina Hawes. Perhaps you were interested in the layout of the house: how it might differ from your friends' home. Perhaps you wanted to see if it was true that Jacob Bisset did not use the upstairs of the property.'

Wyland tinkered with the cup, revolving it again with a bony index finger. 'To the best of my recollection I did not visit this man's house.'

'Keith Hawes-' Hallows changed course again -'he's a very old friend?'

Leaning away from the table, Wyland indulged in a slow stretch, arching fatigue from his back. 'Yes. We became friends at school.'

'So how do you square that friendship with making a play for Gina, his wife?'

'Bad guess, Superintendent,' Wyland reproved quietly. 'Don't taint me with the behaviour of others. If I had felt any attraction to Gina, I would have cleared out. As it was, I don't know how Keith stuck her. She was self-opinionated, tight-arsed and tight-fisted. But, let's face it, this thing, love, is pretty strange. He was devastated by her death.'

'Was Sally a jealous woman? Did she believe you were having an affair with Gina?'

Wyland's eyes narrowed: 'You amaze me. What avenues are you trying to drag me down now?'

'Sally was suspected of killing Gina Hawes and Carol Reynolds. Carol, for no better reason than that she happened to be there. Did you encourage her? Did you weave an elaborate alibi for yourself, anticipating that Sally would act out her jealous rage? And did you foresee she would walk beside the Nean in a state of remorse, before following your plan and meeting you later at Victoria Crescent – where you murdered her?'

There was a dismissive snort. 'Sally drowned,' Wyland said.

'Do you speak from personal knowledge?'

Wyland scowled impatience. 'No. How could I? I wasn't there. I echo, sadly, what was put about by the media.'

'Do you?' Hallows paused when the only sound was the distant banging of a door. 'So let's come back to Victoria Crescent. The body of a young woman has been discovered.'

He watched keenly but the doctor's dark eyes didn't alter. It was impossible to gauge Wyland's reaction. 'I'm inviting you to stay at Abbots Hill overnight. We'll resume our talk in the morning.'

Wyland stood up to his full height, like a lath compared to Hallows, but taller still. 'Unless you're arresting me, I'm going home,' he said calmly. 'I'll return in the morning with my solicitor. Kindly unscramble your thinking by then – it stinks.'

Hallows watched Wyland's receding figure thoughtfully. Wyland was certainly cool, and a very cool character had dealt in murder. So what had he learned from their toing and froing? This. That. But nothing solid to suit a crown prosecution.

Ferret glanced through the Incident Room's open door and saw something new. Two time charts had been displayed side-by-side for comparison. Coming closer, Ferret saw that Hallows had had the Linda Thorne time table placed alongside DI Merrison's chart of the Briers Way deaths.

Why these two? She backed away. Oliver's name featured on one.

In a room nearby, Scott waited. He had a street map spread and ready.

His considered her with tired eyes. Chalk-faced this evening, but then probably so was he.

Ferret threw her handbag on to a chair. 'Organized?'

'Yep.' And he talked her through what was arranged. 'Frank Lilly lives at number two Brithwell Road and Will at number twelve.' The two properties were part of a row of twenty old terraced houses that backed on to a rough lane and allotments.

'The knock's at dawn. Six of us at the fronts. Three DC's to each of the two back gardens. If the brothers make a run we'll have'm. I've issued descriptions of our two charmers: narrow heads, greasy fair-brown hair, blue-grey eyes, short sideburns otherwise clean shaven, flat cheeks, cleft chins and thin cocky mouths. Frank is the shorter though they're close as peas . . . House searches are sorted. OK?' She nodded and he added: 'Fancy some grub at the Dog?'

'When I've rung the hospital. Martin Falder should have had his op. I'll meet you in the yard.'

Outside a mist had descended to settle at streetlamp height. It hung like gauze, filtering each lamp's glare, making more intensely dark those shadowed doorways and back alleys that were usually simply gloomy.

'Is this going to thicken, Scotty?' She frowned at it and hugged her raincoat closer.

'Forecast said it wouldn't last.' They crossed moist pavements for the pub. 'Glad young Falder's OK.'

She was walking to the Dog out of habit. She had lost her appetite since leaving the library.

Carrying their beers, they grabbed a table as it was vacated.

'The brothers shouldn't give any problem.' Froth bearded Scott's eager mouth and he licked it off.

Unresponsively she eyed the food placed in front of her. Cottage pie and . . . This was a mistake.

She felt him watching her dawdling fork and deliberately encouraged conversation. 'What do you make of Barraclough?'

'A qualified bore but, that apart, putting a job the brothers' way doesn't make him iffy. It's true, the brothers do spend half their lives in the betting shop. Born losers, they'd go for the dosh Barraclough was offering. What we're getting is what we see: an inflated middle-aged man with a public reputation to protect.'

'Without Bisset's murder we could have let the brothers roam for longer.' She speared a pea, but was in no hurry to carry it to her mouth.

'Bisset had a good half of somebody under his nails. If they have scratches, we're home and dry. And they might talk.' With his plate cleared his eyes remained on hers, still well mounded.

Minutes passed and little changed. 'Chuck it in, Ferret. Go home. You're bushed. I'm bushed. And we've got an early start tomorrow.'

Chapter 2

It was approaching eight-thirty when Ferret plodded up the stairs to see Hallows. She rounded his door and faced particularly stern eyes.

'You've learned already – we lost the brothers. The fog came down again just as we went in. They took off over the roofs of the terrace. We heard them. Couldn't see a thing. Legged it across the allotments. We found a bill of sale for a blue Astra. We're circulating the registration number and watching the main exit roads from the city.'

She stood by for the official sharp rebuke and studied the top of his wiry-haired head as he growled about giving proper consideration to the weather and of tying up officers who could be otherwise employed.

'Sorry, guv.'

Hallows did not harp on. He understood the loss of face: could appreciate her frustration. Instead, he reached for a file.

She tried reading the name upside down, but Rob Curtis's neat writing was too small. There didn't appear to be a 'y' there. It didn't look like *Oliver Wyland*. She took it she was to hear nothing of the previous evening's interview.

He had two photographic enlargements in his hand: 'You'd better take a look at these prints before you think of seeing Josh Elwood.' Careful laboratory work had produced more detailed evidence from the ash in Linda Thorne's grate. He continued, 'You'll remember Elwood's tone in his letter to Saville, a dislike for what Saville was suggesting. Well we now know what they used to force Bisset to move. SOCO found a portion of an envelope which contained a photograph. The lab have worked on what remained of both.

He passed her the first of the two enlargements.

The flames had eaten their way across an A5 envelope, dying at the point where a name and address had been written. Ferret read: *DSupt.Hallows, Abbots Hi . . .* She looked up, her grey eyes questioning.

'I can confirm the writing is Elwood's.' He handed her the second print.

Anticipating the worst, Ferret sealed her expression and looked down.

The fire had been choosy over what it had left and what it had burnt.

There was ecstasy on Bisset's face, agony on the young boy's, and from what else remained, it was clear he had been penetrated.

She passed it back and for a minute cupped her face in her hands.

He saw her fingers shake and smelt elemental fury.

'Go and have a coffee, Liz – and keep away from Elwood until . . .'

'. . . until I can resist *clouting* him. How dare he express concern and then do damn all!'

At nine-forty-five Oliver Wyland, accompanied by solicitor, Jon Odell, entered Abbots Hill police station and experienced the same opening routine as on the evening before.

Curtis ushered them into an interview room and offered tea or coffee.

Wyland glanced at Odell, who shook his head, which was not surprising since they had only just left Peel Square's coffee shop where Odell had devoured breakfast as they had conferred.

And, as before, Curtis slotted tapes into the recording machine. It would be Curtis's voice that would describe who came, went and other visual details.

Wyland adjusted his long legs beneath the table, let his hands relax in his lap and waited.

Hallows came in, carrying a thin folder.

He knew Odell. A smart dresser, arrogant refined features, a pleasant but forceful manner when he chose. It interested him that he was representing Wyland. They appeared as chalk and cheese: Odell in bespoke charcoal-grey suit and Wyland in jeans, open-necked shirt and chunky sweater. People who were more county usually engaged Odell, but perhaps, like Wyland, he was a member of Patronus. Perhaps that was why Wyland had asked him to oversee fair play.

Hallows pulled out his chair and glanced at Wyland surreptitiously in the process of getting settled.

Wyland was certainly clever enough to plan and execute murder, but whose murder? Linda's? *Vicky*'s? The DNA results on Kennet's scalpel blade should be through by mid-morning. Richard Webber would have to wait until this afternoon before he learned whether *Vicky* was his sister and if he could at last mourn.

Hallows rested his elbows on the table and, confronting Wyland, wondered if the man had managed to sleep last night.

He said: 'Dr Milo and Linda Thorne appeared to have hit it off. Like to comment?'

'You have been shopping around, Superintendent.' Wyland smiled lazily. 'I offer you a fact for your collection. No one likes Milo, who gathers and dispenses gossip, and I can't believe Linda was an exception. I imagine he was trying to discover if Linda and I were an item. He's always fancied he knew who I was sleeping with, but he's never progressed beyond suspicion.'

Hallows merely nodded, but a statement taken from Neville Howard had suggested much the same of Milo.

'You had a meal with Linda Thorne at the Mitre.'

'Bar grub, nothing special.'

'Eating together is sociable; it breaks down barriers.'

'A well known fact.'

'So she would have let you into the house without hesitation. She knew you – would have recognized your voice over the security intercom. How did you threaten her? You frightened her. You made her talk, Dr Wyland. You made her tell you where the photograph of you and Sally was hidden, together with the other papers she had taken from Elwood's office.'

Wyland answered with slow tolerance: 'I did not leave the pool, Superintendent. When Linda Thorne died, I was swimming. I know no more about her death than those few facts this morning's papers have given me.'

Meeting a steady gaze, Hallows said: 'Suffocation was the word they used. What image does that conjure, Dr Wyland?'

Wyland thought about the question. 'Children trapped in fridges. Miners trapped below ground. The stuff of bad dreams, particularly for the claustrophobic.'

Hallows nodded as he reached inside the folder and withdrew a SOCO photograph. 'Shall I remind you how Linda looked when you left her?' He glanced down, but he needed no reminder of the details: Linda tied to the chair, a butterfly of elastoplast across her lips, the plastic bag over her head, a damp red curl against her cheek, the vibrant hair flattened. He placed the photograph before Wyland and watched.

Wyland kept his eyes on Hallows, then at last gave in. With a sharp insuck of air he twisted his head away. The skin below his eyes tightened, the flesh tones paled.

'Rendered lifeless, ugly, because she had found a snap of you and Sally. You have admitted that Linda Thorne threatened you over this affair with a student. You had infringed university rules. You could lose research funding, at worst, your job – but did she go further? Had she concluded you had killed Sally? Was it: pay up! or she'd come to us? There can hardly be a stronger motive for her murder, can there?'

Wyland appeared unable to look down at the table again despite the SOCO photograph having been removed. He focused beyond Curtis's shoulder on some speck on the wall. 'I did not kill Linda. I did not kill Sally,' he stated austerely.

Hallows regarded the averted face thoughtfully. He glanced at his watch, then pushed back from the table. 'We'll take a break.' He saw Odell register a moment of surprise. Wyland, he hoped, would now reflect on that so far covered and worry.

He followed the accepted courtesies: 'Would you both like coffee while you wait?'

Odell, who could enjoy being detached since no demands had yet been made on him other than being present, said yes, vigorously. He accepted for Wyland too, who appeared to have wandered off on some introspective jaunt.

'No mistake-' Curtis said -'the SOCO photograph of Linda Thorne upset him.' He swung the door of the Incident Room back to let Hallows through.

'Doesn't point to him being responsible.'

'True. But it's the only thing that has raised much of a reaction so far.'

With all eyes turning their way, they were treated to a sudden expectant silence. Hallows shook his head. 'This is going to be a game of patience and we've only just begun.' Seeing Kennet, he crossed to where he stood in front of the Linda Thorne and Briers Way timetables. 'So what have you spotted?'

'Hawes, Wyland and Elwood were at the Leisure Centre on the evening of Linda Thorne's death and also on the evening of the fire at

Briers Way. But the timing is more complex for the evening of the fire. Hawes and Elwood met at seven-thirty, then separated for a while. Elwood played badminton while Hawes went to the gym. Wyland arrived at eight and joined Hawes in the gym. Hawes completed his workout and went for a sauna and shower. Wyland and Elwood met in the showers around nine and then joined Hawes in the pool at ten past.'

'OK.' Hallows turned to Curtis: 'So what strikes you about these activities?'

'Lack of back up. It's like their time in the pool when Linda Thorne died.' Curtis had been comparing statements with supporting testimony. 'We've no one prepared to say they saw them actually swimming. Ten years ago, only Elwood was covered up to the swim. He was playing a doubles match. Plenty of witnesses. Wyland arrived late at the Centre, apparently detained at the university. First search and I've found no confirmation of this. He and Hawes spent much of the time until they swam, independently. They were seen in the gym and Hawes was seen entering the sauna, but it was a busy evening, and everyone questioned was rather vague about time.'

'Right. Anything else Rob?'

'Sightings of women in both cases. A woman by The Laurel's drive and a woman – Sally Webber? – walking by the Nean. Wyland was dating Anne Hawes . . .' Curtis oscillated his hand suggesting conspiracy.

Kennet watched his tone: nothing stressed. Hallows and Curtis would pounce. 'Anne Hawes is clear. Plenty of witnesses at the Mitre. And when Sally Webber took her walk, Anne was partnering her father at a small college dinner. Witnesses again.'

Hallows said: 'I want timings, Roy. How long from A to B, at a walk, at a run . . . Quiet exits from the Leisure Centre . . . You know what I'm after.'

'Yes, guv.' Kennet handed him an envelope. 'The DNA result on the scalpel blade.'

Hallows began to slide out pages. 'So tell me,' he invited.

'The profile of the blood on the blade matches the profile of *Vicky*.' Kennet had no qualms at sounding a trace triumphant. 'I believe she died in that greenhouse at the end of Hawes's garden. The blade being used to remove her head. Still can't think why, though. Or where it was left.' He frowned disatisfaction: 'Can you?'

Hallows rubbed his heavy jaw absently. 'After talking to Wyland I have the brewings of an idea. Remind yourself of recent statements. I'll be with him again in half an hour, join us if you can.'

Wyland's and Odell's empty coffee cups had been removed when Hallows, with Curtis and Kennet, returned to the interview room.

The unease Wyland had exhibited had passed. He looked bored yet relaxed, almost as if he might go to sleep. Only his eyes were alert.

Earlier questions were repeated, identical answers given.

'How would you define ambition, Dr Wyland?' Hallows quietly asked the unexpected.

Wyland threw off lethargy. He sat forward, propping his elbows on the table. 'Ambition: a determination to achieve success in a chosen field. Will that do?'

'Does it diminish or increase with time?'

The question interested Wyland. 'I can't answer for my friends – or for you. However, for myself now, I'm more content to float with the tide than to row against it. I've established a solid reputation in what I do. Career building is rather like constructing a house: get the foundations right and you're away.'

Hallows nodded. 'So Sally would have been more of a threat to your career than Linda?'

There was a long forbearing sigh from Wyland. 'If you think Sally was blackmailing me, you're so wrong. She was open spirited, entirely without guile. And what would she have gained from blackmail? I was at the bottom of the career ladder. I had uncertain prospects and no money.'

'Unlike your friend, Mr Hawes.' It was Kennet.

Wyland considered the DCI, close to his own age, and gave an unexpected chuckle. 'Now, yes. Keith's made his money work, but he started off as broke as me.'

'Another ambitious man,' Kennet said.

'We're all ambitious. You want to make Superintendent before your red hair fades, don't you? Some of us make it. Keith had a dream that's become a reality.'

'Helped along now by his wife – nice lady, Mrs Hawes,' Kennet said conversationally. 'Unless I misread the signs, it looks like a real love match.'

'You judged it right. Good proof that what we value most doesn't have to be money.'

Hallows said: 'Marriage didn't work out for you?'

'No.' A wistfulness entered Wyland's eyes. 'Kate's affection for me went the way of the languishing rose. However,' he added briskly, 'she's happy now with Josh.'

'And that's important to you?'

'Of course it is.'

'So when Mr Elwood confided that Linda Thorne was blackmailing him, you were prepared to help. You forced her to tell you where she was hiding letters, photographs, and when you had put a match to them, you killed her.'

Wyland shrugged off a sudden impatience. Returning Hallows's gaze, he said flatly: 'I did not kill Linda Thorne. And if Sally is dead, and I've seen nothing in the papers that said you've found her body, I'll be very, very sad. I remember Sally as a sweet-natured woman, and in not knowing what happened to her, I've enjoyed the hope that she is still alive and well.'

Hallows leant forward, his eyes inscrutable beneath beetle-brows. 'There is a body, Dr Wyland. Details have not yet been released. You've admitted you stayed at Keith Hawes's house. We have reason to believe that the young woman we have found was killed behind the drawn blinds of the greenhouse.'

Wyland was forced to close his eyes for a moment; the only betrayal of acute distress.

Hallows rose slowly. 'Go away and have lunch, Dr Wyland. Discuss what you have to discuss with Mr Odell and be back here at three.'

Wyland had lost all sense of time and turned to Odell questioningly.

'Come on,' Odell ordered, keen to stretch his legs and eat.

'In – out. In – out. What's Hallows's game?' Wyland asked as the traffic din in Peel Square hit them.

Odell pointed to the coffee shop opposite. 'He's testing ideas.'

'Testing them at my expense!' Wyland snapped with unchecked feeling.

*

Ferret walked unannounced into Elwood's office. He was forewarned of her anger: she closed his door with a thrust of her foot.

'You've got something to tell me, Josh.'

He had already decided he must confess, but it was to be to Hallows – a man. 'And if I have-' he hedged -'why to you?'

'I'm the officer investigating the death of Jacob Bisset, not Superintendent Hallows. So let's get on!' She was so wild with him, she couldn't care a damn for his embarrassment.

Gearing himself up, Elwood rubbed his jaw that so readily coloured – as he knew it would, which made explaining worse.

He turned obliquely away: 'Whenever I was near Victoria Crescent, I used to call on Bisset. Grandfield were agitating for a sale. Their offers were becoming more and more generous but he continued to be as stubborn as hell. I was losing patience and on this occasion I knocked and walked in without waiting to be called. He was sitting at a table with an album which . . .'

She interrupted for a description.

He said: 'Leather bound, a locking strap, large, thick, heavy – very heavy.'

'OK.' She nodded for him to carry on.

'It looked as if he'd been arranging photographs. He closed the book quickly. There were some prints lying loose. He pushed them underneath it. One escaped. It fluttered to my feet. I picked it up. He forbade me to look at it, but I did of course. It was of Bisset and . . .' He tried dodging detail.

She was deliberately cruel: 'Speak out, Josh.'

He talked quickly to have it done with. 'He was buggering a young boy. I felt angry and sick! I thought back – could see Patrick, an innocent of twelve. I pushed the photograph into my pocket, rushed back here and was preparing to send it to Superintendent Hallows when Charles Saville walked in. I needed to talk to someone, shout out my disgust. Saville was bloody cool, but then he hasn't got children. He pointed out that Earle's would feel the draught if Grandfield took future business elsewhere. I've been ashamed of giving way ever since.'

She had wondered how much he would lie, and there was immense relief in being certain she heard the truth. She had thought of him as a friend and sometime in the future she liked to hope something of that could be restored.

'Can you guess why I'm so mad with you?'

He shook his head.

'That boy was one of many. Bisset was part of a pornography ring. We could have had a decent chance of catching the others if you'd been higher-minded.'

Pure horror contorted Elwood's face: 'Oh, my God!' He needed to walk, take deep breaths, fight off a rush of nausea. Springing up, he forgot his leg until the pain bit. He cried out.

She was not disposed to crow over so much discomfort: her rage had been spent. Opening the office door, she called out, asking that they be brought coffee.

He had dropped back into his chair and she leant against the wall, looking down at him. To his surprise, she said: 'You should be grateful to Patrick, Josh.' His brow arched questioningly. 'You had perfect motives for murdering Linda and Bisset and he's given you the best of alibis.'

'Patrick has?'

'Badminton, Josh. You've become a temporary cripple. You couldn't have sprinted from the Leisure Centre. And Bisset's killer showed agility. Made nothing of nipping through a window.'

The fog had long ago cleared. As Ferret dodged between pedestrians on her way back to Abbots Hill, she wondered where Bisset's odious album was now. It had not been found in either of the Lilly brother's houses.

A horn blasted as a car bore down on her.

'The brothers!' Scott yelled from behind the wheel and shoved her door wide.

'Where?' She sprang in and lurched back as his Passat pulled away.

'Heading south,' he said, 'from Mawes Hill. Spotted our check point – did a U-turn.' He eased up only at an intersection. 'Two cars pursuing. Thought we'd join the fun.' His unattractive face creased in a grin.

The car radio crackled between them.

Lead car: 'Blue Astra, Eastcourt Road. Left turn, entering Reform Street.'

'Lovely!' Ferret slapped her thigh. 'They're off home ground. Mustn't lose them in the desolate mega-maze of Whitburn.'

'You think that's where they're heading?'

'Wouldn't you? Twenty or more buildings, vast as hangars, with every door nicked for firewood. They give a whole new meaning to drive-in.' She called Control: '. . . further attending cars – focus Whitburn and deploy. Out.'

Lead car: 'Southwell Street – right – entering Burleys Way.'

'Scotty! Go for Union Street! There's a chance we'll get ahead of them.'

Left, left, right, then a roundabout, left again . . . the wail of pursuing sirens closer.

Lead car: 'Right – entering Bull Road. Junction: Left, left, left! Jennings Street.'

Jennings Street: a right would bring the Astra into Union Street, a terrace of boarded up houses with immediate access across Wharf Way into Whitburn.

Wharf Way: straight, forsaken, dead of people, dead of traffic. Entering from its west end, Scott hit the gas. Half a mile ahead, a crossroads. Right from Union Street, left from Whitburn.

As they eased back for the left, the Astra shot across their path in a flash of blue.

Scott burned rubber. The Passat surged forward into Whitburn, dividing the two police cars from the Lillys.

William Lilly, twisted around in his seat, saw the Passat skate in behind.

Frank Lilly made a right, entered the gaping mouth of the loading bay of Collinson's, tyre-screamed through the empty, rain-puddled hulk, powered out, shot across a service road, roared into Emersons, snaked around its few remaining walls, bumped down stepped levels and cannoned out on to a concrete track.

The police cars had fallen back but the Passat remained glued. Staying on the road, Frank crushed his foot down and felt more thrust. He needed distance before swinging left into the warren of Granger's buildings. Get in there, make some sharp turns, cut the engine, and they could hide up while the bluebottles blew past.

Bracing for the turn, he abruptly tugged the wheel back. A police car waited just off the entrance. Suddenly the network of Whitburn came alive: headlights blazed as cars broke cover on either side. Behind them the Passat was eating separation. Ahead the brothers saw a high brick wall.

'Bloody coppers can't climb!' Frank roared.

He swung hard right; braked alongside the wall. They were out, then up on to the car roof as the Passat swerved to a halt. As one, the brothers' jumped, gripped coping, heaved up and rolled over.

As the brothers disappeared Ferret and Scott stepped from their car.

They knew the area. They heard the expected: a very loud splash.

Springing nimbly from the Astra to the top of the wall, Scott looked down. His honest laugh filled the darkening day.

The brothers' flailing arms were reaching for buoyant flotsam in the stagnant waters of a redundant dock.

For the third time in less than twenty-four hours, Wyland reported to the front desk at Abbots Hill, and for the third time DS Rob Curtis came to collect him, with Odell, and conducted them to the interview room.

Hallows appeared, but without DCI Kennet this time. As he settled himself, the big man surreptitiously studied Wyland. The casual lethargy was still there but the act was as thin as paper. Wyland looked ill.

For an hour questions and answers revolving around Linda Thorne were delivered and replied to as before.

'Did you really not like Gina Hawes?' Hallows asked out of the blue.

'No. She and her twin sister were totally different.'

Wyland was volunteering information. That was significant and Hallows prompted: 'A twin sister? In what way different?'

'Stella was considered to be the black sheep. At sixteen she had a baby which was adopted. I could believe she was a kind, happy-go-lucky girl, though I didn't know her till much later, of course. In contrast Gina was cautious, reserved, precise. They had a wealthy aunt, an only relative. The aunt died when they were in their twenties leaving everything to Gina. Not a penny-piece to Stella who was then working in the States. She flew over for the aunt's funeral and stayed for about six weeks. Keith wanted Gina to share the inheritance, it was substantial, but Gina refused. Not, she would have it, out of avarice, but simply that the money should not be risked or squandered as Stella might do. Gina made her a small gift of a couple of thousand, bought her some good clothes and then waved goodbye.'

'Stella returned to the States?'

'Yes. She flew back to get married. Gina, Anne and I drove her to the airport. Keith couldn't take time off from the hospital, whereas we were free, the university was down for Christmas.'

Wyland continued: 'I feel sure Keith's solicitor, Sears of Sears & Scully, contacted Stella when Gina died. She didn't return for the funeral. Anne might know why. I think she and Anne corresponded for a while.'

Hallows said: 'Did Stella ever talk about the baby and how the adoption had been arranged?'

'She spoke of the event as a fact but without details.'

There was a heavy knock at the door. A PC delivered a whispered message to Hallows, whereupon he walked out.

Having halted the interview temporarily, Curtis followed.

Wyland glanced uneasily at Odell: 'What now?' he murmured.

Hallows hurried to his office where he found Richard Webber trying to make light conversation with the constable who waited with him. His nervousness was very evident. He rubbed his hands together in an odd massaging action.

'Am I too early?' Webber asked.

Hallows felt something of Webber's tension himself. What they would hear would be pivotal to the idea forming in his mind. It was almost four-thirty: 'No,' he said and encouraged Webber to take a chair. 'DS Curtis will bring the DNA result here as soon as it arrives. I must, however, caution you again to be prepared for disappointment.'

Webber glanced down at his kneading hands, pulled them apart and flattened them on his thighs. 'I'm ready for that. At least I know the enquiry is active once more. That brings another kind of hope.'

Footsteps sounded and Webber's eyes darted to the open door.

Curtis entered, shot a warm nod to Webber and handed a sealed envelope to Hallows.

Webber's present nightmare was ended.

'She's not your sister,' Hallows said. 'The mummified body found at 6 Victoria Crescent is not that of Sally.'

Tragedy, relief, uncertainty, a rush of emotions passed over Webber's face. He took a deep breath, then said forcefully: 'So we go on! You do believe that Sally is dead?'

'Yes.'

'So where is her body? Do you have any idea?'

'I'm fairly certain of what happened to her, but I must ask you to be patient. I promise to tell you as soon as I'm able.'

Wyland stretched, sighed and looked wearily about the stark room. There was absolutely nothing present except essential furniture. No pictures, no bright posters. Nowhere for the mind to escape. He wondered how much time Liz spent closeted here as an inquisitor. The prospect didn't daunt him, but rather made him respect her specialized ability more.

Odell, who had used the interval to write a letter, capped his pen as Hallows entered.

Hallows did not plant his hard bulk on a chair. Instead he delivered the unexpected: 'I'm not going to detain you any longer today, Dr Wyland.'

Wyland gaped surprise, then pulled himself together. 'Some sense at last,' he said drily.

In Hallow's mind there was an echo. He recited no more than what was customary: '. . . must remain available. Thank you for your co-operation.'

Wyland gave a rueful snort. 'Did I have a choice, Superintendent? More to the point . . .' he asked with sudden intensity '. . . did my being here advance the course of justice?'

Hallows eyed him thoughtfully as he swung a chair back ritually under the table. 'How would you like me to answer that, Dr Wyland? Perhaps I'll say this. You attach a great deal of importance to friendship. Can you continue to live with yourself if you are not a friend to truth?'

Wyland walked unhappily from the building. He had a scientific, logical mind and Hallows had coaxed him along routes he could not now ignore.

Since his youthful flings and from his time with Kate, correctness and fairness had become greatly important to him, yet here he could do nothing, say nothing more. He had honoured truth: it had all been said. All he could do now was to hope to the centre of his soul, that his reasoning was flawed.

As Odell and Wyland parted in Peel Square, Hallows returned to the Incident Room. He wanted to tell Liz that Wyland was no longer in the hot seat, but he hadn't the time. Instead he read the many notes written on a white-board with felt pens:

The Laurels/The Nean. A Woman – Who? The name of Anne Hawes was noted there and then crossed through.

A detective was on his way to interview Sears, Keith Hawes's solicitor. Copies of wills were being applied for. Stella's baby, almost an adult now, would be sought as soon as they had more information. Anne Hawes and Stella had been in contact: he must talk to Anne.

Hallows called to where Kennet and Curtis were in discussion: 'Rob, ring the Fitness Centre. Ask Keith and Anne Hawes to call here on their way home from work.'

The Lilly brothers parted with their wet, stinking clothes in the medical suite at Abbots Hill. They said very little while waiting the short time to be examined, other than demanding a brief each.

Directly she was told they had been passed fit to be detained, Ferret had them held separately and then joined the doctor.

'They weren't in the water for long,' she said.

'An indisputable fact. Their body temperature was perfectly reasonable.' He exchanged his white coat for a smart single-breasted jacket. He preened a little and shot cuffs before saying: 'Look on the desk.' Arranged neatly on his blotter were back and front view body charts for two persons. He had shaded in numerous elongated areas on the necks and lower arms. Arrows linked these with closely written notes. 'The scratches are grouped. They run parallel as you would expect from fingers clawing downward. They're too old to be argued as collected today, of an age that would correspond to when your Jacob Bisset died. The brothers made no objection to these being photographed. DNA profiles will confirm the Bisset connection, or otherwise: the two agreed to give blood samples in the presence of their solicitors.'

'Good, that's one wrangle less.' She turned to leave, and then appeared to have an afterthought: 'Are they likely to mind being kept apart?'

'A guess, not an opinion: they'll hate it.'

Her mouth slid into a sly smile: 'Love you. *Ciao,* doc.'

Ferret chose to confront Frank Lilly while Scott questioned William. Two hours later when the brothers had been taken to cells well apart, they compared results.

Scott said: 'To picking up youths from the bus station, and to Slade, and the fire at ViewPoint, all I got repeatedly was: *"Don't know what yer talking about, squire.'"* And other than saying they clean windows at Green Vale, William's denying any knowledge of knowing or speaking with Jacob Bisset.'

'Frank parroted his brother.' Ferret pushed her hands in her trouser pockets and leant into the wall. 'So much puffed-up confidence despite the prospect of being in an identity line-up this evening. Danny, the other lads, and the Hillington butcher are ready. Have you let DI Turley know?'

Scott nodded. 'But even with evidence rolling in, and a probable positive DNA match with Bisset, will they talk?'

'Depends how secure they feel about promises. I can believe somebody has said: serve your time and I'll see you right.'

'If so, knuckleheads!'

'Lonesome knuckleheads, I hope. It could be to our advantage, Scotty, that they're as close as a handshake. Unable to confer they could get twitchy. One might rethink his lot and choose to lever responsibility for Bisset's death on to a third person.'

Early evening, and to the Haweses' surprise they were shown into different interview rooms on their arrival at Abbots Hill. Anne found herself facing Hallows while DCI Roy Kennet spoke to Keith.

'Mrs Hawes-' Hallows felt the full attention of direct fine eyes -'I have some questions for you that may seem a little strange – ancient history in fact – but please answer them as best you can. Ten years ago I believe you met Gina Hawes's sister, Stella.'

'Yes. Old history, indeed.' A passing frown marked curiosity. 'She stayed with Gina for a while.'

'Did you write to each other when she returned to the States?'

Anne nodded. 'Regularly until she had a family. We exchange just an annual letter now, at Christmas.'

'I believe your husband inherited a great deal of money from Gina, Gina having inherited from an aunt. I know Stella was excluded. Didn't Stella bear a grudge, first against Gina and then against Mr Hawes?'

Anne's instant dismissive smile gave this the lie. 'Stella liked Keith. She knew he made every effort to persuade Gina to share their aunt's bequest. He did as much again when Gina died. His solicitor contacted Stella. She rejected the offer.'

'Unusual.'

'No -' that open smile again -'not when Stella had married her boss who had gone on to take control of the firm. She saw Keith's need as being greater than hers. She knew of Keith's ambition, it was long standing. She wished him luck in the venture.'

'But Stella didn't return to the States entirely empty handed, did she? Gina had given her some money?'

Her expression suggested she wondered how he knew. 'In proportion to the amount Gina had received, it was very little.' She frowned. 'Very little, indeed. It was two thousand, I believe, and a trousseau . . . mostly underwear, if I remember correctly.'

'Something expensive?' Hallows asked casually.

'Lareine. Gina had developed a liking for it.'

'Lareine: a man's choice when buying for his wife, mistress, lover . . . Did Mr Hawes buy it occasionally for his wife?'

She smiled: 'Keith's generous, but you can't be generous to that level when nearly all of what you earn goes on the mortgage. That was how it was for him then. Gina and Keith maintained the financial habits they had agreed to before she inherited. The new money was salted away in a personal savings account. I would think Lareine was her only extravagance.'

'What was she saving for, the next generation?'

'Perhaps, though Keith has never been keen to have children. I can't,' she added simply. 'I'm not sad about it. I suppose the Fitness Centre could be said to be our child.'

Hallows met a parallel here: Isla, of a similar age to Anne, could not have children. She had told him before they'd married. He loved her, had never hankered for what might have been.

He said: 'I'd like Stella's surname and address.'

'I'll ring it through to you from home.'

'I understand Stella had a child when she was sixteen. He, or she, would be around eighteen by now. For reasons I can't disclose, I need to trace this young person. Can you give me any details?'

'Not really. When we were at the airport, killing time until her flight back to the States was called, we looked around the shops. Stella suddenly mentioned the child's birthday. It was the season, you see; they were decked out with tinsel and glitter. She wondered if the adopting parents had kept the names she had chosen. Holly Stephanie: born on . . .'

'Boxing Day,' Hallows presumed. 'Also St Stephen's Day.'

'Yes. Probably the single reason why I remember such crumbs. Will they be of help?'

'Indeed. Now earlier, you spoke of Mr Hawes, working to pay the mortgage. That was for the house in Victoria Crescent?' She was nodding. 'Was he on the staff of University Hospital at that time?'

'Yes. As I was later. We worked there until we bought the house that became the Fitness Centre.'

'Did either of you know Huey Alcott?' he asked. 'He worked for the hospital's security department-' she was looking puzzled -'and was dismissed for drinking while on duty.'

'Oh, him! I heard about the scandal from Keith. The poor man lost his job sometime before I worked at the hospital. I saw him in the grounds once or twice.'

'Why do you say, poor man?'

'His wife had died of cancer. Hospitals are like villages, Superintendent, there are no secrets. Everyone knew the man had started drinking. Keith said he should have been offered counselling, not thrown out. Why are you asking about him?'

'He died recently. Do you recall hearing of a fire in Victoria Crescent?'

'Yes. Somebody had been sleeping rough . . .' Understanding entered her eyes. 'Huey? How very sad.' It was obvious the regret was not fabricated.

'Accidental death was recorded, but there are some loose ends. The fire appeared to have spread from the grate. He was probably very drunk and not too careful. Do you know if he smoked?'

'I've not the slightest idea.'

'I only ask because we couldn't find evidence of matches or cigarettes, you see.'

'Perhaps they got burnt in the fire.'

'That's my feeling. Maybe your husband will remember. DCI Kennet will ask.' Hallows shifted his feet as if about to rise and then paused. 'There is one thing more. Linda Thorne – all those meetings your husband had with her – how did you hear?'

Tiny furrows gathered at the outer corners of her eyes. 'Friends told me and so did Keith.'

'Sensible man, telling you-' Hallows was standing at last and she followed -'innocent encounters can so often be misconstrued.'

He was not mistaken, uncertainty had deepened the lines. Opening the door, he thanked her warmly for giving her time. Over warmly? he wondered, to appease his own sense of guilt. He had no liking for what he had started, but faced with a cluster of murders, you used what tools you had.

Back in his office, he stretched for his phone, stabbing out his brother-in-law's home number.

'Iain? Can I see you at the hospital tomorrow, early?'

'What about? Not the PM we did on Linda Thorne?'

'No. On the Briers Way deaths and the mummified body.'

'Ah . . . Make it eight-thirty.'

It was there as an undercurrent – the excitement in Sinclair's voice.

Keith Hawes had faced similar questions to Anne and had unreservedly given information.

Kennet, rounding up, asked about Huey Alcott.

'The hospital behaved deplorably,' Hawes said. 'He needed help. His job was the only thing holding Huey together.'

'My final question, Mr Hawes, and thanks for your patience. Did Alcott smoke?'

Hawes spread his hands in a gesture of not knowing.

Kennet, bringing the husband to join his waiting wife, walked with them to their individual cars parked in the square. He watched her leave and wished achingly for the unattainable.

Alone in his car, Keith Hawes worried about Anne. He was certain Hallows had said something to disturb her. She seemed very taut when they were reunited. He would not have her upset. He'd tell Hallows as much when their paths next crossed.

Anne, driving behind her husband, remembered Hallows's voice. 'All those meetings your husband had with her . . . Sensible man, telling you . . .

Had there been an affair? Common sense told her that was rot. But doubt was the very devil at embroidering the worst of pictures. She tried to summon up the strong, critical, advisory tones of her father, but tonight, possibly because she was very tired, his wisdom remained out of reach.

As they made supper together, she put on a show of being bright, asking about his questions and comparing them with hers: 'Were you asked about Huey Alcott? Superintendent Hallows wondered if he smoked. I said I didn't know. So sad, dying all alone.' As Linda had, her mind chimed.

'Few of us can choose where we die.' He was lifting broccoli from a steamer into a warm dish. 'All we can hope is that it's quick.'

Linda's name slithered on to her tongue: 'Linda . . . did she die quickly? I haven't heard.' She moved away from the grill and crisping cutlets.

'Nor me.'

'And she's taken her secrets with her.' She turned to him, her voice brittle: 'That kiss . . .'

'Forget her, woman-mine.' He reached for her hand but she stepped back. 'Her kiss was a theatrical gesture. She's dead, Anne, don't raise the dead between us.'

Her fingers had begun to drum on the table. 'I wish she hadn't died. At least I could have asked her.'

'Asked her what?' he said patiently.

'If you had slept with her . . . if you were sleeping with her?'

Hawes breathed out in a controlled sigh. 'That woman was nothing to me. And you do know it.'

'Do I? I don't know what I know, right now. I hear myself, but I hear the words of others louder.' Her heart was beating faster. She was stepping into the vortex . . . swirling into semi-hysterical accusations that could eventually, after hours of needling, bring him to anger. An anger of words alone, an eruption that would frighten, silence, shake away doubt, then lead her back to tranquillity.

PART FOUR

Chapter 1

Sinclair had the appropriate reports lined up on his desk when Hallows arrived, looking grey around the eyes as if he had slept badly.

'Too early for tea, Mike?'

The kettle had begun to pipe steam. 'I'm tempted but this visit has to be particularly swift.' Hallows tugged a chair alongside Sinclair's, sank down heavily and pulled a sheet of paper from his pocket. 'I have here our detailed description of Sally Webber. I want to compare her particulars with the physical descriptions you have for Gina Hawes and *Vicky*.'

'Simplicity itself.' Sinclair turned pages of two files. 'We use a somewhat similar form.' He arranged the three forms in parallel then leant back allowing Hallows to read.

Hallows worked through the headings: Sex, Race, Age, Weight/Build, Height, Eyes, Hair, Scars/Marks . . . plus other outward physical factors before blood group and dentition. The PM forms continued with internal anatomy and physiology.

'Well?' Sinclair prompted, after too long a silence.

'Forgetting the dentition, we have details that read the same for all three names.'

'True, but the dentition can't be ignored.'

'No, not ignored *or* taken for granted.' Hallows saw a gleam enter Sinclair's sharp eyes. He went on: 'Gina Hawes had been savagely attacked with a knife, so savagely that her head had been severed. *Vicky* has no head. Like to make a medically based comment?'

Sinclair's fingers flew over the PM notes for both cases. 'Cool. Macabre,' he murmured. '*Vicky* and Gina: both bodies decapitated in exactly the same region and not a chip to the bones at the severance point.'

'How much skill would have been needed?'

'Just basic medical knowledge. In the Briers Way case, the fire would have served its purpose – smoothed out the edges, as it were.' Sinclair kicked a heel and propelled his chair from his desk. 'You'll be wanting these details presented in an instantly digestible form.'

'Yes. I'm holding an Incident Room meeting in an hour.'

With a regretting glance at the kettle, Hallows left, but his step was lighter. The route forward was at last fully mapped.

Close to nine-thirty, leaving the brothers to reflect on their lot after being picked out in the identity parade, Ferret drove to University Hospital. In her bag she had one of the vile photographs Slade had taken of Martin Falder. She hoped it could remain there, that he would talk unprompted.

He detached himself from radio headphones as she dumped a basket of fruit on his bedside locker. It nuzzled against juice, mints, books, tissues, those disconnected items considered essential for a short spell confined to bed.

He thanked her as she tugged the curtains closed then brought a chair near his pillows.

She kept her voice low: 'I've been talking to some boys: fourteen, fifteen, sixteen-year-olds. They've shared your experience.' He shut his eyes momentarily. 'They were picked up at the bus station, doped . . . I know, in detail, what happened to them. Now, the photographs-' his eyes darted to meet hers, wide with concern -'yes, we have them. It is essential we hear your story, Martin. If there are some things you'd rather keep for my sergeant, I'll arrange it.'

'I've been *trying* to forget,' he snapped in a whisper. 'I've spent four years trying to bury what happened and now you want me to unearth it – why?'

'This is how it runs. We have in custody the men responsible for picking up lads. The photographer and the house-owner are dead. One other, I believe it to be only one, is free and enjoying the profits from their activities – the same man who indulged in unnatural acts. There are videos as well as stills.'

His eyes shifted to the frame that kept bedding off his leg.

While she ached with sympathy for his embarrassment, she pushed on: 'You're an adult now, Martin. I need your help if we're to go to court. I have to find and seize all those films. I need a lot from you. As a responsible adult are you going to help me?'

Resigned, he nodded. And since he had lived the details as often as day follows night, he spoke unfalteringly: 'I was waiting for friends. A guy and I got talking. He bought Cokes. I began to feel muzzy-headed, then hot and sweaty. I was helped into a house. Bright lights, cameras. I felt detached – floating. I couldn't stop any of it, the poses, the rape. He *hurt* me.'

She thought about the appalling pity of it all: a shy youth, driven to run, not talk, driven to bottle up sordid details where they could fester and stunt living; and the agony the obscene act had heaped on the parents, left frightened, unknowing and abandoned.

She offered a short break. She heard the clink of china beyond the curtains. An orderly was bringing round hot drinks.

'What would you like? Coffee, tea, chocolate?'

His face lost some of its gravitas. 'Chocolate. Thanks.'

She fetched it with biscuits and begged a coffee for herself. She was grateful for its heat, not its thin quality. As she sipped she offered advice: 'You must tell your dad, Martin.'

'I can't.'

'He reads the papers; he knows what goes on. He's probably been nursing an accurate idea of why you ran for a long time. And he'll be looking elsewhere for blame,' she stressed. 'He'll make it easy for you. Tell him soon. You'll feel so much better when you have.'

She watched him paddling his spoon in the chocolate's dregs.

'Perhaps – when I'm ready.' He reached for the headphones: 'Is that it?'

'No. I know you've had enough, but don't start ducking now, you've done so well. I want to talk about the man who hurt you.'

His jaw set, hate coarsened pleasant features.

'Martin, square your loathing. I don't have to spell out why I have to catch him: leopards don't change spots. Did you learn his name?'

'No.'

'Never mind, just tell me what he looked like.'

'I don't know! I couldn't look round and then Slade pulled a cloth bag over my head.'

Down, deep down inside her, she could have screamed with frustration. Yet her voice betrayed nothing of this: 'I see-' she spoke gently, patiently - 'well, spend some time thinking how else you might remember him.'

Close to ten, quietly elegant Anne Hawes, dressed in a dark suit, high-necked cream silk blouse and medium-heeled shoes walked swiftly into Abbots Hill. She approached the desk sergeant: 'May I speak to Detective Superintendent Hallows?'

He rang through, but it was Kennet who appeared.

'Will I do?' His smile was intended to put her at her ease, but its root lay in sheer pleasure.

'I promised an address. Then I forgot to ring it through. Will you apologise? It's for Stella, Gina Hawes's sister.'

'Of course, though I'm sure an apology is unnecessary.' She looked uncertain, as if there could be something else to say if Hallows had been there. Or maybe she was inhibited by their surroundings – a large space with a ring of chairs screwed to the floor. On impulse he suggested: 'Have you time for a coffee? There's a café on the other side of Peel Square.'

'Yes – yes, just about.'

When seated at a corner table, with full cups in front of them, he studied her over steepled fingers. She was pale and taut, and very dark around the eyes. 'I don't mean to be ungallant, but you look tired.'

She shrugged slightly. She was not going to be offended by the truth. 'Are you married?' she asked unexpectedly.

He shook his head. A heavy wave of red-brown hair slid forward and he swept it back impatiently, highly conscious of being observed.

'Is it true -' a smile flickered -'are you quick tempered?'

'I'm better now than I used to be.'

Satisfied, she harked back: 'I'm tired simply because I didn't sleep.'

'Marriage, lack of sleep – and tempers?' he murmured, before venturing: 'Is there a connection? Have you and your husband had a row? I thought marital tiffs were supposed to clear the air.'

'I was edgy. It might have helped. Keith's very placid.'

'It takes a lot to get him going?'

'Yes.'

'So you still feel like a coiled spring?'

'A coiled spring – how perceptive of you.' She sat for some moments in silence, ironing the edge of the table cloth with her thumb.

'There was something else beside the address, wasn't there?' he prompted. 'Was that to do with the row that never was?'

'No. Superintendent Hallows asked me if Huey Alcott smoked. I didn't know, but in Sainsbury's this morning, doing an early shop, I met someone, a security guard who I thought had worked with Huey. I – I don't know whether I've been too forward but I asked him if he remembered. His name is Stan Price-' Kennet made a note -'he's retired now. He said Huey definitely didn't.'

So that had been the worry: over-stepping the mark. How many people would have been concerned enough to act? How many would have considered they might have marred an investigation? He offered peace of mind: 'No problem. You did right.' As he slotted his pen away, his eyes were on her slender hands. 'You don't smoke either, do you?' Her fingers, warming around her cup were free of nicotine stains. 'How about your husband?'

With a nagging burden disposed of, she was suddenly relaxed with him. She broke into a grin: 'Lord, no! Keith can be very impolite about tobacco.'

He found himself chuckling in response. 'So your cars don't stink. I notice these things now, you see. I've given it up. No more half empty fag-packets and matches littering my ageing Ford.'

'Ah, do I hear the crow of the converted?' She teased, then drained her cup. 'I should go, Mr Kennet. I've a patient to see shortly.'

He walked with her to the corner of Peel Square, watched her cross towards a car park and then turned back. He wondered about Hawes who evinced love: was he really so good for her, or was there something deep that encouraged an anxiety? Whatever . . . there was a vulnerability about her that demanded a hug.

So many people gathered, and yet such a silence.

In expectation the Incident Room's teams waited for Hallows to speak.

On a sharp nod to Curtis, Sinclair's promised data chart was projected in giant detail on to a wall screen. Headings: Sally Webber, Gina Hawes, *Vicky*; these against Age, Height, Weight, Colouring. Comparisons could be made at a glance.

'I'll present you with my hypothesis,' he began, his deep voice firm with certainty. 'We can argue about it when I've finished. Gina Hawes was a young woman of somewhat stern and decided views. She inherited a large sum of money which she was not disposed to share or to risk. Patience might have won her over – and our man has considerable patience – but another woman of greater charm, warmth, magnetism came on the scene, and the scales dropped heavily against Gina. But how to get rid of her yet appear blameless? An extraordinary plan was evolved. A woman of identical appearance was needed and through a friend, and Patronus, he met her. I speak, of course, of Sally Webber. Remember, only blood grouping and dental records could help us to establish the identity of a body at that time, particularly one ravaged by fire.

'Our planner was able to check blood group details in hospital medical records, they were near to hand, but teeth presented a far more difficult problem – for a while. Then he saw the matter as simplicity itself to resolve. He would simply swop heads.'

There was an extended gasp, but no one interrupted.

'I believe it was Gina Hawes who was killed in the greenhouse at the foot of her garden at Victoria Crescent. You'll recall DCI Kennet's team found a broken scalpel blade there. Her head was severed and taken to Briers Way. Sally and her friend were killed. Sally's severed head was replaced by Gina's. Jewellery was exchanged, appropriate for the woman who was supposed to have died there. I suggest an item of Sally's was taken – a shawl – and then slow fuses were set, which would transform the old house into an inferno.'

Kennet listened, saw the murderer in his mind's eye and knew Hallows was right. A knot tightened like a ligature in his chest.

'The planner-' Hallows continued -'did not have a great deal of time at this point. He took Sally's head to the hospital in a surgical-waste disposal bag. He added it to other material for incineration. Unfortunately for him, he ran into Huey Alcott on his normal security patrol. Our planner is a good talker, he could have presented logical reasons for his being there, but Alcott might have started to think about the encounter again while DI Merrison was making inquiries into the Briers Way deaths.

'Alcott had to be got off hospital property. Alcott's growing addiction to alcohol, following the death of his wife, had to be fed. Word was received that Alcott had spirits in his locker. He was dismissed. A sympathetic "friend" began supplying him with drink to ease his sorrow and disgrace, an expense that continued until Alcott's death.

'Keep in mind that Gina liked to wear Lareine underwear, not your chain-store product. The planner had already decided how to dispose of Gina's headless body. He was familiar with Jacob Bisset's domestic arrangements. He's strong, audacious, and leaving the body in an upstairs cupboard was not a problem. The killer felt certain the body would remain undisturbed for years: Bisset had sworn he would never move. That held true until he was forced out ten years later.'

Kennet should have felt elation: he was hearing a remarkable piece of exposition, a result of some damned clever thinking, but instead his imagination presented him with a nightmare that revolved round her.

Hallows was saying: 'An aside here: our planner had to think quickly when he learned that Grandfield had bought Victoria Crescent. He couldn't be sure to what degree the body would have decomposed. A fire would be the simplest answer and it wasn't likely to be noticed until it had got a good hold. And why not, at the same time, be rid of Huey Alcott? Alcott liked to sleep in quiet corners, away from others. Number 6 was not yet boarded up. The simple lock could be easily released with a few minutes of patience, and the door left on the catch. A word in Alcott's ear when he was not too sozzled to listen and he was bound to seek it out as darkness fell. As we know, Alcott perished, but one of our patrols spotted the fire earlier than had been anticipated. The mummified body, wearing pants and bra by Lareine, was untouched by flame or smoke.

'Following the then accepted death of Gina in Briers Way, the planner knew he would be an automatic suspect. He not only conceived for himself an alibi that would be difficult to disprove, he went further. He placed Sally beside the river. Sally was said to have been depressed. It would not be unreasonable to believe she could have killed and then committed suicide while tormented by guilt.

'Sally was, in every respect, a victim. She was down, not depressed. To misquote: word of her mental state was greatly exaggerated. Suggestions had been planted in minds. Fiction was accepted as fact.

'She was down because she had lost the companionship of a man for whom she had affection if not love . . . Oliver Wyland. Wyland was double dating. The second woman was Anne Howard, now Mrs Hawes. You may disagree, but I believe the planner hinted to Anne that Wyland was seeing another woman, meaning Sally. Anne told Wyland that he must choose between them. The planner's gamble paid off when Wyland dropped Sally. Sally reacted normally in such a circumstance, after all, rejection hurts.

'Our planner was only too familiar with university procedure. When a student's work dropped off due to emotional problems, Gina Hawes was always called upon to have a chat. The scene was set. When Gina said she was going to visit Sally at Briers Way, the action began.'

Hallows paused. He expected a question and it came from a DC.

'Sir, if Sally was dead, how could she have been recognized by friends, walking by the Nean?'

'Remember they were at the Riverside Inn while Sally was seen on the tow-path on the opposite bank. How do you recognize people who are some distance away from you? I suggest it's more by association. Height, build, and what they're wearing. Everyone linked a particular shawl with Sally. It was the drape of the shawl her fellow students recognized.

'Just in case any of you remain in doubt over the identity of the man I've been calling the planner, let me show you this.' He nodded to Curtis standing by the projector.

Dazzling, vibrant with colour, a poster burst on to the screen. *The Importance of Being Earnest* was being advertised with the additional proclamation: *Keith Hawes as Lady Bracknell.*

Not a voice of dissent, but a strong murmur of acceptance came from the listening officers.

Kennet said nothing. Anxiety flowed through his veins, not blood.

Hallows could feel the energy levels rising in the room. With much evidence gathering to be done, every drop of adrenalin would be needed to keep up the momentum.

'Sir-' an officer at the back of the group -'the victim, *Vicky*, was pregnant. Did that have any relevance to the crime, do you think?'

'If Hawes knew Gina was pregnant, it might have given an additional spur to his plan to get rid of her. A baby, when he was no longer in love with the mother, could have been seen as a further complication. But, to give Hawes the benefit of doubt, it was quite possible he didn't know. Only he can tell us.'

He gave them space to talk before concluding:

'We've already noted that the Leisure Centre features as Keith Hawes's alibi for Linda Thorne's death and for the Briers Way killings. You've established he would have had time when he was supposed to be swimming, to cross to The Laurels. And a woman was seen. He's not tall. In raincoat and headscarf, glimpsed at night, he could convince passing traffic. I want to know where those clothes came from and how he's disposed of them. It's the dustbins hunt!' There was an amiable and expected groan.

A WDC signalled to Hallows: 'Sir, the clothes could have been theatre gear.'

'A strong possibility. Check it out.'

The big man moved on. 'Now we'll consider ten years ago. From Merrison's time-charts you can see, against the Briers Way deaths and the sighting of Sally by the Nean, there are periods while he's supposed to be at the Leisure Centre, when Hawes is invisible. Make dummy runs, triple check, remember Hawes's defence will go all-out to shred what you have.

'Lareine. Get some statistics. How many women of Gina's age would be likely to have been wearing . . . You know!

'We need to take a hard look at Hawes's financial arrangements, but that will have to wait till we charge him. Keeping Alcott in booze must have cost a packet. We'll need proof of a ten year commitment.

'However, before we can become more than an irritant to Hawes, we have to get DNA confirmation that *Vicky* is in fact Gina. Gina's twin sister had a child. I want Gina's niece found. If we hit a blank, we'll contact Gina's sister, Stella.'

'Sir?' It was the WDC again. 'Why did Hawes kill Linda Thorne? There must have been more to it than protecting his friends.'

It was a question common to them all. The noise level dropped.

'Hawes has an Achilles heel – his wife.'

'His wife!' Kennet's mind echoed.

'Anne, a sensitive woman, admits to a fault: the evil of doubt. Hawes would do his utmost to protect what was special to them. He adores her beyond-' he paused, wondering how this would be received -'life itself.' There was silence and then a grunt of acceptance from the hard-nosed crowd. 'I imagine he fell in love with her at their first meeting, when Oliver Wyland brought her to Victoria Crescent.

'It would be useful to know how she came to work at the hospital. Did Hawes manoeuvre so that staff vacancies were brought to her attention? Did he contrive to have her canvassed by other staff? Hawes couldn't act himself, not as a widower stricken with grief. Coming to know Hawes in here-' he tapped his head -'I wouldn't be at all surprised.

'As you're all aware, I've put Dr Wyland through the mill. I'm certain now that he's been an innocent in all this deception. He's been sent on his way with much to think about: could be he's grappling with his own suspicions. He was genuinely fond of Sally, and Hawes has been a close, long-standing friend. Facing the ultimate truth is going to bring him a lot of grief.

'While you're chasing evidence, I intend to have a series of talks with Mr Hawes. I don't expect any result. My purpose is underhand. The only pressure likely to rattle him will come inadvertently from Mrs Hawes.' Hallows's roving gaze found Kennet. Fury stained his face. 'When she begins to add two and two. When she begins to question.'

Hallows waived reflecting on the reason for Kennet's anger. Instead he opined: 'I don't believe – I don't think Mrs Hawes will be in danger from her husband.'

Kennet doubted: felt ice expand in his gut.

Keith Hawes was asked to come to Abbots Hill after lunch.

He was amiable as usual, except for two grumbles. He reminded Hallows mildly that his patients would not be pleased to have appointments changed. The second complaint was more forceful. He reproached Hallows for unsettling Anne on the previous evening.

Curtis awarded Hallows a mental tick as Hallows made appropriate apologies.

The questioning centred on the evening Linda Thorne had died.

Two hours later, they parted company.

Returning to the Fitness Centre, Hawes found Anne anxiously wanting to know why he had been called and what he had been asked.

'Just routine questions about our swimming. Nothing to worry about, woman-mine. Let's have tea.' Slapping hands together enthusiatically, he ran up stairs to their sitting room.

'Why you?' she asked when the door was closed.

'Well, having discarded Oliver, it had to be my turn or Josh's. Obviously Josh is to be last.' He smoothed the frown from her brow with an affectionate finger. 'Don't worry, and don't be surprised if they want to see me again, that's routine too. Hallows and Merrison are bound to work in a similar manner.'

'Merrison? But he was involved with Gina's death, why mention him?'

'Because, having been subjected to Merrison's attention, I feel I know them all. Have we any biscuits? Talking has made me darned hungry.'

Ninety minutes later, Hallows and Curtis walked through the doors of the Fitness Centre.

Anne answered the receptionist's call, coming forward looking utterly perplexed. 'You've only just parted, Mr Hallows. Keith's with a patient right now.'

'We can wait.' Hallows smiled. The smile was sincere. His words, however, would be of a subversive nature.

Once in the sitting room with the door firmly shut, she said: 'Now, what is this all about?'

'It's important I find out who murdered Linda Thorne. Wouldn't you agree?'

'Most certainly! But why talk to Keith? He was with Josh and Oliver for the entire evening.'

'It's a matter of elimination. Dr Wyland is in the clear, now it's your husband's turn. I imagine he suggested that?' His dense brow arched expectantly.

'Yes. But it does seem a waste of time to me. What about this woman the papers were describing. Shouldn't you be hunting for her?'

'Oh, we are,' Hallows confirmed strongly. 'It's a pity she was only glimpsed. We have little to go on. Someone of your, or your husband's height.' The emphasis he had placed on husband had been subtle, sufficient to give a slight echo when she re-examined their entire conversation later. 'Thank you for Stella's address, by the way. I'm hoping I won't need to get in touch. There's a chance we can confirm identification from another source.'

Her eyes lit with curiosity: 'Have I missed something? Identification?'

'I'm sorry, my fault. I'd assumed you knew we found a woman's body in number 6 Victoria Crescent.'

Her mouth opened with confusion: 'But you found a *man* at that house. Huey Alcott.'

'True. But upstairs in a cupboard were the mummified remains of a young woman.' He laid out facts, starkly, sparing her nothing. 'She had been folded into the cupboard like a discarded doll. Left there, almost naked, ten years ago. She was ten weeks pregnant – and her head had been skilfully removed.'

'Oh!' Anne started away clutching her arms in an eruption of shudders. 'That's awful. Horrible!'

'Indeed it is. I'm facing a cluster of deaths: most certainly we have an abominable business.' A woman mutilated and a baby dead: how those words would chime in her mind. And he tasted guilt, she had such a capacity to empathize. Emotionally, she appeared as fragile as a paper boat. 'So you do understand why I must leave no stone unturned.'

'Yes,' she said distantly. 'What an open invitation to bad dreams.'

'I see I've been very clumsy. Believe me, Mrs Hawes, it doesn't please me to upset you.'

Keith Hawes strolled into the sitting room with an easy assurance, and sent Anne away with a kiss on the cheek. He pointed to chairs for the detectives and took one himself, sinking in to it to tweak his trouser creases and cross his legs. He arched an eyebrow at Hallows as if signalling that the interview could begin.

During the next two hours, Hawes remained unquestionably relaxed.

Hallows focused initially on the likeness between Gina and Sally, and on Wyland's affair with Sally. In context, Hallows let drop that the woman found in Bisset's house had been pregnant. The big man watched Hawes keenly.

'That's very sad, Superintendent.' Hawes didn't flicker an eye. 'Quite dreadful, in fact.'

Hallows remained left in the dark wondering if Hawes had been surprised or not. He would return to the pregnancy when Hawes was eventually charged.

The questioning progressed: his relationship with Linda, his life at Victoria Crescent, his attitude to Gina's new wealth, how he met Sally, the night of the fire . . . And the answers flowed with no deviation from previous statements.

Curtis had listened to many a liar, but with Hawes it was different. Hawes spoke with such consummate sincerity, it was as if he actually believed every word he voiced. And hard-headed Curtis found himself unexpectedly spooked.

'I'm afraid, Mr Hawes,' Hallows was winding up, 'I'll have to trouble you again. I'd like you to attend Abbots Hill tomorrow morning just to tie a few more ends.'

Hawes clicked his tongue in a rebuke as he moved out of his chair with the soft agility of a gymnast. 'I have patients booked with me for tomorrow, Mr Hallows. Is it really imperative? The evening would be better.'

'The morning, Mr Hawes,' Hallows repeated.

For the first time Hawes frowned. 'Oh, well. Short notice though to find a locum.' He smiled again. 'So, I'll see you tomorrow.'

Unlike Wyland, Hawes did not speak of bringing his solicitor.

DS Rob Curtis was unusually quiet as he drove from the Fitness Centre.

He took the main road. It was congested but its many traffic lights regulated the flow.

He had listened to Hawes's cheerful, forgiving view of Linda, of her joining him for lunch at the Mill and of her breezing up to him and Anne at the Latimer. There was so much about meals coming from these interviews.

Linda had eaten with Oliver Wyland. She had eaten with Neville Howard too. Well, it was part of the pattern. She had no interest in cooking. He had seen for himself the limitations of her larder. She'd had no use for an oven . . . an *oven*.

'Jeeze!' Curtis hit the brakes. The car pitched to a halt as the lights changed.

'Watch it!' Hallows barked.

'God, guv! I know how he did it.'

'Did what?' Hallows said with an icy tolerance.

'Hawes frightened the shit out of Linda with a spray-can of oven cleaner.'

Hallows screwed around, scowling into Curtis's face: 'Go on.'

'She didn't have an oven, but I found a full can in her flat. You don't use oven cleaner on a microwave.'

There was a blare of a horn. The lights had changed. Curtis gathered himself and moved off. 'I can see it plain as bloody daylight. When Linda opened her front door, he had the can levelled at her eyes.'

A harsh suck of air passed through Hallows's teeth.

Curtis anticipated him. 'I'll have it checked for prints. His won't be on it, but I bet my pension hers will.'

At Abbots Hill, Kennet had been chafing to speak to Hallows. They coincided in the Gents.

As Hallows concluded washing, Kennet rubbed soap into his hands with a furious energy. 'I hope you're right about Hawes not harming his wife.' He glared at Hallows in the mirror. 'I'm worried spitless.'

'How do you think I feel?' Hallows's heavy jowled reflection scowled back. 'But what choice do we have? None, none at all.' He snapped on the metal wall drier and raised his voice above the drone. 'As clever bastards go, Hawes is above average. Collecting enough hard evidence for one prosecution, be it Linda, Gina, Sally or Alcott, is going to push us to the limit.' The drier cut off. His volume dropped. 'Anne Hawes is the only one who'll get us in with any kind of a chance.'

Kennet shook his wet hands like a dog with a rat. 'I still think it's a hell of a risk . . .'

The outer door banged closed behind Hallows's departing back.

'*Damnation!*' Kennet roared. He slammed out, striking the dryer with a mighty sideways thud.

It shuddered, yawed, then squealed against the tiled wall as it dropped from sheared screws to swing gratingly from its wire.

Hallows found a note on his desk written on personal paper. He read:

The Lilly brothers might as well be sitting in a vacuum: I hear nothing. We'll see what tomorrow brings. Liz.

He had a lurch of conscience. This communication had very little to do with the brothers. Here was a heavy hint: *remember me?* He owed Liz information about Wyland.

He rang her office. Scott answered.

'She's gone home, sir. Do you want her back?'

'No, no, it'll keep.' But it wouldn't. He abandoned his desk and drove to Quay House where a light glowed behind closed curtains in her sitting room.

He pressed the security button: 'Liz, it's Mike Hallows. Got ten minutes and a beer?'

'Yes, to both.'

He sank wearily into the largest of her easy chairs and filled it. With the beer in his hand and the first sip taken, he gave her a summary of the Incident Room meeting. 'Hawes is in the frame. Oliver Wyland admitted to being an idiot when young, but we've all been down a similar road at a similar age.' His amiable glance dared her to disagree. 'But I've no reason to think he hasn't been principled in recent years.' He saw a fleeting glower. 'It's called maturity. So what's he done to offend?'

'That's private.'

'OK, but more recently you got uptight over something?'

She didn't have to tell him, but tonight they were friends not colleagues. She said: 'There's a poem – damned if I'll recite the pertinent three lines to you, they're personal. Oliver would quote them! But when you had him in for questioning, I had a compulsion to know the fourth. It runs: *In his eyes foreknowledge of death.* It's now I remember that Oliver originally linked the poem with Hawes, quite innocently. Reading those words when Oliver was under suspicion, well – I was rattled.'

'An acceptable reaction.' There was something about his mouth that suggested a smile. He took a swallow of beer and then added pointedly: 'If you're keeping in your heart a *blind desire*.'

'You know it,' she accused.

'Isla reads poetry as an escape from teeth.' The smile, so rarely seen, came out.

Chapter 2

Frank Lilly yawned ostentatiously as Ferret, followed by Scott, walked into the interview room.

Scott showed new, sealed tapes to Frank and his solicitor, Percy Judd, then removed their wrappers and slotted both into the recorder.

Ferret, meanwhile, pulled out a chair, smiled sweetly at Mr Judd, saccharinely at Frank and unhurriedly made herself comfortable.

'Interview commencing at-' Scott glanced at the clock -'nine-thirty a.m. Those present . . .'

Ferret only half listened while she studied Frank Lilly's face. It was an empty page. His tongue chased a scrap of late breakfast around his teeth, then he picked at a molar with an irregular, yellow finger-nail. His hand, when it dropped back on the table top, caught her attention. It had a slight tremor – very slight – that had not been there before. She felt a flutter of excitement.

'Morning Frank. Missing William?' she began brightly. 'Not a bad day outside. There's a slight breeze. It's dry, not particularly cold, sun's trying its best to come through from a light cloud covering . . .'

'Spare me the weather forecast,' he drawled lazily.

'Oh, I thought you'd like to know what you're missing. It'll be a long time till you feel rain on your face again. You'll be a really old man. As to number of years . . . well, judges are being urged to get tougher. Oh, yes, you'll probably be bald, crook-backed and in need of a walking stick, when you're finally released.'

He said nothing. His almost closed eyes suggested he had left home.

From his sour mask of a face her eyes slid to his hand. It continued to tremble.

She said: 'Can't see why you want to be noble. The guy you're covering for won't care a toss about you once you're banged away. Let me guess: he's promised you money for silence. Well, he's not going to invest it, not for you. While it's providing a healthy monthly return for him, you'll be slopping-out on an even more regular basis. And when you do emerge again on to our traffic-locked streets, your paymaster will have vanished. There'll be no chance of breathing down his neck, begging for what was yours.' She sighed: 'Oh, Frank. it's sad, tough, but there, that's human nature. No loyalty, you see. No guarantee. People will always let you down.'

The other hand had joined its partner. Frank's coarse-skinned fingers had linked and right thumb plucked, trembling, at left.

She reached into her trouser pocket and withdrew a folded sheet of paper. 'I've made a draft list. Thought you'd like a reminder of what you're going to go down for.' She laid it between them, smoothing it open. 'A4, and covered closely with my tolerable writing. *And* it continues on the other side.' She turned it over briefly.

'I'll read it through. Ready? Procuring boys for pornographic films and immoral acts: they're queuing up to tell the judge. Doing over Stan Parkin for the purpose of theft. He's much better. Did you know? Feeling more than a little piqued too, since he's been forced to neglect his business.'

Frank Lilly opened his mouth as if about to speak and then thought better of it.

Any misplaced word about Parkin could drop him right in it. The papers had given no details of the beating or theft.

She went on: 'Next, setting fire to photographic premises at Hillington, namely, ViewPoint, with the intention of killing Slade. You were seen! Right place, right time, no argument. We can connect you with Slade at Victoria Crescent, and Devin Slade died. You can't get more final than that.'

Acting out tedium, Frank Lilly stretched his back then resumed a slouch. He seemed unaware of his mobile thumbs.

'What, not bored, Mr Lilly? Prison's boring: year, after year, after year, doing nothing. Shall I move on to your criminal zenith? I speak of Jacob Bisset. Bisset, who you hauled out of bed and smothered with a pillow. He put up a struggle, didn't he? Bet you hadn't bargained for that. You went tip-toeing across his carpet in your stockinged feet to steal his album, and then you were into a fight. We've got some excellent photographs of your scratches. You left a good portion of yourself embedded under his nails. Makes for very convincing evidence.' She wondered if he was holding his breath: his thumbs were still, standing up like two coat pegs. 'You'll know what I'm getting at, I'm sure, as you're a man who keeps abreast of science. The DNA results are through, Frank. You're matched perfectly. You're tied to Bisset's death more securely than a bungee jumper likes to be tethered.'

She was certain: his sallow skin had paled.

She said: 'Who sent you to steal Bisset's album, Frank? Who made sure the window was unlocked? You and William have played his errand boys for years: yes? And then everything started getting very complicated. Are you really prepared to carry all the blame? And for what? Empty promises?'

She fixed him with a pitying stare, then suddenly stood.

It was to his obvious surprise. In a revealing moment a wave of confusion crossed his face.

'I have a hospital call to make.' Would he think, Parkin, and sweat anxiety? 'We'll have another talk this afternoon.'

In fact Ferret was to visit Martin Falder.

Martin lay on top of his hospital bed fully dressed apart from his trainers, the leg of his jeans split to above the knee to allow for a thick dressing.

'So they're about to throw you out,' she said. 'Great feeling, isn't it? Here, have these. I think hospitals encourage hunger.' She dropped a large bag of mini Mars on to his stomach.

'Voice of experience?' He watched her nod. 'Breakfast was hours ago.' He ripped the bag open. 'Want one?'

'You bet.' Learning that Oliver Wyland was no longer under suspicion had done wonders for her appetite, if not for Oliver himself. He had rung her as she was leaving home.

'Read my letter, Liz?'

'Yes.'

'Can we meet then?'

'No. Don't think of taking a step near me for at least a year.'

'Oh, come on, Liz. How else am I to say sorry.'

'That can be an employment for your mind over the next twelve months.'

Now, perching on Martin's bed, she bit fiercely into the chocolate. Contrary to her recalled irritation, Martin looked gleeful. 'I presume you're going home with your dad. You'll meet Rosie. She's a real chatter box.' She paused, made a ball of the Mars wrapper and pushed it into her jacket pocket. 'You know why I've come, what I'm hoping for?'

'You're out of luck, Miss Ireton. Can't remember anything useful about the man. Not a thing.' He met her eyes squarely.

'OK,' she said. 'I'm off. See you sometime at your dad's.' Martin Falder, she decided, was too sensitive to make a successful liar.

She ran into Reg by the lifts. He was wearing a grin wider than any clowns, and she laughed outright. 'Your face speaks volumes. Your son's going to be spoilt rotten.'

'Why not? We've got some years to catch up on.'

'Are you dumping work for a few days?'

'Yep. Brooke House is going on nicely. I can take time off. Not many small jobs on at the moment either. I'll call on Councillor B. when we leave here. He won't sulk at a small delay.'

His feet were shifting in a happy, impatient dance.

'Oh, get on!' She chuckled, dismissing him.

Ferret and Scott stood in the interview block corridor, locked in independent thought.

The Lilly brothers, feeling the chill of betrayal, had sneezed up a name.

'Are they stirring up trouble, do you think?' she said at last. 'If we go about this the wrong way and he's in the clear . . .'

'. . . he'd let the press have us for dinner.'

She stared at the floor in a sort of limbo induced by doubt and surprise.

'There's means and opportunity,' Scott said. 'He was visiting Green Vale with other councillors on the afternoon of the day Bisset died. He could have dropped in on Bisset: pulled the curtains, tampered with the window.'

Her mind was beginning to click back into gear. 'Yes . . .' Memories surfaced with a zip of energy. 'Slade enjoyed a very private joke. He used the word putto.'

'Well, he's plump enough, but if he's our man, an angel?'

'Perhaps that's what tickled Devin Slade's humour.' She had started to walk – quickly – almost running. 'Fix the search warrant!'

*

Lester Barraclough seethed indignation and invited them in.

'The Lilly brothers said that! They accuse me of dealing in pornographic videos. This is absolutely preposterous. What if word got out? I'm up for re-election next May. And now you have to search?'

'Once an allegation has been made . . . Be assured we'll be extremely discreet.'

He began to mellow. 'Let's have it done with then. Not your fault, I know. You're in a difficult position.'

'Thank you for seeing it that way. Might I suggest we go in your kitchen, it'll be quieter there? My officers will leave it till last. You might like some tea. While we wait for the kettle to boil you can tell me what you know of the Lilly brothers.'

He favoured the idea of tea. As she closed the kitchen door her team were flowing into the old property.

Barraclough had gained his second wind and he talked plentifully of his occasional dealings with Frank and William Lilly.

The time arrived to vacate the kitchen for the conservatory. 'Ghastly mess still,' he murmured. 'My builder, Falder, dropped by this morning explaining a delay. His prodigal son has returned. The young man had a nasty accident, though this morning he made light of it. Falder's very happy. There was a lot of laughter.'

'Sir-' a DC stepped forward -'I've made a list of your video film library. Would you check the items and then sign. We'll return them as soon as we can.'

'No rush, I'll be too busy to view this week. Council business. I'm on a number of committees.'

Ferret's toes curled. Barraclough sounded overweeningly self satisfied. She said: 'We'll have to take your computer and disks as well.'

'I can manage, Chief Inspector. I've only advanced a few steps from the quill. Just use it for writing letters.'

She left him with the DC while she made her own tour of the tiny house. It was a man's home, no frills and flowers. Furniture was at a minimum: hand crafted and expensive. He owned a modest number of clothes, also expensive. There was little hung on the jasmin-white walls: two mirrors, three oil paintings of equestrian events and a Rowlandson's print, a caricature of Prinny out for a canter with a dozen other stylish bucks.

She concentrated on the cupboard, occupying part of the sloping roof space, that had been converted into an office. His computer had already been removed. On a shelf above the small desk were three box-files filled with receipted bills, bank statements and associated correspondence. At Abbots Hill these would be checked concurrently with a full financial investigation. In the top drawer of the desk she found his house insurance policy, up for renewal, and new bills for fuel oil and electricity. There was a letter from a Helenborough garage reminding him that his BMW was due for its service. The middle drawer contained solely council related papers. She flicked through them and moved on. In the bottom drawer were personal effects: photographs, two of Barraclough as a boy, the rest were press shots of him attending civic occasions. Also a copy of his will, birth certificate, his parents marriage lines, his passport and a yellowing degree certificate in public administration. That was all.

She returned to Barraclough: 'We're leaving now, sir. Thank you for your cooperation.'

He spread his plump hands in an open gesture of acceptance.

At the front door they saw the last of her team drive away as Barraclough's cleaning woman came through the gate. Moving towards Scott's car, Ferret's and the woman's paths crossed.

The woman was tugging off her jacket and smoothing her apron.

'Not a bad day,' Ferret said brightly, falling back on the banal.

'No wind to dry me washing. Just as well with him at it.' The woman's head jerked towards the noisily working, but invisible woodsman. 'Bonfires all the time: smelly things. Get some wind and he'll send us all up.'

Ferret ducked further conversation and dived into the car.

At Abbots Hill video players were being set up *en bloc* in a recreation room. By late afternoon the tedious job of checking Barraclough's video library had begun. One joker turned his sound up for a few seconds. The strains of *The hills are alive* . . . drifted along the corridor to where finance officers had started to calculate returns on Barraclough's hefty portfolio of stocks & shares.

Chapter 3

Two days had passed and Barraclough had heard nothing from Abbots Hill yet, which was as he expected. The arrival of the police had not unduly concerned him. He had earlier moved damning evidence from the house.

He had always been careful, left nothing committed to paper, and addresses which DCI Ireton would assuredly exchange her eye teeth for were well beyond her ken. Moving money had never been difficult either: the dead letter box at his disposal saw notes and cash flowing as blamelessly as any high street bank.

The Lilly's talk would be regarded as floundering spite. Slade would have been the only weak link and Slade was dead.

Barraclough placed a spark guard in front of the settling embers of his log fire. The wind was getting up as forecast, so it would be expedient to execute the final act this evening.

He pulled on the dark boiler suit he had bought that afternoon. Clothes for all occasions, he murmured to himself. Later it would be formal wear appropriate for his Planning sub-committee's meeting.

Making himself comfortable at his kitchen table, he began to separate sheets of newspaper, rolling some into spills and crumpling others.

Keith Hawes had spent more time at Abbots Hill during the last two days than he had at the Fitness Centre. While he, however, remained apparently unperturbed, Anne was not so blessed. While she waited for Keith to read and sign his latest statement, Hallows would appear and treat her to one of his chats.

She liked Hallows: it was not what he said at the time or the manner of his saying it, it was the after-thoughts that he provoked that were the problem. He would trigger analyses.

This evening, matching the speed of her car to her husband's as he led the way home, she moved from thinking of Linda Thorne's intrusion into her marriage to looking at the nature of the marriage itself.

Keith idolized and indulged her, yet such infatuation was both wonderful and suffocating. With everything being done for her and with her she had forfeited every shred of independence.

Unlike his, her passion was not all consuming. She loved him because she was loved. And while she had blossomed from his affection, she recognized she would thrive in response to any sincere warmth of feeling. It went with her being somewhat insecure.

This devotion of Keith's – what had she done to earn it? Absolutely nothing. She was a very unexceptional woman. She had reasonable but unremarkable looks that could be enhanced by a good dress sense and she was hard-working, cheerful and sympathetic to others' needs. Nothing unique here, thousands of people had the same qualities.

She was as ordinary, and with all the same values, as DCI Kennet. He had his faults – his temper, and his good points – consideration, and wonderful brown eyes when he let you see them.

What did one look for in choosing a partner? She ranked tender affection, friendship and loyalty as essentials ingredients.

Loyalty? her mind repeated, and she sensed Hallows pushing her to define. Devotedness: Keith was devoted to her. Reliability: he had that reputation. Steadfastness: when he set his mind to a task he would see it through. Trustworthiness . . . Her mind locked on Linda Thorne. Doubt, the devil that dogged her was there again.

She had tailed Keith through Roxleigh and into Witley Lane. He slowed and entered their drive to park close to the garage. He would put his car away after they had eaten. Hers would have to remain outside until the woodsman had taken his tools from her garage.

She stepped out and immediately felt the wind. Dry leaves skipped against her legs. Her skirt ballooned. A huge beech chafed and tapped its thinnest topmost branches. She looked up, but could see nothing just now of its crown. Scurrying clouds were playing hide-and-seek with the moon.

She caught up with Keith as he crossed to the front door, the recurring question on her lips.

'What did Superintendent Hallows talk over this time?'

Hawes slid his key into the lock. 'It was mostly about Sally Webber.'

'So what exactly did he ask?' Instantly she regretted pressing him. He was very tired. A low hall lamp accented every line of fatigue on his face.

'Give it a rest, darling,' he said, rather more forcefully than usual. 'Let's forget Hallows for this evening.'

'Difficult -' she attempted some humour -'when we've seen so much of him. He's as good as living with us. I'll get changed,' she added, shrugging off her coat.

While she entered their bedroom and pushed the door to, Hawes made the rounds downstairs. He pulled curtains, turned on lights and then ambled after her to take a shower.

He paused opposite their bedroom door and sagged against the wall:

'Anne, shall we have supper on a tray tonight? I'm not particularly hungry, just feel like crashing out in front of the TV.'

'Yes. Poached egg, salad . . .?' she called back.

'That's fine. I'm presuming Hallows will leave us alone for what remains of this evening,' he said facetiously, but she noted an unusual sharpness which made her pause in belting her trousers. 'He and I are sounding like a couple of parrots, we've repeated ourselves so many times.'

'A parrot . . . yes.' A polo shirt replaced her cream silk blouse. She pushed high heeled shoes into the wardrobe and slipped on loafers. 'I hear the same things too. He asked several times about Sally's build, her similarity to Gina. Then he mentioned her blood group.'

With the tip of his toe he nudged open the bedroom door: 'What about her blood group?'

'If known at the hospital how accessible would it have been?'

'And what did you say?'

She skimmed a comb through her hair: 'I said anyone working there could have looked it up.'

'Yes, anyone,' he echoed.

She made a humorous grimace: 'Well, you would have had no cause to.'

'Certainly not.'

Something of his tone made her look at him more intently. 'So why did he ask, Keith?'

He strolled into the room. 'No idea. What else did he say?'

'Oh, he spoke about Patronus and the play. He hoped the tickets were selling well.'

'They are. Was he hinting he'd like some?'

'Maybe. He was interested in the amount of effort that's put in by the drama group. He wondered if you took the part of a woman under duress – friendly duress, of course.' She chuckled.

Hawes came forward and trailed a casual finger along her cheek. 'Sally, then the play – what else has been said?'

'He always speaks of Linda. Tonight he started talking about dry cleaning.'

'How rum!' He laughed, but his eyes showed no amusement.

Her mind was elsewhere for a moment: she had tossed her handbag on to the bed. She must tidy it away. She carried on: 'Dry cleaning in connection with smoking. He said his clothes picked up the smell at work. His wife complained.' A rough nail bothered her and she took a file from her dressing table drawer. 'He said attending the scene of house fires always left a taint that was equally disagreeable.'

'As do bonfires.' Hawes peeked through the curtains to see theirs. From the edge of the copse, the faintest glow marked the fire's dying embers.

'But they're not the same.' She put the file away.

He turned to confront her: 'Yes, they are.'

'No,' she smiled, 'I remember last time, when I took your coat and suit to the cleaners just before our house-warming, they didn't smell of Lucy's Guy Fawkes fire, as you grumbled. They smelt sooty, acrid, as if you'd been . . .' She heard herself. She *heard* herself. Her mouth dried: 'Keith . . .?'

'Yes?'

'Huey Alcott.' His eyes were strange to her: she was reminded of a hawk.

'What about him?'

'He died in a house fire.'

'Apparently.'

'You were late home.'

'I often am. Tom Wheaton had a late appointment.'

'Not so late against the time you got home.'

He spoke quietly as if they were discussing a time to eat: 'When did you start checking my working hours?'

Ice was forming in the pit of her stomach, but she went on. She required the truth. 'After you received the tie from Linda Thorne. That's when I started worrying that, after all, you might have been seeing her. And then I remembered when your clothes had carried the smell of smoke. Did you go to Victoria Crescent to meet Huey Alcott? Had you been giving him money?'

'Now and then.'

'Was the house alight, Keith, when you arrived? Was it? Superintendent Hallows keeps on about Huey smoking and that a smoker needs matches. He's hinting at an arsonist – an arsonist needs matches.'

'Undoubtedly,' he said coolly. 'So where are you taking us?'

'Matches . . .' she murmured. 'I found matches.'

Quite suddenly, his hand whipped forward and closed around her arm: '*Where?*' he hissed.

'You're hurting!' she yelped. He slackened his grip a mite and she continued breathlessly, 'The night you took Josh his invitation card. I was looking for my glove and I found a box under my seat in the car.'

'I thought I'd looked everywhere for it.' He frowned. 'Where is it now?'

'In my bag.'

Walking her to the bed, he took the bag with his free hand and shook out the contents. The almost full box plopped on to the quilt. 'You don't want me to go to prison, do you, Anne?' He picked it up and rattled it. 'A shameful piece of carelessness. This is the only thing that will send me there.'

She forced an even tone: 'You did kill Huey.'

'No. According to the inquest, he died of smoke inhalation.' He paused. 'Am I still hurting your arm? Sorry, woman-mine.' And he slackened his hold further. 'I'll tell you the truth, Anne. You're my love and you can be my confessor, the keeper of secrets. The fire was necessary. I had to get rid of Gina, you see. There was a risk that too much of her remained.'

'*Gina!* That wasn't Gina they found?'

'Yes it was. Did you think it was Sally?'

'You-' she choked revulsion -'you cut off *your wife's* head!'

'I had to. I had to fool them.'

'But *why* kill her?'

'I wanted to start the Fitness Centre. With time she would have come round, but then I met you. You haunted my every thought, woman-mine. Loving you brought a sudden, wonderful clarity of vision. It became obvious, what I had to do.' With his free hand he lifted hers, turning it gently to kiss her palm. 'My love, I have made you happy, haven't I?'

She began to cry. Huge tears spilled slowly down her frozen face.

'Oh, woman-mine, please don't,' he begged and letting go her arm, he reached into his pocket for a handkerchief.

With the pressure removed, she came to life. Driven by primal terror she slammed the door on him, pelted down stairs and dashed from the house.

He was fit and he was fast.

That knowledge spurred her forward, skidding across the loose stones of the drive.

With no keys for the cars she headed past them into the wood.

She heard the assured thud of Keith's feet as he met the gravel. She would never reach Barraclough's cottage. Ahead was the stable. The bonfire blazed momentarily and she saw the door was open. With an explosion of energy, she stretched the distance between them and dived inside. Immediately she was in the midst of a thicket of furniture. Dropping to her knees, she slithered between table legs and chairs, crawling into their heart.

The rough floor vibrated. He had arrived at the door. Crushing her arm across her mouth, she muted gasps for air and became transfixed.

A match was struck . . . those same fearful matches. 'Where are you, woman-mine? Anne? I won't hurt you, my love. I wouldn't have anyone hurt you, darling. Linda Thorne was giving you pain. I couldn't allow that.'

The match fluttered and died.

She was no longer anchored by terror. Such fear could not be indulged. An uncluttered basic instinct to survive mattered now. She had to get out.

Those seconds of light had helped. She now had some idea of what was around her. She had seen a route to the front wall. Once there she could feel her way along a line of iron hay-baskets and the rough brickwork to the door. But would he come in a little way, giving her space to make a final dash?

A second match blazed and then a third. He began to inch in, moving towards a less tangled corner. There was a clatter. A small cascade of video cassettes landed by his feet.

He kicked them aside, the match died and she began to slide forward.

Another match burned.

She froze, committing to memory where she was. There was a pile of scrunched newspaper to her right. She glimpsed *Victoria Crescent Fire* ... and felt a wave of nausea.

In the fluttering light he soft-crooned her name, coaxing her to come out.

The match faded and in the darkness she slithered on, terrified of brushing against rustling paper.

'Anne, come out, my love ...'

Light again. She could see he had moved down a narrow corridor of furniture. Shortly that route would be blocked. He would have to turn – return to the door.

The flame shivered in a sudden draught and vanished. Snaking forward, her hand met the wall. Listening for the rasp of the next match, she eased upright. An iron basket, prickly with stale hay, jutted into her path. She traced its rim, then almost yelled as her fingers stubbed against something large and hard.

Unexpectedly she heard his louder breathing. Horrified she realised he had already moved back towards the door.

She heard the rattle of a match, the box closing ... Petrified of being seen, she grasped the heavy object.

As brilliance flared, she struck at him.

Hawes lost balance. Furniture parted, then closed, as he began a slow backward fall. The light died as he grasped wildly at things to stop himself, bringing down an avalanche of video cassettes.

Anne ran out of the building to a rolling clatter of noise. She aimed for the lane. At the drive's edge, she realized she still carried the weapon and flung it away.

Opposite was the bridle path to the centre of the village.

As she raced and tripped over ruts through the tunnel of bare trees the moon emerged to light her remaining way.

She could have slowed. As Keith Hawes fell, his head had struck the corner of a log-box. Out cold, he lay buried beneath toppled furniture and video tapes.

Barraclough opened his back door and listened. He wondered for a moment if he could hear someone running on the road, but it lasted so short a time he dismissed it as a trick of the wind in the trees. Holding a small torch and carrying a cardboard box containing candles, wood wool and firelighters, he crossed into Hawes's wood.

This was his second visit to the stables. Earlier he had distributed little mounds of kindling paper.

Once inside he worked quickly. By the time the candles had burned down to light the paper, wood wool and then the firelighters, he would be arriving in Helenborough.

Having seen that each candle was burning bravely, he closed the stable door and quietly lowered the locking bar.

There was one final thing to be done before he left for the council meeting. He dropped thin twigs on to the hot embers of the woodsman's fire, then added thicker material as they caught. With a strong wind blowing, capable of carrying sparks, it provided an obvious reason for the stable to have caught fire.

By his car, he tugged off his boiler suit, rolled it and sealed it in a plastic bag. He would lose the suit in a dustbin in town.

Gasping for air, Anne collapsed into Oliver Wyland's arms as he opened his front door.

'My God, Anne! What's happened?' He lifted her into a chair, hardly recognizing her with her filthy clothes and ruddy tormented face.

She was struggling to stand.

'Stay put,' he ordered. 'Get your breath.'

'No!' Her voice rasped from exertion as she grabbed at him and tugged herself upright. 'I have to see Superintendent Hallows *now!* '

The need for haste spared Wyland from asking questions where he feared the answers. In three minutes his Citroën was in Deep Lane, his speed reckless, his finger on and off the horn, warning.

Four miles beyond Roxleigh he scudded to the left and braked in a lay-by. She was shuddering with an arctic cold that crossed the divide to touch him.

'What ha . . . ve you st . . . opped for?'

'You're in shock: if you shiver much harder you'll fragment.' He lunged for something on the back seat, found a huge car rug and immediately began wrapping her in it.

Kennet forgot his jacket. He sprang down stairs in his shirt sleeves, pounded along the corridor and yelled for a DC to follow.

As he ran into the front lobby his heart gave a hideous lurch. Anne was swathed in an immense tartan rug, her hair was wild, her eyes huge and black, her face a greenish-ivory and streaked with dirt. She sat clutching at the rug and leaning into Wyland.

A grimace from Wyland conveyed his ignorance of what had happened.

'Mrs Hawes?' Kennet bent, then dropped on to one knee. He put a hand on trembling icy fingers, then lifted her chin. Her skin was so translucent she might have been bled dry. 'I'll get a doctor!' He turned to direct the DC.

'*No !*' Her voice exploded.

He swung back.

'I've n . . . no physical injury.' Mindful of his extreme tension, she forced speech through violently chattering teeth. 'I un . . . under . . . stand shock. Just get Mmm . . . Mr Hallows and bring . . . me t . . . ea, hot, hot tea.'

He brought his face close to hers: 'Anne-' fiercely worried, he didn't care that her first name flew free -'no bruises, cuts, lumps or broken bones?'

'None.'

'OK!' To the DC he said: 'Get Hallows. Then tea to Room 2.'

To Anne he said: 'Are you too wobbly to walk? There's a reception room close by with an easy chair.'

'I'll get there.' Letting go of the rug, she fastened on to his offered arm and stood.

The coldness of that slim hand penetrated his shirt sharp as a burn. He was branded for life.

Kennet allowed her just time to sink into the chair: 'I have to ask now, did you flee because your husband confessed to a crime?'

'Yes.'

His mind racing, he dashed away. What was Hawes likely to do? Snatch for his passport and scram, or dare the devil and look for Anne? He ordered two patrol cars to Witley House, a watch mounted at all exits from the country and then, suddenly thinking Hawes might check Anne's father's home, he sent detectives to keep surveillance there.

He met Hallows arriving and briefed him.

Anne's tea had been brought. Wyland had helped to steady the cup and she drank without spillage. The second cup she managed on her own.

With a large pot provided, Hallows poured her a third and one for Wyland and himself. Then he took a seat close by her.

Kennet sat at the side of the room. His hand hovered over the ON of the tape recorder. He was taut with protective zeal, ready to pounce on Hallows if the interview became too much for her, and sod the consequences.

As surprising to herself as to them, she mustered an iron control and told her story swiftly and clearly. The confession, the stable, the cassettes, the weapon – a heavy leather-bound book, and the breathless flight in the dark to Wyland's house. Kennet listened and imagined with an accuracy that comes with loving, how she would have felt through it all.

He glanced at Wyland as she concluded. Wyland looked haggard and Kennet suspected that if Wyland did not have Anne to worry about, nausea would take over. The blunt reality of Hawes's barbarity would take some stomaching.

'Does Anne have to stay here?' Wyland said.

Hallows asked her: 'Will your father be at home?'

'I think so.'

'Then, Dr Wyland, drive Mrs Hawes to Mr Howard's house.'

'Are you going to Witley House?' she asked him.

'Yes, as soon as I've made a phone call.' He must contact Liz Ireton. When she heared of Barraclough's use of the stables she would want to act fast, secure evidence and bring him in. He said to Anne: 'DCI Kennet will bring you news later.'

'Of an arrest . . .'

'Of an arrest,' Hallows repeated and left her with Kennet.

Kennet accepted there would be no supporting her on her way to the car. She was exhausted but not unsteady now. He had to presume those brief minutes when she had taken his arm would be the first and the last physical connection between them. She was leaving Abbots Hill with emotions tightly corked. No doubt she would sob in her father's arms – such an anguish to hear, such a privilege to bear.

The Citroën moved rapidly off. Kennet remained stock-still until it had disappeared. His emotions too had been contained. Now he spun on his heel as anger erupted: anger directed at Hallows.

Hallows turned from the phone to find Kennet a railroading pace away.

'A word in *private*, sir.'

Kennet marched to Room 2, and threw back the door.

With the signs familiar, Hallows urged himself to be patient. 'What's biting you?' he said stonily and elbowed the door closed.

'*You* risked her neck. I warned you! We could be investigating Anne Hawes's death this evening.'

'But we're not.'

Livid colour flamed upward from Kennet's throat. 'You said you believed Hawes wouldn't hurt her, but he chased her into that hell-hole.'

Hallows regarded him stolidly. Kennet's point was valid except – in his opinion – wrong, and he said so quietly: 'Keith Hawes would never have harmed her. I believe he thought he could persuade her to keep his secret. He's very arrogant, as you must have seen.'

'But she *ran*.'

Kennet could push one, Hallows muttered to himself, but two of them blowing steam would achieve damn all. He said: 'He would have considered that no more than a reflex to surprise; a slight blip. He believes in his powers of persuasion. He was sure he could have talked Gina into parting with her money. He persuaded Alcott that it was all right that he was in an off-limits area at the hospital. Persuading Anne to protect their marriage would be no problem, in Hawes's view.'

Kennet listened: Hallows was nobody's fool. Maybe, just maybe he was right. And his pulse rate began to drop. He said with less aggression: 'She would never keep quiet. She would never stay with him. She wouldn't be able to bear him near her.'

Watching the barometric colour subsiding, Hallows said: 'I know that. You know that. But Hawes's opinion? Anne is his wife, she loves him, she'll stay: as a couple they are invincible. His is a grand case of self delusion.'

'It's all hypothetical . . .'

The door shot inward.

'Sir! There's a fire at Witley House.'

Lofty flames danced along the roof-line of the stables and roared out through gaps in the brickwork. They reached upward, snatching at overhanging branches. An acrid smell was carried hither and thither by the gusting air, and another that was sweet and strongly resinous.

Kennet had sprung across hoses being run out and sprinted into the house to check for signs that Hawes had taken off. Alone, Hallows picked his way in the glare towards the stable. Fire was a frightful and beautiful creature and he was filled with the fear and pleasure of it now.

Behind him he heard a rapid measured footfall. A constable joined him. The two halted at the brink of intense heat. Smoke swirled, obscured, then departed in waves. A hose swelled and hardened as water flowed. 'So what happened?' Hallows asked.

'We arrived to arrest Mr Hawes and found the cars as you see them on the drive, sir. The house door was open, but there was no sign of him inside. Two of us went to check Councillor Barraclough's cottage. He wasn't there. Two others had started a search, working their way into the copse. We were about to join them when the stables went up. It just exploded in flame. I've never seen anything like it . . . nor want to again.'

There was an oddness in his voice. Hallows looked at him sharply. In the cruel brillance of the fire, he saw a face contorted with distress.

'Sir, we were over there-' he pointed -'when we heard this terrific whoosh. Flames leapt from every cranny. I ran towards the building. Heaven know's what for, there was nothing I could do. And then . . . God, its awful.' He choked. 'I heard a man screaming.'

Hallows's stomach flipped over: 'You *what?*'

'The door was barred. It was too hot – we couldn't get near – we couldn't open it.'

'My God!' Hallows turned, took an agitated step closer to the stable. In a swirl of smoke and steam his view was cut off. 'Barred did you say?'

'Locked with a strip of metal – and the man screaming and yelling.'

Hallows stood powerless and appalled. Hawes? Surely this wasn't Anne's work? He couldn't have misjudged her – could he?

Water surged from another hose. It sprayed high, cooling glowing twigs and branches. He felt the constable, rocking with misery.

Never Anne? She wouldn't have shut her husband in? Then Hallows remembered, and his confidence rallied. She had described newspapers, not bundled but crumpled, and words that had been hideously meaningful: *Victoria Crescent Fire . . .* A headline that was recent. This fire had been set. Someone, not Anne, had planned it. Barraclough?

Hallows turned back to the constable. He loathed asking but had to know: 'What was the man yelling?'

'It sounded like: "Anne! Help me, woman-mine!"'

Hallows drew an unsteady hand across his mouth. The wind changed, the stable became visible to him again and as they stood in the relentless, shimmering orange glow, the stable door in skeletal form was there for him to see with the bar in place.

Those words would haunt the constable. And when he was called at the coroner's court, Anne would hear them: she too would be haunted for the rest of her life.

The young constable still rocked. He needed a diversion. Hallows said: 'Call Control for me. A message for DCI Ireton. Councillor Barraclough to be charged with arson and murder.'

Left alone again, Hallows, leant into a tree. Tonight he felt crushingly old.

The light was going. There was more steam than flame now.

He moved. He had a purpose. He tracked along the route Anne had described and arrived at the point where the drive opened opposite the bridle-path. He began searching, called for a torch and found what he sought beside a dense shrub.

'Well, Liz,' he said in a undertone, 'the video cassettes will have gone, but you have Bisset's album.'

Midnight. The clocks in the city chimed in a new day above the constant hum of traffic. In Hallows's office a light burned and the room smelt foully of smoke released from his discarded jacket.

'Barraclough's vanished!' Ferret was too high on anger and disappointment to sit down. She stamped her feet on worn carpet in front of his desk. 'We went to the Council Chambers, but no one had seen him despite his car being parked in its usual place. I've had officers running all over the Civic Centre. Not a trace of him. Scott and I checked the cottage. Empty. No clothes missing, his passport was still in his desk. Beside it was a bundle of money – eight hundred pounds. I've impounded both.' She slowed up, frowning: 'Who skips without money?'

'Circulated his description?'

'Yes, it'll be in the *Mercury* at midday and on TV in the morning. "Missing, wanted for questioning in connection with a fire."'

He grunted acknowledgement. 'It doesn't console, but he's too well known to be lost for long. The album – I've sent it to Fingerprints. You could be lucky. Barraclough's might be inside.'

A ruminative silence followed. In Peel Square late-night revellers were out-noising passing cars.

Their laughter made a hideous juxtaposition to what she was thinking. 'They were bringing out the body when we got to Witley Lane. How has Anne Hawes taken it?'

'Don't know yet.' He stood suddenly. He wanted to roar down to the larking crowd to *shut up*! Instead he shooed her towards the door. 'Go home, Liz. If Barraclough materializes, you'll be reached.'

'And you?'

'When I've seen Roy Kennet.'

'Guv, was Oliver present when you talked to Anne?'

'Yes. He looked gutted.' He watched her mouth purse sympathy. 'Now go.'

Thirty minutes later, Hallows recognized Kennet's footfalls. They were slow tonight, the tread of a man who had played Death's emissary.

Strain makes deep rivers of every line on a face. Kennet's was no exception. Dark fissures crazed the grey landscape of his skin: freckles had entirely disappeared. His eyes were more hooded than ever and the message on his pinched mouth read: don't ask.

There would be time enough to talk. Hallows reached to the back of a cupboard and took out an almost full bottle of whisky and two glasses. He poured a good nip in each, lifted both and passed one to Kennet. 'I declare us off duty,' he said.

Given choice, Ferret never rushed breakfast. Coffee, cereal, fruit juice and sometimes, like this morning, a boiled egg with toast soldiers, shored up the body while giving uninterrupted space to think.

She had received no news of Barraclough. She turned from speculating where he might be, to considering the money found in his desk. Eight hundred pounds. They had counted it, noted quantity for each denomination, slid it back into its band quickly and passed it to the impounding officer at Abbots Hill. The band? She was sure it had not been a bank's band. It was plain . . . almost.

Eyes closed, sipping coffee, she tried to see it. A dim smudged stamp. Yes! Kempe's.

Hallows stood upwind of the woodsman's bonfire as SOCOs trowelled and sieved debris. Like winnowings, the fine dust blew and coated a nearby holly.

An officer considered remnants in his sieve and beckoned to Hallows. 'A buckle, sir.'

Hallows peered at scorched metal absent of leather or cloth. 'From a woman's garment do you think?'

'From its size, I'd say so. A raincoat maybe. Any help?'

'Patronus's theatrical costumes department are missing a woman's raincoat. Hawes had access.'

Hallows looked from the buckle towards the soot-streaked carcass of the stable. Hawes was now with Iain Sinclair. Soon Iain would be at work with his scalpel with Hallows obliged to attend. It was the smell he dreaded.

The officer also considered the stables. 'I'll be surprised if we find evidence for DCI Ireton there.'

Having witnessed the intensity of the fire, Hallows was bound to agree.

What was Barraclough's connection with Kempe's when he had claimed not to be a gambling man?

Ferret left Scott and a team of search officers to invade the betting shop while she called on Martin Falder.

Mrs Falder, all smiles, with fair-grey curls kept tame by an Alice-band, showed her into the sitting room. Martin reclined regally on a settee, his injured knee supported on a wealth of cushions.

'How're you doing?' Ferret asked.

'OK. My leg's not quite so sore. Here – I've had a card from the retreat.' He reached amongst mail scattered on the floor and passed it to her.

It was of a balloon airlifting a happy bear. Grinning, she opened it. 'Nice words. They're missing you.' And she put it on the mantelshelf. 'Will you go back there or join your Dad and become a builder?'

He shrugged indecision. 'I like it at the retreat. I enjoy growing vegetables, looking after the hens and goats.'

'Your Dad wouldn't want you to do something you didn't enjoy.'

Mrs Falder nodded vigorously.

'Where is Reg, by the way?'

'Not doing work for Lester Barraclough!' Mrs Falder said tartly. 'We saw the news. He's just popped to Brooke House to see in a load of timber.' She took a brisk step away: 'You'll excuse me, Miss Ireton, I have to collect Rosie from a friend.'

Mrs Falder's departure suited Ferret. This was not a social call. She sank into a comfortable chair and was reminded she had enjoyed only a few hours in bed.

She said: 'You were going to do some memory chasing, Martin. Made any progress?'

He was grimacing at his leg. 'No,' he said and began shifting his hips in a slight cautious manoeuvre to reposition it.

'Are you sure?'

'I said no.' He closed his eyes, wincing at a zip of pain.

'OK.' She considered him shrewdly. 'We'll try again in a day or so. Have you told your Dad yet why you took off?'

'Yes. He took it all right. A quiet bloke, my dad.'

'Yes, a good bloke. Now if you do remember . . .'

'. . . I'll get in touch.'

'DS Scott will call to take your formal statement.'

'Right.'

She accepted today's impasse and returned to the neutral topic of the retreat. 'The nuns have promised me dinner,' she said, rising to leave. 'Don't know when I'll get there though.'

In the front garden she met Rosie with her mother.

The child asked: 'You going now?' The small delicate mouth remained puckered with the question.

'Yes. Do you want to come with me to my car?' Ferret looked to Mrs Falder and received agreement. The child's small, soft hand slid into hers and gripped possessively.

While Mrs Falder watched from the gate, Ferret, with leaping, bobbing Rosie, crossed the yard.

'Did you have a party yesterday, when Martin came home?' Ferret asked.

'No,' Rosie had begun to rub at the scar on Ferret's hand. 'Daddy had to go out and Granny's got to come. We're going to have toffee ice cream.'

'Mmmm.' Ferret laughed. 'Sounds really good.' With her free hand, she found her keys. 'Better run back to mummy now.'

Rosie started her trot away, then stopped, turned and blew a kiss.

Ferret accepted it as no more than a gentle parody of affection but, nonetheless, she experienced a wholly unexpected warm flutter of response. She was not, however, so happily disposed to Martin. He had lied. He had dodged eye contact. Well, he would discover she could be a persistent nag. To close this sickening case she had to secure all loose ends.

It had been dark for some while when Hallows emerged from the post-mortem and prepared to get changed out of surgical greens into his day clothes. Armed with Sinclair's spare soap and shampoo, he stepped into the shower and started to work up a mildly fragrant lather. He had taken prudent measures, stuffed cotton wool into each nostril. Hidden under his mask, no one had known.

He pressed out water from his hair, rinsed again and repeated the exercise. With the water off and the thick foam sluiced away, the distance between himself and the first visual shock of seeing the blackened victim in pugilistic attitude had lengthened. He now considered what Sinclair had said.

The dental record confirmed that the victim was Hawes. Samples of blood showed a high level of carbon monoxide present. This, together with the presence of soot particles in the lungs established that Hawes had been alive when the fire had started. There had been a high leucocyte count in the region of lower arms and thigh showing that burning had occurred here before death. But Hawes had actually died from the smoke generated within the stable – from carbon monoxide poisoning. He would have had no sensation of what the fire did to the rest of his body.

On entering Sinclair's office to have his usual cup of tea, Hallows found Liz Ireton and Curtis waiting for him. He scowled irritation. 'I need a quiet brew. What is it?'

'We've found Gina Hawes's niece, guv,' Curtis said. 'She's still called Holly Stephanie. Lives in York, but she's here at Helenhall: a second year student.'

'Well, I'm damned. What circles we turn in.'

'I've squared it with the lab to start running a test today, and arranged for her to be at Abbots Hill in-' he shot his cuff -'forty minutes. The DNA result will be through before she goes down for Christmas. She's very laid-back, guv. Knows she was adopted. Doesn't mind giving blood to identify a relative. I left telling the why of it to you.'

'Thanks,' Hallows said dryly.

Ferret waited until Curtis had breezed away. 'Lester Barraclough is Ivor Kempe's business partner – a very quiet business partner. None of the staff there knew. I want a favour, guv.'

'Oh, do you now?' He plugged in the full kettle.

'Scott found a computer at Kempe's which Ivor says has nothing to do with him. It belongs to Barraclough. It doesn't work.'

'Is Kempe in on the Bisset-video racket?'

'I'm pretty sure not. Ivor Kempe might be a wiz when it comes to racing, but I think everything else completely passes him by. According to him, Barraclough supplied the money to start the business and that was his sole function. He popped in through the back door now and then to check the books, and to collect plump envelopes left for him. Cash I presume.'

'So what about this computer?'

'I wondered if Barraclough removed a component for security purposes.'

'Our lab people can check it out tomorrow.'

'I can't afford to wait. I'm convinced the hard disc holds the mailing list. A lot of people are going to throw a sweat when the full news of Barraclough breaks. I want them collared before they destroy evidence. There have been enough fires! Permission, please, to call on Sam Westcott's expertise.'

'You're being unusually scrupulous about asking.'

'He's been done for hacking.'

'What!' The kettle clicked off.

'Come on, guv. I've got nothing on this case except Slade's stills.'

'Necks on blocks,' Hallowed muttered. 'OK. But watch him.'

Hallows was not to be kept reflecting on the wisdom of his decision for long. Holly Stephanie had scarcely left him for the waiting haematology technician when Ferret rang through.

'Jackpot!' she said breathlessly. 'Four hundred names, most of them off our patch.'

'Nicely confirms Barraclough's role.'

'In part. I have yet to link him with 6 Victoria Crescent. And where the hell is he?' she fumed.

Three days after her first visit, Holly padded confidently into Hallows's office alongside Curtis to hear the result of the DNA profile. Looking up, Hallows was reminded of the image he had built of Sally. Youth, vivacity and now, flowing at considerable length from Holly's attractive neck was a silk Isadora Duncan scarf.

She was as much angry as distressed when she learned that the mummified body was that of her aunt, Gina Hawes. 'What a rotten, absolutely rotten and insulting way to die.' She glowered, then sighed and regarded Hallows with dark thoughtful eyes. 'What will happen to her now?'

'Her solicitor will get in touch with Stella . . .'

'My natural mother?' she interrupted.

'Yes, to discuss funeral arrangements.'

'I'd like to go to the funeral.'

'Then I'll give the solicitor your address.' He took a guess at what else she might be thinking. 'If you want to meet Stella, I'll mention that to him too, but be prepared for her not to feel able to agree.'

She nodded amiably: 'I've read the books – I've got the messages.'

'Is there anything else I can do for you?'

'Don't think so.' She rose. 'Must go, if that's all. I'm packing. Moving into a house next term. Sharing with two others.'

With a sense of déjà vu, Hallows went cold. Maybe she saw something of dismay on his face, for she said with a laugh:

'It's not a dump. My dad and the university have vetted it.' And with a wave she waltzed out of his office.

Four weeks had elapsed since Hawes had died. Martin Falder had returned to work at the retreat and Barraclough was still being sought for questioning.

Kennet took a diversion to work in order to do some essential shopping. He had loaded his single large bag of provisions into his car when he spotted Anne Hawes pushing an exceptionally laden trolley.

He had not seen her since the inquest and then only from a distance. Then and now he thought she looked desperately thin.

Was he blighted for having brought bad news? he wondered, and details of that grim visit to Neville Howard's house returned for the thousandth time. Wyland had already left when he rang the bell. Howard had ushered him into a cosy unpretentious sitting room where Anne sat woodenly, staring into space. Howard must have expected the worst. Watchful and protective, he sat close beside her on the settee.

To be on their level where he could face her, Kennet had to sit down himself. The most available chair brought their knees almost touching. Across the narrow gap he could feel her misery.

He began simply: her husband had died.

He knew she would ask how and dreaded it. The question came.

'The stable caught fire,' he said.

Her fingers began to work, locking and interlocking. 'How? Those matches? I don't understand. I only hit him with a book. Why didn't he run out?' And then she became very still. 'Mr Kennet-' her eyes rested on his -'what exactly did happen?'

How could he lie, and how could he tell the appalling truth?

He must pick his way: no sudden moves to capsize their boat. 'He didn't run out because he must have been unconscious. Someone – someone came after you left. He barred the door. I believe your husband would have died from smoke inhalation.'

'Barred it?'

'Yes.'

'Oh, God. How do you know?'

'I'd sent officers to the house . . .'

'So they got Keith out, but the smoke had been too much.'

'No.

'Go on,' she said.

Her eyes were locked on his and he knew at that moment she had to hear everything. There must be no shocks in the coroner's court. 'They heard him calling briefly, and then he must have passed out, but . . . they couldn't open the door, there was too much heat.'

She started trembling and her father's arm went about her.

'What did he call?'

Kennet wished he were anywhere else on earth but here. He said gently: 'I'm told it was: "Anne, help me, woman-mine."'

She choked, staggered away from them, ran upstairs and started to scream. It was the most awful God-forsaken noise.

Howard had rushed after her.

Kennet, bathed in a fierce cold sweat, heard the noise become muffled as Howard must have held her.

It seemed like hours later, Howard reappeared. 'I wanted to call a doctor,' he had said, 'but she wouldn't have it.'

And now Kennet watched her struggling to steer the heavy trolley. He hesitated, then walked towards her. 'Can I help? Or would you rather I went away.'

Immediately she said, 'Mr Kennet! Help would be welcome. And for your peace of mind. I don't believe in shooting the messenger because the news is bad.' She pointed to her car and he took the trolley. 'My father, as you can tell from all this, has a hearty appetite.'

'So you haven't returned to Roxleigh.'

'No, not even for clothes. Kate Elwood fetched personal things. I shall sell the house without ever stepping inside again.'

'And the Fitness Centre?' She had unlocked the boot. He lifted and carefully stowed boxes and bags.

'I need to work – keep busy. I'm going back shortly. Pa's going to look after the admin. side.'

'Don't overdo the hours.'

She smiled for him, the smallest, gentlest of smiles. 'Oh, Pa will put on the brake.' She looked at the empty trolley. 'I must get rid of that.'

'No, that's OK.' And he had walked away wondering why he couldn't have said something useful.

Later, in Hallows's office, he said casually, 'I saw Mrs Hawes this morning.' He wanted to talk. He wanted to be drawn, to get his tongue round the subject of her. He wanted to talk with someone who wouldn't be gabby.

Hallows showed no obvious sign of a pricking interest. He continued to apply his signature to the top one of a sheaf of forms.

'She's going to sell Witley House.' Kennet's second statement was followed by a prolonged moody pause. 'She'll be worth a bit.'

Hallows had wondered about Roy Kennet. He had been markedly subdued since the time of Hawes's death. Hallows put down his pen, folded his arms and looked at the DCI pensively: 'Are you lining me up ready to bite?'

A grin flittered over Kennet's face. 'No.'

'Right. So does the money put you off?'

'Yes, yes it does rather. Raises questions. Can a cat look at a queen?'

'Personally, and given that we're considering some time ahead, I can't see what you're worried about. She has the characteristics of a Tuesday's child.'

'What?' Kennet frowned.

'Hell's bells! You can be exasperating at times, Roy. Birth*days*. Tuesday's child is full of grace. You know: elegance, kindness, compassion. Besides which, she's a woman who gives time to friendship. Do I encourage you? I'm damn well trying.'

'Yes . . . and no.' Kennet gave way to a relieved chuckle. 'Saturday's me.'

'Ah! Saturday's child works hard for its living. Well, the lady could think your references are better than those idlers who'll be swarming around her as if she's their honey pot.'

Chapter 4

Ferret felt Hallows's presence. Her sense of space in her office, albeit that the room was small, seemed suddenly diminished. She looked up from working to see him swing a chair forward.

'You're going to the theatre tonight.' He settled himself directly in front of her.

'Am I?' she said off handedly.

He placed a ticket for *The Importance of* . . . on the page she had been reading. 'It's the last performance, Liz. Patronus do a damned good job raising money for local causes. The fact that they continued with the show was right. See it.'

'OK,' she muttered unwillingly.

'Is it because of Wyland that you're not keen?'

She leant back in her chair, cradled her neck in her hands and deliberately looked at the ceiling.

'Liz!'

'I'm not going to answer that. I'm not in the dock.'

It was time they had this talk. He was tired of them all having to play messenger boy. 'I'm pissed off with this thing between you and Wyland.'

'This thing,' she growled, glaring at him, 'is personal.'

'If only it were. Curtis, Scott, me, Kennet and the duty sergeant have been fielding phone calls from him for six weeks. Six whole weeks – the entire time that Barraclough's been gone. Six weeks of you being intentionally unavailable – either at the retreat with Martin Falder or at Hillington with Turley. Six weeks of us saying: "She's out. She's on her way out. She should be back soon. She'll ring you back." But you never do. God knows he's not one of my favourite people, but I'm beginning to feel sorry for the guy. I can't think what he's done to be sent to Coventry for so long.'

'Who says I haven't spoken to him?' she snapped.

'*He* does. What are you going to do about it, Liz?'

She stormed to the window, took refuge glaring at the afternoon shoppers scurrying through Peel Square.

He joined her.

'Stop quizzing me, guv.'

He too watched them, heads forward, moving with so much purpose. 'Soon be Christmas,' he said less forcefully. 'Couldn't you meet to negotiate an armistice?'

'I don't want to see him.'

'Why? You don't now dislike him so . . .'

'Drop it!' She made a fist. She wanted to thump his vast chest. Instead she snatched up her bag and ran. 'I'm OUT! Martin's at his father's place. I'm there.'

'Liz!' he shouted after her. 'Get it sorted.'

Ferret could hear Rosie's laughter as she parked her car in Reg Falder's yard. She followed the sound, walking to the fence enclosing the back garden. Martin was playing ball with the little girl, rolling and chasing it, and showing no signs of having had an injured knee.

'Martin,' she called.

With exasperation he banged the ball away. 'Will you get off my back!'

Rosie looked startled, then apprehensive.

He gave her a quick apologetic smile: 'Go inside, Rosie. I'll call you out again in a minute.' Her brow furrowed absurdly as she did as bidden.

He approached the fence and said, with exaggerated softness: 'Get this clear, Miss Ireton, I can't help you identify the man, not now, not ever. I liked you when we first met, but now you're driving me up the wall.'

'Do you think I like badgering you? But you're lying. I know you're lying. Listen Martin, I have to know if the man I suspect is guilty, or if I have to look elsewhere. If elsewhere, I'm in a whole new ball game. I'm worried! The passing years make no difference to that kind of pervert. He'll do to others what he did to you. He has to be caught.'

He turned from her, leaning into the fence. 'I remember nothing,' he said.

Ferret slipped into her seat as the house-lights dropped.

She was nervous and furious at being so. Why couldn't Oliver have played the butler? He'd be on and off, out of her sight much of the time, not stirring emotions in every act.

The curtains parted: a long limbed man on the stage sprawled elegantly across a chaise longue. His first lines were well delivered.

The play progressed and Ferret found the words and action took precedence. Oliver was thankfully lost in character.

Outside, however, she made no further attempt to please Hallows by stepping through the stage door. Instead she dodged the leaving crowd who chattered and dawdled under street lamps, and began her short walk to Quay House.

She entered a road of small fashion shops which ran at right angles to the High Street. There were fewer people here. Mostly couples, arms wound round each other. They sauntered to the numerous bars, boasting live music, which had sprung up recently in the smaller side streets.

Footsteps sounded and retreated. Footsteps that were light, others heavy. The pavements echoed with the ebb and flow of people. Her mind elsewhere, she scarcely listened.

Suddenly her arm was grabbed, fingers digging into bone. She was borne back, thrust against plate glass, a small figure dwarfed by a languid, trendily clad dummy whose vitrified eyes gazed down on the victim unimpassioned. Pinned there by a huge hand terrifyingly near her throat.

She heard a woman's shriek of alarm: 'Reg!'

Focusing, close range, Ferret stared into the unrecognizable and furious face of Reg Falder. He had lost pounds. His skin hung in slack folds from facial bones now made visible.

'A word!' He pulled her forward, then slammed her back against the glass which flexed and shivered. 'Stop pestering Martin. I won't have it. I won't have him harrassed. No stirring – no opening old wounds. He's bled enough, God knows.'

She gulped air and snarled: 'Let go of me, Reg!'

He hesitated, released her, but didn't back off.

In an adrenalin rush she stormed: 'Your son's withholding information. There's been a degenerate, living in Helenborough, who's enjoyed a charmed life, raping young men and boys with complete impunity for years. I want him identified. Be clear, I am never, never, going to give up until I have him in the dock! I will not accept this wall of silence from Martin. If he wants me off his back, he's got to talk.'

Falder made no movement, neither blinked nor spoke, just stared at her.

Mrs Falder appeared frozen too, overwhelmed by her husband's extraordinary behaviour.

Ferret shifted her feet slightly. 'Go home Reg. Take it easy. Martin's twenty-one, it has to be his problem.' And she slid along the face of the glass out of his reach.

She cut across the road before looking back. Reg Falder remained motionless.

Syncopated jazz was filtering through a partially open door. The sound was interleaved with Mrs Falder's weeping.

Christmas was a week closer. Some hopeful had hung mistletoe in the lift at Abbots Hill. More people seemed to be using the stairs.

Ferret opened a carton of orange juice, took a glass from a desk drawer, blew it clean and poured. Barraclough had still not been sighted and a new case file lay open. Having quenched her thirst, she returned to it.

Afternoon slipped into evening.

A copper coin bounced on the page in front of her. 'My thoughts are worth more than that,' she said, meeting Scott's eye.

He owned an earthy chuckle. 'In that case, I'll have it back. I fancied a bite at the Dog and Duck. How about. . . ?' The internal phone rang and he turned his thumbs down in expected defeat.

He tried reading her expression as she took the short call. Puzzled, perhaps?

'So have we just missed dinner?' he said.

'I'm not sure. Reg Falder wants to see me. Duty sergeant says he's in an odd state – restless. Come on.'

Reg Falder had been shown into Interview Room 1.

'Reg-' she took a chair facing him -'what's the problem?'

The restlessness had gone. He was absorbed by his own large hands spread flat on the table, the calloused fingers fanned into spokes. He viewed them with a detachment that suggested they weren't his own.

'Reg?'

'You're still looking for Barraclough?' She nodded. 'Did he start the fire which killed that Hawes bloke?'

'We believe so.'

'Do you have anything else on him?'

'I'm supposed to ask the questions, Reg. We have suspicions, yes.'

'Like what?'

'I'm not at liberty to say.'

'But you reckon he's a bad bloke . . . apart from the fire?'

'Between us, yes.'

He turned his hands over, surveyed the palms, scratched at a residue of dried paint.

'Reg?'

He wet his lip and for the first time looked at her. 'The day I collected Martin from hospital, I called to see Barraclough.'

'To delay his repair job. I remember you saying you would.'

'He was happy enough about it. He came to the car – had a word with Martin – made some sort of a joke – had a laugh.'

She remembered that odd treble of a laugh, how it brought hairs rising on the back of her neck.

'Martin was very quiet when we got home.'

'Shy, I expect, after being away so long.'

'Not that, though he was nervous. He told me everything soon after – why he'd run away. It came tumbling out. Sobbing he was – made my heart bleed.'

'Reg, I'm sorry, but I'm glad he could talk.'

'And now – now you're hounding my son.' His skin glowed. He dragged at his collar, sweat breaking out on hand and neck. 'It can't go on! I won't let it!'

'I told you why.'

'It was Barraclough!' The name exploded from his mouth. 'Barraclough was the one.'

'Barraclough raped Martin?'

'Yes!' He slammed his horny fist against the table. 'Martin remembered his laugh. That high cackly laugh.'

She sagged back with frustration: 'And now he's got away.'

'No.'

'We've looked everywhere. Believe me, we've. . .'

'No. He's not far from here.'

'Oh, come on! He's probably got his feet on some sunny shore.' Given that Falder hadn't looked so ill, so cadaverous, she might have indulged in a scornful laugh.

'He's not far away,' he repeated. He began patting his chest. 'I'm big – well I was. I've lost some weight lately – you've noticed.' He saw her nod. 'Built a bit like a wrestler. It's from the work, but I'm not a violent man, very slow to cut up rough, always have been.'

She could believe it.

'But . . . Well, inside – when Martin told me it was Barraclough who had done that to him – I went mad with pain. It was a pain like no other. I couldn't handle it. I made out I had an emergency job to see to. I knew Barraclough had a Planning Committee meeting. I waylaid him as he left his car. I forced him into the van and drove him to Brooke House. I tied him up. Gagged him. Put him in one of the fireplaces – laid some bricks. I think Martin might have guessed.'

Her mouth hung open. 'You walled him in?'

'Seemed like justice at the time. He has to be dead, Miss Ireton.'

'Oh, Reg,' she whispered. 'You fool!'

Early evening three days later, after a morning when the magistrates had ordered Reg Falder to be remanded in custody, Ferret shrank from going home. For once she was thankful her desk groaned under paper. It gave an obvious reason for her remaining.

Once alone in her flat Rosie, Martin, Mrs Falder and Reg – all their sad, sad faces would impose themselves on her mind. She would see them reflected everywhere. Every polished surface would hold an image. 'If only . . .' she said aloud.

'If only's get you nowhere,' Hallows answered snappishly from the doorway. 'You did all you could. You're not the only soldier on the field. You would have heard me or Scott loud enough if there were loopholes in the enquiry. You are going to go home. I repeat: get something to eat and go home. I know you of old. Off your grub since Falder came in. Well, I'm not having an underweight moping copper on my team. I give you half an hour to be out of here. That's an order.'

He didn't wait for an argument.

She muttered curses after him. Why couldn't he mind his own damn business?

She drove through Peel Square, dodged taking the road to Quay House and found herself on the Riverside Inn road.

The inn's car park was irritatingly full. She happened on a space then walked mechanically into the carvery, took a tray and settled for the first thing offered. There was one small table empty by the window.

She set out cutlery and her plate and began picking at a roast potato.

She saw Rosie's face in the shiny bowl of her fork, and a lump swelled in her throat. Stupid fool. Emotional idiot, wanting to cry in public.

Her table shuddered as someone moved in. 'Oh, for *heaven's* sake!' she accused.

'Sorry! Long legs.'

She looked in disbelief. 'Oliver!

'Long time.'

'What the hell are you doing here?'

'Following you. Obeying your boss's instructions.' He placed a mixed grill beside cutlery.

'Mike Hallows had you follow me?' She dragged an angry finger across a wet cheek.

'He rang. Said to watch out for flying flak.'

'I think I'll put in for a transfer.'

He took no notice, began eating and then made something of considering her hardly touched plate.

She growled: 'Don't *you* start on about food.'

'Wouldn't dream of it.'

She met his eye. There was amusement there – and something else of more depth. She looked back at her plate: spiked a couple of peas.

'I should give up that particular battle,' he said casually. 'Perhaps you'd fancy a fork full of apple pie?'

She glared at the table: 'I don't see any apple pie.'

'A small detail that can soon be remedied.' And he signalled to a distant attentive waitress.